CW00393093

Copyright © 2022 P .

All rights

The characters and events portrayed in this book are fictitious. Any similarity to real persons, living or dead, is coincidental and not intended by the author.

No part of this book may be reproduced, or stored in a retrieval system, or transmitted in any form or by any means, electronic, mechanical, photocopying, recording, or otherwise, without express written permission of the publisher.

ISBN: 9798807631732

Cover design by: Rachel Tyler Artwork

With grateful thanks to all those friends and family members who encouraged me to finish this book but mostly to those who were the first to read it and gave such helpful feedback (Derek, Ty and Mike).

Extra special thanks to my wonderful wife, Mags, who read it in a day and had over thirty excellent suggestions, virtually all of which made it into the finished manuscript.

If you like the cover art please check out @RachelTylerArtwork on Facebook.

(They're available for commissions.)

Table of Contents

Chapter 1
Introduction

When something bad happens, people use the expression 'it's the end of the world' or if they like to think bigger, or are a bit over-dramatic, they might say 'it's the end of the universe'. From my experience one of the major problems with 'the end of the universe' is just how often it's almost actually happened. You really would be surprised how often something threatens to wipe out, well, everything. Sometimes the impending disaster has been averted, sometimes it has been postponed until a plan to prevent it has been devised, sometimes it has been mitigated for, with terrible losses, but one day it may actually happen.

The expression 'it's the end of the universe' is hyperbole, after all what is really meant is human life in this galaxy, but somehow the expression 'the end of the galaxy' hasn't caught on. Humanity has settled a large part of the Milky Way, but hasn't yet travelled to our nearest neighbouring galaxy. Despite our Earthbound ancestor's absolute conviction that 'we are not alone' not one single sign of sentient, or even animal, life has ever been discovered outside Earth.

I work for The Organisation, which had, and still has, the sole purpose of ensuring the continuity of human life in the galaxy. It's the ultimate big-picture scenario. There are teams of the brightest and best beavering away, using the smartest technology ever created, running complex statistical analysis on the entirety of human activity to predict where, when and sometimes how the galaxy might end next. That wasn't my job though, I couldn't calculate the statistical likelihood of it raining in the afternoon, I worked in the field. I got information from the Barbs[1] and went to investigate, to see if the predicted disaster was actually happening. Then working in co-operation with the Barbs, I took appropriate action. We all knew the whole universe, let alone this galaxy, would end someday; it's the first thing you learned on day one when you joined The Organisation. No-one, even after hundreds of billions of hours of

---

[1] Back-room boffins, BRBs or colloquially Barbs.

calculations and advanced simulations, had found a way to prevent the heat-death of the universe. Entropy is as irreversible as it is irresistible. But fortunately, it is also *very* far off in the future[1], so far in fact that by the time we actually get there we'll probably all be heartily sick of the whole thing and be glad of the chance to stop. We knew, ultimately, we were bound to fail so therefore we redefined success. Success to us was ensuring that the thing that finally did end all life was entropy all on its own and not an artificially created genetic mutation, a virulent matter-eating virus, someone trying to create synthetic black-holes to use as a power source, or an irresponsible time-traveller interfering with human evolution[2]. I enjoyed my job, there was lots of travel to interesting planets, the pay was good and then there was the whole ego boosting saving the galaxy aspect. It was occasionally dangerous work and we did lose field agents. Not many retired unscathed either mentally or physically. Most of us coped with the work for a decade or so before we'd had enough and either retired or were reassigned to a desk job back at headquarters. Field agents very rarely became Barbs; the skill sets were just too different. I'd been out in the field for almost fourteen years, so was one of the most experienced agents still operational.

I was currently on board a commercial starship that had recently departed the planet Mirth on its way to Coronnol. I was about to investigate a scientist who was suspected of having a really good chance of ending all life the galaxy.

---

[1] Approximately 10^{100} years. That's so far off that no matter when you're reading this, it's pretty much the same amount of time in the future.

[2] I only made up the time travel scenario, I helped stop the other three impending disasters in the last few years. The Barbs considered that nothing was more likely to actually beat us and end human life than time travel, so we all fervently hoped it remained absolutely impossible.

Chapter 2
Coronnol

Doctor Maldonaro Octavius Jones[1] was one of the galaxy's foremost Astrophysicists. She had worked hard and distinguished herself in the eyes of her peers. No-one outside certain rarefied academic communities would have heard of her but within them she was a rock-star. Her first major breakthrough was when she designed the first successful warp stellar probes. These used a miniaturised version of a starship's hyperspace drive to allow the probe to take samples from the core of a star. The probe would accelerate towards the target star before engaging its hyperdrive in two short bursts. The first caused it to vanish from normal space, to instantaneously travel through hyperspace and reappear inside the star for the smallest possible fraction of a second then the second burst would carry it safely to an orbiting lab where the probe's readings and samples would be analysed. As the probe shielding improved the probes were able to remain inside the star for longer and longer, until the data she was obtaining revolutionised stellar mechanics. She was responsible for much of the current detailed understanding of how stars worked internally and had written extensively on stars near the end of their life. She had been the lead researcher in a team that successfully predicted, years in advance, and then recorded and analysed a supernova as it actually happened. Twenty-five years of her adult life had been devoted to astrophysics, the majority at the same university. She had grown up on Mirth but after graduation had moved across the galaxy to the university planet of Coronnol for her Doctoral research and had stayed. Mirth wasn't exactly a backwater, it was one of the first thousand or so planets settled by humans, so it had an ancient and

---

[1] During this period of human civilization everyone had three names, the first they chose themselves at coming of age, which almost always had a diminutive variant used by close friends, the second was chosen by their parents at birth and finally the family name which was passed down by parents. When parents with different family names became bondmates (or married as it was archaically known) they chose one or the other of their family names to be known by or quite often picked a whole new name to represent the new family unit.

respected culture but was known more for its artists and philosophers than for its scientists. Coronnol on the other hand, a relatively recently terraformed planet, was a melting pot of both cutting-edge research and solid reliable well-regarded academics. If you earned tenure there you could spend your life digging deep into whatever field of scientific research fascinated you. Jones fitted in like a hand into a glove.

All of this information and much more was contained in the briefing package I received while I travelled from Mirth to Coronnol. I'd visited Doctor Jones' home planet to get some background on her as a person, to meet family and friends discreetly and see if I was dealing with a lunatic, a maniac or, even worse, an idealist[1]. What I'd found out about Jones wasn't very helpful. She had no surviving immediate family still on Mirth and the distant relations, childhood friends and old colleagues I found who did remember her had only unhelpful phrases such as 'a quiet studious person' or 'she mostly kept herself to herself' or 'she really focused on her work' to offer me. Everyone liked her but no one seemed to know her particularly well personally. It appeared she'd managed to get through the first twenty something years of her life without making any enemies or even that many friends. She didn't appear to fit the profile of someone who would be linked to ending human life in the galaxy, but perhaps she was simply very good at hiding her true nature.

I neither understood nor particularly cared about the mechanics of how stars worked let alone what caused them to die. A broad general scientific understanding was required for field agents but we had neither the time, nor generally, the inclination to become a specialist in any one area. What we all had though was a much higher than usual level of skill with Infosys[2] and related technological matters but that was a requirement for the job. I knew some stars became red

---

[1] A lunatic would do dangerous things without realising the consequences, a maniac would do them despite the consequences and an idealist would do them *because* of the consequences.

[2] Infosys – A portmanteau word made from the words 'Information' and 'System'. Infosys is the standardised civilization-wide communication and computational platform. No single planet or conglomerate controls it, it's a resource for all of humanity. Every world is linked, using hyper-space relays, to it. The computing and storage is distributed across thousands of worlds for maximum resilience. In ancient times, when Earth was the only planet humanity lived on, its very earliest and most primitive iteration was known as 'the internet'. But that's like comparing a primitive cave painting to a 3D interactive hologram.

giants as they aged and could then go super-nova before eventually collapsing into a black-hole but the length of time involved was enormous. It wasn't something that would bother any inhabited solar systems, so far as I knew. Only planets orbiting relatively young stars had been settled, as red giant stars didn't typically have habitable planets in orbit around them.

I moved over to the window in my basic but spacious cabin to watch our approach to Coronnol. I'd never been there before and while, in one sense, if you've seen one planet you've seen them all, I'd always enjoyed approaching the latest variation on the big blue marble. You may be surprised to hear that virtually all inhabited planets look superficially very similar; they're approximately half to two-thirds water, have a largely nitrogen/oxygen atmosphere, rotate once on their axis somewhere in between twenty and twenty-eight hours, and have roughly one 'g' of gravity. So they are all blue with white clouds and are approximately the same size. Until you are close enough to spot a continental land-mass you'd be hard pressed to tell them apart. Some like my home world have a slight greenish tint to the blue and a pale orangey/red/pink tinge to the clouds due to the different balance of salts in the sea water and a redder than usual sun. Few, only a very few, inhabited planets have much larger than usual ice caps or deserts because when space travel is easy and there are, to all intents and purposes, an inexhaustible number of planets to settle on why would you choose one that would make living on it any harder than it needed to be?[1] My home planet does have one unusual feature that made it stand out from the majority which is that it's a counter-spinner, or 'countie' as the vernacular would have it.[2]

I stared at Coronnol. We were approaching the southern hemisphere but the cloud cover was minimal so I could see a large landmass. It was vast. It stretched from the southern pole in a haphazard crescent shape westward up to the widest point near the equator before tapering off eastward to a chain of small islands, that

---

[1] Terraforming a planet can take anywhere from several decades to three hundred years and while it's happening only a handful of specialists live on it to supervise the process. Some say the settlement of the galaxy is what finally cured humans of their institutionalised short-termism.

[2] Counter-spinners make up less than 0.1% of all inhabited planets. They rotate the opposite way to the direction of orbit around their sun than is usual. This means the sun rises in the west and sets in the east. This makes outdoorsy people very uneasy especially when out hiking, camping or sailing on a planet with a spin different to the one they grew up with. Townies tend not to even notice.

were currently invisible to the naked eye, about mid-way from the equator to the northern pole. The southern end of the continent was mostly white, which meant it was covered in ice and snow and I dearly hoped that Doctor Jones' department wasn't based there. Spending the next few days or weeks freezing cold wasn't an attractive prospect. Infosys informed me that the distance from the main spaceport to the Astrophysics department was three hundred and eighty-four kilometres, the journey would take under an hour and that the spaceport was not, thankfully, in the polar region but somewhat north of a mountain range in a temperate zone. We were now close enough to be able to see some detail which included plenty of lush green land north of the snow and we were noticeably heading towards there rather than the polar region. I touched the button to blank the window and headed for the couch to made myself comfortable. A bumpy landing was unlikely as the weather was so clear but better safe than sorry, plus this could be my last half hour of quiet contemplation for a while.

The landing was as uneventful as expected and I disembarked with the rest of the passengers into the spaceport terminal. A quick scan of my cuff[1] and a retinal image check got me through the cursory immigration procedure and I headed for the Mag[2] station. The cuff guided me to the correct platform where I had only a short wait for the next Mag to the capital city of Transium which was where the Astrophysics and Physics departments were based. As you'd expect for one of the leading university planets the Mag system was first class. The seats in the pods were wide and comfortable and most faced in the direction of travel. I picked one next to a window and clipped my seat belt on. The familiar surge of acceleration from the magnetic propulsion was one I enjoyed although I knew some people found it unpleasant. In almost no time we were doing over five-hundred kilometres per hour and the

---

[1] The Infosys interface is worn on the wrist and is referred to as a cuff. Mine was a particularly pleasing gold and silver interlocking pattern of my own design. It projects almost any number of screens of user selectable size and opacity, which always remain conveniently positioned in front of the user, no matter how much you move your arms. Interaction is by either voice or by touching the virtual screens.

[2] Most planetary travel other than within a city is by Mag. Mag is short for Magnetic Vacuum Transit. It's a chain of pods that travel through extremely low-pressure tubes on magnetic tracks. It is environmentally sound, efficient and very fast. Cruising speed varies from 500 kph to 2,000 kph depending on the distance between stops.

industrial and commercial landscape around the spaceport was vanishing behind us. The Mag I was on was an express which meant Transium was the first stop. According to Infosys it was a coastal city with a temperate climate that was very popular with visitors to Coronnol.

The scenery was quite beautiful. The Mag line was staying low down near sea level but lush farm land stretched far off, on the right-hand side, to the mountains that were shrouded in wispy cloud. The landscape was cut through with the occasional river or road and dotted with small towns and villages. The nearby ones flashed past in almost an instant, gone before I even had a chance to notice them properly. Lining many of the rivers were what looked like vineyards so I supposed there must be plenty of wine produced on Coronnol but as I had no experience of farming, or agriculture, I was clueless about what the other crops might be. The left-hand side was mostly unbroken forest but, as the trees came to within a hundred meters or so of the Mag, they were just a blur and no individual species could be identified.

It wasn't long before there came the slight dip of deceleration and a quick glance at the information panel near the Mag door showed us arriving at Transium in ten minutes. A few minutes later the trees on the left side of the Mag thinned out and I could see the coastline. The land the Mag tube was on rose twenty meters above sea level and was running in a broad arc, following the bay, to the city. The beach was pure brilliant white sand and I could see plenty of people out enjoying the sunshine and the water. It wasn't overly crowded but it seemed popular enough. The city was quite close now and I could see the gleaming glass of dozens of high-rise buildings each one subtly different in shade and design but all towering over the trees that interspersed them. I expected the Mag to dip below ground, as that was standard practice, and sure enough the interior lighting came on and moments later we were in a tunnel. The Mag slowed quite sharply then stopped in a brightly lit and colourful station. I had arrived in Transium and I was about to meet Doctor Maldonaro Octavius Jones.

Chapter 3
Meeting the doctor

My cuff guided me from the station up a couple of short flights of stairs to the surface and across an extremely well-tended park to one of the tallest buildings in central Transium. The reception desk had the usual building directory on the wall, and my cuff glowed gently when I waved it over the desk to indicate it had linked to the building's database. The Astrophysics department occupied almost the whole building and the cuff showed me that Doctor Jones was on the one hundred and sixth floor. The express elevator took me straight to her floor where I knocked on the large frosted glass door, that had her name etched into it, as there didn't seem to be any contact patch or intercom system to request entry.

'Come in,' said a woman's voice from within.

I pushed open the door and stepped inside.

'I'm looking for Doctor Maldonaro Octavius Jones,' I said, even though I recognized the woman before me.

Doctor Jones was standing behind the desk. She looked to be about mid-forties in age, was tall, athletic and well dressed in fashionable subdued forest shades with a jet-black cuff on her left wrist. Her skin was a smooth healthy mid-brown colour and her hair was short, glossy and black. She did not look like a stuffy academic who spent her whole life buried in books or squinting into some obscure scientific instrument in a lab. She looked much more like the sort of person who spent a great deal of time outdoors, possibly hiking up mountains.

'That's me,' she said brightly, 'how can I help you?'

I had a very comprehensive and easily corroborated cover story about being a science journalist doing a series of articles about prominent scientists from Mirth. It was easily corroborated because The Organisation had me registered, using various aliases, at any number of magazines, periodicals and local news stations all over the galaxy.

An article I wrote appeared at least once per month. Not that I wrote any of them, our junior Barbs did that as part of their training.[1]

'Doctor Jones, my editor arranged for me to spend some time with you for an article I'm writing. I'm not due to interview you until tomorrow but as I've just arrived in Transium I thought I'd pop in and introduce myself. I'm Cemeron Argalion Pike, or Cem to my friends. Please call me Cem or Cemeron. I like to keep things informal.'

I'd chosen the Pike alias because the articles published under that name were positive, upbeat and generally showed their subjects in a good light. They weren't quite puff pieces, but they weren't far off. I was also certain she would have checked me out before agreeing to meet me, so a friendly persona would be more likely to get a warm reception from Doctor Jones. Sometimes being combative and hostile got results but I preferred to at least start off friendly, I could always get tougher if required.

She came around the desk and held out her arm, I did the same and we briefly linked arms at the elbow.[2]

'It's nice to meet you Cemeron,' she said smiling and seemed to mean it. 'How long will you be with us here in Transium? I hope they've put you in a decent hotel?'

'I'm booked in for a week at the Fortitude Tower just a short walk from here,' I answered. 'I've been living and working on Mirth for a few years now but this is my first visit to Coronnol.'

It was a good hotel and much better than some of the places I had stayed recently.

'Lovely. We could have dinner there tonight if you like? The roof top restaurant is wonderful.'

'I'd like that very much, but surely you have plans already?'

'Nothing that can't wait. You must tell me all the latest news from Mirth. I haven't been home for years and it's very easy to lose touch, even with this,' She raised her wrist and wiggled her cuff. 'Is eight o'clock alright with you?'

---

[1] I'd even won a couple of minor journalistic awards. I'd had to turn down a personal appearance at the ceremony though as I hadn't even read the articles I'd allegedly written.

[2] A standard greeting for strangers and acquaintances on most planets. Close friends and family members might hug or even kiss but meeting someone for the first time you would never touch, skin to skin. That would be considered extremely inappropriate.

I told her that was perfect, made the standard excuse about being tired from travelling and needing to unpack. We said goodbye, but not before I surreptitiously planted a tiny Spycomm[1] on the underside of her desk. If she was up to no-good I needed to know if she was working with anyone else. I doubted someone as clever as her would be stupid enough to use university facilities to communicate with them or to do it over an unencrypted line but I never rule anything out. People can be both incredibly clever and moronically stupid at the same time depending on their training and experience. I was hoping dinner tonight might present me with the opportunity to plant one on her person but that would be considerably trickier.

As I walked out of Doctor Jones' building into the park I had the sudden feeling I was being watched. I paused, apparently to check my cuff, and took a careful surreptitious look all around me. There were a few, innocent enough, small clusters of people sitting in the sunshine enjoying the park, but the only people on their own were a tall thin bald man striding purposefully up behind me, heading in the direction of the Mag station, an elderly woman sitting on a bench under a tree reading a book and a middle-aged man on the far side of the park who was glancing around him, possibly waiting for someone. I knew I'd never seen any of them before and that I would definitely recognize them if I saw them again. Sometimes the feeling means something, sometimes it doesn't. I was a stranger in the somewhat insular world of the university, perhaps I was being watched but just because I was unfamiliar rather than for any malign reason. To be on the safe side I took a circuitous route to the hotel. I stopped in shops and browsed, I doubled back a few times, I even got as far as the beach where I bought an ice-cream. After about an hour I was pretty sure that if anyone had been following me I'd have noticed them.

When I arrived at my room on the one hundred and fortieth floor of Fortitude Tower my cuff automatically unlocked the door and I was very pleased to see my luggage had arrived safely from the

---

[1] A pinhead sized audio bug. We use them a lot. They're sound activated and record everything in a room in extremely high quality. The recording is compressed and transmitted in a short burst a few times a day to avoid detection. Listening in live is much harder due to the power drain and the likelihood of detection. The power cell in our Spycomms lasts up to two weeks and then the whole thing biodegrades into a tiny barely noticeable amount of harmless dust.

spaceport. I could easily replace the clothes and personal items but some of the more interesting things hidden in the case would be very hard to come by. I used my cuff to do a basic scan of the room for eavesdropping devices and found nothing obvious. I could do a more thorough scan should I need guaranteed privacy, but disabling any devices would tip my hand to the person who'd placed them. I unpacked quickly, took a long hot shower and fell asleep within minutes. My cuff was set to wake me at seven o'clock. That would give me time to review the Spycomm's recordings before dinner.

Chapter 4
Dinner with a view

I woke up a few minutes before seven, feeling refreshed by my nap and cancelled the alarm. The virtual screen projected from my cuff had a small blue dot pulsing at the top right corner meaning the Spycomm had transmitted at least one batch of recordings. I propped myself up comfortably on the bed and listened. It was short and not remotely informative. There was a brief call to the restaurant to book a table for two at eight o'clock tonight made just after I left the office, there were two calls to her laboratory; the first to check everything was ready for my tour tomorrow and the other a few minutes later to see if some equipment had arrived and finally a call to someone called Danatis to discuss something scientific that I did not understand about her latest paper, that was about to be published, and to ask him to escort me to the lab tomorrow. A quick check on Infosys revealed that this was Danatis Mercutio Randolf, a junior colleague whose Doctoral work was being supervised by Jones. So absolutely nothing out of the ordinary.

I got dressed in what I hoped would be appropriate semi-formal attire and headed for the rooftop restaurant. I took the stairs as it was only ten flights up and the exercise would do me good and help give me an appetite. I wanted to be there early so I could observe Jones' arrival. I could watch her body language and try to work out if she was nervous, edgy or otherwise uncomfortable. The rooftop restaurant was called Forts and when I approached the Maître D to introduce myself, I was surprised to discover that Doctor Jones was already there even though I was thirty minutes early.

The restaurant was circular. The floor overhung the roof of the building by several meters and was completely transparent as were the walls and the domed ceiling; with just the thinnest metal latticework supports visible. The tables around the edge of the room looked as if they were standing on nothing, suspended in mid-air over a hundred and fifty-story drop. I didn't think that would make for a relaxing evening for most people but I imagined it would be extremely popular with thrill seekers. The rest of the tables were arranged in concentric circles, each circle raised about half a metre

13

higher than the one outside it, so that everyone in the restaurant got a perfect uninterrupted view. I followed the smartly dressed server up the curved ramps that flowed smoothly up to each tier of tables until we reached the top where there were just four tables for two and seated alone at one was Doctor Jones. She stood up as I approached and we linked arms again briefly.

'So good to see you Cemeron' she smiled again 'Isn't it a wonderful sight?'

She gestured expansively around as if the city were her own personal creation. I had to admit it was stunning. The Fortitude Tower must have been the tallest building in the city and appeared to be right in the centre.

'Yes. It's quite a sight,' I agreed

'The tower is at the exact centre of the original city,' Jones said, 'It used to house the Astrophysics Department's offices, administration, lecture and conference facilities but during the last major expansion fifteen years ago it was converted into this hotel. Laurence Howarth Fortitude founded the university here on Coronnol, so there are a lot of buildings named after him. The exact centre of the city is now somewhat east of here due to expansion. We're obviously unable to expand westward because of the ocean.'

The city was laid out in concentric circles, the tallest buildings at the centre. Five major thoroughfares radiated out from the central point and there were parks scattered liberally throughout. The sun would be setting soon out over the ocean. I imagined we were in for a superb sunset as the weather was still clear and virtually cloudless.

'When the new Astrophysics building went up there were a few who wanted it to be taller than the tower. It was a matter of academic pride I suppose.'

'You disagreed?' I asked.

'I sided with the majority who insisted that it would unbalance the whole city centre. There's a lot to be said for balance, wouldn't you say? Aesthetically that is. So, our building has a larger diameter but is just slightly shorter at one hundred and twenty floors. This gives us the extra space we needed.'

A waiter approached and asked if we were ready to order drinks. A light touch on his cuff produced the menu and wine list, he flicked them deftly with a finger, first to Doctor Jones and then to me. My cuff glowed briefly indicating the menu was now available so I opened it.

'I always like to try something local when I go somewhere new,' I said. 'I saw vineyards from the Mag on the way here from the spaceport. Are the local wines any good?'

'The Transium region is famous for its red wines,' said Jones pre-empting the clearly affronted local waiter. 'We'll have a bottle of the eighty-eight Mardonne. If that's alright with you?'

I indicated I was happy to bow to her local knowledge.

We ordered our meals and watched the sun sink towards the sea, sipping on what turned out to be an outstanding glass of wine.

'Have you always been a journalist?' she asked me after a few minutes of companionable silence.

'Yes, I'm afraid so,' I replied. 'Writing was the only thing I showed any real talent for at school. I enjoyed science, especially physics and technology, but knew I was better at writing about it than doing it.'

This was certainly true of my alias but in reality I had shown a propensity for deception and recklessness that combined with a talent for technology would in almost any previous age have resulted in a career as a criminal. Fortunately, a talent spotter for The Organisation got wind of my mischief before it got too serious and I was recruited.

'I read your recent articles before agreeing to meet you. I found two particularly interesting. The one about the team at Scarlastion[1] was fascinating. It's not my area of expertise at all but I think you did well to explain their research for those unfamiliar with it, I certainly found it enlightening. Also, the work being done by our friendly rivals at the University of Theslis[2] into black holes is extremely exciting and could have quite an impact on some of the work we do here.'

Fortunately, I had read the last four or five articles published under the Pike alias, that much at least was required for my cover, anything further back than that and I could easily pretend I couldn't remember.

'Do you really think the team at Theslis will be able to get some kind of probe beyond the event horizon and successfully retrieve it?'

'I don't know for sure, but if anyone can then I think Doctors Wharton and Brice can...'

---

[1] Scarlastion is home to the galaxy's leading biomedical research facilities.

[2] Theslis is one of the oldest science universities in the galaxy. It is very venerable and highly regarded but considered a little stuffy and 'safe'.

She was interrupted by the arrival of our first course. The food smelled amazing and looked like art. Fortunately, it also tasted absolutely fabulous[1].

'The other article you mentioned was about replacing the cuff with an implant so we can control the Infosys link directly with our brain wasn't it' I said. 'It seemed rather far-fetched and answering a question nobody is really asking. But the team there are convinced it'll be revolutionary.'

'How do you personally feel?'

'Oh, I'm quite happy with my cuff,' I said with a smile and jiggled my left wrist.

'So am I. I'm wary of tinkering with the brain. The law of unintended consequences so often applies.'

'How so?' I asked her.

'Oh, I don't want to get into it now. It must seem strange that someone whose life has been devoted to science and reason should be wary of progress but in this instance I am.'

She suddenly looked embarrassed and appeared to be keen to change the subject.

'Please, carry on,' I encouraged with a smile, 'I won't laugh.'

'No. It's ridiculous,' She said shaking her head emphatically, 'Tell me about Mirth, what's it like there these days?'

She'd shut that door for now and I didn't want to be too pushy so as the next course of our meal arrived, I talked about Mirth. I had spent just enough time there to ensure if Jones checked up on me it would appear that I had a life there. I'd read up on some of the cultural highlights and hoped I could exaggerate and elaborate on my minimal experience of the art galleries, theatres and gardens.

We were interrupted by a brief warm sonorous bell-like tone which Doctor Jones explained was the announcement that sunset was imminent.

'The restaurant knows that almost no-one wants to miss the sunset,' she said, 'but it's easy to be caught up in the food or

---

[1] Virtually all food is vegan. No one has killed or exploited an animal for food for many thousands of years, so far as I know. The little meat that is eaten is grown artificially in nutrient farms, it has no central nervous system and therefore no consciousness. People who do eat meat tend to only eat it once or twice a month as the incredible variety of fruit and vegetables available is so delicious, healthy and nutritious.

conversation. The bell discreetly gives us a moment to pause and watch it together.'

Even if you've seen a thousand sunsets on a thousand planets a sunset into the ocean was always special. No one was eating and every head in the restaurant was turned to the west. Well almost every head. There was one that wasn't. One head was staring our way but I wasn't sure if its owner was staring at Doctor Jones or at me until our eyes made contact and she didn't look away. She was glaring at me with considerable ferocity. It was the elderly woman who had been reading in the park earlier in the day.

Chapter 5
The grand tour

I lay on my bed in the hotel room thinking about the old woman from the park and the restaurant. I was certain it was the same person. When our eyes had met and I'd seen that ferocious look, a look of almost hatred, it had been only momentary then she had appeared to get her emotions under control. I had smiled and nodded to her as if we were perhaps acquaintances then turned back to my conversation with Doctor Jones. The rest of the meal had been as spectacularly good as the starter and I didn't catch the old woman looking in our direction again. She finished before we did and left the restaurant. I was desperate to follow her but couldn't do so without it appearing extremely rude and odd. If there was anything significant in it I was sure I'd be seeing her again and if not, if it was just my imagination or a coincidence, then I wouldn't.

I had used my cuff to generate a reasonably good likeness of the woman and sent it to The Organisation for a facial recognition match. I didn't expect an instantaneous reply. It was only a likeness and that would reduce the efficiency of the search[1]. The intelligent search systems would start here on Coronnol then move back through my personal mission itinerary and, to be safe, Doctor Jones' travel history before widening the search outwards. I was also going to get a lot of false positives. I muted the cuff's alerts on this particular item so I wouldn't be disturbed in the middle of the night.

I hadn't managed to plant a Spycomm on Doctor Jones during the meal, which was a little frustrating, but I'd hopefully have a better chance tomorrow when I was given a tour of her department and was able to start the interview proper. I took some of the usual precautions before I went to bed. I set up a pair of small automatically activated force-field generators from the secret equipment hidden in the luggage. One in front of the bedroom door and one in front of the window. Nothing ruins a good night's sleep

---

[1] With a galactic population that was somewhere between a few hundred million to three billion people per planet and roughly twenty-five thousand inhabited planets that was a lot of faces to match.

more than unpleasant people bursting into your room trying to kill you. If anyone did open either the door or the window, by force or by stealth, the force field would activate preventing their entrance and my cuff would wake me. I wasn't expecting trouble but I knew I'd sleep deeper and for longer if my subconscious was relaxed, and now the encounter with the old woman had me wondering who else had an interest in Doctor Jones' work and why they apparently hated me.

I awoke refreshed ready to face the day just before eight o'clock the following morning. I wasn't in a rush as my appointment wasn't until ten. I deactivated the force fields and packed them away and ordered a spectacular breakfast to eat in my room. I wasn't in the mood for company and I could enjoy the view and eat in peace.

I checked my search results and a few dozen close matches had been found but only five of them were here on Coronnol and none in Transium itself. None of them were close enough matches to be the person I'd seen.

After a long hot shower I dressed fairly casually and headed down to the lobby and out across the park to the Astrophysics building. There were no familiar faces to be seen anywhere. As I approached the reception a young man stood up from the waiting area and waved to me.

'Cemeron Argalion Pike?' he said, 'I'm Danatis Mercutio Randolf. I'm part of Doctor Jones' team. She asked me to meet you and escort you to the facility. The main lab is on the edge of the city.'

He turned and walked back out of the exit so I followed him. He was almost impossibly tall, over two meters I estimated, and thin as a rake. He had a long loping stride that meant I needed to walk quite briskly to keep up.

'We'll go by bubble,' he said, indicating the row of vehicles under a covered alcove just to the side of the entrance.

The bubble, a common surface transport that was in use galaxy wide, could seat between one and four people depending on size. As the name indicated it was a transparent sphere that could roll in any direction, the seats inside remained anchored in the upright forward-facing position by a small gravity generator. The occupants could render the sphere opaque if privacy was required; the occupants could see out but no one outside could see in. They were smooth, quiet and comfortable, but their use was discouraged if the destination was within reasonable walking distance.

He offered his cuff to the nearest one and it lit up with a soft warm glow and a large section of the curved transparent side popped out a few centimetres and smoothly slid upwards following the contour of the sphere. He had to fold himself almost in half to get inside then he slid over to the far seat. I followed him rather more easily before the door closed silently behind me.

'Astrophysics Lab Two,' he said into his cuff.

The bubble rolled smoothly out of the alcove and headed through the park at walking pace until it reached one of the five roads radiating from the centre of the city, it then sped up considerably.

'It's a bit too far to walk when you're on a tight schedule,' he said apologetically, 'But I walk it quite often, I don't always use a bubble.'

'I'm not here assessing your commitment to personal fitness,' I said with a smile.

'It's just that I don't want you to think I'm lazy.'

I decided to change the subject.

'How long have you been working with Doctor Jones?' I asked.

'For. Not really with,' He nervously corrected me, 'I'm just one member of her team. I've not got my Doctorate yet. But all being well, later this year…'

He tailed off and glanced nervously about as if trying desperately to think of something interesting to say, or possibly wondering if he was allowed to say something he wanted to.

The city was now whizzing by at about fifty kilometres per hour and the buildings were getting noticeably shorter as we neared the outskirts. One in particular caught my eye. It was single story, squat, rectangular and very plain. It was utterly at odds with all the other buildings in the city. There was a strange looking logo or symbol and the words 'Primitive Meeting Hall' were written above the wooden door.

'You have Primitives here on Coronnol?' I asked.

Randolf looked to where I was pointing.

'A few, barely more than a handful I expect. They built that themselves by hand, contravening all planning statutes, a few years ago. The city government has been arguing, in court, to get it demolished ever since but they keep appealing on the grounds of freedom of expression.'

The Primitives were a sect that had a scattering of devotees all across the galaxy, albeit in vanishingly small numbers compared to the general population. I was hazy on their belief system but knew they were anti-technology. The Organisation had never considered them a threat on the dual basis that they were so few in number and they eschewed almost all technology; to end the galaxy would require either a lot of people and/or a lot of advanced technology. People mostly considered them to be harmless cranks and subject to some gentle mocking if they were considered at all.

'I am surprised. I wouldn't have thought there was any anti-technology sentiment here in this bastion of progress.'

'They occasionally do a silent protest outside one campus building or another, they hand out leaflets telling us we should discard our cuffs. They seem harmless, if a bit odd.'

'Do you spend a lot of time at the lab we're meeting Doctor Jones in?' I asked, just to get the conversation back on topic.

'Sometimes I feel like I live there,' he said, 'Not that I'm complaining. It's amazing work and an honour to be a part of it.'

'How are you involved in Doctor Jones' work, what is your specialisation Per[1] Randolf?' I asked.

'Oh, my Doctorate is all about what will be a revolutionary breakthrough in hyperspatial technology. It's very exciting. I'm sure you understand the basic principles of hyperspatial travel? Well, my research is a whole new way to calculate a hyperspatial portal. The new method improves calculation time, accuracy and it allows portals to remain open. It's really very exciting.'

He gabbled on so I tuned out and let it wash over me. I had almost zero comprehension of the mathematics involved in plotting a hyperspatial journey or how a hyperspatial portal was opened. I just took the technology for granted as had trillions of people for tens of thousands of years. The hyperdrive had hardly changed since it was invented other than the physical machinery had shrunk. The earliest known hyperspace ships had been gigantic, with approximately ninety-five percent of the ship being the fuel and the hyperdrive itself. These days a hyperdrive could be fitted into a ship for four people and only take up five percent of the space. The ones I'd seen were just large grey metal boxes. There was nothing to see, no moving parts that I was aware of. I didn't understand how anyone

---

[1] The title Per is universally used to formally refer to someone who doesn't have an occupational or academic title such as Doctor. It's short for Person. It's gender neutral and finally did away with the archaic Mr., Mrs., Miss or Ms. that restricted people's perceptions of gender and identity for millennia.

could get excited about speeding up the already lightning-fast hyperspace calculations.

The bubble had now left the main thoroughfare and was navigating around some smaller paths and slowing down considerably. Soon we were back to walking pace and a huge low curved building appeared at the top of a gentle climb up a hill. The bubble stopped outside large glass double doors under an elegantly sculpted protective canopy then the hatch popped out and up. I clambered out followed, somewhat awkwardly, by Randolf. As the bubble hissed quietly away, to park itself next to two or three others nearby, the doors opened and Randolf ushered me inside.

There was a small reception desk with a plaque above it informing visitors that Professor Malvus Arthur Crenshaw had opened Physics and Astrophysics Laboratory Two some five years previously. I'd no idea who he was but I presumed he was quite important. There were double security doors on either side of the reception area which was tastefully if sparsely decorated. There was no one waiting at the reception desk. Randolf tapped his cuff, as he did so I set mine into record mode. A virtual screen lit up on the desk and he entered some codes which were now safely recorded for if and when I needed them[1]. You never know when a thing like that could come in handy.

'Please raise your cuff in this direction please,' he said indicating the screen.

I did so and my cuff glowed briefly.

'You'll be able to get through the security doors for the rest of the day now. Everywhere I have access to, which is pretty much everything, except for the hard radiation workshops and other secure locations. The radiation labs are very dangerous if you're not accompanied by a specialist and as we don't really use them in our team you won't need to go there.' He was gabbling again. I wasn't sure if it was because he was just nervous or if he was trying so hard not to give something away that he was blurting out everything else.

He strode off to the left-hand doors which opened as we approached and closed with a solid sounding clunk behind me as I followed him. I activated the mapping feature of my cuff as we headed through the doors. Whatever else I saw today I wanted to

---

[1] Cuff are usually unable to record the activities of other cuffs, for privacy and security reasons. Cuffs issued by The Organisation had no such limitations.

know how much of the building I'd really seen and especially if there were any parts of it they'd been keeping me away from.

The corridor curved gently to the right and was brilliant white. Every ten metres or so there was a window on the left to the outside world and on the right to workshops, laboratories and offices. Randolf chatted away explaining the contents of the rooms, even the ones that were self-evident to a non-scientist like me. After a hundred meters or so the doors we had come through were no longer visible.

'Is the building circular?' I asked

'Yes. Most of Transium is based on circular or curved shapes. Coronnol architects don't appear to like straight lines very much.'

'Are you not from Coronnol?' I asked

'No!' he laughed, 'Can't you tell from my accent? I'm from Fortuna.'

I had noticed a slightly odd accent but hadn't been able to place it. Everyone assumed their little corner of the galaxy was famous but apart from a few dozen really remarkable worlds none were, galactically speaking.

'How long have you been living here?'

'Almost six years now. You should have heard my accent when I first arrived. I must have sounded like a terrible stronky.'

I had no idea what a 'stronky'[1] was and wondered if I should look it up when Randolf suddenly turned right through a set of frosted glass doors with Doctor M O Jones etched on the left-hand pane. There were several closed opaque doors at intervals to the left and right so I had no idea what lay behind those. At the end of the narrow corridor another set of frosted doors opened as we approached letting us into the lab itself where I saw Doctor Jones surrounded by a small team of people all dressed similarly. It appeared she had excellent hearing as she turned to greet us as soon as the doors opened.

'Cemeron, Danatis! Good to see you both,' she looked up at Randolf, who towered over her, 'Thank you for escorting our visitor here.'

She approached and held out her arm to link with mine. I noticed Randolf half raise his arm ready to link but he realised Doctor Jones was already turning away and quickly lowered it again, scratching an imaginary itch.

---

[1] I looked it up later. It's *very* rude.

'Let me show you round,' she called over her shoulder as she headed for a large bank of complex looking machines on the far side of the vast lab.

The group of people she'd been talking to had all drifted away. Some left through various exits and some were now working quietly at who knew what at the various workbenches scattered around the room. The room was curved as I presumed all were, but it was at least fifty meters deep from outer to inner edge, and a hundred meters or more across. I presumed there was no top floor to the building as the ceiling was very high so I was surprised there were no skylights to make the most of natural daylight.

She noticed me looking up.

'No skylights I'm afraid. Security reasons; we don't want anyone looking in at what we're doing here. In fact the whole building is shielded.'

'Is what you do in here that sensitive or secret?' I asked.

I was quite surprised at the comment about the building being shielded. That would be an important piece of information if I had to return here on my own, uninvited.

'Rivalries between academic institutions are as bad, if not worse, than commercial ones, Cemeron,' she answered, 'There are one or two other universities who would give their eye teeth for a good look at our research. While the ideal is openness and transparency the reality is we have to maintain a degree of security until we're ready to publish to ensure due credit is received.'

The next two hours passed in a head spinning whirl of names, jargon and complex technology. I understood very little of it but was impressed by her enthusiasm. She certainly appeared to be a good leader, she knew everyone's name and exactly what they did for her, and also knew enough about their personal lives to at least make it look like she cared. I felt like I'd walked about five miles by the time we returned, through the main lab, to one of the rooms behind an opaque door that turned out to be her office. It had two comfortable sofas, a coffee machine on a stand, a large bookshelf[1] covering most

---

[1] Amazingly printed books were still popular, for leisure purposes or for display, all across the galaxy; the invention of the cuff, a few hundred years ago, notwithstanding. They've not been made from dead trees and animal hide for millennia but a love for the feeling of weight and solidity in reading matter is clearly deeply ingrained in the human psyche. Nothing beats a good quality cuff and Infosys when researching, working or creating as far as I'm concerned.

of one wall and a small desk and chair. Another wall was dominated by an intricate two-dimensional rendering of a planet seen from space entitled Planet Earth. I wasn't very familiar with Earth. I knew it was humanity's original home but I'd never been there either as a tourist[1] or for work. The continent facing the observer dominated the globe, it started in the southern part of the northern hemisphere and was very wide, stretching almost from edge to edge, then it tapered sharply on the left-hand side down to a point not too far from the southern pole. I had no idea what it was called.

Doctor Jones produced two coffees and took the sofa facing the door. I sat in the other. I had noticed as we went round the facility that Doctor Jones had only talked about the research and work that her subordinates were engaged in. She had very carefully avoided revealing what she herself was working on. Possibly she was just modest but I considered that quite unlikely.

'We're due to have lunch with most of the department's staff shortly,' she said, 'Would it be alright to start the interview after that?'

I agreed readily as I was quite hungry by that point. We finished our coffees and I followed Doctor Jones to a large open cafeteria on the outer wall of the building. This had a simple curved glass exterior wall looking out onto the grounds but the ceiling was composed of a multitude of differently shaped glass panels in subtly changing hues all tessellated neatly together in a complex almost organic pattern. Although the panels remained stationary, they changed shape occasionally. That plus the way the colours migrated slowly around made it look alive, almost as if it was moving underwater.

'That ceiling is incredible,' I said

'It's by Fibrilla Carlos Ikoku, one of the leading glass and light artists on Mirth. I recommended him to the university when we were planning this building. I remembered his installation at the Planetary Library in the capital where I lived as a child. I decided if I was ever in a position to commission something by him then I would. He's quite elderly now and semi-retired so I imagine this was one of his

---

[1] Earth is now principally a tourist destination and conservation park. There's almost no industrial or commercial activity. As the only planet in the galaxy to have evolved a thriving, diverse ecosystem as well as intelligent life, it is preserved, protected and maintained extremely carefully. Biologists. ecologists, and terraformers are those most interested in it. I couldn't imagine why an Astrophysicist was interested.

last large works. I adore it and eat in here as often as I can, just to enjoy the light.'

We helped ourselves from the extensive buffet and then joined a group of mostly familiar faces at a large round table, many of whom already had their meals but were waiting politely for us to join them. The food was excellent and there was no talking 'shop' during the meal. Mostly people talked about music, sport, family and the day-to-day trivia of life. In fact, anyone talking about work was gently rebuked and steered off the topic. The second time this happened I glanced at Doctor Jones.

'Balance again I'm afraid. I mentioned last night that I believed it was important, and the work/life balance is one of the most important of all. We try to ensure meal times are social occasions and that as many from the team as possible get together each day. It builds a sense of community and shared purpose when you know each other as people and not just as a set of job functions. I don't make distinctions between technicians and researchers or administrative staff and maintenance crew. We are all part of this department, part of this university. We all contribute and our contributions are all valid and important. If someone mentions work, we don't snap or shut them down, we just remind them and move on. If anyone has something urgent that cannot wait, they take the person they need back to the lab to talk there.'

She seemed sincere. I didn't get the impression this was purely public relations spin or, worse, some kind of over-zealous control. As someone who was always working when undercover I almost envied this opportunity to disengage but I also knew I lived for the adrenalin thrill of living a double life.

A short pale man with thinning sandy coloured hair, scraped artlessly across his bald patch, sitting a little further anti-clockwise round the table from me moved his empty plate, stood up and picked up his drink and came to sit closer, presumably so he could talk. I had been introduced to him earlier and he had excused himself immediately so I had no idea what he did at the lab. He smiled as he sat and introduced himself.

'Per Pike, I am Doctor Julius Markus Grippe, did you enjoy your tour?'

'I remember you Doctor Grippe. Although I didn't get to talk to you or find out your role in this amazing place.'

'I'm Doctor Jones' deputy director. I'm a physicist. The Physics and Astrophysics departments are very closely linked. We have a joint director of the two departments. When there's an Astrophysicist in charge the deputy is always from the Physics department and visa-versa. I help oversee a lot of the work here. I specialise in quantum mechanics and gravitational manipulation fields. Did you come here on a Starlight class ship?'

I told him that I had.

'The artificial gravity modules on those were designed by me, and my team,' he added the last bit on as almost an afterthought, 'They're a great improvement on the old ones. They use approximately two-thirds of the power and produce a much more stable and focused field. I don't imagine you had space sickness once during the voyage?'

'No, I didn't,' I agreed, 'but I rarely do, I travel a lot with my job.'

'Almost all space sickness, that isn't psychosomatic, is due to slight variations in the grav field, did you know that? We won an award for that design. They're gradually replacing all the grav generators on every modern starship.'

He was beaming with pride.

'Gravity has always been an interest of mine,' he said, 'I'm originally from Cestus. Have you heard of it?'

'No, I'm afraid I haven't'

'Our gravity at sea level is just over one point eight 'g', which explains my short stature. It's the highest 'g' of any inhabited planet that I'm aware of. We don't have many skyscrapers or tall people.' He glanced down the table to Randolf, who even sitting down was obviously taller than anyone else in the room, 'Per Randolf wouldn't even be able to stand if he came home with me but here on Coronnol I feel as light as a feather for a few weeks until I re-adjust. Perhaps you should come for a visit sometime? Anyway, I just thought I'd introduce myself. There's a lot more going on here than Jones is likely to show you.'

Without even a glance at my host he stood up and finished his drink then headed for the exit.

'I apologise for him,' said Doctor Jones, 'He was my only serious rival for head of the departments. When I was awarded the post I offered him the deputy position and hoped we could mend fences but sadly it hasn't worked out. We rarely speak but fortunately our work has little overlap so we don't need to be together often.'

Once lunch was over I spent an hour or so talking to Doctor Jones back at her office about her career starting with her first recognized breakthrough, the warp stellar probe, which she was very happy to discuss and ending with a major academic prize she'd been awarded the previous year before I posed the question I'd been waiting all day to ask.

'What are you currently working on Doctor Jones?'

She paused for quite a long time and seemed to be having difficulty deciding whether to tell me or not.

'I'm between projects right now,' she said, 'I have several ideas but I've not determined which is the most likely to be interesting long term. There are some terrific opportunities opening up in extra-galactic mapping that look promising.'

I was absolutely certain this was a lie. For one thing it was far too vague and nebulous for a hands-on researcher like her and for another I couldn't conceive how anything like that could end all human life in the galaxy. She was definitely keeping quiet about something and I would have to find a way to discover what it was. Perhaps Doctor Grippe would be able to help with that.

Chapter 6
Making plans

We chatted about some inconsequential matters and I thanked Doctor Jones for her time and arranged to meet her again in a couple of days to fill in any gaps and show her the first draft of the article. I also took the opportunity to plant a Spycomm in her office before I headed back to the reception area. I still hadn't been able to get one on her person but I expected I'd have at least one more opportunity to do so.

The weather was clouding over and according to my cuff it would take about an hour and a quarter to get back to the hotel on foot. I decided to walk as there didn't seem to be much chance of rain[1]. The footpaths were well tended and not very busy. Either most people had taken a bubble or I was too early for the end of day rush. I set a reasonable pace back towards the city and decided to use the exercise time to review any further Spycomm transmissions and check my facial recognition search. There was no blue dot for the office in the Astrophysics tower as Doctor Jones must not have been there today but a purple dot for the office at the lab was pulsing gently. I pulled a small earpiece from its compartment in my cuff and popped it in my ear so I could listen in private. Once again, I was mildly disappointed to hear nothing but routine calls to work colleagues. The facial search was throwing up plenty of false positives but each was getting further and further away from Coronnol, plus none had left their home planet recently enough to have been here. I cancelled the search as it was just a waste of time. My generated likeness must not have been accurate enough or perhaps the old woman had been disguising her true appearance. If I saw her again I would ensure I got close enough to capture an image with my cuff.

Back at the hotel I transmitted the recording of my interview with Doctor Jones back to the Barbs, so they could get to work turning it

---

[1] Every ten or twenty years someone claims a major breakthrough is just around the corner in weather control technology and it always turn out to be hokum. On a planetary scale there are simply too many variables in too many systems that are simply too powerful. The best we can do is accurately predict the weather so we can prepare for its extremes.

into a first draft of the article I was supposed to be writing. I pulled up the map of the facility that my cuff had recorded. The cuff's default virtual screen was about twice the size of my hand, but a pinch at the corner and I could drag it out as large as I wanted. I expanded it to over a meter square and set it to be fully opaque so I could see the image clearly and in detail. I started with an overhead plan view where the walls were traced in blue, doors were marked in green and my progress around the building was shown as a faintly pulsing yellow line, with the pulses indicating the direction of travel. I rotated the image to put the main entrance at the bottom and sped up the playback until the yellow line arrived back at the bottom. We had covered a large portion of the left-hand side of the circular building, weaving in and out of rooms around the large main lab before skirting around the top of the circular core to get to the right-hand half of the building then we had continued clockwise round the edge in the outer corridor. The inner rooms on the right side comprised the physics department's radiation labs and we'd only looked in through the windows without going in. The cuff had marked their walls in red, as it could clearly detect the presence of radiation. The line then cut back below the central core to the left side before heading to Jones's office then to the cafeteria with the amazing ceiling, which was right at the top of the building opposite the entrance. The line then retraced itself back to Jones' office then back to the entrance. Looking at the map I realised that without the cuff I would have been absolutely certain I'd seen everything short of the central core, which would typically be the power facility and probably not really of interest, but the map showed a blank space big enough for a medium sized room between the cafeteria and the main lab. We'd skirted it a couple of times but I'd never seen a door and crucially neither had the cuff's sensors. This meant it must be very carefully shielded. I was certainly going to pay a return visit tonight.

I ate again in Forts restaurant. This time I asked for a table on the transparent floor on the outer edge but sadly they were all booked up and I had to settle for one concentric ring in. The view was still amazing and by the end of the meal I was quite glad not to be sitting above such a long drop. Seeing the drop from where I was seated was dizzying enough. I saw no-one I recognised in the restaurant all night.

I set the force-fields and then got to bed as quickly as possible so I could catch at least a few hours' sleep, as my cuff was set to wake me just before one a.m. I anticipated a busy night.

Chapter 7
Night time excursions

My alarm roused me from a deep sleep but the excitement soon kicked in and I felt fully alert. I packed away the force-fields, and gathered a few items I thought might be required including an additional cuff and headed downstairs to the lobby.

There was no-one about at all, the last few drinkers in the bar had given up for the night and the overnight cleaning crews were nowhere to be seen yet. I headed towards the bubble parking by the Astrophysics building and pointed the spare cuff I was wearing on my right wrist at the nearest one. The cuff was programmed with an entirely different, fictional, identity of a Transium citizen. I didn't want to leave a trail showing the Pike identity making nocturnal excursions. I put in the Lab building as the destination and set the bubble's glass to opaque mode as we set off. If anyone was watching they wouldn't be able to see who was riding. I sat back and relaxed until the cuff showed I was five minutes from my destination. I stopped the bubble, re-programmed it to return to its parking bay in the city and got out before it spun around and headed off the way it had come. The rest of the journey would have to be on foot as I had no idea what surveillance beyond the obvious might be in use. I pulled out a soft tightly wrapped package from my pocket. It unrolled into a complete one-piece overall-style suit which I pulled on over my clothes. A headpiece covered my head and face and tight-fitting gloves enclosed my hands. I squeezed a patch on the right wrist and I felt the suit shrink to a snug fit all over. I knew anyone who looked at me would see someone in janitor's overalls plus the face on the head piece looked nothing like mine. The chameleon suit[1] was a handy item and one of the best pieces of field

---

[1] The chameleon suit is made up of a pale almost colourless material that works like a single flexible screen onto which any image can be displayed, this combined with sophisticated shaping and stiffening technology allows the wearer to be a considerably different body shape and have different facial features. It can't make you taller, shorter or thinner than you are but it looks completely realistic until the observer is within a few meters. It was rumoured a new higher quality one was due soon that

equipment The Organisation had. Once wearing it I was unrecognizable, the suit could be programmed with any number of different faces, the fingerprints on the gloves were randomly generated plus the suit trapped any trace of my own DNA inside it.

After a short walk I saw the entrance to the Lab ahead. It was brightly lit, which might mean people were still at work somewhere inside or it might not. I decided to track around the building and enter via the cafeteria. I had seen doors in the glass wall there. It took a few minutes to get there and fortunately the room was in complete darkness. Clearly nobody was eating there overnight. I raised the spare cuff to the door pulled up the screen and entered the codes my own cuff had recorded Randolf using to enter the building. There was a short pause then the door unlocked with a barely audible click and it swung open. I followed my own cuff's map to get as close as I could to the secret room that must exist within the blank space I had seen on the map. I arrived at a normal looking section of wall. I ran my fingers carefully over it feeling for hidden catches, hinges or door edges while my cuff scanned for shielding technology. I found nothing. The corridors were dark, but not completely black, the lighting was in some kind of night-mode. All the windows were opaque as I guess there was nothing to be seen in the grounds at night. I followed my cuff round to the next point where my tour had intersected the secret room. This was in a machine room where several stellar probes were being modified for some kind of experiment whose details had been explained to me while I just nodded along. This time my cuff detected a slight energy signature on the expected wall. I raised the spare cuff and tried the entry codes Randolf had used, without a great deal of expectation but it was worth a shot. Nothing happened. Getting the door open easily now depended on whether the door was a standard security product, as used by those with valuables to hide, or if it was the university's own custom design or even a design by Doctor Jones herself. The Organisation had acquired back-door codes to virtually every major security product on the market and the ones that didn't already include a back-door workaround we had developed hacks for. If it was a custom-made door then I could be in for a long night. I brought up the hacking menu on the cuff and selected security doors, hatches and windows then set it trying combinations, beginning with the

---

would work well enough to use face to face.

most complex and expensive and working its way down from there. I doubted anything worth hiding here would be protected with a cheap door. The cuff flickered gently to indicate the number of attempts and after about thirty minutes and eighty-six tries had hit on the right door, a Stanton-Mayes, one of the best security doors around and unhackable to anyone but us. I double checked there was no-one around, drew a stunner[1] from my pocket and triggered the door opening sequence. It was something of an anti-climax, there was no escape of steam, no alarms started ringing, all that happened was that a door sized section of wall popped two or three millimetres proud of the rest of the wall and a handle lit up with a soft glow. I pressed it and the door swung outwards smoothly. I raised the stunner and checked inside the room. It was dark and, so far as I could tell, unoccupied. I took out a small cylindrical hand-held scanning tool from my pocket. It was about eight centimetres long and about one and a half in diameter. I tapped it on my cuff and they both glowed briefly. The cuff screen lit up and I selected the appropriate function, scanned for surveillance equipment and when I couldn't detect any I went in cautiously and closed and locked the door behind me. I didn't want to be disturbed while I was in there. As I entered the room the lights faded up to normal brightness automatically.

This room was definitely what I was looking for. There was a large holo-image on one wall showing an animation of a star changing from a yellow sun to a red giant before exploding into a supernova. There were parts for some fairly complex equipment scattered across the work benches, some looked intact and some looked partly assembled, or maybe, disassembled. Best of all there was smallish red rectangular device I recognized as a secure storage and processing unit, or SSP. An SSP allowed highly sensitive work to be done using Infosys as it encrypted everything passing through it and the only way to decrypt it was to be in this room. Every SSP was unique, location aware and could not be accessed remotely. Even if I removed it to work on elsewhere it wouldn't give me access. I would definitely not be able to crack the security on that in the time available, they were extraordinarily difficult, even The Organisation would need quite some time to do it. I recorded detailed scans of all

---

[1] A small hand-held weapon that could be set to do anything from paralyse someone for a few minutes while keeping them conscious all the way up to the maximum power setting that would knock someone out for a whole day. I usually kept mine at the lowest setting.

the equipment around the room and then very carefully attached a small device very similar to the audio Spycomm to the underside of the SSP. Whenever the SSP was in use this Spycomm would analyse the communication between it and the cuff linked to it until it could work out how to replicate the access codes. That could take a few days depending on how much the SSP was in use. Once the encryption was broken, I would have to come back. I decided I'd seen enough and although I had no idea yet what I'd found I wouldn't be able to analyse it any better here than in the hotel. I opened the door carefully, stepped through and pushed it closed. It slid flush with the wall and the illuminated handle went dark. It was as invisible as before. I turned in the dim light and started making my way out of the machine room towards the corridor. I wanted to visit the building's core, even though in all likelihood it was simply the power distribution systems I needed to be sure. I'd just stepped out into the main corridor when a vicious blow to the back of my head sent me reeling and bounced me off the opposite wall.

Chapter 8
Fight or flight

O nce again I was extremely grateful for the equipment The Organisation provided. The chameleon suit, as well as being an efficient disguise, had some minimal but effective armour built in. The blow was heavy enough to crack an unprotected skull but even through the suit it still stunned me. All the lights, even the minimal night lights, were off in the main corridor, it was almost completely pitch black. I had dropped the stunner somewhere when I'd been hit but looking for it now was pointless and, even worse, dangerous. The first priority was to avoid getting hit again. The suit's armour wasn't going to keep me safe from many more of those kinds of blows. My head was pounding and I could taste blood, I must have bitten my tongue, but I knew I needed to get up quickly and tackle my assailant or make a run for it. Getting to my feet was hard enough so running really didn't seem to be an option; my legs were rubbery and I was dizzy. I leant against the wall peering into the dark trying to spot my assailant, a shadow moved in the darkness and something hard, probably a metal bar or rod, hit me on the side and knocked me back down. I rolled quickly away on the floor until I had a few metres between me and my unseen assailant. I forced myself upright despite my spinning head and swallowed the blood, spitting it out was not an option from inside the suit's hood. Even if it were possible, I wouldn't want to leave my DNA at the scene. I couldn't see my attacker but hopefully I might be able to hear them. I took a cautious silent step forward, heading back towards where I thought I'd first been jumped, holding my breath to give myself the best chance of hearing something. I took another step, then a third. I heard a sharp intake of breath to my left like someone readying themselves and turned in time to see a very faint glint from a long metal tool. They'd taken far too big a back swing so I stepped inside the incoming blow and their hands hit me on the shoulder instead of the bar hitting my head. I grabbed two handfuls of their clothing and using my forward momentum I span round and dropped backwards to the floor pulling down with all my strength. Already off balance from their swing my assailant flew over me and crashed heavily on the floor behind dropping the tool which clattered away. Now we were both unarmed I had more of a chance. I span round on the floor and kicked out hard to where I'd heard them fall and felt my foot connect with something soft, probably their stomach. There was a cry of pain from my assailant and I scrambled to my feet ready to kick again. Whoever this was they were in good shape, as they too were up and ready. My eyes had adjusted to the darkness but still I couldn't make out any details. They were just a slightly different shade of black, panting and breathing heavily. I sensed more than saw the wildly swung left-handed punch, which I only just dodged. It was followed by a flailing right which missed completely as I had backed away out of range. Whoever this was they were strong but they weren't a fighter. Violence wasn't something The Organisation encouraged but it was occasionally necessary, so I had received a lot of training and had more than a little actual experience. With a frustrated cry my shadowy assailant lunged towards me both arms outstretched, presumably hoping to grab me and get me down on the floor where they could finish me off. In my woozy state I doubted I'd get up again if they succeeded, so instead of retreating, which they would have expected, I moved towards them and at the last second stepped to their right. Their momentum didn't allow them to change direction mid-charge and I easily brushed their outstretched arm aside, span quickly and pushed them in the back with all my strength. They hit the wall of the corridor at full speed and I heard a crunch which sounded awfully like a bone breaking, then they slid to the floor moaning. I needed to ask this person some questions. I approached them cautiously but before I got the chance to ask anything, I saw a faint pattern of lights appear on their cuff and then every alarm in the building went off. The sound was deafening and the corridor was filled with flashing light. My assailant staggered to their feet, they were dressed in a one-piece ski suit complete with ski mask, the front of which was covered with blood. They might have broken their nose when they hit the wall. They were also cradling their left arm tight to their body, it definitely looked broken. The left hand was slack and at an odd angle. They turned and staggered off down the corridor towards the main entrance. I considered chasing them but decided running into campus security or the police would be quite likely. At least the flashing lights helped me find my stunner, which I pocketed and then I headed back to the cafeteria as quickly as I could manage. I certainly wasn't going to be able to investigate the core tonight. Once I'd let myself out into the grounds I headed for some bushes, that would allow me to keep out of sight while I made my way to a path back to Transium city centre. I reprogrammed the chameleon suit with an entirely different identity, an overweight elderly man in workmen's overalls. The suit wouldn't pass for real up close but at a distance of more than ten meters, or on surveillance video, it would be good enough.

Five minutes later I was feeling a little steadier on my feet. I hadn't seen any activity at the rear of the building but the alarms were still ringing. I used the spare cuff to summon a bubble as walking all the way back wasn't really an option. Within a minute or two I saw it gliding towards me and I clambered in, set the glass to opaque and headed back to the city centre. I didn't head for the hotel; I'd set the Mag station as my destination as I hoped that would be busy enough even at this hour for me to go unnoticed. The bubble parked itself at a different entrance to the one I'd used the other day but I soon found the public restrooms and slipped out of the chameleon suit in one of the cubicles. I triggered the suit's autodestruct and flushed the rapidly dissolving dust down the toilet bowl. I checked the back of my head as well as I could in a mirror but I couldn't see or feel any blood in my hair, just a very tender spot that would no doubt ache for a few days.

Back in my hotel room I rigged the force-fields again, checked myself thoroughly for any other injuries but aside from the splitting head-ache, a bitten tongue, a bruised back and shoulder I seemed fine. I took a couple of pain killers with a large brandy from the minibar then soaked in a long hot bath until the adrenaline had dissipated enough for me to climb gratefully into bed. It was past four in the morning. I cancelled my alarm, set the room's do not disturb feature and fell fast asleep.

Chapter 9
Recruiting an ally

I woke at about half past nine with the taste of dried blood in my mouth and a dull ache in my head. I ordered breakfast in my room again, and while I waited I did some careful stretches and exercises to ease the stiffness in my right arm and shoulder. I had a nice lump on the back of my head, but my hair hid it sufficiently. I couldn't see anything too wrong in my mouth, just a slight swelling on one side of my tongue that should soon go down, and I had a nice new bruise on my back from being kicked. I felt really stupid for allowing myself to not only get caught by surprise last night but also for not even finding out who it was that attacked me or why. If it was someone at the lab I didn't imagine they'd be able to go in to work today with a broken arm, someone would be bound to ask questions. It was too late to watch the morning arrivals and spot who was missing, plus I had no idea of anyone's schedule, so not turning up at the lab could have any number of innocent explanations. The only person I felt I could rule out was Danatis Mercutio Randolf, my attacker was a lot shorter than two meters. They were strong, that was for sure, and physically fit. They'd recovered surprisingly quickly from being kicked, hard, in the stomach and had been very stoic about breaking an arm. The ski attire didn't help me with identification as I'd seen several shops selling such items near the hotel because there were multiple popular ski resorts in the mountains, a short Mag ride south of Transium. There was a knock on the door that I hoped was my breakfast arriving. I deactivated the force fields and picked up my stunner before opening the door. It was my breakfast, I thanked the waiter and took it eagerly, I was starving.

I needed an ally inside the lab, that much was obvious, but I couldn't tell anyone the truth about who I worked for. Randolf seemed the most likely candidate to recruit as he couldn't possibly be the person who had attacked me, he was quite junior and he seemed very insecure and eager to please. I knew exactly what lie to tell him to get him on board. I called the university and made an arrangement to meet him for lunch at my expense at a beach front restaurant. It was one I'd seen two days ago when I did my walk about ensuring I wasn't being followed. Now I had at least the beginnings of a plan I could enjoy my breakfast. I followed that with the hottest shower I could tolerate before dressing and lying back on the bed to rest.

It took a few minutes to send all the images and data I'd gathered last night to the Barbs for analysis along with as much information and conjecture about my attacker that I could remember. I also checked my three Spycomms. The audio bug in Jones' city centre office was still silent, she clearly didn't spend a lot of time there, but the one in her office at the lab had already recorded several conversations. Unsurprisingly they were mostly about the alarms going off last night and the surveillance system having been disabled, which was interesting. I hadn't disabled the system, so my assailant must have. Doctor Jones had been most concerned that security should be tightened especially near the machine room and that everyone's access codes should be revoked and new ones issued before the end of the day. That would make a return visit using Randolf's stolen access problematic. The SSP had not been accessed yet, which given the disruption the new security concerns were generating wasn't particularly surprising either.

I was still pretty tired so I decided to nap until my appointment with Randolf. I delayed sleeping just long enough to re-enable my force fields and then crashed out into dreamless sleep.

The restaurant at the beach was fairly busy when I arrived, ten minutes or so before my rendezvous. I asked the waiter for a secluded outside table and I chose a seat that put the restaurant's wall at my back and gave me an uninterrupted view of the beach and all the available approaches. I ordered a local coffee, strong and milky without sweetener, and waited for my guest. He arrived on time, and was easy to spot as he towered over everyone else around. I stood up as he approached, smiled and said hello, then we linked arms briefly.

I gestured to a nearby waiter.

'Please order a drink first and then we'll decide what to eat.'

'Just a mineral water on ice, please,' he told the waiter and looking at me added, 'I don't drink anything other than water during the working day. I need a clear head with no stimulants or toxins affecting me.'

He seemed slightly embarrassed by this confession.

The waiter returned with his drink and flicked the menu to our cuffs.

'How would you feel about the sharing seafood platter?' I enquired.

'That would be great.'

'Wonderful. We'll have that and I'll have a half bottle of the Mardonne to drink. Are you sure you won't join me in a glass of wine?'

He emphatically declined with a shake of his head. But I indicated the waiter should bring a second glass anyway.

'Just in case,' I said.

We chatted about the weather, swimming in the sea and other inconsequential matters while we waited for our food. Fairly soon a pair of waiters returned with two large serving dishes loaded with food, some of which I recognised and some I didn't. One waiter pointed out an unfamiliar seaweed-like item and explained it was one of the few native plants that was both edible and delicious. I poured myself a large glass of wine and toasted Randolf's good health. I knew the sharing meal plus our pleasant friendly conversation would be putting him at his ease, making him feel we were friends and on the same side. I felt bad about what I was about to do to him, but I couldn't see another option without breaking protocol completely and telling him the truth. I waited until we were well into our meal before I explained the reason for meeting him.

'Per Randolf,' I said conversationally, 'I'm not a journalist, and I never have been. I'm an undercover police officer. A very senior one. I'm investigating Doctor Jones for serious misappropriation of funds that were donated to the university for research. I used your access codes to gain entry to the building last night in order to look into her private records but before I could find anything incriminating, I was attacked by an unknown person whose arm I broke during the confrontation. You're going to help me find out who that was and what has happened to the missing money.'

The reaction was exactly as I expected. His hand froze midway to his mouth with a forkful of food. All the colour drained from his face and all he managed to stammer out was a feeble 'What?'

'I think you heard me Per Randolf,' I said in my smoothest but most implacable tone, 'Here's my credentials and my authority to investigate in any way I see fit.'

I pulled up the bogus ID and warrant on my cuff and flicked them over to him. His cuff flashed briefly and he opened up the documents and read them with his lips moving slightly.

I continued eating, then looking at his pallid complexion, I poured him a small glass of the wine.

'Are you sure you won't have a drink now?' I asked.

He picked up the glass with two shaking hands and downed it in one, almost choking on it.

'I haven't done anything wrong,' he pleaded, 'You have to believe me. I'm completely innocent.'

'I know,' I said, 'That's why we're having lunch together here instead of talking in an interview room at police headquarters. I'm not trying to trick you into a confession or waiting to arrest you.'

He breathed out and a little colour appeared to come back into his cheeks.

'I'm asking for your help,' I said, 'You are in a perfect position to supply me with the information I need to either expose Doctor Jones as a thief or, better yet, exonerate her and find out who really has embezzled the missing funds.'

'I'm not sure I'm comfortable informing on the Doctor,' he said.

A little life and defiance were creeping back into him now that he was over the initial shock and had realised I wasn't accusing him of anything.

'You forget Per Randolf.' I said, 'According to the access logs it was you that entered the lab via the cafeteria entrance in the middle of the night and then left the same way a few hours later. I think you may find that rather hard to explain. Either you broke in or you gave someone your access codes so they could break in. Obviously, nothing physical was stolen, so they know it wasn't a theft in the traditional sense but Doctor Jones did explain how secure the building is and how there are many other universities that would be very keen to gain access to your unpublished research. If it helps motivate you a little more, I'd have absolutely no hesitation in depositing the sum of one hundred thousand credits into your personal account, money which would easily be traced back to, say, the University of Karnack?'

'That's blackmail!' he cried.

'Please Per Randolf keep your voice down. And no, it isn't. It *is* the threat of blackmail though; I'll give you that. But it needn't come to that. I just need your help. You'll be doing your civic duty in assisting an officer of the law. I can't manage this whole platter by myself, so I would also really appreciate you eating some of it.'

I continued eating and particularly enjoyed the seaweed even though, rather oddly, it tasted of barbequed meat. Randolf looked thoroughly miserable and was picking at his food listlessly.

'What do you want to know?' he finally asked.

'Firstly, I need to know what Doctor Jones' secret project is. Secondly, I need to know who is working on it with her. Thirdly, I need to know who should have been in the lab today but didn't turn up. A broken arm can be fixed pretty rapidly with a tissue regenerator but it will still be obvious for a day or so. I need to find that person quickly before the evidence is gone. Oh, and I need you to plant one of these on Doctor Jones.'

I placed a small sealed transparent box containing a tiny Spycomm on the table between us.

'What is it?' asked Randolf.

'I'll show you,' I said.

I stood up, moved round behind him brushing my hand across the back of his neck slightly as I passed him then returned to my seat.

'What was that about?' he asked nervously.

I pointed to the tiny device in the box, wafer thin and with a diameter of only a few millimetres.

'I just planted one on you,' I told him, 'It's called a Spycomm. I can hear all your conversations now for at least the next week, maybe two. The back of the neck is the best place to put it. You put the Spycomm on your finger, brush lightly on someone's skin and it transfers over and is activated automatically. It changes colour to match the skin tone of the person it's planted on and it won't wash off. It's harmless and it biodegrades once the power supply is exhausted.'

'I c-c-can't bug Doctor Jones!' he cried.

'You can and you will. Please remember that you are already implicated in the break-in. By now they will have realised it was your code used to gain entry in the middle of the night. Just tell them you have no idea how your codes were compromised, promise to be more careful about security in the future and get me the information I need. Remember I can easily escalate your apparent involvement but you will be under the microscope for a little while, so act naturally. Assuming you agree to help I'll let the local police know that your access codes were found for sale on Infosys, along with those of a few other researchers. I'll say they'd been obtained by some mischievous InfoTech students testing security protocols, one of whom got greedy and tried to profit from the test. We'll let it be known they've all been suspended and the culprit disciplined. That will satisfy the police and the Astrophysics department. The InfoTech department is on the other side of the planet so I doubt anyone will care to follow up to see if it's true.'

'Who *are* you?' he asked.

'As I said, I'm a very senior police officer and I'm investigating a very serious matter. I have the authority to proceed as I like. And at the moment this is how I'd like to proceed.'

'All right I'll help you,' he said, 'but I'm absolutely certain Doctor Jones hasn't embezzled any money or done anything unethical. She's an incredible talent and completely devoted to this university and to her work. She'd never do anything to compromise it.'

'I sincerely hope that's true,' I said, 'I like her too but well over ten million credits is unaccounted for and that's a huge sum. A scandal like that coming out publicly would badly damage the university's reputation and destroy the careers of anyone implicated in, or even associated with, it. I want a quiet, publicity-free, resolution and with your help I'm sure that can be achieved.'

'But if I could just talk to Doctor Jones…' he began.

'Let me make it absolutely clear that you cannot, and will not, speak about this meeting, who I really am or what I've asked you to do with *anyone*.'

He didn't look convinced.

It'll be fine,' I said 'You'll be fine.'

I smiled reassuringly.

He pocketed the Spycomm and glumly resumed eating. I can't say the conversation sparkled after that but I was confident he was going to help me.

Chapter 10
Conference

I was walking, by a random and erratic route, back to the hotel when I felt my cuff vibrate in the specific pattern that indicated an urgent communication from The Organisation. I flicked a screen on and kept it very small so only I could read it. The message said...

'Probability of life in the galaxy ending has increased. Are additional resources required? Report progress ASAP.'

That was a surprise, I felt like I was making progress. It could be that the danger had increased precisely because I *was* making progress. If whoever tackled me last night was involved in the potential cataclysm it could be that they felt I was a threat to their plans and had accelerated them. If so then it was increasingly likely I was dealing with an idealist, someone who knew exactly what they were doing. It was hard to imagine how someone could be willing to destroy virtually all life in our galaxy but if I couldn't find out more and quickly it might actually happen. The Organisation had only dealt with one or two idealists in its history. Most of the time we prevented tragic accidents or the occasional lunatic who didn't comprehend the danger of what they were doing.

I sent back a message that I was making progress, now that I had an inside source, and asked for a conference with the duty Barb on the images and data I'd acquired while in the secret room at the lab. I couldn't see the connection between the apparently innocent work being done at the Astrophysics Lab and a galaxy-wide cataclysmic event.

Once back in my hotel room I secured the door and windows again then using the scanning cylinder I swept the room for listening and recording devices, the cuff could detect simple bugging equipment but this could detect anything. I wasn't surprised to find a small camera fitted at the top corner of the room above the window, its fish-eye lens would cover the whole room; I disabled it so it would appear to be simple equipment failure. Most hotels installed cameras to ensure any damage done to the room or any crimes committed in them could be traced back to the guest responsible.

They were meant to have safeguards to prevent the recording of nudity or sexual activity but I wasn't one hundred percent convinced there wouldn't be a way around that restriction, so when in a hotel for personal reasons I always disabled them. I found no evidence of any other surveillance technology, not even something like our Spycomm that was mostly passive. Our bug scanners were constantly updated so it was unlikely anyone had developed anything they couldn't detect. I then set the scanner to scramble mode, popped the earpiece out of the cuff and into my left ear. This conversation needed to be completely private, only I could hear the earpiece and the scramble mode would make my words unintelligible to anyone listening in through the door or walls.

I called The Organisation and once they'd confirmed my identity, that I was alone, shielded, and verified using code words that I was not being coerced, I was connected to the Barbs. An attractive androgynous very dark-skinned face topped off with dyed bright red short hair appeared on the cuff screen. I stretched the screen out so it was life size, to make it possible to see the whole of the person at the other end. I knew them well; we'd worked together on many investigations and we were very good friends. They were one of the smartest people I knew and I felt better knowing that Kastagyr Devon Marshall was backing me up.

'Kas, it's good to see you!' I said and I meant it.

'Cem[1]. It's good to see you too,' they[2] said, smiling broadly.

'Have you had time to draw any conclusions about the equipment I scanned and sent you this morning?'

'For your information it's early morning now. You sent it in the middle of the night, our time, but as you know I don't sleep much so my team and I have already got a few ideas. Most of the equipment is similar to Doctor Jones' solar probe tech but much more advanced. There was what looked like advanced heat shielding, guidance and hyperspatial circuits but exactly what differences there are between those parts and the standard probe we don't know yet. There were three items that we presently have absolutely no clue about, we're attempting to create simulated versions of them from your scan but that will take some time. They could be anything from a coffee machine to the mythical solid matter transporter[3]. The Spycomm you

---

[1] An agent is only ever referred to by their active alias when in the field.

[2] In common with many non-binary people Kastagyr used they/them pronouns.

[3] Transporting a solid object by dematerialising it, sending the energy somewhere

placed on the secure storage and processing unit has reported in and it's almost fifty percent of the way through decrypting the access link, so someone has been using it most of your afternoon. Hopefully before the end of the working day tomorrow we'll be able to send the access codes to your cuff and you can return and find out what's going on in there.'

'That's good news about the SSP,' I said, 'but returning will be trickier now that they know there has been a break-in, thanks to whoever attacked me. Security has already been beefed up. I've now got someone on the inside, so he'll have to help me get back in. Those parts being for a new model solar probe makes sense as the hidden lab is off a machine room and it had several probes in various states of assembly in it. I guess you would want to keep the new versions of the tech secure and away from prying eyes. One problem is that I don't know if my attacker saw me find the lab. They hit me coming out of the machine room, but they may have been watching me for some time and waiting until I'd re-sealed the hidden door.'

'Try as we might we cannot find any connection between this equipment, Jones' published research, her or her team's personal connections, friendships etc and the results from The Machine here showing such a high likelihood of disaster. To say we're worried is an understatement.'

The Machine that Kas referred to is The Organisation's primary analytical algorithm. It takes in vast quantities of data, via Infosys, from every inhabited world. Economic, social, political, scientific, anonymized personal messages, everything, and it uses a method of temporal quantum analysis to predict a set of likely futures for the galaxy. It deals in probabilities and the output is always changing but once a likely future catastrophe becomes statistically significant the investigation teams swing into action. Occasionally a new catastrophic future with a high probability appears suddenly and without warning, and then we have an emergency scramble, like this one. The Machine is usually able, with such high probability futures,

---

else and re-assembling it has so far remained in the realm of science fiction. No-one is able to scan at the subatomic level with the required resolution to perfectly codify anything but the simplest of elements; for any complex matter the data storage and transmission requirements would be in the billions of terabytes, the power needed would also be astronomical; and with a living being there would be no getting away from the ethical conundrum that you would be destroying, or murdering, someone and then creating a copy of them elsewhere that may, or may not, be precisely identical.

to pin down the planet the trouble starts on and often the key players but that doesn't leave us much time to prevent it.

'Keep me posted if The Machine spits out anything helpful,' I said, somewhat redundantly. It wasn't like they'd keep it to themselves.

'Take care, Cem,' Kas said, and then hung up.

I decided to call Randolf, I needed a look at the core of the building and he could legitimately show me around. He wasn't happy about my request but I couldn't sit in my hotel room waiting for the cataclysm to get more and more likely, plus he'd been back at the lab for a few hours now and should have had time to check out who was unexpectedly missing.

I packed a few items and headed down to catch a bubble back out to Astrophysics Lab Two.

Chapter 11
Many happy returns

On the way there in the bubble I replayed my conversations with Jones, Randolf and Grippe in my head. Looking for something that would give me a clue to what was going on. I knew someone had said something that had since become significant but I couldn't remember what it was. I closed my eyes and pictured each of them in turn and listened again to their voices, not just the words said but the tone, the emotion, the emphasis. Randolf had talked the most but he hadn't said anything that shed light on my problem, had he? I didn't have an eidetic memory[1] unfortunately but I could remember the tone of voice particularly well. Randolf had been gabbling excitedly or possibly nervously a lot of the time. I assumed he was nervous about how he and his mentor, Jones, were going to be portrayed in my article, or if he was even going to be mentioned at all. Perhaps he knew more than he was letting on. When he'd given my cuff his security clearance in the Lab's reception area, he'd said

'You'll be able to get through the security doors for the rest of the day now. Everywhere I have access to which is pretty much everything except for the hard radiation workshops and other secure locations.'

This must mean he knew about the secret lab but didn't himself have authorisation to access it as I'd mapped no off-limits areas other than that one plus the radiation workshops. Perhaps his nervousness was related to the fact that he had, in fact, gained entry to the lab, knew more than he should and thought I was investigating him on Jones' behalf? That could explain his relief when I recruited him to help me investigate her.

The bubble pulled up outside the Lab and I climbed out and was greeted by an even more nervous than usual Randolf.

'Per Pike. Now really isn't a good time for another tour! Things are a bit frantic here today after last night's events.'

---

[1] What used to be called a photographic memory. Not for the first time I wished I had that ability.

'Relax Per Randolf. May I call you Danatis?' I said.

'Dan. Most people call me Dan.'

'Dan. I just want to talk to you and have a look at the core of the building. It is the power distribution and management centre isn't it?'

'Yes. There's nothing of interest there. Why do you need to see it?'

'Thoroughness. Come on let's go.'

I strode off into the reception and he had no choice but to follow me. He pulled up the access code system at the reception desk again. This time I didn't bother surreptitiously recording him, if I needed the codes I would just ask him. I pointed my cuff in his direction when asked and a brief flash showed I was authorised.

He set off through the right-hand doors, subconsciously, or perhaps consciously, keeping me away from Jones and we headed in towards the building's core at the first left turn. It didn't take long to get there. We arrived at a heavy metal door festooned with warning symbols and notices about the dangers within. Randolf raised his cuff, but the door didn't open automatically. He had to enter some additional information first.

'I have to verify my access at this point - if you don't know what you're doing in here it could be very dangerous.' he said.

The door slid open soundlessly and we both stepped through. There was a narrow corridor between banks of equipment that led to the very centre of the building. Heavy insulated cables ran around in complex patterns on the ceiling and the air was extremely cold. I could see my breath every time I breathed out. Randolf was shivering already. The corridor ended at the exact centre of the building which was a meter high, four-meter-wide circular installation set into the floor made of grey metal. All the cables and pipes in the room ended, or more accurately started, here. A ring of heavily insulated connecting brackets joined them to the top of the grey metal core.[1] Surrounding this core was a circular walkway and on the outside edge of this were curved control panels covered in small display units, lights and switches all facing inwards to the core itself. There

---

[1] Most large buildings get their power using heat conversion from the molten core of the planet. Thermal extraction rods are driven down through the crust to the hottest part of the planet and this heat is converted to electricity. All generator buildings are linked to each other in a grid so that power is evenly distributed planetwide and to smaller buildings where such a system is not easily installed. It's inexhaustible, and environmentally sound. The top of the unit is kept very cold to improve the efficiency of the conversion equipment.

were four ways out, the corridor we'd just walked through and three others equally spaced like the cardinal compass points.

Pulling the metal cylindrical scanner from my pocket but keeping it hidden in my hand I tapped it on my cuff to start the scan of the room. There were a couple of standard surveillance cameras but nothing complex and certainly nothing to indicate this was anything but the power core for the building. I switched the scanner to scramble mode as this would not only mask our voices but make the cameras temporarily useless.

'Per Randolf. Dan,' I said, 'I know there's a hidden lab just off the machine room on the far side of the building. You've been inside it but I presume you don't have regular access. I think you know what's being built in there and I think you know what it's for.'

'I didn't break in!' he protested, 'They told me to go there. They needed my help.'

'I'm not accusing you of breaking in. I'm sure you've been told not to discuss the contents of that room. But the fact is I have been in it, I know it exists, so no more secrets.'

'What's that thing in your hand?' he asked, always the curious scientist.

'It's something to keep this conversation private. That's all you need to know. You're going to tell me everything you know, right now, or you're going to walk out of this room under arrest.'

'Grippe swore me to secrecy!' He protested.

I glared at him and his Adam's apple bobbed a few times as he swallowed, trying to decide if he could talk about it.

'The special projects lab is for senior members of Doctor Jones' team only,' he confessed miserably, 'I've been in there once. I think only Jones, Grippe and one or two others are allowed in. They needed help with my new hyperspace calculations, the ones I told you about, so they called me in once to check their equipment was getting the right results. I didn't even know the room existed until that point. Really, I didn't.'

So, Doctor Jones had been lying when she told me she and Doctor Grippe rarely spoke and had virtually no overlap of responsibilities. What were they building together and why were they hiding it?

'What equipment did you help with? Tell me everything.'

'I don't see how this relates to missing funds!' he practically squealed the last part.

I gazed steadily up into his eyes, he towered over me, but I held his gaze unblinkingly until he gave up and looked away.

'It's relevant because I say it's relevant. Now stop stalling and tell me what you know.'

'You understand that Interstellar travel is only possible because of the hyperdrive, right?'

'Obviously,' I muttered.

'Well for millennia we've used the same equations to open a hyperspatial portal, and set the course through hyperspace to the destination. The maths is horrendous. The early settlers of the galaxy had to wait hours, if not days, while their primitive computers did the calculations, and the bigger the jump the more accurate you needed to be and the longer it took to get it right. If you messed it up you could end up with only part of your ship entering the portal, tearing your ship in half, or you could re-appear in normal space but light-years from your destination and have no fuel for further jumps so you'd die when your air, food or water ran out; or you'd re-appear so close to a planet or a star you crashed on it or got burned to a crisp. You could even re-appear inside one...I can't imagine how horrible that would be.'

He looked faintly sick at the prospect.

'Okay,' I said, 'thanks for the history lesson. Why is this relevant?'

'Well, our modern ships don't carry fuel in the traditional sense, just a small rechargeable power cell and Infosys does the hyperspace calculations in a matter of seconds. That's partly why we travel in several jumps, to allow the cell to recharge directly from a nearby star. The galaxy is so well mapped we have the majority of routes pre-calculated. In hyperspace there are fixed points that are anchored to the gravity well of a star in normal space. That means even though the solar systems are all moving relative to each other the hyperspace calculation for the trip from, say, Fortuna's star to Coronnol's is the same each time, even if in normal space they have changed their relative position.'

'Okay. I get it,' I said and encouraged him to continue.

'So, we jump through hyperspace from star to star, recharging the power cell at each one for the next jump. This is how we can get all the way around the galaxy so easily. We do dozens, or maybe even hundreds of jumps, through hyperspace. All easily calculated by Infosys in seconds. If there's a supernova or a new star is created then the calculations all change, but only a fractionally and Infosys can work out the change easily. But this is also why we're trapped in *this* galaxy!'

'I'd hardly call us trapped,' I said, 'the galaxy is enormous.'

'It is. But sooner or later we are going to run out of planets we can terraform. Then what?'

'We'll have to settle the next galaxy. What's the problem?' I asked somewhat grumpily.

I couldn't see how any of this was relevant but Randolf seemed to be following a thread in his own long-winded way.

'We can't,' he said flatly, 'we can't get there. Well, we can't with the equations we use currently. It's just too far to jump in one go. There's no way to accurately calculate a safe exit point from hyperspace near to a star in any other galaxy. The maths just isn't up to the distances involved because we don't know any of the fixed hyperspace points for any of the stars outside our own galaxy. I know what you're going to say next, we'll jump there in multiple shorter jumps, right?'

'I was about to say that, yes,' I admitted.

'It can't be done,' he replied only slightly smugly, 'There are no stars, so no fixed hyperspace points in interstellar space which makes the maths tricky for a jump into the interstellar void, but just about doable with Infosys. But because there are no stars there's no way to recharge the ship for the next jump and we cannot design or build a ship that can store enough power to make that many short jumps. It'd be bigger than a city but with only enough room for a crew of about four or five. Also, once we're out of the galaxy, after the first jump, we lose the connection to Infosys. Then we're back to having onboard computers to calculate the subsequent jumps which will be very slow and add even more bulk and even higher power requirements. We're just not going to colonize another galaxy that way.'

'I'm guessing you have a solution?'

'I hope so. As I said I've got a completely new system of hyperspatial calculation that has two effects. The first is that we can open a hyperspatial portal that stays open, instead of the instantaneous blink we use to move a starship now, this would act like a kind of wormhole, linking one part of space to another and a ship could just fly in and re-appear at the destination without having an onboard hyperdrive. Ships would be simpler and cheaper. We can send as many sensor probes through the wormhole as needed to map out the nearest stars in the next galaxy ready for full sized ships to make the jump. The second effect is that we can calculate the exit point with much greater accuracy. It may even be possible to create the wormhole boundaries within the atmosphere of a planet. If that works out then we may not need starships at all. We could fly in using some kind of airship and arrive in the atmosphere of the destination planet!'

He was quite excited now and I had to admit it sounded like a complete game changing breakthrough. Clearly when he'd talked to me about the maths in the bubble on the way to the lab yesterday I hadn't really listened to him, and certainly hadn't realised the implications of it at all. To be fair though it did also sound like pie-in-the-sky science fiction.

'So that's what they're building in the secure lab?' I asked, 'A new hyperdrive?'

'Yes. Well, I think so. They were using Doctor Jones' solar probes as a basis for the test units because they're the most physically robust devices available. They can survive in the heart of a star so they should be able to take any physical stresses we can imagine. Doctor Grippe is in charge of the engine build with a senior engineer on loan from the Astro-Engineering campus, but Doctor Jones is the project lead. I created the mathematics but don't have the engineering or applied physics needed to take it beyond the conceptual or theoretical.'

'Why is Grippe involved? And if he's in charge of the build why isn't he in charge overall?'

'Grippe is one of the galaxy's foremost experts on gravity. A hyperspace portal is created using technology very similar to artificial gravity waves and the wormhole portal will require the most precisely focused waves imaginable. He's not in charge, although he desperately wants to be, because it was Doctor Jones who read my preliminary paper and saw the potential in my research. She convinced me to come to Coronnol to use it as the basis of my Doctorate. She saw the practical applications of what I just thought of as a better solution to a complex mathematical problem.'

'How close are they to getting it working? Have there been problems, accidents, anything not going as planned?'

'I don't know. Both Doctors Grippe and Jones are extremely secretive and cautious. I'm a mathematician and theoretical physicist not an engineer or astrophysicist. I programmed the mathematical equations for them both and left them to it. They call me back in when they need them revising, that's all.'

I glanced around the room. We'd been here long enough, probably too long, with the cameras out of action and sooner or later someone would come to investigate.

'Okay Dan. That's all really helpful. Once again let me remind you that you're not to talk about this conversation with anyone. Absolutely nobody. I'll know if you do. Remember the Spycomm I planted on your neck at lunch time.'

'I won't, I promise,' he said glumly.

I turned the scanner off and slipped it back into my pocket as we headed out through the maze of pipework, cables and equipment. We were both shivering uncontrollably now, but before we left the power core, I had to ask him one more question.

'Dan, who didn't show up today who should have?'

'I checked the schedules and there're about twelve people who are normally in who weren't here. But all of them were either teaching, at the administration building in the city centre, or had the day booked off already.'

'Anyone here who looked like they had a recently broken arm or nose, any swelling, bruising, difficulty breathing?'

'Well because I had lunch with you,' he said a bit testily, 'I didn't see everyone in the cafeteria. But I saw most of the team during the course of the day and I saw nothing untoward.'

'Okay. Get that Spycomm planted on Doctor Jones today,' I said.

He left me at reception and headed back through the left-hand doors towards the main laboratory.

I still wasn't feeling up to the walk back to the city so I hopped into a spare bubble. I wanted to talk to Doctor Grippe but he was one of the people not on site today. According to his schedule he was in his office at the physics department building, in the city centre, this afternoon after a busy morning teaching undergraduates.

It was getting late and I doubted he'd let me talk to him now but I could at least schedule a meeting for tomorrow. I called him at his office and he answered in audio only.

'Doctor Grippe, it's Cemeron Argalion Pike. We met yesterday.'

'Ahh yes. The journalist. What do you want?'

'I'd like to meet with you, tomorrow if you've time. You said there's a lot more going on than Doctor Jones is likely to show me and as I'm always looking for my next story perhaps you could fill me in?'

'Tomorrow might be difficult. I've a very busy day tomorrow.'

'The day after? I'm not here much longer than that and I really would like to speak to you about your work.'

'No. The day after is even worse. Back-to-back lectures and a charity event in the evening. Look, if you can meet me early tomorrow, for breakfast, I could squeeze you in for half an hour or so.'

'I could do that,' I agreed

'Astrophysics Lab Two again then. Breakfast for seven thirty in the morning. Don't be late.'

He hung up abruptly. I sent a message to Kastagyr telling them we needed to talk as soon as I could get back to the hotel and arrange a secure environment. I closed my eyes and napped the rest of the way back.

Chapter 12
Working breakfast

I'd briefed Kastagyr on the new hyperdrive system outlined by Danatis when I got back to the hotel room and secured it. They confirmed that it sounded like an astounding breakthrough but was certainly plausible which meant Danatis was unlikely to be lying. The unidentified equipment the Barbs had been trying to simulate from my scans did appear similar to the control systems for a hyperdrive generator. Now they knew it was designed to create a stable wormhole it should make further analysis much easier although without a complete understanding of Danatis' new equations there was no way to make a functional replica. Unfortunately, we still had absolutely no idea how the creation of wormholes through hyperspace or more accurate jump calculations could precipitate the end of the galaxy. I ate alone in my hotel room and got an early night as I wanted to be fresh for my breakfast with Doctor Grippe.

My alarm went off at five thirty which gave me plenty of time to shower, dress and walk the hour or so back to the lab. I needed time to think and the walk would do me good. It was summer in the southern hemisphere so the days were long and started early. The weather was cloudy but Infosys thought there was only a five percent chance of rain and I made good time. As I walked through the city centre to the footpath that led out to the laboratory complex I had the familiar itching feeling that I was being watched again but I couldn't see anyone obviously following me. There were quite a few people walking the same paths but I didn't recognize anybody and no one seemed to be paying undue attention to me. It seemed the people of Coronnol took their physical exercise responsibilities seriously as plenty of people were pushing themselves quite hard in the runner's lane. I only paused to look around a few times, mindful of my need to be punctual, and even launched a microdrone that followed me in a spiral orbit getting up to four hundred meters away from me before working its way back. I watched the facial recognition footage from the drone on my cuff but saw nothing to worry about. The problem with walking to a popular destination was that some people would be walking the exact same route and I wouldn't be able to distinguish their commute from them following me. I recalled the microdrone and slipped it back into my pocket as I approached the lab's main entrance at seven twenty-five exactly. There was no sign of Doctor Grippe or anyone else to greet me but as I walked into reception a virtual screen lit up. Grippe's balding head appeared on it.

'Per Pike,' the recording said, 'please make your way through the doors to your left and follow the corridor to the cafeteria at the opposite side of this building.'

As I neared the door I heard it unlock then it opened as I approached. Clearly Doctor Julius Markus Grippe did not particularly care about the human touch and was happy to let the reception sensors detect the return of my cuff to the building. As I passed the doors with Doctor M O Jones etched on the frosted glass I tried them, out of curiosity, but found them locked. Doctor Grippe must have programmed only the doors between reception and the cafeteria to unlock for me. As I entered I saw the ceiling was showing a completely different set of colours to my last visit. This was predominantly yellows, whites and blues which pulsed and shifted in an energetic but still soothing way. I wondered if it had different colour schemes for different times of the day or if it was random. It certainly reminded me of the sky on a bright summer morning. I saw Grippe sitting alone at the end of a large table and headed over to join him. He looked up and acknowledged my arrival with a slight tip of the head. He already had a light breakfast in front of him and he'd started eating.

'You'd best get something quickly if you want to talk,' he said, 'You're late.'

I headed for the buffet and stole a quick glance at my cuff, it was seven thirty-one. I selected a similar light breakfast, mostly fruit and something I hoped was yoghurt, and headed back to sit next to him.

'I assumed you meant to be here at the building by seven thirty…'

'Why would you assume that?' he said, 'I always breakfast at seven thirty precisely. You should have allowed enough time to traverse the building, make your selection and be seated.'

He glanced over the contents of my tray, as if looking for something to disapprove of, but as it was virtually identical to his there wasn't a lot he could complain about.

'You've now got just over twenty-five minutes. Don't waste it.'

'In that case your statement about the other interesting things happening here intrigued me,' I said 'What is going on that Doctor Jones wouldn't want to tell me about?'

He stopped eating for a moment and gazed levelly at me, then carefully and innocently swept the room; I presumed to ensure there was no-one close enough to hear us.

'I have the greatest respect for Doctor Jones,' he said and I just knew there was a but coming, 'but her focus is almost exclusively on Astrophysics projects. This is...sub-optimal. We are a combined department and physics projects will always have more impact on everyday life. Astrophysics is cerebral, academic, it's important I grant you, but when a physics department makes a breakthrough there's a chance it can change the fundamentals of life.'

He resumed his breakfast. I said nothing. I just waited. I could feel he was bursting to tell me about something, presumably the hyperdrive wormhole project.

'How long did it take you to jump from Mirth to Coronnol?' he asked.

'About thirty hours,' I answered.

'No. The jump itself. If you exclude the lift off, landing and manoeuvring.'

'I don't know exactly,' I said, 'a few minutes I suppose per jump. The take off and getting into orbit takes half an hour or so, the same for landing. We did the journey in thirteen jumps as it wasn't a direct route and had a few stops. We also docked with another ship after the second jump so some passengers going to Artelon could disembark. Then there's recharging the hyperdrive in orbit around each sun for a short while.'

'So the jump calculations and the jumps themselves are a matter of minutes. The other twenty-nine hours and change is wasted time.'

'If you choose to think about it like that then yes, but it's still incredible. You can't even see Mirth's star in the night sky from Coronnol, it's so far away, and we did the journey in less than a day and a half!'

'But imagine if we could speed that up. It's physics that will do that. Not biology, not chemistry, not psychology or geology or any other ology and certainly not Astrophysics. Just plain old physics.'

'How much faster can we make take-off and landing? Even with artificial gravity there's inertia to contend with and no-one but professional pilots or thrill seekers want to feel significant motion effects. Then there are the relativistic problems of travelling at any significant fraction of the speed of light. Is it possible to coax significantly more speed from the normal-space engines without running into that issue? Hyperdrive recharge time is down to between half an hour and an hour in orbit around a sun, how much faster can you make that?'

'I'm not talking about those things!' he snapped angrily, 'I'm talking about a fundamental change. Of course those things take time, even though we've perfected the systems over generations and pared the timings down to the super-efficient minimum. I'm asking you to imagine something else, something entirely different in approach.'

'If you're talking about matter transportation...' I started to say but he interrupted.

'Absolutely not! That will almost certainly never happen. At least not in the way it's been proposed previously. What I'm saying is you need to be back here in about four to six weeks. We will have something to show you that will astonish you. I'm certain of that.'

He smiled an extremely self-satisfied smile which faded abruptly.

'Well we will if Doctor Jones can get her head out of her Astrophysics obsessed ass and avoid any more distractions.'

'Would one of the distractions be all the excitement of the other night? The break-in?' I asked.

'Who told you about that?'

'People talk Doctor Grippe. Rumours fly around, especially in close-knit communities like university departments. Do you suspect a rival university was trying to get a look at your project?'

Before he could answer a short heavy-set man with a bald head, an extremely bushy beard and vast moustache approached the table. He wore a pristine white lab coat and had both hands firmly pushed into the pockets. He looked uncomfortable approaching us and walked in an extremely stiff and self-conscious manner. He completely ignored me, and with a cough and a nod of his head indicated he needed to talk with Doctor Grippe.

Grippe stood up and moved slightly away from the table and they had a whispered conversation. Grippe looked extremely angry. The bushy-bearded man looked momentarily cowed then I saw a flash of something, maybe hated or contempt in his face before he composed himself.

'Excuse me Per Pike,' he said, 'but I need to go a little early. My colleague needs me in the lab. Doctor Bertrand Farley Gernard meet Cemeron Argalion Pike, a journalist visiting the department.'

The man reluctantly turned to me, completely ignored my offered linking arm, and without meeting my eyes muttered something that sounded like 'A pleasure to meet you' but he certainly didn't sound sincere. It was considered very rude not to link arms but the man was clearly uncomfortable disturbing us, which perhaps revealed just how fearsome Grippe was within the department.

'Thank you for your time Doctor Grippe,' I said, standing up, 'I will definitely take you up on your offer to return and see your breakthrough, whatever it turns out to be.'

'I'll be in touch, finish your breakfast,' he said, waving me back down. 'Your cuff will allow you to exit via any available route for at least another hour.'

He and Doctor Gernard hurried away leaving me alone at the table, but the rest of the cafeteria was getting quite noisy and full. I looked around wondering if I might catch sight of a familiar face but neither Jones nor Randolf were around. I finished my breakfast and headed back to the main entrance.

Clearly Grippe and Jones did not get along. Jones was working on something connected to the hyperspace wormhole but was mysteriously unrelated to space travel and was keeping it top secret. Grippe was charging full steam ahead with a space travel revolution and was clearly desperate to brag about it. I wondered if Gernard had come over to interrupt specifically to stop Grippe from telling me everything, from the look of his physique I guessed he too was from Cestus. It would be vital to Coronnol University's continued success to be able to announce the breakthrough properly and reap the benefits of all the publicity. Randolf was the creator of the mathematics that made the potential hyperspace revolution possible but was being kept on the periphery by both Jones and Grippe, and possibly also by his own lack of assertiveness and ambition. He was far too diffident and nervous to be the public face of a project this important. So far so very academic soap opera but nothing to indicate galaxy ending calamity.

Back outside the main entrance I was torn between walking back to the city centre and riding in a bubble. Walking often helped me think and I needed to work out who it was I'd been fighting with in the corridor. Until I could fit that into the picture, I was flying blind.

My feet decided for me and I found myself on the winding path out of the laboratory gardens towards the main footpath back to the city. It had to be an inside job because no one else could have disabled the security system or triggered the alarm. But who was it? There were fewer people on foot now, I guessed most people had already started work as it was now past eight o'clock in the morning. I pulled the earpiece from my cuff, popped it in and checked the two Spycomms in Jones' offices. The one in the city centre still had no recordings of her and the one at the lab started out with more routine calls about parts, conferences, budgets, the enhanced security since the break-in until finally something interesting even if I had no idea of the relevance. She took a call from a Doctor Intriligator at the university observatory. Jones thanked them for finding suitable red giant and white dwarf stars in neighbouring uninhabited solar systems and fast-tracking permission that would allow her to move forward to the experimental phase. If I hadn't been so lost in thought I might have noticed the large opaque bubble moving past me and I could have reacted rather better. The hatch slid open and two people wearing breathing masks jumped out and sprayed something in my face. I was already slipping into unconsciousness as they roughly bundled me towards the rear facing seats and all I could manage was to lock my cuff and slip the microdrone out of my pocket onto the ground before they closed the hatch.

Chapter 13
Unpleasant conversations

I woke up with a start. It was so sudden I knew it wasn't natural. Someone must have administered an antidote to whatever gas they'd used to knock me out in the first place. I kept my eyes shut and tried to work out if I had been injured at all. I was propped up sitting on a hard surface leaning against a corner where two walls met. Tensing my muscles and shifting position didn't trigger any new pains to indicate recent violence, which was good news relatively speaking. I cautiously opened one eye, then the other. Nothing changed. Either I'd gone blind or I was in complete darkness. I wasn't tied up and I seemed to be still wearing the same clothes. My cuff was gone so I had no way to be certain how long I'd been unconscious. It didn't feel long. I wasn't feeling hungry so it seemed reasonable to estimate no more than an hour or so.

'Hello!' I called. 'Is there anybody there? Where am I? What do you want?'

I guessed a journalist's inquisitive nature would prompt them to ask questions first and if they'd been in a few tight spots they'd be unlikely to panic straight away. Keeping my cover intact and playing the part of Cemeron Argalion Pike to the best of my ability seemed like the best choice for now.

I stretched, rubbed my face and ran my fingers through my hair and in doing so discovered to my surprise the earpiece was still in situ. It was very small so perhaps they hadn't noticed it. The microdrone had been the only piece of incriminating evidence that I might not be who I claimed to be and I could probably have explained that away as photographic equipment in a pinch, but better safe than sorry.

'Hello!' I tried again. 'I'm awake. Could I have a glass of water please?'

Nothing.

I carefully got to my feet and used my fingertips and slow cautious steps to establish I was in a small metal room approximately three meters square. I couldn't find an obvious door but there had to be one and I had no idea how high the ceiling was.

Why had they woken me up if they were then going to ignore me? I sat back down. I could think of only one reason that made sense. They wanted to frighten me. If I was asleep I wasn't afraid. They hoped I'd start panicking because then I'd be much easier to manipulate.

I rolled onto my side, closed my eyes and decided to have a nap. I wasn't going to play their game. I waited and within a minute or so a bright beam of light shone directly down from above me making a small circle on the floor about a metre away. In the circle of light was my cuff. At least I now knew that I wasn't blind, I was just being kept in absolute darkness.

'Unlock the cuff', demanded a synthesised voice. Someone wanted to keep their identity secret.

'No.' I replied as inoffensively as possible.

'Unlock the cuff!' insisted the voice.

'No. I won't,' I replied, 'Why don't you just ask me what you want?'

'We want you to unlock the cuff. You will do it.'

The circle of light snapped off as an ear-splitting noise erupted from all sides, a high-pitched oscillating wail combined with ringing alarm bells, screams and a rhythmic subsonic pounding beat, it started to be physically painful within minutes. I lay on my side with my hands clamped over my ears, for all the difference that made. The sound lasted maybe five minutes then stopped as abruptly as it had started. I was gasping for breath. I'd never heard anything like it before, it was a brutal assault on the senses. I could once again hear my breathing and the sound of my body changing position in the darkness but I was sure I'd be hearing that noise in my imagination for some time. I shuffled back up into a seated position and leant against the corner of the room.

'Will you please tell me what you want?' I called out into the darkness.

In answer the circle of light flicked on again illuminating my cuff, still lying on the floor.

'You know what we want,' came the synthetic voice again.

I slid my right shoe off my foot, gripped it by the toe end, then with all my strength I smashed the heel down onto the cuff as hard as I could, over and over again until the intricate latticework of silver and gold was mangled and deformed. Once it was smashed beyond repair I pulled my shoe back on.

'Now are we going to have a sensible conversation?' I asked defiantly.

The circle of light vanished and the hideous sound restarted. If anything it seemed louder than before. I clamped my hands over my ears and determined to wait it out, curled up in the foetal position. Whoever was operating the equipment had poor impulse control and a mean streak. I hoped those were character flaws I would get a chance to exploit at some point but the first order of business was to get out of the cell. I was completely out of ideas in that regard and it was hard to think straight while enduring the sonic torture. The sound felt like it was inside my body forcing joints apart, loosening teeth, making me feel physically sick, and I was starting to worry about permanent hearing loss.

It stopped suddenly and I gasped involuntarily with relief. That had definitely been longer than the first time and my ears were buzzing and ringing.

'Thank you,' I said.

I reached out in the darkness to where my cuff had lain in the circle of light but it was gone. Either someone had come in while I was curled up or there was some sort of hatch in the floor.

'Who do you work for?' asked the voice.

'I'm Cemeron Argalion Pike. I'm a freelance journalist currently working for The Science Review on Mirth,' I answered.

There was a lengthy silence.

'Who do you work for?'

'If you're going to keep asking questions that I've already answered this is going to take forever. Am I under arrest and if so on what charge? Galactic law specifically forbids torture and while some planets interpret this law somewhat flexibly, I didn't think Coronnol was one of those. I'm happy to answer any questions I can, but I'd prefer to do that in more civilised surroundings and with a legal representative present.'

The sound started again but this time the room was also lit up with intense flashing brilliant white light, turning on and off in a crazed random pattern. I screwed my eyes tight shut but even then it was so bright it was visible through my eyelids. I had the choice of putting my hands over my eyes or over my ears. I curled up again and tried to wrap my head in my arms. I concentrated on breathing evenly and attempting to shut out the shattering noise and blinding light. It was certainly a clever way to torture someone as I would have no bruises or other physical marks to use as evidence later, unless they kept it going long enough to either blind or deafen me.

The silence and the darkness finally returned. That session had seemed to last forever but I supposed it was only about an hour. I felt sick, weak and shaky. I could see spots dancing in front of my eyes in the blackness and the buzzing and ringing in my ears was far worse. I was sweating profusely which was also extremely unpleasant. I pushed myself up into a sitting position and waited in the silence, breathing heavily until my heart rate slowed to something like a normal speed.

'I had to break the cuff,' I said, 'A journalist cannot reveal sources or allow their privacy or confidence to be breached. It would be the end of my career. I'll answer any questions I can, within those parameters. I won't press charges for torture or wrongful imprisonment. I'll even leave Coronnol and never come back if that's what you want but I don't understand what law I've broken or what you think I've done.'

'We are not the police and you are not a journalist. You are not writing an article about Doctor Jones. Who do you work for?' asked the same synthetic voice.

'I'm Cemeron Argalion Pike. I'm a citizen of Sellion living and working on Mirth. I am a journalist and I am here writing a story about Doctor Jones for a journal on her home planet. You can contact the Science Review offices on Mirth, hell, you can check my credentials at any number of journals, publications or broadcasters. I won an award for my article on Scarlastion's neuroelectronic research. Frankly I'm sick of this, now get me out of here and...' at this point I was cut off as the noise and light started up again.

It went on and on. The sound pounded through my head and seemed to reverberate off the inside of my skull, the light waited to blind me or drive me crazy if I was incautious enough to open my eyes even for a moment. I curled back up as small as I could with my hands clamped over my ears and my face pressed to the ground.

I had lost all track of time and only a growing thirst gave me any clue how long I'd been there. My captors seemed determined to keep this session going until I cracked and I knew that point was inevitable sooner or later. It was impossible to sleep or rest and no human being can survive lengthy sleep deprivation even without a constant sonic and visual barrage. Assuming they gave me water to keep me alive I had a few days at most before I could resist no more.

I forced myself to uncurl. I had to do something. Find some way out. I slipped out of my top and wrapped it round my head so that at least I could have my hands free. The soft opaque material might protect my eyes from the light and deaden the sound enough to prevent hearing loss. I started with the wall right next to me, methodically sweeping my fingertips over every centimetre starting as high up as I could reach and working my way down and then along to my right. The metal was smooth and the first wall revealed nothing, nor did the second. On the third though, about half way along I could just feel a slight join; the barest suggestion of a seam or break in the smooth metal. I traced its outline and it was door shaped, approximately two meters tall and just over a meter wide. There certainly wasn't a handle on my side so I had no idea if it was a purely mechanical door mechanism or something fancy and electronic. I continued my survey along the fourth wall until I was back where I started. The door on the third wall was the only thing I could detect by touch.

The dizziness was getting worse. I guessed hunger and dehydration combined with the noise was responsible. I felt my way back to the outline of the door. I threw all my weight against it but felt nothing except a pain in my shoulder. I tried a few more times all as equally unsuccessful. I sat down and braced myself as best I could and kicked the door, right where the seam was. I put as much force into it as I could muster but I was just sent sliding backwards on the smooth floor. I couldn't even hear my shoe connect with the door over the deafening siren. I tried a few more times to kick, alternating which vertical seam I was pounding away at. After a few kicks I ran my fingers over the joint to test if anything had changed but I wasn't affecting the door one tiny little bit as far as I could tell. I kept going until I was exhausted and then eventually lay back on the floor to rest. Sleep was impossible.

After what felt like hours the noise and the light both stopped.

'You cannot break out. There is no escape. There is only answering the question. Who do you work for?'

I sat up and shuffled across the floor until I was by the door and leant against it. I unwrapped my top from my head and wiped the sweat off my face with it.

'When I get out of here I am going to find you, whoever you are, and I am going to kick your ass,' I snapped angrily.

'You cannot break out. You cannot find us. Answer the question. Who do you work for?'

'Screw you.' I muttered. 'I'm not answering any questions.'

'You will,' said the voice, 'Everyone does. Eventually.'

The noise and light started again. I re-tied my top around my head and clamped my hands over my ears. I tried to think of happier times. Time spent with Kastagyr and with others from The Organisation. Time spent travelling, sightseeing. Time spent loving and being loved. I'm not a machine. I have feelings and there have been people I've encountered that I have given serious consideration to having a long-term relationship with, but the job has always come first. It's hard to establish a really trusting relationship when you can't even tell someone your real name.

Silence and darkness returned as suddenly as it had the previous times.

'Who do you work for?'

I ignored the question.

'Who do you work for?'

The problem with a synthetic voice was the lack of nuance, subtlety and emotion. The problem was mine though. I couldn't tell if my refusal to answer was infuriating my captor or not.

'Who do you work for?'

'Asked and answered. You're wasting time.' I replied.

'We have all the time we need.'

'Not if I die of thirst or hunger, which I admit isn't imminent but I could really do with a drink now.'

'Who do you work for?'

'Why don't you speak to me yourself? Are you frightened I'd recognise your voice?' I shouted.

'Who do you work for?'

'Screw you.'

The sound and light started again. I curled up small and tried to turn my attention back to positive thoughts and happy memories but concentrating was becoming harder. I was getting a very painful headache and the nausea and dizziness were affecting me quite badly now. I had certainly lost all track of time. I must have eventually passed out.

I was snapped alert by a thump against the door I was leaning on. At first I wasn't sure if it was real or just a change to the subsonic harmonics of the appalling noise. Then it happened again and then again. Someone was banging on the door. I span round and kicked the door rapidly with my heel three times, then again three more times. I still couldn't hear anything and I didn't dare remove the cloth from over my eyes. I could see enough through my closed eyelids and my clothing to know the crazed randomly flashing light was still going. I knelt up and put my palms against the door. I couldn't feel anything. I pushed the door but it didn't move. I needed to get ready. If my captor was coming in then I was going to have to fight. The second the door opened I needed to get through it, it might be my only chance. They must have been banging on the door to make me move away. Perhaps it opened inwards. That would make sense. It would be stronger and more difficult for me to force it open from the inside. I struggled to my feet keeping one hand on the door. I felt it move very slightly. I braced myself. The door started to open, but outwards. I shoved it hard and lunged through, colliding with someone on the other side. I grabbed them and spun them round roughly and we both fell down two or three steps and then slammed into the floor with me on top. I found their neck and pinned them down with one forearm across the windpipe while with my free arm I punched them in the stomach repeatedly until they stopped struggling. I rolled off them and pulled the clothing from my eyes. The noise coming out of the metal room I'd been in was still deafeningly loud but at least there were normal lights on and I could see. Lying next to me was a man dressed in a Coronnol police uniform. Dark grey from head to toe, with a white sash and a small embossed gold badge on his chest. I checked his pulse and his heart was beating well. He was only unconscious, thank goodness. I looked around me. I was in a large almost empty room in the centre of which was the metal cube standing on half-meter-tall legs. There were two steps leading up to the open door which had a locking wheel on the outside. I stood up, pushed it shut and spun the wheel. Thankfully this cut the noise down to a fraction of the volume. I looked around, trying to see the way out.

Before I had a chance to go any further a tall stocky man in a very smart dark green suit came around the corner of the metal cell, he had his hands out palms up indicating he was no threat.

He spoke but I couldn't hear him. My ears were buzzing and ringing too much. I pointed to my ears and shook my head. He pulled a gold badge similar to the police officer's from a pocket and showed it me.

'Per Pike,' he shouted, 'I'm Chief Investigator Andrews. I got a message from Per Marshall about your situation. You're safe!'

He glanced with concern across at the police officer lying on the floor. He used his cuff to signal for medical help as he knelt down beside him to check for a pulse.

'He's okay,' I said, 'He's just unconscious.'

Some medics arrived to tend to the officer as Andrews took my arm and led me round the cell and out through some doors and down a maze of curved corridors until we left the building. It was night outside and it was raining. I stood in the rain with my face up to the stars and enjoyed the feel of it pouring down my face. There were police ground vehicles and an ambulance nearby as well as several police officers, all keeping a respectful distance. A medic approached and pulled a scanner from a kit bag and started to check me over. I asked for a drink and someone passed me a bottle of water. My ears were still ringing and buzzing but I could now hear Andrews as he explained.

'I got a message from the Coordinator General about six hours ago,' he shouted, 'telling me that someone called Kastagyr Devon Marshall, from a confidential branch of the galactic service, had been in touch informing them that a citizen was being held against their will. Apparently when you smashed your cuff an alert was sent to your headquarters that included your last known location and they went into action. We received your name and image and started to look for you. We were warned to be cautious as you could be in danger so the search had to go rather slower than we would have liked.'

'Where are we and what time is it?' I asked, looking around me. I didn't recognize the place.

'It's just passed midnight and we're on the outskirts of Transium,' said Andrews. 'It's a warehouse complex. These buildings are rented out for storage but this one is currently not supposed to be occupied. The location given to us was only accurate to within a few square kilometres, the metal cell shielded your cuff quite effectively.'

I looked behind me and saw paramedics bringing the unconscious officer out.

'Please will you pass my sincere apologies on to that officer,' I said, 'I didn't know who was opening the door and didn't dare take any chances. It seemed likely to be my captor coming to finish me off.'

'I will,' he said.

'Did you find anyone else in the building? I was being interrogated by someone who was using a synthesised voice. I presumed they were nearby but I guess that's not necessarily the case.'

'No. I'm afraid there's no sign of anyone else in or around this building. We have a forensic team ready to scan thoroughly for trace ID evidence though.'

A uniformed officer approached from the building carrying something. She spoke to me but I couldn't make it out. I saw Andrews explain and she tried again.

'Excuse me Per Pike,' she shouted, 'We found the remains of a cuff in the hatch in the floor. Was this yours?'

I looked at the wreckage in the box she was carrying.

'I'm afraid so. May I have it back?'

'It is now evidence so we'll need it for forensic examination,' she said.

'That won't be necessary Examiner Carlton,' said Andrews taking the box from her and handing it to me.

She nodded reluctantly and headed back to join her colleagues who were busy securing the crime scene.

'I've been told that your name is not to appear in the case file, that you're not to be questioned and we're to cooperate with you in any way we can. I don't like it but those are my orders,' said Andrews.

'Chief Investigator Andrews I don't want to keep you in the dark any more than necessary but I'm really tired and hungry. I'm happy to leave your people to secure the building. Could you give me a ride back to my hotel? I'll gladly meet with you tomorrow to discuss the matter further.'

The medic reluctantly agreed I could go as he couldn't detect any permanent damage to my hearing. He tried to convince me to spent at least one night in hospital for observation but I declined. I headed to the largest ground car assuming, correctly as it turned out, that it would belong to Andrews.

Chapter 14
Investigations

A ndrews dropped me off at the hotel and the concierge intercepted me to explain that the lock on my door had been overridden by the police and that they had discovered the room and its contents had already been quite badly damaged by someone conducting a thorough search. Consequently, I had been moved to a different room on another floor where my luggage awaited me. I headed up to the new room and was surprised to see a police officer stationed outside.

'CI Andrews' orders,' he said when I questioned him about his presence, 'Until he's sure you're safe there'll be someone outside the whole time you're here.'

I went inside and saw my luggage on the bed. I dropped the box with the smashed cuff next to it. The lock on the case was broken but checking through it I couldn't see anything of significance missing, although some of my clothing had been ripped. The hidden compartment in the case was intact and still opened with a scan of my thumb and inside all my special equipment lay undisturbed. Whoever searched my belongings wouldn't have discovered anything incriminating as it was impossible for anyone but me to open that compartment, and forcing it open would trigger a self-destruct sequence that would leave no trace of the contents. I dropped the smashed cuff into an empty compartment and pulled out the scanner and set it to block the in-room security camera then took a spare personal cuff out and slipped it gratefully onto my wrist, I'd felt naked without one. I gently stroked the silver and gold and felt it activate. It glowed with a flickering pattern showing the synchronisation to Infosys was active and then the virtual screen lit up and connected to The Organisation. Kastagyr's worried face filled the screen which I quickly stretched out to life size, I needed to see them properly.

'Are you okay?' they asked.

'I am now, thanks to you and your security protocols,' I answered, 'If the cuff hadn't sent that alert and if CI Andrews' team hadn't been so efficient it could have been a different story.'

I gave Kas a brief but concise run down of the events of the day.

'I need some food and sleep now,' I said, 'Can we talk further tomorrow?'

'Sure Cem,' they said beaming a genuine smile, 'sleep well. Call me in the morning, whenever you're ready.'

They broke the connection and I opened the minibar and found the largest bottle of ice-cold beer it had and drank it while ordering some food from room service. I don't remember what I ordered, just that I didn't each much of it; I was too tired.

I set the force field up despite the police officer guarding the door, moved the case into the wardrobe, dropped the empty box into the bin and sank into the bed grateful for the relative peace and quiet. I hoped the buzzing and ringing in my ears would reduce significantly by the time I awoke.

I didn't wake until after eight o'clock. I was ravenous. My hearing was certainly better, but definitely not back to normal. There was a fuzziness to it. I retrieved the scanner and set it to medical mode. I've no medical training or experience beyond basic emergency first aid but The Organisation had access to the best technology in the galaxy. The cuff showed me how to scan my head and the results were sent to the doctors back at headquarters. While I waited for them to get back to me I had a shower and decided I wanted breakfast with a view. There was a different police officer on duty outside my door so I asked his name, and he introduced himself as Examiner Pascal. I invited him to breakfast. As he was bound to follow me up to the restaurant anyway he may as well join me instead of sitting watching me from a different table.

We rode up together in the lift. My new room was on the one hundred and thirtieth floor and I couldn't face twenty flights on foot particularly without something in my stomach first.

There was a table right at the outside edge on the transparent floor available so we took it. The view was incredible. We were on the side of the hotel facing out to sea and it was a glorious sunny day. The long shadow of the Fortitude Tower pointed towards the distant horizon where the pale blue of the sky blended into the rich dark blue of the sea. There were a few pleasure craft visible a kilometre or so from the shore. It was an idyllic scene. I would very much have enjoyed a day off down on the beach, swimming, relaxing, eating and drinking, but I had far too much to do.

'Have you eaten yet this morning Examiner Pascal?' I asked.

'I don't usually eat breakfast Per Pike' he replied, 'I'm happy with just a coffee.'

'Nonsense! You can't leave me to eat alone. That's not sociable, not sociable at all. I'm paying so go to town.'

The waiter approached and our cuffs lit up with the menu. I was starving so ordered a large hearty cooked breakfast that was very heavy on the mushrooms and fried food but Pascal couldn't be persuaded to stray beyond a couple of small pastries with his coffee. In the morning I only drink tea so got myself a large pot of my favourite blend.

'I can't have breakfast with you and call you Examiner Pascal,' I said, 'My name is Cemeron, or Cem to my friends. What can I call you?'

'I'm Robin Darion Pascal, but everyone calls me Rob.'

'Excellent, Rob. Now we've ordered what shall we talk about while we wait? How long have you been with the police? How do the ranks work here on Coronnol? I'm not sure where an Examiner fits in.'

'I've been in for three years. I used to work in the family business but it wasn't for me and I joined the police with their blessing.'

'And the rank?' I asked.

'A new recruit is a Probationer for a year, then you spend at least a year as an Assistant Examiner. I've been an Examiner now for a year but in two to three years I'll be able to apply for Senior Examiner if I want to. That's as high as uniformed front-line officers go. I can transfer to the Investigation Division if I don't want to be a Senior Examiner, or to the Coordinator's Office. I'm hoping to be an Investigator. The Coordinators are management, administration and strategy, no frontline work. I'd have to start as an Assistant Investigator then maybe after three years or so Investigator, then Senior Investigator and then perhaps Chief Investigator. There's only one Chief Investigator per city, with usually five to ten Senior Investigators reporting to them, depending on the size of the city.'

'So for me to have CI Andrews out in person last night was quite the honour then?' I asked.

Pascal seem genuinely surprised.

'The CI came out in person last night? I've never even met him.'

Our food arrived and we tucked in. I caught Pascal looking at mine every now and then and decided he had just been polite when he chose the pastries. Which was his loss. He'd have to learn to be more assertive if he was going into the Investigations Division.

'What did they tell you about me?' I asked.

'Only that threats had been made on your life, that you were a journalist and that we needed to be on our guard,' he patted the side pocket of his uniform jacket, 'I have a regulation stunner tucked away in here and authorisation to use it.'

'Then you've no idea about what happened to me yesterday?'

'No. Why? What happened?' he asked. He was either genuinely in the dark or he'd missed his calling and should have been an actor not a police officer.

It seemed CI Andrews wasn't keen for it to be general knowledge that a foreign national had been kidnapped, tortured and interrogated by persons unknown on his watch.

'Oh, nothing of interest. It's all probably a fuss about nothing,' I said, 'What are your orders once I leave my hotel room?'

'I was told that you are recommended to stay in your room for the time being.'

'And if I don't want to stay in my room?' I asked as innocently as possible.

'Then I'm supposed to report your destination to my Senior Examiner. They'll decide if I need to accompany you.'

We finished breakfast and headed back to my room, where I left Pascal to resume his post outside. I assured him the next time I left the room it would be to meet CI Andrews. Before then I needed to talk to Kastagyr and The Organisation's doctors

With the security camera once again disabled I contacted Kas. They discussed the events of yesterday with me, trying to work out if there was any way to determine who had kidnapped me. We agreed that the chance of this being unconnected to the person I'd had the fight with was slim, but we couldn't be sure if they knew they'd tackled the same person twice. My chameleon suit should have protected my identity during the fight and perhaps they'd targeted me simply because I was a nosy journalist asking questions they'd prefer didn't get answered. It was frustrating feeling so much on the back foot.

We were interrupted by the senior doctor at headquarters who told me that she had programmed my med-kit to synthesise a drug to repair the auditory nerves that had been over stimulated and slightly damaged yesterday. I was rebuked for not contacting them immediately upon my release and the dangers of nerve damage were emphasised. I pressed the med-kit's injector against the side of my neck as directed and a quiet hiss signalled the medication had been delivered successfully. She reassured me that the scan showed little to worry about and the medication should ensure no permanent hearing loss. Within a few minutes I was relieved to feel the fuzziness clearing away.

Before signing off Kastagyr had one excellent piece of news to impart, the Spycomm I'd attached to the SSP had completed its analysis and I would now be able to access it from within the hidden lab. I thanked them again for looking out for me and reassured them that I'd try not to get kidnapped or beaten up again.

I then contacted Chief Investigator Andrews and arranged to meet at the warehouse in half an hour, I also requested that Examiner Pascal be returned to normal duty. I couldn't have him tagging along.

Once I was safely in a bubble headed to meet Andrews, I checked the audio Spycomms. As expected, there was nothing of any great interest from Jones' offices but I was pleased to see that the one I'd given Randolf was now active. He had managed to plant it on Doctor Jones.

The Spycomm's intelligent filtering was set to ignore any personal, or irrelevant conversations. I'd set the filter to highlight anything concerning wormholes, hyperspace, secrets, Grippe and one or two other key words and phrases. If nothing interesting arose then I could listen to everything, including anything personal, if I felt that was necessary[1].

The most interesting thing Jones talked about was during a conversation with Randolf and another academic called Doctor Intriligator. She was planning to test a new wormhole probe and was going to a different star system, one with a red giant sun, tomorrow. The department's research ship was being prepped. She wanted Randolf to accompany her in case the mathematics needed tweaking and she didn't want Grippe knowing anything about it. I was going to need a ship to follow her. I sent a message to the Barbs requesting the urgent dispatch of a fully equipped scout vessel to the spaceport here. I would also need to speak to Randolf and get a tracking device to him. It was impossible to follow someone through hyperspace as

---

[1] I'd cracked one investigation purely because the subject talked in his sleep, so all his careful precautions against giving himself away during the day time ended up being for nothing.

there was no indication, while in normal space, of which direction or how far the hyperspace jump would be. Jones had not said the name of the star system she was going to and there were far too many red giants in the galaxy to attempt to find her by trial and error.

The bubble slowed down and I set it back into transparent mode. I could see the warehouse block the cell was in ahead. Outside was a police ground car and Andrews' personal car. Two uniformed officers were standing guard at the entrance, somewhat redundantly; as I could see a force field generator protecting the doors. It wasn't as small or inconspicuous as mine but there was no mistaking it. I presumed there were similar devices at any other entrances or exits.

I got out of the bubble and looked around. Andrews got out of his car. He was dressed in a dark blue suit today. It must have been expensive because he was tall, maybe five centimetres taller than me, and although heavily built it fitted perfectly. He had a sensible short haircut that was still mostly light brown but showed some greying at the temples. He wasn't bad looking if rather too serious. He nodded to me and the officers then used his cuff to deactivate the force field before heading inside without a word. I presumed I was to follow him.

I caught up with him as we headed along the traditional Coronnol curved corridors. Even purely functional buildings like this warehouse adhered to the planetary design aesthetic it seemed.

'Did you sleep all right?' he asked eventually as we entered the room the cell was in.

'Yes. Yes I did, thank you.' I answered.

He looked surprised.

'I'm not sure I'd sleep for a week after what you went through yesterday,' he admitted.

'I think being exhausted was a large part of the reason,' I said 'that and having a drink before turning in.'

We arrived at the cell.

'We've run full ID forensic tests on it,' Andrews said, 'other than what we presume were your finger prints and traces of DNA inside the cell there was nothing readable outside. We would like to fingerprint you and get a DNA sample to check.'

'Please just forward your findings to Per Marshall,' I said. 'They'll compare them for you. I'm not permitted to hand those over to planetary authorities.'

He scowled at this.

'Every outside surface that could have been reached by human hands and all the surroundings had been sprayed with an organic solvent that has destroyed any trace of DNA. Whoever locked you in there was very efficient and very clever. I doubt this is the first time they've done something like this. I'm puzzled as to their motive.'

'They wanted me to unlock my cuff so they could access all my personal data, I refused and decided it was safest to destroy it in case the sensory torture got too much and I gave in.'

Andrews stared at me quizzically.

I didn't elaborate.

'Is it commonplace for freelance journalists to be kidnapped and tortured for information?'

'I've never heard of it happening before. We may get attacked verbally or occasionally physically but that's very rare and usually only in a certain sensationalist type of journalism.'

'Which makes me wonder what this was really all about,' he said, 'and who you really work for.'

I said nothing. I climbed up the steps and looked into the cell. The door had been left open after the examination and there wasn't anything of interest to see.

'How's the officer who opened the door?' I asked

'He's fine. Some bruising and a mild concussion. He'll be back to work in a few days. I wouldn't say he's your biggest fan. He was only trying to help.'

'I'm glad he's okay,' I said.

'Is it usual to be proficient in hand-to-hand combat in your line of work?' he asked.

'I wouldn't say I was particularly proficient.'

'He described the choke hold you used to pin him down and the way you subdued him in quite some detail. At least up to the point he blacked out. If I understood him correctly you managed that while blindfolded. You could very easily have killed him, had you wanted to.'

'This sounds suspiciously like you're questioning me Chief Investigator,' I said, 'I was under the impression you'd been specifically instructed not to do that?'

'Not at all. If I were questioning you Per Pike I would have read you your rights. You'd have legal counsel available to you, and given the seriousness of the matter we'd be doing it in an interview room where all of this would be on record. No, this is just a conversation.

I'm only trying to assess if this perpetrator is likely to pose a broader threat to society or if this is really all about you, and if once you leave Coronnol I can forget all about it.'

He paused and then added 'You are leaving Coronnol quite soon I imagine.'

There was definitely an undertone that suggested it would be a very good idea if I did and a very bad idea if I didn't. I didn't respond. I didn't want him arresting me despite his orders, especially as I needed to see Randolf and get to the spaceport before Jones departed on her mysterious trip.

'I am curious what else they may have asked you after you destroyed your cuff,' said Andrews, 'because it seems odd to keep torturing you if the only thing they were interested in had been destroyed hours before. Why would they do that?'

'I really couldn't say,' I answered, 'sadistic pleasure?'

'We're checking the nearby buildings and all the paths into this facility for cameras we can legally access. We may spot a pattern in the comings and goings to help us pinpoint whoever set this up. Someone went to a lot of trouble to get this cell. You're fortunate to have friends in high places who could raise the alarm. How do you know Per Marshall?'

I didn't answer.

Andrews sighed, and showed me the access hatch in the base of the cell that allowed items to be passed safely into and out of it.

'These hatches are why the cell has to be mounted off the floor. You place your tray of food, or stolen cuff, into this receptacle on the side of the cell, press the button and it is moved underneath and up through the hatch in the floor. There's no way for the prisoner to shoot anything through, or to grab someone who gets too close. The same procedure works in reverse. An Examiner found your smashed cuff in the receptacle. One of our tech people had a look at it before we passed it back to you. She said she'd never seen one like it, a custom-made cuff with lots of extra circuits in it and no manufacturer's name or any part numbers to be seen. Which is interesting, wouldn't you agree?'

I didn't answer. I couldn't tell Andrews the same lie that had worked so well on Randolf. He wouldn't fall for that. Being a police officer himself, and the most senior one in the city, he'd spot it for a lie in a heartbeat. I needed something plausible but outside his experience if I was to deflect his natural investigative instincts. Something close enough to the truth but not too close.

'Chief Investigator Andrews you are obviously not going to stop pushing at the boundaries of your orders so I may as well take you into my confidence,' I said, 'I am a journalist, but that's not all I am. I work very closely with the Intelligence Division of the Galactic Fleet. A journalist can get access to people and places an Intelligence Officer could not. They provided me with the special cuff, it has one or two features unique to the Intelligence Division. They suspect someone in the Astrophysics and Physics Department is working on unauthorised weapons technology. They had several of the senior researchers consult with the Fleet some time ago on a number of secret projects and the suspicion is that someone has taken some of the ideas and are planning on producing their own variant which they will sell to the highest bidder.'

He looked sceptical but allowed me to continue.

'The Galaxy is at peace but in some regions it is a fragile one and tensions run high. One of the Fleet's primary missions is to keep the peace, arbitrating disputes as a neutral party, and ensuring agreements are kept. They use force only when all other avenues have been exhausted and then sparingly. If a planet or group of planets were to get hold of superior weapons technology to the Fleet, then that role would be in jeopardy. Per Marshall is my supervisor at headquarters. I'll call them up and they can confirm all of this if you like.'

He nodded so I placed the call to The Organisation.

'This is Pike. Please could you put Kastagyr Devon Marshall on the line with myself and Chief Investigator Andrews?'

A few moments later I heard Kas' voice so I switched to visual and stretched the screen out to life size so Andrews and I could easily see Kas.

'Per Marshal please would you explain my relationship to the Galactic Fleet and my investigation here on Coronnol?' I asked.

Kas and I had long ago implemented a policy that if I ever asked for them by their full name and included the fact that someone was with me that they would play along with whatever I said.

'How much have you told CI Andrews?' asked Kas.

'Everything,' I said, 'He knows I'm working undercover for the Galactic Fleet's Intelligence Division looking into possible links to illegal weapons manufacture by someone here at the University.'

Kas looked extremely angry and started to tear into me.

'Per Marshall,' said Andrews, interrupting. 'Please don't blame Per Pike. I've been pushing and pushing to understand the situation here, and Per Pike eventually had to explain. If there's anything illegal going on here, which I doubt, you will have my department's full cooperation.'

'I'd expect nothing less CI Andrews, but you must understand we have protocols and procedures for civilians like Per Pike to follow. And that does not include taking planetary authorities into their confidence without clearing it with me first. At the Fleet Investigation Division we use civilians from time to time but only when necessary and under close supervision. As this investigation is now compromised, I will need to reassign Per Pike and have someone else take over. I trust I can rely on you to maintain confidentiality on this matter? Should the investigation bear fruit we will of course hand all evidence over to local law enforcement to make any arrests, as stipulated in the Fleet Charter.'

'I understand completely,' said Andrews, 'absolute confidentiality is guaranteed.'

Kas terminated the connection.

'I'd really like access to any security camera footage you get of the area,' I said.

Andrews shook his head.

'I'm sorry but as you're being reassigned, I cannot release that to you. It will have to go through channels or to your replacement, if they contact me at headquarters. I cannot have you pursuing those responsible for personal reasons.'

It seemed he had been pretty convinced by our story but he was no fool so I was also sure he knew he wasn't being told the whole story.

'What happened to me yesterday felt pretty personal!' I said.

'You should return to the hotel and make preparation for departure. I wish you all the best Per Pike but please don't take matters into your own hands,' he warned.

I gave him a non-committal answer and headed back out to the entrance where I found the bubble still parked where I'd left it. I jumped in and headed back to the hotel.

Once safely back in my room with the cameras disabled I pulled up one of the less standard features in my cuff's repertoire. It consisted of an interface that should allow me access to the university's Infosys domain. Their security was good, which was to be expected when one of their larger departments was InfoTech. They'd beefed up the standard protocols with several layers of customised protection but as I may have mentioned a field agent's primary skills had to include an expertise with Infosys. It took me about half an hour but I was able to access the University's procurements system and found that the Psychology Department in Ghisto, which was in the next major city to the north, had ordered two of these standard prison-type cells several weeks ago. A quick check with the manufacturer showed they'd received the order for two, to go to a Ghisto address, then an amendment had been sent through to deliver a third one to a fictitious company here in Transium but that change had only come through four days ago. The day I arrived on Coronnol. Next I called the Psychology Department, pretending to be from the manufacturer, to verify that the two they'd ordered had arrived, and found they were both accounted for and being used for isolation experiments and they knew nothing about a third tank. Someone had amended the order information. Someone within the University. Someone who expected there might be trouble and was quite happy about using unscrupulous methods to interrogate anyone they suspected. As I'd discussed with Kas earlier, this person was likely to be the same someone who had disabled the security cameras at the labs, fought me and then triggered the alarms the other night. It made sense. The chances of there being two unconnected conspiracies at the same time was tiny. It was either one person or a small group of people working together, probably two but at the most three. It was almost impossible to keep anything truly secret once even three people knew about it. The evidence of something very untoward happening at the University was stacking up. Frustratingly none of it was pointing to Doctor Jones specifically, or to anyone else either. Nor could I establish a connection to the impending end of the galaxy.

I called Randolf and told him I needed to see him later in the day and not to make himself uncontactable. I needed to get back to the spaceport, according to my cuff the scout ship I'd ordered was due shortly. It was time to check out. It was unlikely I'd be coming back to the Fortitude Tower. I packed the few personal items I had in the luggage, got a stunner to keep on me in case someone attacked me again, and made sure the broken lock on the case worked well enough to at least keep it shut even if I could no longer lock it. I'd need to keep the luggage with me this time as I wasn't using a commercial carrier who would handle that for me.

I headed down to the reception where I settled my outrageously large bill with a simple swipe of my cuff and, carrying my luggage, walked briskly to the Mag station. It was nearing lunch time so I grabbed a large coffee and a few local delicacies to eat on the Mag from a fancy pastry stall in the station itself. I hadn't recognized any of the items for sale so had asked for two savoury ones and two sweet.

I arrived at the spaceport about an hour later. I'd only had to wait a few minutes for a Mag going in the right direction and I'd thoroughly enjoyed my lunch especially as I'd seen nothing suspicious and I'd recognized no one.

Once I was out on the platform the cuff led me in a different direction to the rest of the passengers. They were all heading for the departure lounges for the commercial starships. I headed for a much smaller section of the port. The charter and private ships were kept well away from the large commercial ones. A small ship wouldn't fare well if caught in the wake of a rapidly taking off starship.

After a ten-minute walk along a gently curving glass corridor, I could see a group of smallish hangars ahead. The corridor widened out into a reception area with a small seating section, a coffee pot that smelled freshly brewed and a desk. I swiped my cuff over the desk and my screen lit up showing a stylised map of the spaceport. There was a softly blinking blue 'you are here' dot and a fine blue line leading to a nearby hanger where my ship was waiting for me. I swiped to indicate I wasn't yet departing Coronnol, so customs and emigration officials did not need to get involved.

I followed the blue line down the corridor until I reached the indicated hangar door which unlocked automatically for me.

The ship was outstanding. It was roughly cylindrical but sleek like a dart, with a small thin bulge running the length of each side where it had retractable wings for atmospheric flight. It was a light matte-grey with no markings of any kind. It was just over ten meters in length, about five metres wide with the wings closed. The front section tapered to a needle point. This model was large enough for three adults to live in comfortably for several days. It was the latest generation of small scout ship and would be fully equipped with everything I could possibly need. I pressed my thumb against the contact patch for a DNA scan, that plus a swipe of my cuff confirmed I was authorised to enter. The hatch opened and a small ladder extruded from the hull. I climbed in and the hatch closed behind me.

The inner airlock door was already open as the ship had detected an external atmosphere so I checked the ship out. To the left was the cockpit area with three seats, arranged in the usual manner with pilot and co-pilot side-by-side facing the controls and the windows. There was a third seat behind the co-pilot. There was a pop-up jump-seat behind the pilot that could be used for a fourth person if required, but it wasn't comfortable for lengthy use. To the right was a door through to the living quarters. The first part was the bedroom with one fixed single bed and two in the walls, that folded down. On the opposite side of the room was a tiny bathroom that comprised a shower, toilet and hand basin. I dropped my luggage on the bed then continuing aft I went through a door into the kitchen, or galley. This was pretty basic and consisted of storage for pre-prepared meals, a special cooker to re-heat them and a fold down table fastened to the wall. There was one more door continuing aft and this led to the final section. This was the workshop and engine room. All the special equipment a field agent could need was stored here plus, in the centre of the room, was the cylindrical grey metal hyperdrive casing that went from the floor all the way to the ceiling. Under the floor were the artificial gravity generators and the engines used when in normal space or for atmospheric flight. Everything seemed perfectly in order so I headed back to the cockpit.

Chapter 15
Fast drop

The Barbs had done very well to get the ship here so fast. I'd only ordered it about four hours ago. It couldn't have been very many hyperspace jumps to Coronnol from the nearest supply depot. The delivery pilot had left me a full checklist to reassure me all systems were fully operational and following standard procedure they'd have headed straight to the commercial departures lounge to catch a starship back to wherever they'd come from. It was possible to send ships by automatic pilot, but it was far faster with a human one. Piloted vessels always received priority take-off and landing when spaceports were busy.

I pulled up a view of the area around Doctor Jones' laboratory complex on the pilot's screen. I had no desire to take the Mag to Transium and back, plus the nocturnal activities I had planned for later today meant a prompt departure from Coronnol might become necessary. The map showed there was plenty of parkland around the facility but no official aircraft landing zone, air travel being fairly rare on Coronnol as it was on most planets. The emergency services would have some flying ambulances to get to patients quickly but they were designed to be able to manoeuvre well enough to land almost anywhere. The scout ship wasn't much larger than an ambulance so I chose a densely wooded area about a kilometre from the lab as the best place to set down and remain unnoticed. I filed a flight plan, with air traffic control, to a reasonably distant city that would pass near to the lab complex and prepped for departure.

The ship wasn't quite fully charged yet but would draw power from the planetary grid while in the atmosphere, so I could go as far and as fast as I liked.

I strapped myself in and called the control tower for permission to take off. I was given a departure token which the ship automatically acknowledged and within a couple of minutes the flight engine started up. The spaceport mustn't have been very busy to get a slot so quickly. I felt the subtle change to the onboard gravity field as the planet's gravity was neutralised by the grav engine, allowing us to lift off. The ship glided smoothly out of the hangar, tipped nose upwards by about thirty degrees and accelerated rapidly to two thousand meters before levelling off. I kept a close eye on the course as I didn't want to overshoot the lab and have to turn around. Looking down out of the window I could see a thin silver filament tracking across the green fields towards the coast, which must have been the Mag tube heading towards the high-rise towers of Transium city centre in the distance. I was much higher than even the Fortitude Tower, but it was pretty easy to spot it, almost smack in the centre of the city. My flight plan curved inland slightly, avoiding going over the city itself. It was almost time to take manual control. I activated a decoy drone that would continue on my flight plan emitting a duplicate of the ship's transponder signal. I couldn't just vanish from the planetary traffic systems without raising all kinds of alarms. The drone would file a change to the flight plan just before reaching its destination, turn around and head back. By then I'd either be ready to break orbit or I would meet up with the drone and continue back to the spaceport with no one any the wiser. I enabled manual control, launched the drone and activated the scout ship's stealth mode. I wasn't invisible to the naked eye. That technology didn't exist, yet. But the matt grey colour of the ship wasn't paint, every square centimetre of the ship was like the chameleon suit. It could change colour or display an image. This allowed the ship to very effectively camouflage itself and blend into the background, unless you were extremely close or knew what you were looking for it would be difficult to see. Stealth mode also deactivated the onboard transponder, a highly illegal act we used all the time in The Organisation. That alone would definitely put me in CI Andrews' bad books. I slowed to fifty kilometres per hour. A glance out of the window showed the circular laboratory complex in the distance to my left, it was tiny from this altitude, and I checked the map. The woods were north east of the lab, so I banked to the right and slowed some more and brought the ship to a halt. I activated the belly camera and looked straight down. I could see the woods directly below me. I zoomed in and checked visually and with a full instruments scan to ensure there was no one about. I didn't want to land on anyone, and I also wanted to set down without being seen. The ship's belly panels were mimicking the sky above, so I was as near invisible as I could be from the ground. Once I was certain there was no one about I pinpointed the landing area and engaged the fast drop landing. This was fully automatic, as I doubted any human pilot would have the necessary reflexes to do it manually. I braced myself and pushed the go control. The ship's gravity engine disengaged and we dropped, in free fall. My stomach lurched into my mouth and I clamped down so as not to lose my lunch. I could feel the panic rise and I gripped the straps holding me tight to the chair. What if the autopilot miscalculated the drop? Did it allow for the variations in the gravity field between planets? From this height it would take approximately twenty seconds before we crashed into the ground at over seven hundred kilometres per hour. There would be little chance of surviving that impact even in this ship. The fancy crash systems could only cushion so much impact force. After eighteen seconds and when only a handful of metres above the ground the engine kicked powerfully back in to bring the ship to a smooth but perfect high-g landing, exactly where I'd marked on the map. The camouflage system instantly mimicked the trees and shrubs around the ship once the window blinds had slid shut. I shakily unbuckled the harness and stood up. An eight 'g' landing was horrible and I felt awful as I headed to the equipment room. I stopped for a much-needed small but strong drink in the galley. While the fast drop landing was supposed to be completely safe, I hated doing them. They did minimise the chances of being spotted from the ground or the air, so sometimes there was no better option if you couldn't wait until night. I'd heard talk that someone was working on a powered dive version, so you would fall even faster than free fall and brake at about the same height from the ground. I had no desire to try that, the g-force on landing would be in the low teens. Most people pass out somewhere between five and eight. I packed a hyperspace tracker and some other important items, including a chameleon suit into a small knapsack and headed out of the airlock towards the lab. As I walked I called Randolf and instructed him to slip out and meet me in the gardens near the canteen in about ten minutes. I estimated I was slightly more than a kilometre from the lab, but I'd rather he was there before me so I wasn't hanging around trying to remain unobserved. The drone would take about three hours to reach its destination, then another three back. I thought six hours was a reasonable amount of time to get everything done.

The walk to the lab was beautiful. Coronnol was one of the most scenic planets I'd been on recently, or certainly this part of it was. There may have been unsightly or run-down areas somewhere but I hadn't seen any. The grass was thick, soft, and a vibrant shade of green. Trees of multiple different varieties meandered along the contours of the ground. Never getting so dense that the light was seriously blocked, but never too far apart. They must have been planted back when the terraforming of Coronnol was almost complete as they were mature but the algorithms used to position them had been extremely sophisticated; the woods felt completely natural and organic. I was starting to perspire a little as the ground rose up into a small hill. It was warm and I had a fair bit of equipment with me. At the top of the hill I had a perfect view down to the lab. The circular building looked spectacular from up here with the late afternoon sun bathing it in rich yellow light. I could see the glass wall of the canteen but the woods I was sheltering in ended at the hill and I would have to get to the rendezvous point across a large stretch of open ground before I entered the relative safety of the gardens themselves. I pulled the chameleon suit out of the bag and wriggled quickly into it. It wouldn't do anything for my perspiration problem but I couldn't help that. I chose a random disguise and walked briskly down the slope. I saw someone in the garden, fidgeting and glancing about nervously. I'd have been sure that was Randolf from the body language even without the fact that he was uniquely tall and thin of all the people I'd met here. I saw Randolf glance my way and then look away dismissively, that meant the suit was working well as he hadn't recognized me at all. I made my way into the bushes and deactivated the disguise before I approached him

'Per Randolf,' I called out cheerily, 'How nice to see you again.'

He looked worried and didn't answer.

'Smile Dan!', I said, 'People might be watching and you look terrified. You're not in trouble.'

I held out my arm and we linked briefly.

'Let's walk', I said.

He nodded and we followed a looping path away from the building through some ornate landscaped flowerbeds and water features.

'I have work to do. I need to get back,' he said.

'You can get back shortly. I needed to give you this,' I said and took a small but heavy rectangular box from the knapsack.

It filled my palm and had just one small sliding switch on the top.

'This is a hyperspace tracking beacon,' I said,' to activate it you just slide this switch here and it'll glow faintly while it's on. Slide it back to turn it off. It'll need to be on for a few minutes to establish your precise location and send that information to me. The light will flash slowly when it's done its job. Once you've made your final jump through hyperspace switch it on, or if you think you can't keep it with you safely then switch it on once you're on board, hide it in your quarters and it'll update me after each jump.'

He took it and slid it into his pocket.

'I'll activate it as soon as I can,' he said, 'but why don't I just tell you where we are? You are listening to everything I say.'

'I'll lose my audio bugs on both you and Doctor Jones when you jump,' I said. 'For some reason I don't fully understand, the Spycomms won't survive the trip through hyperspace I think it does something to the microscopic power supply.'

'Well the three of us are leaving at nine o'clock in the morning from Transium spaceport,' he said.

'Who is the third?'

'It's Doctor Gernard. I'm not sure why he's coming instead of Doctor Grippe. All the equipment is already on its way to be loaded and Doctor Jones will be heading down there shortly to supervise. Doctor Grippe found out about the trip and is furious that he's not been invited but protocol means he can't ask to join us, it would be a tremendous loss of face to admit he wants to go and wasn't invited.'

I told him to find things to do so he could stay until everyone had left for the day then to exit the building through the cafeteria, where I would meet him.

I wandered back to a secluded part of the garden and made sure I was out of sight before reactivating the chameleon suit's disguise. Randolf had estimated it would be a couple of hours for the majority of the staff to leave. Then I could get back to the hidden lab and check out the secure storage and processing unit and maybe finally find out what was going on.

I was bored but relieved that it was only an hour and a half later that I saw the door to the cafeteria open and the lanky figure of Randolf standing there peering anxiously out into the gardens. I quickly crossed the strip of grass to the door and he jumped and looked startled.

He started to protest that the building was closing and I couldn't come in without an appointment. He hadn't recognized me in the suit, and just stared when I spoke to him before finally he realised who I was.

'Where did you get this technology?' he asked.

'It's part of the standard field pack,' I answered, 'it's pretty good, from a distance, isn't it?'

He nodded and agreed he hadn't noticed anything odd until I was a few metres away from him.

'You should leave,' I said, 'I can take it from here. I want you to carry on as normal with Doctor Jones and I'll be in touch when you get back to Coronnol'.

He headed off across the garden to the footpath back to Transium city centre. It was a clear warm summer evening so it should be a pleasant walk.

I pulled the door shut behind me and headed back to the machine room that led to the hidden laboratory.

Outside the machine room I activated my scanner to check for security upgrades. There was a new camera hidden above the door on the inside recording anyone accessing the hidden lab but that appeared to be it. It was a simple matter to block it but it did mean I'd have to get the Stanton-Mayes security door open quickly before a faulty camera drew someone's attention. I hurried across to where the hidden door was and pulled up the access system on my cuff. I selected the codes I'd used last time and the door didn't budge. The handle didn't appear in the wall and nothing lit up. I started scanning and discovered that it was no longer a Stanton-Mayes door. It had been replaced by an even more expensive and upmarket one. This make, Excelsior, didn't have a back door code on file that we could use to override the lock but I could calculate a code given some time. The hacking system on the cuff's screen showed the connection to the door and I started generating codes and analysing the door's responses. I was anxious about the disabled security camera but I had no choice but to stay right next to the door. The Excelsior wouldn't accept commands from a range greater than one metre as part of its security features. My screen flickered as I tried combination after combination each time learning a little more about the algorithm used to keep intruders out. After a nervous forty minutes I thought I had enough so I got my hand-held stunner ready, just in case, and triggered the unlock command. The outline of the door lit up green and it smoothly slid out from the wall a few millimetres and then swung open slowly under its own power. I stepped back to allow it to open fully, keeping the stunner pointed into the hidden room.

I scanned the room, but no cameras had been installed in it since the other night. More importantly there was nothing in there. Nothing at all except the few work benches that had been there before. There were no partially assembled probes, no tools, no notes, no documents, no personal items and worst of all no SSP. Doctor Jones must have either moved everything to another location or taken the SSP with her to use on her field trip. This had been a massive waste of time.

I touched the contact patch on the door and watched it slide smoothly back into place and vanish as if it didn't exist. I stepped back out into the corridor and deactivated the camera blocker before making my way back to the exit.

Chapter 16
Pursuit

I was fuming as I trudged back to the scout ship. I was mostly angry at myself for not guessing Jones would take the SSP with her if she was planning to conduct some extensive field testing. Even though I couldn't have gained access any earlier it was still frustrating to have missed my chance.

Once back at the scout ship I packed away the chameleon suit and other equipment and made myself something to eat while I waited for the decoy drone to get back to Transium. I'd sent it a command to speed up, which had cut the four hours that remained of its decoy trip down to just under two.

Once the drone grew close, I made my way to the cockpit and prepared for take-off. A quick scan of the area showed that no one was around so I set an intercept course that would allow me to smoothly bring the drone on board and then continue on to the spaceport. I opened the shutters on the cockpit windows just as my stomach turned a momentary somersault when the antigrav activated. We were at tree top hight already and then the nose tipped upwards to allow a rapid climb to catch up with the drone at its cruising altitude. As soon as it was safely back on board I disengaged stealth-mode so the transponder on the scout ship was re-activated. Air traffic control would have been none the wiser about my little detour.

I had already decided not to spend the night on Coronnol. I definitely felt safer on the scout ship. I requested permission to enter orbit prior to leaving the planet and was assigned a departure token almost immediately. The navigation system showed my ascent to orbit started above the spaceport, so I was treated to one final fly-by of Transium city before entering the orbital spiral[1] that would get me out of the atmosphere and to the edge of space. I slotted into the

---

[1] To maximise the number of take offs and landings all ships are assigned to one of the many spiral patterns that guide them to and from orbit. So long as everyone sticks to the correct rate of ascent or decent in their spiral multiple ship can use the same one. A spiral is one way traffic, it's either going to or from orbit, never both. It's the reason commercial ships blank all windows and viewports as they take off or land. Watching the planet spin can make even seasoned space travellers feel sick.

spiral and saw a few ships ahead of me higher up and one below me that must have just taken off. All were similar in size to my scout ship; the commercial liners would be much slower and use a spiral with a greater diameter to reduce the motion effects on the passengers. The sunset looked pretty good from this altitude but my ascent was so rapid the sun was struggling to get below the horizon. The navigation system emitted a low chime to warm me I was nearing the end of my spiral and would need to plot a new course. Coronnol had no natural moons that I could wait in orbit around so I requested a polar geo-stationary orbit as I didn't want to go far from the planet and polar orbits weren't usually much in demand. The next planet out from Coronnol's sun was an eight-hour journey, which was far too distant.

Once orbit was established, I checked my messages and was pleased to see the first draft of the article on Doctor Jones had been completed by the Barbs. I skimmed it quickly and was pleased with it, the tone was about half way between a fluff piece and a serious report on her astrophysics career, which suited the established Pike style well. I compiled an accompanying note and forwarded it to Doctor Jones expressing my hope that she would be satisfied with it and that I would let her know when it was to be published.

I got myself a good stiff drink and headed aft to the living quarters. I undressed, climbed into bed and got comfortable propped up on some pillows before I checked the Spycomms recordings. Once again nothing from the city centre office, I wondered if she ever used it, and nothing from the office in the lab. The personal Spycomm wasn't flagging up any recording matching my search filters which I found astonishing given how close she was to field testing. I disabled the filter and started the playback from the first conversation in the morning. It was a less than fascinating account of her having breakfast with someone, I didn't know who, the research had indicated she had no bondmate. I supposed that didn't stop her from being in a relationship or having a visitor. I sped the playback up to the highest speed I could and still understand it. She wasn't a chatty person. She only seemed to talk when she had something to say. I'd got to the point in her day when she'd arrived at work and suddenly her voice was replaced with the low hiss of white noise. I paused and rewound before replaying that section at normal speed. One moment she was speaking to someone about lecture schedules and then there was a slight change in the quality of the ambient noise and then static. She must have entered a room that had a scrambler. She was extremely cautious. The scrambler wasn't to the same level of sophistication as ours, which generated innocuous speech for listening devices to record, but it was effective as it stopped anyone from hearing the conversation. I searched all previous recordings, since Randolf planted the Spycomm on her, for the white noise and found about a dozen instances. That explained why I'd heard nothing significant about her project. Whenever she'd been discussing it she'd done it with the scrambler technology active. She couldn't possibly know about Spycomms, only The Organisation had tech like that, but she had been paranoid enough about rival universities to be careful of a security breach within her own laboratory. It wasn't incriminating exactly but it was certainly suggestive that she was fully involved in something she was frightened of anyone finding out about. I dimmed the lights and lay down to sleep, grateful I didn't have to worry about force-fields, intruders or being kidnapped while on board the ship.

The following morning I was up early. My cuff was still on Transium time but in polar orbit the time was moot. From the cockpit I could look down and see the terminator[1] separating the night half of the planet from the day. While I was eating my breakfast I received a message from Randolf letting me know that they were about to take off. I hoped he'd planted the hyperspace tracker properly. I checked the ship's systems and was pleased that a night in orbit had fully charged the ship and I would be able to jump to wherever I needed to. Coronnol control gave me permission to break orbit and I moved slowly away from the planet in a gentle curve into the planetary plane. I estimated at least thirty minutes before Jones' ship could make a jump. The question was would she jump more than once? If she was going a long way it was customary to split the trip into multiple smaller jumps, just to be cautious. I would have to wait at least thirty minutes after the tracker signalled to see if she had jumped again.

My cuff glowed and coordinates appeared on the navigation controls showing the tracker had detected a jump through hyperspace. I located the star system and wasn't remotely surprised that its designation meant nothing to me. Millions of stars meant nothing to anyone at all and this one was in an uninhabited system

---

[1] A terminator is a line, visible from orbit, that divides the daylight side and the night side of a planetary body.

according to Infosys. I watched the clock countdown and at thirty-five minutes exactly they jumped again. It was a small jump this time to a system reasonably close to the first one. I restarted the countdown and when forty minutes had passed, with no further signals, I plotted my own jump coordinates and engaged the hyperdrive.

The pattern of stars outside the window appeared to flicker for the tiniest fraction of a second and was replaced with an entirely different one. This was the only way you could tell a jump had been successful without checking Infosys or the ships navigation controls. Human beings could feel no significant sensation when passing through hyperspace. I started scanning for Jones' ship. Infosys informed me that this too was an uninhabited system. Neither this system nor the previous one Jones had stopped briefly at had an appropriately sized planet within the goldilocks zone[1]. This one had two small solid planets far too close to the large red sun to be life bearing then three gas giants much too far out. It took me half an hour to locate the ship as Jones had dropped below the planetary plane and moved closer to the star, presumably to avoid any meteor or micro-planet debris, to get her ship recharged. I ensured the scout ship had its stealth tech fully activated before following her down and manoeuvring myself to within a few kilometres of her. The sun was old. Much older than Coronnol's, Mirth's or my own home planet's. I wondered if there may have been other planets closer to the sun that had long ago been swallowed up by it. This sun probably wouldn't even have a goldilocks zone.

My instruments detected a launch and I tracked a solar probe leaving Jones' ship and accelerating toward the sun. It stayed on my screens for only a couple of minutes before apparently winking out of existence. I presumed it had jumped through hyperspace into the star as that was what her original probes were designed to do. I had no instruments capable of detecting the probe in the heart of a star. I would just have to wait and see what happened next.

Hours passed and as far as I could tell absolutely nothing at all was happening. Jones' ship stayed exactly where it was, in orbit around the giant red star. I stayed five kilometres away observing. I

---

[1] The goldilocks zone, properly known as the circumstellar habitable zone, is the perfect orbit for a planet to be in where temperatures and solar radiation will be such that water can exist in liquid form and carbon-based organic life is possible. Most yellow suns have such a zone, but not all will have a planet in it.

was tempted to call Randolf, to ask what was happening and how long we were likely to be here but I didn't want to risk it. He could be busy with Jones and would find it very difficult to explain why I was contacting him. Eventually when the boredom was almost total, I decided to try and connect to Jones' ship's systems. If I could interface with her ship I might be able to find out what was happening. As was a requirement for all space capable vessels there was a unique registry number on the side[1]. I scanned it and did a search in The Organisation's database for any known security vulnerabilities that I could exploit for that type of vessel. It was a pretty common ship, a Delios Explorer, and only moderately secure. They weren't used by the military or other security conscious organizations. Most customers were universities or private companies. It was only slightly larger than my scout ship. I transmitted some codes that should allow me to discover if its security had been enhanced or if it was standard, depending on the response. I received nothing back, which was odd. Usually at the worst I'd get some kind of access denied message and a warning that my attempt to contact the ship had been logged. I tried again with the same result. Either the InfoTech department on Coronnol had completely re-designed and upgraded the security protocols on board or there was something very wrong. I decided to move closer. If there was a problem then the ship's collision detection system would most likely be off-line too. I engaged my engines and headed directly for Jones' ship at a steady pace. When I was a kilometre away my collision alert sounded and I had to repeatedly override the automatic pilot that was trying to change course. At five hundred metres the collision alert was getting louder and more insistent. At fifty metres every light in the cockpit was flashing red and I almost felt like I was back in the torture cell in Transium the alarms were so loud. By this point Jones' ship ought to have moved away from me automatically so I knew something was very wrong. I backed off to a kilometre to silence the alarms and tried to contact Randolf. There was no answer. I tried Doctor Jones and got no response there either. I put a call through to the Astrophysics Department back on Coronnol and asked to speak to someone on her team. I kept the call audio only. I didn't want anyone at the other end knowing I was on board a spaceship.

---

[1] The Organisation's ships did not comply with this regulation. Our ships would display a unique and fake code as and when required as part of the camouflage system.

'Astrophysics Department. This is Mayday Telium Sands how may I help you,' said a voice.

'This is Cemeron Argalion Pike, I urgently need to contact Doctor Maldonaro Octavius Jones. I've tried contacting her directly but I'm getting no answer.'

'Doctor Jones is currently unavailable Per Pike.'

'I know she's busy. What I'm worried about is the fact I cannot contact her or Danatis Mercutio Randolf who I believe is with her. Please would you just contact either of them and let me know they're okay?'

'When Doctor Jones returns, I'll let her know you've called,' said Sands.

I could feel anger and frustration boiling up and took a deep breath.

'This is a matter of life and death. I cannot explain to you why or how I know this. You have to trust me. I need to know if you are able to contact either of them and find out if they're okay. I'm not asking to be put through. I just need to know they're in good health,' I said through clenched teeth, 'so please do it now.'

'Please hold,' said Sands.

It's widely believed that death and taxes are the two universal constants. It's not true there are three and the third is that Doctor's receptionists are always uncooperative. I waited. Two minutes passed and then another two. The line remained silent. Finally, after almost six minutes I heard Sands come back on the line.

'Per Pike, we are unable to contact Doctor Jones or anyone with her. How did you know there was a problem? I've got Doctor Grippe here wanting to talk to you.'

I hung up. I didn't have time to explain to Sands or Grippe even if I felt it was safe to do so. I had to get aboard Jones' ship and quickly.

Chapter 17
Rescue

Ire-started the engine and quickly headed back to Doctor Jones' ship. I engaged the docking system so that the collision detection was overridden. A Delios Explorer, like all commercial makes and models of ship, uses a standard docking system. The problem would be if their ship was disabled, through accident or by design, the automatic docking mechanism might not work properly and I would have to do it manually. The scout ship pulled alongside the Explorer at about twenty metres out and then started edging sideways until the two ships were almost touching. I switched the controls to station keeping and jumped out of the pilot seat and ran through the bedroom and kitchen to the workshop. There were three space suits. They were universal ones so could adjust to fit most people. I slipped my cuff off and placed it on the workbench as I wriggled into one as quickly as I could, then replaced the cuff back on my wrist. The airlock door was flashing a warning that there was no atmosphere outside the ship. I jabbed the acknowledgment button, opened the door, stepped inside and sealed it behind me. I could see Jones' ship through the window. Their airlock ought to have been lit up as it detected the presence of my ship and the two docking rings should have been connected to each other making a perfect air tight seal. I switched my docking system into rescue mode. This was specifically designed to allow a connection to a disabled ship. My docking ring extended further out until it touched their ship's hull and then the magnetic nodes engaged making what I hoped was a good seal. I pumped the air out of the airlock and opened the outer door. The moment I stepped out of the airlock I became weightless, the artificial gravity only worked within the ship. I gripped the handrails and pulled myself the few meters to Jones' airlock.

I looked through the window but it was completely dark so I couldn't see anything. I activated the head torch on my helmet and was relieved to see the inner door was closed which meant I could safely open the outer one. I pulled the control panel on the hatch open and pressed the manual override button. Nothing happened. It seemed the ship was completely without power. I twisted round and pulled myself back to my airlock. Once inside the artificial gravity made me feel reassuringly substantial once more. I opened the maintenance hatch and unspooled a power line and towed it with me back to Jones' airlock. I shoved the plug at the end of the line into the socket below the switches, which thankfully all lit up. I tried the manual release again, this time the door opened. My ship could provide power to the airlock but I doubted there was an easy way to provide power to the whole ship. Once I was inside I closed the airlock and then realised I was still floating; even the artificial gravity wasn't working in Jones' ship. I pumped air into the lock, opened the inner door and floated through into the ship. I flipped open my faceplate and called out.

'Doctor Jones? Per Randolf? Can anyone here me?'

There was no answer, but it was a bigger ship than mine so it was possible they simply couldn't hear me. I pulled myself awkwardly along the short corridor that branched right to the body of the ship and left towards the flight deck; it was too large to be called a cockpit. I was going to have to search the whole ship. The flight-deck door was open and from the harsh light of my head torch I could see there was no one in there. All the seats were unoccupied and everything was dark, there were no instrument lights, not even emergency ones, on the control panels. These ships were high quality and extremely safe, Delios didn't make cheap ships, there would be backup systems and plenty of redundancy built in. Something catastrophic must have happened to cut off all the power. I turned around and headed back into the main body of the ship. I didn't know the layout but typically the working quarters would be on the same level as the flight deck with the living quarters on the upper deck. I decided to search this deck first, if anyone was alive then they'd presumably be trying to restore power in order to call for help. I floated aft pushing open any unlocked sliding doors to check inside the rooms, which was difficult as I had no real leverage while in microgravity. The locked doors would have to wait, but I pounded on them and called out in case anyone was trapped inside. Nobody answered me. I continued working my way aft. The engine room would be right at the back of the ship. By the time I got there I was heartily sick of having no artificial gravity, almost literally. I was feeling nauseous and exhausted in almost equal measure. The door was locked and wouldn't budge. I banged on it as hard as I could in my gloves.

'Is there anyone in there?' I shouted.

There were three loud bangs and a muffled voice replied.

'Hello! It's Danatis Mercutio Randolf. Is that Per Pike? I'm stuck in here with Doctor Jones. We came in to try to restore power, without success, and the door closed behind us. Can you open it?'

'I'll try,' I replied.

There were no handles, the doors slid back into the walls, and would normally open automatically as you approached. I would need a magnetic grip or a crowbar or something similar if I couldn't restore power. I checked all around the door and found the service hatch with the manual release and prised it open. I expected the release button would do nothing and wasn't surprised to be right, but helpfully there was an auxiliary power socket below it.

'I'm going to have to get some equipment from my ship,' I called, 'I'll be back soon.'

'You have to hurry,' Jones called through the door, 'We could all be in grave danger here. There's no time to explain but please be as fast as you can.'

I made my way as quickly as I could back to the airlock, which wasn't very fast. It's almost impossible to be in a hurry in microgravity. I snapped my faceplate shut then once inside I pumped the air out before I opened the outer door to make my way back into my own airlock. It was a major relief to be able to stand up and feel my normal body weight. I unspooled more and more cable from the maintenance hatch and hoped it was long enough to reach all the way to the engine room. When the cable stopped unwinding with a sudden jerk, I knew I'd pulled every last metre out. It lay in coils about my feet with the other end still plugged into Jones' outer airlock door.

Now I had to work out how to get it through the sealed airlock on Jones' ship. The only way I could think of doing that was by opening both doors which would mean I'd be relying on the docking ring seal and the strength of its magnetic connection to Jones' ship's hull to stop all the air venting into space.

I took a few deep breaths, savouring normal gravity, and then stepped back out into weightlessness. As I floated to Jones' ship, I unplugged the cable from the outer door and towed it into the airlock and reconnected it to an emergency power socket. Now for the moment of truth. Jones' ship was larger so it made sense to fill the docking ring with air from that one rather than mine. I activated the pumps and waited until I had a normal atmosphere. Cautiously I snapped open the faceplate and listened. I could hear a very slight hiss coming from where the docking ring was stuck to the hull. There was a leak but hopefully not a big one. I checked the pressure and it was only down a tiny fraction from normal. I would have to hurry though. I opened the inner door and headed back to the engine room towing the power cable with me. It was even harder to make progress one handed pulling a heavy cable and it was at least five minutes before I arrived sweating and panting back at the engine room. I pounded on the door and called out.

'It's Pike. I'm back. Are you okay?'

'We're fine,' replied Jones.

'Do you have any space suits in there?'

'Yes. I think so. Why?'

'You need to put them on. The airlocks are open and if the docking ring seal goes then we've got a huge problem. I'll get this door open as soon as you're ready.'

I plugged the cable into the auxiliary power port and was relieved to see the control panel light up. I quickly disabled the automatic opener. After a few minutes I heard a bang on the door.

'Per Pike, it's Danatis. We're suited up. But have you seen Doctor Gernard? He's not in here with us.'

'When did you last see him?'

'In the main lab which is the second door aft from the cockpit. He could be hurt.'

'Who else is on board?' I asked.

'No-one, it's just the three of us,' said Jones.

'One thing at a time,' I said, 'let's get you safe first. Close your faceplates and stand by.'

The lab Gernard was in was behind one of the locked doors that I hadn't been able to check inside. He hadn't replied to my knocking or shouting, so I guessed he was unconscious or worse.

I snapped my faceplate shut and triggered the manual door release. The door slowly slid back into the wall and in the light from my head torch I could see two figures on the other side. Randolf looked very uncomfortable. Even an adjustable space suit would struggle to accommodate his extraordinary height. He was bent over crouching uncomfortably as Doctor Jones' waved him through then she followed him.

'I'm leaving the cable plugged in for now,' I said, 'as we'll be able to pull ourselves along it, hand-over-hand to get back to my ship. Once you're safe I'll come back and disconnect it.'

I grabbed the cable and started making my way back to the airlock pulling myself along, hoping they were following.

We'd only gone ten metres or so when suddenly I was spun round violently and was swept along the corridor like a balloon in a gale. The cable slipped out of my grip, I tried frantically to get a hold of it but it was no use. I just kept tumbling and bouncing off the walls. The docking ring seal must have failed which meant all the air in Jones' ship was rushing out into space, carrying us with it. As I was spun around and around I caught glimpses of Jones and Randolf several metres behind me also being buffeted along the corridor but it looked like they still had hold of the cable. I guessed their lack of confidence in microgravity had ensured they had kept a much tighter grip on it than I had. I was now fairly near the airlock and if the docking ring had disconnected completely, I was in danger of being ejected straight out into space. I saw the T-junction approaching, the left turn led to the airlock and straight ahead lay the flight deck. I slammed into the wall and had the wind knocked out of me. I was starting to slip headfirst along it towards the open airlock and couldn't get focused enough to grab the power cable. I was going outside, like it or not.

A hand grabbed my foot and I looked back to see Randolf at full stretch. One hand holding the cable, the other gripping my ankle. The pull of the atmosphere leaving Jones' ship was finally diminishing, and after a few moments I managed to grab hold of the power cable myself and waved my thanks to Randolf. The suit intercom crackled and I heard Doctor Jones' voice.

'Are you okay?'

'Yes. Thanks to Per Randolf,' I gasped.

I was still feeling the effects of hitting the wall at quite some speed. I was glad Jones had worked out how to activate the intercom. Now we were in a vacuum we couldn't open the faceplates to talk.

'What happened? Why did the seal break so abruptly?' she asked.

'I don't know,' I said, 'I can't see anything. It's too dark.'

I pulled myself the last few metres to the airlock and shone my head torch out towards the scout ship. The docking ring was completely disconnected from Jones' ship and had almost completely retracted back into the scout ship's hull. I could just make out, standing in the airlock trying to disconnect the power cable from the maintenance hatch, a figure in a space suit. It could only be Doctor Gernard.

I used my cuff to scan for his suit's intercom and saw the connection activate.

'Doctor Gernard,' I called, 'what the hell are you doing?'

I could hear his breathing but he didn't answer. He was grunting and panting with the effort of pulling on the cable. He'd obviously had enough of trying to work out how to correctly disconnect it and was now using brute strength. He had both hands around the cable and he braced himself by planting one foot on the wall at the side of the maintenance hatch and then heaving. The power cables were strong but I didn't know if they could withstand this. Gernard was from Cestus which would make him extremely strong indeed. I heard him cry out in rage or pain and the power cable stretched a little and then snapped. He shot backwards and slammed into the far side of the airlock. Once he'd scrambled to his feet, he turned and looked across the void at us.

'You're not going anywhere Gernard,' I stated calmly, 'my ship won't open the airlock for anyone but me.'

'We'll see.' he said.

He tapped on the control panel and the outer airlock door closed smoothly hiding him from view.

I felt a tap on my shoulder and turned to see Doctor Jones indicating her cuff. I saw her change the intercom channel so I did the same thing on mine and Randolf followed suit.

'Now Gernard can't hear us I have a mountain of questions, but all of those can wait. We have to either get this ship working or we need to get into yours otherwise we are going to die sometime in the next hour. This sun is going to become a supernova.'

'What?' I exclaimed, 'Why are we in orbit around a sun so close to exploding?'

'I'll explain once we're safe but the short version is Gernard is responsible for it. This sun ought to be stable for millennia. Can you fix this ship or get us into yours?'

'I'm sure I could fix your ship,' I said, 'but not in less than an hour.'

Getting control of my ship should be pretty simple. I outlined what I was going to do and how I expected Jones and Randolf to help.

I switched the intercom channel back and hailed Gernard.

'Doctor Gernard, this is Cemeron Argalion Pike. I know you can hear me. I'm going to give you one chance to open the airlock and exit my ship. One chance only. After that whatever happens is down to you. I'll try not to hurt you but I have no intention of letting the three of us die here so I can make no promises regarding your safety. Open the airlock, now!'

I put as much authority and command into my voice as I could muster and hoped he would respond to it. All I could hear was his breathing and him muttering something rhythmically under his breath that I couldn't make out. He didn't answer.

I pulled up the cuff's ship control interface. One of the many great things about our scout ships was they could be remotely piloted from a range of a few kilometres. I programmed a complex sequence of moves.

'Doctor Gernard, I'm sorry but you brought this on yourself.'

I tapped go and watched, fascinated, as the scout ship moved away twenty metres or so and then started to rotate about its longitudinal axis. After four or five revolutions it was spinning quite fast, it would be very unpleasant to be in that airlock and was about to get worse. I watched the hatch rotate down to the bottom and vanish from sight then come up over the top, as soon as it was facing us directly it sprang abruptly open and a space-suited figure was ejected out directly towards us. The ship slowed its rotations to a stop and started to close the gap between us again. I watched as Gernard span towards us and then crashed roughly into Jones' airlock. I was ready, as were Jones and Randolf. Gernard seemed to be unconscious so we used the broken power cable to tie him up as tight as we could. I aimed myself at the scout ship airlock and pushed off. Once inside I reactivated the onboard gravity, I'd had to turn it off in order to shoot Gernard out of the airlock, and manoeuvred the ship until it was as close as possible to Jones' so they could step aboard dragging Gernard between them.

The airlock outer door closed and the inner one opened. I flipped open my helmet and watched Jones and Randolf do the same.

'Follow me please,' I said and I headed right, through the bedroom and galley, to the workshop.

The semi-conscious Gernard offered no resistance as he was dragged along. We got him into the workshop and I found some extremely strong restraints and pushed him down into a sitting position on the floor against a bulkhead and fastened his wrists behind his back and secured him to it. No human could break out of those, not even one from Cestus.

I opened his helmet and checked him over with a medical scanner. His eyes were half closed and he was mumbling incoherently, but he was in no danger of dying. His head slumped forward and he passed out. I removed his cuff from his wrist and locked it in a secure storage compartment. I didn't want him signalling anyone by voice control if he woke up.

'Okay. Let's get out of here,' I said.

I pushed past Randolf and Jones and headed quickly back to the cockpit

.

Chapter 18
Explanations

Once in the pilot's seat I immediately noticed the sun looked different. It was definitely brighter than before and also looked much closer. I checked the ship's station keeping and according to the distance between us and the planets we hadn't moved closer, that meant the sun was expanding. There was a lot more activity on the surface of the sun according to the instruments and a warning light was flashing alerting me that I was dangerously close.

'Per Pike, we must go right now,' said Jones, who had followed me to the cockpit and dropped herself into the navigator's chair.

Out of the window the sun slipped away to the right as I turned the ship and accelerated away.

'Is the next star system far enough away?' I asked.

'I don't think so, no.'

I launched a surveillance probe and then programmed the navigation system. There was the usual wink of the stars, but this time they only shifted position slightly instead of changing completely.

'We're approximately thirty light years away now,' I said. 'This system's star is directly behind us and the one we just left is the extremely bright one up there.'

I pointed to a bright dot, then pulled up the surveillance probe's video feed onto one of the cockpit monitors. The sun was clearly brighter still and expanding. The planet in the innermost orbit had been swallowed up and the next one out was being scorched to a cinder.

'What is happening to that star?' I asked, 'Why is it going supernova?'

'I can't tell you. It's classified,' replied Jones.

'Really?' I said incredulously. 'After just saving your lives that's your answer?'

Randolf arrived in the cockpit. He'd removed the uncomfortable spacesuit and he sat himself down in the remaining chair, he still looked nervous.

'Are we far enough away now?' he asked.

'We are. We're safe here. But Doctor Jones does not feel inclined to explain.'

I glared at her.

'As explanations are on the agenda perhaps you'd care to explain how you happened to be nearby spying on my experiment?' Jones shot back at me angrily.

Randolf looked increasingly uncomfortable.

'It's a good job Per Pike was here, or we would be dead now,' he said, pointing at the screen.

We all watched as the star's surface began pulsing with rapidly shifting brilliant yellowish white patches. The warm red glow was gradually swallowed up as the bright patches expanded and then joined together. Suddenly the screen went brilliant white and then black.

'Was that it?' asked Randolf.

I rewound the feed to just before it had blanked out then slowed the playback down to a fraction. We watched as the last of the red vanished and the now white surface expanded to fill the screen shooting vast columns of stella matter out in all directions before a moment of static then nothing.

'Yes,' I said,' that was the probe being destroyed by the sun going nova. If we sat here for another thirty years or so we would see it out there.'

I pointed up to the bright dot.

'So what happened?' I said, 'I take it this isn't the result you intended?'

Jones didn't answer so we sat in awkward silence for a few minutes. Eventually she spoke.

'I don't trust you,' she said to me. 'How did you find us?' she turned to Randolf, 'Are you working for Pike, or are they working for you? And why did Doctor Gernard try to leave us behind?'

'I helped Per Pike to find us,' admitted Randolf, 'I had a hyperspace tracker in my quarters.'

He turned to look at me and said 'You say you're some kind of police officer, but now I'm not sure what kind exactly.'

It was now Randolf's turn to feel the heat of Jones' silent anger.

'I can help,' I said, 'but only if I know what's going on. I am a police officer, of a kind, but I can't really give you any details. I lied to Per Randolf to coerce him into helping me. The most I'm willing to say just now is that there is a dangerous conspiracy somehow related to the work you've been doing. As I didn't know anything about your research, who on your staff might be involved or anything very much, I arranged to interview you in the hope I'd be able to find out what was going on. The fact that you almost died out there makes it extremely unlikely either of you is involved but Doctor Gernard is going to have some difficult questions to answer when he wakes up.'

I showed Jones the same police credentials that I'd shown to Randolf when I'd recruited him. They seemed to convince her somewhat.

'I'm sorry I lied to you Per Randolf', I said, 'but as I had no idea who I could trust I couldn't reveal the real reason I was interested in the Astrophysics Department's research. That was why I fed you the story about fraud and a potential scandal, I knew it would motivate an honest person into helping and a dishonest one would become obvious as they tried to hinder my efforts.'

'What was Gernard trying to do?' asked Jones. 'He is the only person who could have sabotaged my probe without me noticing, but I have no idea why. We started getting strange readings from inside the star almost as soon as the wormhole opened, but I didn't realise what was happening until it was too late.'

'I don't know either but it would help to know why you would want to open a wormhole inside a star,' I said.

'It all started when I read Per Randolf's equations and theories about stable hyperspace wormholes. Not for the obvious transportation reasons that I'm sure Grippe has been telling you all about, but because I saw the chance to do something incredible, I think of it as stellar engineering. Like everything else in the universe stars age and eventually they either stop emitting heat and light and become a dark dwarf or they expand and then explode as a supernova. I suspected Randolf's wormhole technology had the potential to prolong the life of certain kinds of star, possibly by billions of years. We would channel hydrogen through a wormhole from the core of one star into another, rejuvenating the target star. Some of the donor stars would go dark but we could massively extend the life of our target stars. Grippe had the necessary applied physics skills, as he is the university's foremost hyperspace and gravity expert. He and I designed the wormhole technology together using Randolf's equations. Gernard built it with help from the engineering department and here we are.'

'That's what you thought of when you read my paper? Not instant space travel but prolonging the life of stars?' exclaimed Randolf.

Clearly this use of his equations and theory was as much news to him as it was to me.

'Not just prolonging the life of stars. Prolonging the habitability of the galaxy. Even though we pick our habitable worlds very carefully, we are eventually going to face the problem of a sun, with inhabited planets in orbit, becoming dangerously old. If we could re-charge that sun from a star in an uninhabited system we wouldn't need to evacuate; and as the galaxy ages this will become more and more of an issue.'

I was flabbergasted. I'd heard of long-term thinking but this was on an almost unimaginable scale.

'You're really trying to find a way to slow down the inevitable death of life supporting stars in this galaxy? But that's billions of years away!' I said.

Now Doctor Jones looked angry again.

'It is yes, but if we don't start finding answers now we might leave until it's too late. By the time the problem is a pressing one and someone starts to research this issue there may be nothing that can be done. I'd rather have a workable solution now that can be further refined over the millennia so that when the time does come human beings are ready.'

'So, what happened here?' I asked pointing at the screen, frozen on the exploding star.

'We picked two stars. A hot young yellow star in an uninhabited system, with no planets in the goldilocks zone, that we named Alpha and a red giant that we named Omega. We stopped off at Alpha briefly to launch the first wormhole probe then immediately continued to Omega. We were supposed to be sending hydrogen from Alpha to Omega slowly over a period of a few weeks. We hoped to detect a change in Omega that indicated a lengthening of its lifespan. There was a high probability Omega would have gone nova in twenty to thirty thousand years, so any change should have been detectable. You see when a massive star, like Omega, has used up all the hydrogen needed for nuclear fusion, gravity causes the inner core to collapse and the shock wave of that collapse makes the outer layers explode and that's what we call a supernova. But Gernard must have reversed the particle filters to remove hydrogen in vast quantities from Omega and send it to Alpha instead. It's the only explanation that fits what happened.'

'It explains what he did to those stars, but not why,' I said. 'We can safely assume if he sabotaged the probes then he also disabled your ship to prevent you from either leaving or contacting anyone. He appeared to have no escape plan so he apparently considered it important enough to die for, and my turning up forced him to improvise to try to stop me from rescuing you.'

'I don't think he was necessarily planning to die,' said Jones.

'What makes you think that? I asked.

'Two reasons. The first is we have to assume he had a reason for what he did, that he's not just suicidal or insane. So if there's a reason then you must be right about there being a conspiracy, therefore the other people involved will need to know if he succeeded or not and the details of how to replicate what he did. He must have had a way to communicate with them or for them to rescue him. The second is rather simpler, he had a space-suit stashed and ready to use.'

'There must have been another ship,' I said, 'somewhere nearby. Watching and waiting for Gernard to disable your ship and then make his escape using the spacesuit.'

'But how would they know where to wait?' asked Randolf, 'You needed a hyperspace tracker to find us.'

'That's because Per Pike's only source of information was you', explained Jones, 'I hadn't explained to you the details of the experiment or shared the location. Gernard knew everything and must have planned this with his associates in advance.'

'Let's see if I can confirm this theory before we go and have a chat with Doctor Gernard.'

I pulled up the ship's sensor logs from the moment I'd arrived at the Omega star until the moment we had left. The scout ships were often used for surveillance and observation so were equipped with the very best sensors available. Everything that could be recorded was recorded. It was just a matter of knowing what to look for. I activated every available display screen in the cockpit and sent a different category of data to each one. I programmed the search to look for correlations between them that could indicate the presence of a ship without an active transponder. We all stared at the screens as the data started scrolling by, but I was certain I was the only one able to make much sense of it.

'Any normal ship would have a transponder beacon that would automatically have been detected by your ship and by mine. The navigation systems rely on this to avoid collisions, and in busy spaceports to determine a ship's priority for taking off or landing. My ship only detected your transponder, so if there was a rescue ship they had illegally disabled it.'

I pointed to a screen showing an accurate representation of Jones' ship in relation to mine and the Omega star.

'I'm starting the search at your ship and using a spherical search pattern that expands outwards slowly. I think it's reasonable to assume that they would want to be nearby so they could rescue Gernard as quickly as possible and then leave.'

Raw data scrolled up the screens slowly for several minutes. Eventually one screen froze, then another and finally another.

'Got them!'

'How?' asked Jones.

'Every ship puts out electromagnetic radiation from the engines, the life support, the Infosys link etc, plus they have an appreciable mass that can be detected if they're close enough and finally there's a visual component. Even if the ship is black it will pass in front of the sun, the stars, other objects and momentarily block them out even if they've turned off all the external lights. These three screens were looking for an incident of each of those things in the same location

The visual display that showed the scout ship and Jones' ship changed as a generic spaceship icon faded in.

'Now we know where they were, I can see if the cameras picked up anything,' I said.

All the screens except the one showing the frozen tableau of ships blanked and I zoomed in on the icon of the rescue ship. Gradually the icon was replaced by an image generated from the various cameras on board. Within a minute we could see a clear picture of a plain grey, angular ship. The airlock facing Jones' ship was already open.

'I don't recognize the design,' I said,' and more worryingly neither does Infosys. It must be a custom-made ship rather than a standard model, so perhaps instead of disabling the transponder it simply doesn't have one. They were about ten kilometres from you, twenty degrees below the orbital plane. It has no markings or a serial number that the cameras could pick up. It's a lot larger than this ship. It could have a crew of ten to fifteen people.'

'What happened to them when Omega went Nova?' asked Jones.

'Good question' I said and wound the timeline forwards on the image.

The mysterious ship suddenly vanished at around the time we had been dragging Gernard into the scout ship. They had been watching and had decided not to attempt a rescue.

'They jumped through hyperspace to avoid being vapourised,' I said.

'Who are they?' asked Randolf.

'I have absolutely no idea,' I said, 'why don't we go and ask Doctor Gernard?'

Chapter 19
Interrogation

We made our way back to the engine room. Jones and I removed our space suits as it seemed unlikely that we'd need them again soon. I asked Jones and Randolf to wait outside then I pulled a stunner out of my pocket, just in case. As soon as I entered, Gernard's head snapped up and a steady stream of angry unintelligible words were more or less spat in my direction. He was sweating profusely, I presumed because he was still in his space suit and he'd been struggling to break free.

'I'm quite happy to stun you, if necessary, Doctor Gernard,' I said, 'but I'd rather not waste my time waiting until you wake up again.'

I moved closer and checked the restraints around his wrists. His left arm looked odd and when I touched it, he flinched in pain and snarled at me again.

'You appear to have broken your left arm Doctor. Would you like a pain killer?'

I didn't wait for an answer but grabbed a med-kit and set the injector to analgesic. It hissed against the side of his neck and I saw him start to relax.

'You can come in now!' I called to Jones and Randolf.

They entered and stayed well away from Gernard.

'We really need to talk about what happened recently on board the research ship,' I said.

'Release me Pike, or you'll regret it,' he snapped.

'Oh, you're going nowhere Doctor Gernard, except to jail for a very long time. You sabotaged Doctor Jones' experiment, which may or may not be illegal but is extremely unethical, you disabled their ship knowing the danger they were in and then you tried to murder all three of us by opening the airlock. And those things most definitely are illegal.'

'Bertrand,' said Jones gently, 'why? Why did you want to make Omega go nova? You perverted my work into something that could be a terrible weapon and left us to die. What possible motive could you have? We've worked together for years. I thought we were friends.'

She seemed genuinely sad and puzzled.

Gernard's rage subsided somewhat as he forced himself to calm down and he tried to regain his composure. The painkiller would be helping. To be able to break your own arm struggling to get free was remarkable, even for someone from Cestus. I was glad the restraints were as strong as they were, if free to move he could probably have overpowered all three of us, possibly even with the broken arm.

'That's an outrageous accusation,' he said, talking to Jones and completely ignoring me. 'We were together in the lab when the lights went off. We forced the door open and I stayed behind when you went off with Randolf to try to fix the power. Unfortunately, I drifted out of the doorway when the gravity failed and it closed behind me. It took me some time to re-open it and by then I saw this ship was alongside and surmised whoever was on board must be behind the power failure. I saw a mysterious figure in a spacesuit trying to break into the engine room so I decided the best course of action was to get into this ship and call for help. I didn't recognize Pike's voice at first which was why I didn't obey their instructions. Why would I do any of the things you suggest? There's no logical explanation.'

It was breath-takingly good improvised lying. I saw Jones and Randolf hesitate for a moment, wondering if they'd made a terrible mistake then I saw Jones' resolve return.

'I'm not stupid Gernard,' she said, she'd dropped the familiar use of his first name. 'Only you or I could possibly have covertly altered the probe's programming to funnel hydrogen through the wormhole in the opposite direction. I know I didn't do it, Per Randolf didn't even know what we were using the wormhole for, and nobody else from the project is here or has sufficient skill with the particle filters to manage it.'

He started to object but I cut him off.

'We know about the rescue ship too, Gernard,' I said. 'My ship is equipped with the very best sensors available and we detected it waiting nearby to pick you up. My arrival complicated things for you didn't it, and you needed to stop us escaping? That's why you disconnected the docking ring and the power cable. You needed to stop us returning to this ship. What was next? I presume your associates were going to come closer and tow my ship further away to stop us getting to it, then bring you aboard before leaving us to be vapourised?'

'Nonsense,' he said, 'absolute nonsense.'

I suddenly had an idea and picked up the medical scanner. I reviewed the readings then scanned his left arm again.

'I wondered how you'd managed to break your own arm. It seemed unlikely you'd be able to do that no matter how hard you struggled. You've actually just re-broken it haven't you Gernard?'

I turned to Randolf and asked 'Was Gernard one of the people not at the lab the other day when I first asked you to help me?'

Randolf nodded and Doctor Jones looked puzzled. Gernard looked worried, for the first time.

'I'm afraid I was the person who broke into your lab a few days ago Doctor Jones, but it was Gernard here who set off the alarms. He attacked me as I was leaving the machine room. He tried to kill me by caving my skull in with a metal bar. We had a fight and I broke his left arm and gave him a bloody nose. He set off the alarms so he could escape before I questioned him, he knew I couldn't stick around with the police on the way. The nose would be easy to fix completely with a tissue regenerator but the broken bone would take longer to heal properly and need several days of treatment. That's why you had your hands in your pockets when I had breakfast with Grippe, you were trying to keep your arm still while the bone healed. Struggling against the restraints just re-broke it.'

Gernard was staring at me, clearly surprised that it had been me he had been fighting with.

I showed Jones and Randolf the medical scan that revealed a partially healed break when I'd scanned him the first time and a fresh break in exactly the same place now. It also showed minor residual damage to the nose.

'I think that's pretty conclusive Gernard. I imagine we could still find some traces of your DNA on the wall where you broke your nose.'

'I work in that building almost every day! My DNA will be everywhere in trace amounts,' he said.

'Not in particles of blood it won't. Perhaps you could tell me who you're working with and why you wanted to make Omega go supernova and we can find a way to be more lenient than would normally be the case with multiple counts of attempted murder?'

'I will tell you nothing,' he spat then he resumed his under the breath unintelligible chanting.

'What is he doing?' asked Randolf.

I didn't know. I fed his speech into the cuff for analysis and was quite surprised by the answer.

'It's a different language, which is rare enough, but this one is an extinct ancient one called Latin and he's praying.'

'He's what?' asked Jones.

'Praying. It's a ritualistic form of communication with a deity. He believes in a god.'

'Not *a* god, the God!' Gernard angrily corrected me, 'show some respect.'

He resumed his quiet rhythmic chanting and I knew we were in real trouble. We weren't dealing with a lunatic doing dangerous things without knowing they were dangerous, nor were we dealing with a maniac who would do dangerous things without caring they were dangerous, we were dealing with a religious fanatic, the very worst kind of idealist, who would do the dangerous things specifically because they were dangerous.

Chapter 20
Confessions

I rechecked the restraints, and then ensured all the equipment in the room was secured away. We headed back into the kitchen but I made sure the workshop door was locked. I was getting paranoid, which didn't seem an overreaction in the circumstances.

'You're the person who broke into the Astrophysics Labs and my machine room?' asked Jones.

She seemed quite annoyed. I hesitated a moment before deciding I may as well go all in and trust her completely.

'I did. Not only that but I gained access to your secure lab behind the hidden door and took detailed scans of all the prototypes and equipment. I planted a decryption device on your SSP which would have eventually allowed me to access your wormhole project data. Although I never got the chance to do so as you brought it with you to Omega, and now I presume it's been vapourised along with your ship. Lastly, I planted audio bugging devices in both your offices, one on Randolf and then blackmailed him into planting one on you.'

'Anything else?' she snapped.

'No, I think that's about it. I congratulate you on ensuring you always used an audio scrambler when discussing the project. Because of that I was completely in the dark about it until your explanation earlier. I did not listen to any personal or, intimate, conversations. Our technology filters those out and we need special permission to bypass that restriction.'

She stormed off towards the cockpit leaving me alone with Randolf. He looked acutely embarrassed.

'Are you hungry?' I asked Randolf.

I was absolutely famished and was going to eat whether he wanted to or not.

'Yes, I suppose so,' he answered. 'Although I don't think I realised I was until you mentioned it. It's been an extremely tiring day.'

He certainly had the gift of understatement. I chose three hearty meals and put them in the cooker. I pressed the button that lowered the table into position and three stools folded out from under the table top. It wasn't stylish but it was usable and just about large enough. Randolf followed me in and sat at the table. He was so tall his head nearly touched the roof when he was standing up.

'The food will be about fifteen minutes,' I said.

I found some whiskey in the drinks cabinet and poured substantial measures into three tumblers.

'I don't drink,' said Randolf.

'I know,' I replied, 'but I wanted to thank you properly for grabbing my foot back there in your ship. It was very brave and I'm grateful.'

We clinked glasses and he cautiously took one tiny sip of his.

'What are we going to do with…him?'

Randolf indicated Gernard through the locked door.

'If he won't cooperate then I'll have to hand him over to my people. They will ensure the proper authorities deal with him. I don't want to do that until it becomes absolutely necessary though, he's our only link to whatever this is all about.'

I heard the shower start up in the bedroom.

'I don't understand that praying thing he was doing. What's it about? Why did he get angry when you said he was praying to a god?'

'I've encountered a few religious organizations over the years,' I said, 'and most are harmless if irrational. They believe there's a higher power or greater intelligence that created the universe and still runs it today, organizing people's lives and ensuring it all follows some grand plan. Some of the religions believe there are many gods, that work together at times and fight amongst themselves at others, like a squabbling family. But most religions believe there's just one God and only they understand his plan and serve him correctly. The praying is their method of speaking to him and also often how they convince themselves that they are receiving answers, it can be calming or energizing or even hypnotic. In ancient times, they believed anyone not actively following their particular God was an enemy, especially those who claimed allegiance to a different god. The true believers could be very dangerous because they also believed in a life after death, an eternal life that was better and more real than this one. That meant anything you did in this life, even if considered immoral or evil, could be forgiven so long as it was all in service to your god's master plan.'

'And they really believe this?' asked Randolf in amazement.

I finished my whiskey and then refilled the glass. Randolf wasn't touching his.

'Some. There's only a very tiny fraction of planets in the galaxy with a significant percentage of the population adhering to a religion, and for most of those it's little more than cultural background. A way of ritualising the key moments of life, such as birth, bonding, separating and death. For some though, a miniscule fraction of that fraction it's absolutely real. Despite there being no scientific evidence for the existence of a higher power, or an after-life, they wholeheartedly believe it to be true. No amount of reasoning with them will change their minds.'

'I've never heard of such a thing in this day and age. I thought the word god was just a mild expletive, left over from ancient times. There are no religions on Fortuna, where I grew up, and I didn't think there were any on Coronnol.'

I said, 'there was at least one on Coronnol, and I seriously doubt he is alone. If Gernard's a member of a fundamentalist cult that believe they alone have the truth and are prepared to go as far as killing people to achieve their ends we need to find out more about them quickly.'

There was a soft chime from the cooker to indicate our meals were ready. I retrieved them and placed them on the table.

'Would you like some water? I know it's your preferred drink.'

'Yes, please. Sparkling if you have it,' said Randolf, as he pushed the almost untouched whiskey away.

I got a bottle of sparkling water for him, a still one for me and one of each for Doctor Jones, as I had no idea which she preferred, and three fresh glasses.

As I sat down the door to the bedroom opened and Jones came in. She'd raided through the clothes stored on board and found a pleasantly colourful but practical outfit that fitted her pretty well. Her short black hair was still wet and shiny. She looked incredible.

She took the remaining empty seat, picked up the whiskey tumbler and sniffed it cautiously before downing it in one. She opened the still water and poured herself a glass.

'I am still furious with you about the breach of my personal privacy, the confidentiality of my research and also with the deception perpetrated to gain access to my lab in the first place. However, I accept on the evidence of Gernard's actions that there may be extenuating circumstances and you probably acted as you felt you had to. I'm willing to try to swallow my pride and help in whatever way I can to get to the bottom of this. After all, you saved our lives and that…creature…in there,' she indicated Gernard,' was about to kill all three of us.'

She opened the lid of her meal. Looked momentarily disappointed but then started eating rapidly.

'Are you going to feed Doctor Gernard?' asked Randolf, between mouthfuls of food.

'I hadn't planned to,' I answered, 'as far as I'm concerned that bastard can starve.'

Doctor Jones gave me a look.

'Not to death, obviously. But it won't hurt him to skip a meal or two. It may make him more inclined to talk. I need information that only he can give me.'

'Are we heading back to Coronnol soon?' asked Randolf.

'No. It wouldn't be safe,' I said, shaking my head. 'This ship didn't have a transponder beacon on that they could detect but they'll have been watching your ship, ready to retrieve Gernard, and must have seen me dock with it and then everything that followed. They'll know that the two of you are still alive and I suppose they'll have seen us bring Gernard aboard. They may not know this is my ship or that it was me who rescued you though. Gernard has had no opportunity to update them. They already suspect that I'm not simply a journalist but they don't have any proof.'

I gave them both the edited highlights about my recent kidnapping, interrogation and subsequent rescue. They seemed appropriately shocked.

I offered Doctor Jones some more whiskey, which she accepted but sipped at this time.

'What do we do now?' asked Jones, 'We can't just sit here and grow old together.'

'I've been thinking about that,' I said, 'I think we have to assume destroying Omega was a test not an end in itself. I can't see how the removal of that one particular star makes any galactic difference. It only had five planets, all uninhabitable and of no particular value. The gravitational changes in removing that star are minimal, Infosys will have updated the hyperspace navigation points within minutes so no-one is going to be stopping off there to recharge their ship and finding themselves incinerated or stranded. So that doesn't leave many options.'

'You think they want to use the hyperspace wormhole technology as a weapon!' interrupted Randolf.

'Yes. I'm afraid I do. But I have no idea what the real target is.'

I stood up and collected the empty water bottles and food trays. They went into the composter[1] and the glasses and tumblers were rinsed out and returned to the cupboard.

Both Jones and Randolf looked horrified.

'You could kill billions of people with this technology and it's quite possible to replicate it if you had Randolf's calculations and my schematics, and Gernard had access to both,' said Jones. 'The final step would be to program the probes in pairs to link the stars together. That's reasonably simple for Gernard, or myself to do, but it would require one of us, or I suppose Doctor Grippe, to teach the process before anyone else could do it.'

She got up from the table and went to the workshop door, unlocked it and went inside. I followed her in case she intended any harm to Gernard. Even though he deserved anything that happened to him I couldn't let her do it. I stood in the doorway and kept watch. She called him a few choice names which he ignored as she rummaged in the locker containing the space suits. After a short while she found what she was looking for and returned. I relocked the door.

On the table sat a small rectangular red object with rounded corners; the SSP.

'You didn't leave it behind then?' I asked, completely redundantly.

'Of course not. The last ten years of my life are invested in this. While I could get another SSP and restore everything from backup that would take time. While you were talking to Gernard in the airlock I returned to the lab and retrieved it, he'd left the door open so it was easy.'

'Why didn't you mention this earlier?'

'I didn't trust you, to be honest.'

'And now you do?'

'I think so. Fortunately, I enabled the highest level of security and auditing on this. All being well I should be able to determine if

---

[1] This broke them down to reusable matter within hours. Any tools or devices I needed to make could be made of this re-usable matter.

Gernard, or anyone else, copied any information from the wormhole project files. That way we'll at least know if the people he's working for already have what they need to proceed or not.'

She tapped her cuff on the side of the SSP and both glowed briefly. A screen appeared in front of her and she stretched it out tall and wide. An access denied message glowed in the centre of the screen.

'I'll just need to update the location protocol. It doesn't recognize your ship as a valid place to be used so won't grant me access without verifying my identity in two different ways.'

Doctor Jones keyed in a long complex passphrase and used her cuff to take a retinal scan. The screen cleared and suddenly there were hundreds of objects visible, she quickly scrolled through until she found the security section and opened it. Her fingers flew over the screen manipulating the search criteria and then she tapped a final command and a please wait icon appeared as the SSP collated the information.

'It'll be a few minutes. I started the search right at the beginning and it's looking for anyone accessing any of the project files other than me and displaying them in detail for any length of time.'

'I presume you had disabled copying already?' I asked.

'Of course. No one can send anything classified to any other SSP or Infosys account. If they tried their access would be suspended immediately and I'd be alerted. The only way to copy the information would be to display it on a cuff screen and then record it using another cuff. That would take a lot of time as there are thousands of files. You'd need a complete understanding of the shielding technology to protect the probe while it's in the heart of a star, Randolf's incredible mathematics and the wormhole generator itself. Plus they'd have to do it out of hours while they were alone.'

Information started to appear behind the wait icon. I could see dates and times and object names that were meaningless to me. The oldest date was approximately three years ago. After about ten minutes the wait icon vanished and about a hundred results had been found by the search. The most recent date was three days ago.

'Well?' I asked, impatient to know what Jones thought.

'I need a moment,' she said and proceeded to open a second screen and compare object names and calendar entries. 'Gernard was copying data almost from the moment he joined my team. He had full access; he was integral to us turning a theory into a practical device.'

Randolf and I fidgeted in our seats and watched her work.

'It's bad news,' she finally said,' I think they've got almost everything. Assuming they have someone with sufficient mathematical skill to understand Randolf's equations and somewhere to manufacture the probes they are very likely to have everything they need to proceed. We only made minute changes to the wormhole calculations since the last time Gernard had unsupervised access.'

'That last date is the night I was in your lab,' I said, 'Gernard must have been copying data before I turned up. That explains why the security system was disabled and why he was there late. He must have seen me arriving as he was leaving and wondered what I was up to.'

I was tired. It had been a busy day. I had to find a way to convince Gernard to tell me what I needed to know but I doubted he was amenable to rational arguments. I went into the bedroom and picked up some clean clothes.

'I'm going to deal with Gernard,' I said as I returned. 'Feel free to stay here or make up the beds if you're tired.'

They both started to come with me.

'I'll do this alone, thanks,' I said.

Neither of them seemed to like it, but they stayed behind as I went aft into the workshop.

Gernard looked pretty terrible. His arm must have been hurting quite a lot by now. Having it restrained behind his back to the bulkhead was not a good position for him. He was pale, sweaty and had his eyes screwed shut.

'Doctor Gernard, would you care for another pain killer?' I asked.

He nodded, so I gave him another dose and saw him relax slightly. I stepped away from him and turned my back, so he couldn't see what I was doing, I pulled my stunner out and adjusted the settings so he would be unconscious for many hours. I shot him from almost point-blank range and his head slumped forward onto his chest. I checked he was really unconscious by gently, and then not so gently, squeezing his broken arm. He didn't flinch at all.

It took me more than a few minutes to unfasten the restraints and then get him out of his space suit. The suit could deal with any bodily functions the occupant required, but he still really needed a shower. I washed him down then checked his broken arm and did my best to set it correctly. I strapped it up and used a tissue regenerator to reduce the time the bone would take to heal then put him into the clean clothes. I had made sure the trousers included an extremely strong metallic mesh belt. Nothing fitted his short powerful build very well but he wasn't going to be in a fashion parade. I fastened his wrists together onto his belt at the front and then the back of his belt to the bulkhead. Another restraint around his ankles completed the job. By the time I was done I was exhausted, he was a big powerful man and it took a lot of effort to move him, but he wasn't going anywhere.

I relocked the workshop door and headed for the bedroom to get a much-needed shower and some sleep.

Jones and Randolf had already pulled the two spare beds down. The lights were set quite low and I could hear gentle snoring coming from Randolf. Jones was sitting up reading something on her cuff.

'What did you do to Gernard?' she asked, flicking the screen off.

'I just cleaned him up and set his arm. He's unconscious though because I did stun him first. I couldn't risk him fighting me, he's much too strong for that. It should wear off in a few hours and then he can sleep or not, as he likes. He's not getting anything to eat until he decides to talk.'

I excused myself and closed the bathroom door and had a shower. The water recycling on these ships was so good it was possible to have a long hot shower. Something that would have been unthinkable in the early days of galactic colonisation. The illusion that my troubles and worries were being washed away was comforting for a time but sadly it was just an illusion. The shower switched from water to warm air and soon I was completely dry. I dressed in some lose fitting comfortable clothes. As I headed for the cockpit I saw Jones had resumed her reading so I didn't disturb her. I needed to update Kastagyr and the others at headquarters.

It took me about an hour to fill them in on everything that had happened. I knew the science specialists at The Organisation would be having a field day with the news about the wormhole technology and I was put under some pressure to send the full details of the mathematics and schematics of the probes.

'Kas, I'm not happy about sending you all that information yet,' I said.

'Why not?' they said. 'You were planning on using the Spycomm to access the SSP just a day or so ago. What's changed?'

'That was when I thought Jones was personally involved in the conspiracy. Clearly, she isn't. She's helping us and I need her to trust me. Taking the information without consent would only further violate the fragile trust we've built up. If and when the time is right I'll ask her, but she's already angry about the lies and deception employed so far, violating her privacy even further doesn't feel like a wise move.'

'How do you plan to make Gernard talk?' asked Kas.

'I doubt he will. Not without considerable coercion. There's nothing in his file to indicate he's been religious or fanatical in the past but that could mean he's a recent convert or that he's been planted in Jones' lab covertly and his background has been sanitised.'

'I'll get started on a deep background check on Gernard. I'll send someone to visit Cestus and interview his family and friends subtly. We'll see if we can find out anything that could explain his actions. I'll also check on his movements on Coronnol, find out who he's been friendly with and what he did in his spare time.'

'Thanks, Kas,' I said. 'That'd be very helpful.'

Kas smiled, a broad genuine smile and signed off with a heartfelt, 'take care of yourself'.

I quietly returned to the bedroom to see Jones was now asleep too. I slipped into the empty bed and flicked the light off and was asleep before I knew it.

Chapter 21
Ungodly or righteous?

The ship's local time was still set to Transium's time-zone. There didn't seem much point in changing it when we had no idea where we were going next. I woke up just before seven in the morning. Neither Jones nor Randolf were around and their beds were neatly made up and folded away. I got up and dressed quickly and headed into the galley.

'Good morning,' I said, 'did you sleep well?'

They were both seated at the table. Randolf had only his usual glass of sparkling water but Jones was eating a hearty breakfast. I joined her. I was always hungriest first thing in the morning.

'I did, much to my surprise,' answered Jones.

Randolf nodded agreement.

I looked over to the workshop door to check it was still locked.

'Don't worry, we haven't been in to see him without you,' said Jones.

'Good. I need you to leave him to me,' I said.

'What are you going to do to him?' asked Randolf. 'You're not going to torture him for information, are you?'

I nearly choked on my food.

'Of course not!' I said. 'Good grief. Just because that's the tactics used by Gernard's people it doesn't automatically follow that we would do the same.'

Randolf looked relieved.

I finished my breakfast and went aft into the workshop.

Gernard started stirring as I pulled up a stool to sit down.

I pulled the earpiece out of my cuff and popped it into my right ear and readied the translation feature. I wanted to understand anything he said even if it wasn't in Inglis[1].

'Welcome back Doctor Gernard,' I said. 'Are you feeling any more cooperative now?'

---

[1] In ancient times the ancestor of the galaxy-wide standard language was known as English. It has absorbed words from several other ancient languages and evolved quite a bit but has been known as Inglis for thousands of years. It would be fairly easy to understand ancient Earth's spoken English but the accent would sound bizarre.

He scowled at me but didn't answer the question.

'I set your arm and used a tissue regenerator to speed up the healing process,' I said.

He looked down at his arm and then tested the restraints holding his wrists and ankles. The veins on his neck stood out as he exerted all his considerable strength trying to break free.

'I wouldn't do that,' I warned. 'You'll break your arm, yet again. The restraints are more than strong enough to hold you.'

He relaxed and glared at me some more. There was a coldness in his eyes unlike anything I'd seen before. Their pale irises contrasted sharply with the dark moustache and beard.

'The destruction of Omega was a successful test for you. I suppose your associates in the rescue ship will have reported the results in your absence but will they care enough about you to try to find you and rescue you?'

I paused in case he felt like responding.

'They're not going to find you, by-the-way.'

I decided to just sit and watch him. We sat in silence for about forty-five minutes. He stared at the floor, occasionally glancing up at me. I stared at him, constantly. Looking for anything in his body language that would help understand him. Setting and immobilising his arm must have eased the pain and he was no longer sweating like he had been the night before.

Eventually I heard him restart the quiet prayer. I activated the translation on my cuff and heard the following via the earpiece.

> 'Earth Mother, judge the righteous, hear my prayer,
> Earth Mother, guide the faithful, hear my prayer,
> Earth Mother, protect your servants, hear my prayer,
> Earth Mother, avenge your enemies, hear my prayer.'

This was repeated three times then he paused. He was still looking straight down. I couldn't see his eyes but I suspected they were closed. He looked up at me and for almost the first time made deliberate eye contact, which he held steadily. When he spoke again, it was still in Latin and it still had the same rhythm as the prayer but I knew he was speaking for my benefit.

> Earth Mother, smite the ungodly, hear my prayer,
> Earth Mother, scatter the unfaithful, hear my prayer,
> Earth Mother, protect your servants, hear my prayer,
> Earth Mother, avenge your enemies, hear my prayer.'

I didn't react. He repeated it three times and then went quiet again. We stayed staring at one another in silence.

'I presume in this scenario I am ungodly and you are righteous?' I eventually asked him. 'Would that be right?'

He didn't answer.

'How would I become righteous in the eyes of your Earth Mother?'

He muttered something under his breath.

'I didn't hear you Doctor Gernard,' I said. 'Could you please repeat that?'

'Gaea would never accept a liar and a deceiver such as yourself. You will never be righteous.'

That was interesting. The cuff had translated Gaea as Earth Mother, but that was possibly a mistake. It seemed Gaea was a proper noun. That was his god's name.

'Are you righteous Doctor Gernard?'

Silence.

'Are you Doctor Gernard? Are you righteous or are you too ungodly?'

He started the prayer again. So quietly it was almost inaudible.

I needed him to answer questions, not just mutter in Latin.

'How's your arm Doctor Gernard? Does it still hurt?'

He didn't answer but I saw him look at the arm and he flinched slightly.

I opened the med-kit and set up the injector with some more analgesic. I also added a little of something else. It was a compound called veraserum, we'd used it on occasion to encourage people to reveal information. It wasn't a truth serum as such but it reduced inhibitions and lowered defences making it much more likely someone would tell you what you needed to know. The injector hissed against his neck and he relaxed visibly.

'Are you ungodly Doctor Gernard?'

He shook his head slightly.

'Doctor Gernard, I need you to answer. Please speak to me Doctor. Are you ungodly too?'

'Not anymore,' he mumbled, 'not ungodly. Not ungodly. Renounced my ungodly ways, on the path of the righteous now. Trying hard to be righteous.'

His eyes looked a little unfocused. I was worried I'd given him too much of the drug. I didn't want him falling asleep on me.

'Doctor Gernard, who was on the rescue ship? Who were you working with on Coronnol?'

His eyes focussed a little and some of the anger appeared in them but he just shook his head.

I tried a few more times to ask him similar questions but he wouldn't say anything. I decided to change tack. He was able to resist direct questioning but oblique questions got answers, reluctant ones, but answers.

'Are you hungry Doctor Gernard? Bertrand? May I call you Bertrand? Are you hungry, Bertrand?'

He seemed to struggle with the answer. Some part of his brain knew he should keep quiet and not speak to me but his body was demanding food.

I fetched a bottle of water and a breakfast meal from the galley ignoring Jones' and Randolf's puzzled looks.

I opened the container and the smell soon filled the room. Gernard's eyes opened properly and locked onto the meal.

'Are you hungry Bertrand?'

'Doctor Gernard,' he snapped. Even in his drugged state he wasn't happy with my informality.

'You can eat when you answer my questions Doctor Gernard,' I said and I put the meal in front of him, but out of reach.

'What about Doctor Jones?' I asked. 'Is she ungodly or is she righteous?'

He resisted answering at first but when I persisted, he finally gave in.

'Ungodly. Ungodly woman. Godless heathen. Ungodly and unrepentant bitch,' he mumbled.

At last, I was getting somewhere. I pulled up the faces of everyone I'd met while I was on Coronnol onto my cuff, making sure the screen was opaque from his side and arranged them so I could just swipe through. I included Jones, Randolf, Doctor Grippe, CI Andrews, Examiner Pascal, and all the staff I'd been introduced to at the Astrophysics lab. I even included the generated image of the old woman from the park, myself and some stock images that he couldn't possibly recognise. I shuffled them into a specific order, blanked the screen then made his side visible. He looked slightly curious when the empty screen lit up in front of him. My cuff would record his reactions precisely.

'Ungodly or righteous?' I said as I flicked the first face onto the screen, which happened to be a stock image. He didn't recognize the face so just shrugged.

'Ungodly or righteous?' I repeated. 'Use your words please Doctor.'

'Dunno', he mumbled, then again as I as I flicked and the second face replaced the first on the screen.

I flicked through each person pausing briefly between each one and carefully watched his expression. Most of the people he wouldn't have known and a neutral reaction would be perfectly normal. The cuff could detect pupil dilation, heart rate, blood pressure, breathing stress, muscle tension and several other physiological readings. He reacted most strongly to myself and Doctor Jones. We were definitely in the 'ungodly' category. He identified almost everyone I expected him to recognize as 'ungodly' and mumbled a slurred 'dunno' for those he didn't and the stock images. I was a little surprised and disappointed when Doctor Grippe was also quite forcibly identified as 'ungodly'.

Only one face other than his own provoked a different reaction, and he immediately tried to cover his slip. I'd have missed it completely without the cuff's slow-motion playback and the sensor readings. It was someone he considered righteous. He'd been about to say the word, I was sure of it, but he'd just about stopped himself before covering with a 'dunno',

He had definitely recognised the face, the cuff confirmed it. His physiological response was unmistakable. He not only recognised it but he knew the person, the only other person beside himself that he considered righteous. It was the image I'd generated of the old woman I'd seen in the park and in the restaurant.

I was going to have to go back to Coronnol. I was going to have to find her.

Chapter 22
Back to Coronnol

I didn't feed Gernard. I gave him a drink of water but took the meal away and put it, untouched, into the composter.

'Didn't he want any breakfast?' asked Randolf.

'Yes. He did. But he's not having any.'

Jones gave me a sharp look.

'I'm not torturing him. He can miss a few meals without coming to any harm. Hunger is a great motivator. I won't let him get malnourished, but I may need more information later.'

'What did he tell you?' asked Jones.

'He didn't explicitly tell me anything. He tried very hard not to in fact. I gave him a small dose of a drug that makes you feel uninhibited, but he resisted. I think he's been well trained.'

'You drugged him?' asked a shocked Randolf.

'It's harmless. It's like being happy and drunk. It makes you feel well disposed to the person asking the questions. You want to please them so you answer. He wouldn't answer anything directly related to his associates; hence he's been well trained. It wears off fairly quickly but I can't use it too often as it is quite addictive.'

'So, what did he tell you?' asked Jones again.

'He recognised someone I saw twice on Coronnol. This is someone he considers 'righteous' when everyone else he recognised is 'ungodly'. This same someone was watching me when I first arrived and was watching us, Doctor Jones, when we had dinner together. It's probably the same someone who was asking the questions when they had me in the torture box.'

'Who is it?' asked Jones.

'I don't know. Infosys didn't recognize the mock-up of their face that I created, but Gernard had no trouble recognising them. I'm going back to Coronnol to find them.'

'But you said it wasn't safe there,' said Randolf.

'Yes, I did. Mostly it isn't safe for you though. I can take care of myself. I will drop you off at one of our bases and then head back. You'll be safe there.'

I saw the look on Jones' face and knew what was coming next.

'I don't know who you think you are Per Pike,' she said, 'but you are not in charge of me, or Per Randolf. I'm not hiding away from these people light-years from my home, unable to continue my work, unable to contact my friends, with my life on hold while you investigate for who knows how long?'

'They may try to kill you again,' I said.

'Then tell the police, they can provide some protection. Or use your own people. I don't care but I'm not going into hiding and I am continuing my work.'

'Would you consent to stay on board this ship temporarily, in orbit? Just for a couple of days.'

'One day. That's all. If you can't identify this person and resolve the matter by then, then I'm taking my chances.'

'Do you feel the same way Per Randolf?' I asked.

He looked like he would quite like to accept protective custody at one of our bases but he didn't want to appear any less brave than Jones so he answered with a firm 'Yes, absolutely'.

'Back to Coronnol it is then,' I said and headed forward to the cockpit.

Jones and Randolf came with me and we crowded into the small space.

I programmed the navigation system to return to Coronnol and we all blinked as the stars flickered momentarily and returned to the pattern that stargazers on Coronnol's southern continent would have been familiar with.

I turned the ship and we saw Coronnol's sun track right to left across the windows until it vanished and the planet itself came into view. A smallish blue disk ahead of us.

'We'll go slowly to give the ship time to fully recharge after the jump,' I said. 'But now I need to know which one of you lives in the more isolated house and if there will be anyone there in your absence?'

They looked puzzled.

'I can't leave Gernard on board,' I explained, 'it's too risky. Plus, I might need him. Therefore, I need somewhere to stash him. Who lives alone?'

'I do,' said Jones. 'I had a friend visiting a few days ago but they left when the three of us took the research ship to Omega. You can use my place; my nearest neighbours are half a kilometre away. Your ship would be able to land in my garden quite easily.'

'I live in an apartment in Transium,' said Randolf. 'You'd never get him in or out unnoticed.'

'Your place it is then Doctor,' I said. 'We'll land in your garden when it goes dark. Which won't be for another eight hours at least.'

The next two hours were busy as I spent them updating Kas and the Barbs. We discussed various theories about who Gernard's co-conspirators could be and what known current religious beliefs were associated with the Latin language or the names Gaea or Earth Mother, without really arriving at any definite conclusions. The last hour before landing was busy preparing equipment and working out a way to get Gernard into Jones' house safely, but the middle five hours dragged by slowly. I didn't want to reveal too much of my plan to Jones or Randolf as I was fairly sure they wouldn't approve and would try to stop me somehow. We ate a fairly quiet meal together half way through the day and I relented somewhat and fed Gernard a small portion. The drug I'd given him had worn off long before and he had returned to his sullen monosyllabic self. He ate greedily and clearly wanted more but I was keen to keep him hungry.

When the time was right I contacted Coronnol control to request a landing spiral and plotted a course from the bottom of the spiral that took us over Doctor Jones' home. I used a fake ID and ship transponder signal so that no one on Coronnol would know it was me returning in the same ship I'd recently left in. The ship could mask the presence of Gernard, Jones and Randolf making immigration believe I was the only person on board. Randolf was nervous about lying to the authorities but Jones was much more practical and understood the necessity. There was simply no legitimate way to explain why we were holding Gernard prisoner aboard the ship, and in case his associates had access to the planetary databases we couldn't reveal Jones or Randolf's return without endangering them.

The landing spiral took almost half an hour but the flight to Jones' home was a brief ten minutes.

As it was now fully dark there was no need for a fast drop landing, So I sent a drone to continue the route I'd requested, transmitting the fake transponder signal, engaged stealth mode and landed in Jones' garden without incident.

'The drone will bounce around between various legitimate reasonably local destinations for the next twenty-four hours,' I said. 'This will give me time to do what I need to do. Meanwhile you'll be safe in orbit, the ship will avoid all commercial orbital spirals and just go straight up in stealth mode and wait for my signal to return.'

'I don't like hiding,' said Jones, 'it doesn't feel right. We should face this head on.'

'I generally would agree, but we have no idea who we can trust or how many other people are working with Gernard. Until we do, I need to keep you safe.'

As we'd discussed, earlier in the day, I drugged Gernard once more, to make him compliant, and between the three of us we managed to get him out of the ship and into Jones' home. She had a useful basement utility room he could be secured in and I refastened his restraints but this time the back of his belt was connected to the waste water pipe, which came down from the kitchen above and disappeared into the ground but looked solid enough to prevent him escaping.

Jones and Randolf reluctantly returned to the ship and I watched as it lifted off and disappeared straight up into the night sky, the camouflage system meant I lost sight of it almost immediately.

I summoned a bubble to get me into the city centre and while I waited for it to arrive I headed back down to the basement to see Gernard. He appeared to be asleep but I wasn't certain. I crouched down in front of him and listened to his breathing. It was slow and steady. The drug I'd given him shouldn't have knocked him out but merely relaxed him enough to stop him fighting us as we moved him from the ship. He suddenly lunged forward, possibly trying to head-butt me, but from his position sitting on the floor he couldn't get any real force behind it. I was also, deliberately, slightly out of range.

'Doctor Gernard,' I said,' that was extremely rude of you.'

'I demand you release me this instant. This is false imprisonment, kidnapping, any number of crimes.'

'It's far too late to play the innocent Doctor, Gernard. You blew up a star and tried to kill three people, and one of them was me. I know you're a religious fanatic and a dangerous one. If the authorities do come and find you it will only be to arrest you.'

I stood up to check the restraint holding his belt to the water pipe was exactly how I wanted it then grabbed the back of his neck to hold him still while I whispered in his ear.

'Also, I'd like you to remember that Doctor Jones and Per Randolf aren't here now to temper my actions. You have no idea what I'm capable of, to get the job done. I may appear to be civilized and cautious but I will do whatever it takes to smash your revolting, dangerous conspiracy and put you, and everyone involved, in jail. I'm going to leave you here with no food and no water while I go and round up your friends. You'd better hope the information you've already given me helps me to find them quickly, or I may not be back in time to save your miserable life.'

I shoved his head forward and turned out the light as I headed up the basement steps. I closed the door at the top, then went out the front door of Jones' house making sure to slam it shut behind me. I didn't want anyone wandering inside and finding him.

The bubble was waiting for me on the driveway and once inside I set the destination as Transium's Mag Station. It seemed as good a place to start looking as anywhere.

Chapter 23
Following

I didn't go far, just out of sight of the house, before I halted the bubble and activated the Spycomm I'd planted on Gernard's neck and the tiny camera I'd put high up on the pipe behind his back. The version of the Spycomm I'd used transmitted in real time, which allowed it to be used as a tracker but made it much more susceptible to detection. I needed to have a live feed of any conversations he might have, there was no use hearing them hours later.

The camera had a night vision mode that showed the scene to be exactly as I had expected. Gernard was wriggling backward and trying to push himself upright onto his feet using the pipe. It was proving difficult and it took him many attempts to get enough traction from his bare feet on the cold tile floor to slide his back up the pole into a standing position. Having his feet fastened together and his wrists fastened to his belt had made it tough for him, but thankfully not too tough. This time I'd fastened each wrist separately to the belt at the front, I didn't want him breaking his arm again while he was trying to escape.

He was puffing and panting and occasionally cursing me and then muttering snatches of prayer.

The belt was very strong. I wondered how long it would take him to work out the best way to free himself. I hoped it wouldn't take too long, he did have a doctorate after all. He thrashed his right arm around trying to break the restraint but soon gave that up as useless. I was glad to see he'd learned his lesson with the left arm and he wasn't doing anything with that one.

Eventually he turned his attention to the waste pipe. He got his feet as far apart as he could, which was only a few centimetres, with his heels either side of the pipe. He leaned against the pipe and then jerked forward with all his strength. The restraint only allowed a tiny movement forward but it should be enough. He did this again and again and gradually I could see the pipe was bending slightly. After about twenty minutes he stopped for a rest. He was sagging forward from the waist with his wrists still fastened to his belt. The pipe now had a distinct kink in it and would probably break fairly soon. He gathered his strength and started synchronizing his repeated forward lunges with a loud yell of rage. After about a dozen more tries the pipe snapped and he hit the ground face first with the restraint hanging loosely from his belt as dirty water trickled from the broken pipe onto the floor.

I wondered, for a moment, if he'd knocked himself out. He had hit the floor with quite a bang. It appeared he was only stunned as he groaned and swore and then rolled over onto his back. I could see something dark on the floor by his head, it was probably blood, he must have broken his nose, again. He was free of the pipe now but still had his feet fastened together at the ankles and his two arms fastened to his belt at the front. He wriggled around so he could get back to his feet by pushing himself up the wall next to the pipe. This took even longer than the first time as the floor was now slippery with dirty water and blood but he eventually got to his feet. He couldn't climb the stairs with his ankles restrained so I saw him looking around for something to use to free himself. There were some tools on the workbench on the other side of the room, but they were out of reach with his hands still fastened to his belt. Eventually he realised the broken metal pipe was his best bet and he started scraping the right-hand restraint rhythmically across the broken edge of the pipe. The restraints were made of a hardened polymer which I was pretty sure would wear away faster than the metal pipe. Gernard just needed to be careful not to accidentally slash his wrist, or I'd have to return promptly to save his life, which would ruin all his excellent hard work escaping.

It took him an hour to cut through the right-hand restraint, but once that was done he was as good as free. Now he could reach Doctor Jones' tools and minutes later he had used a cutting tool to release his left arm and sever the restraint on his ankles.

'Now Doctor Gernard,' I said to myself, 'where are you going to go?'

I saw him climb the stairs and then he vanished from sight. He had no cuff, and therefore no easy way to contact anyone. I'd placed a couple of other cameras around Jones' house. I soon picked him up in the kitchen. He got himself a large drink of water and then raided her cupboards for food. He ate whatever was to hand that didn't need cooking; fruit, bread, a rather fancy looking box of chocolates that was still sealed shut. I hoped it wasn't a special gift from someone.

He then went looking for shoes, he must not have relished walking to Transium in bare feet. Doctor Jones' feet were much smaller and daintier than Gernard's. There was absolutely no way he was going to find any that even came close to fitting so he put multiple pairs of socks on to protect his feet and then headed out the front door. It didn't take him long to get his bearings. He must have been to Doctor Jones' house before or at least known where it was, as he started striding towards Transium.

I was a little disappointed that he hadn't shown enough resourcefulness to work out a way to contact anyone or summon a bubble, as now I would have to follow him on foot. I set the bubble to return to its depot, got out, quickly got into my chameleon suit and settled into a steady pace behind Gernard but far enough back for him to be unable to see me. If we were going all the way to Transium we were in for a lengthy walk as we were about eight kilometres from the centre. For the first hour we stayed on the main path to Transium centre. There were no other people about, it was the middle of the night. The illumination on the path was automatic and came on as you approached and went out again after you'd passed. This meant he was always bathed in light and he could see clearly one lamp forwards and one back. The lamps were about thirty meters apart. The chameleon suit hid me from the street lamp's sensors. If he turned around, he wouldn't see another set of lights coming on behind him. For a man without shoes he set a reasonable pace. As we neared the outskirts of Transium he turned off the main path and started heading along an unfamiliar route. My cuff showed the area ahead to be mostly residential so I guessed he was either going home or meeting someone.

Soon we were on residential streets which annoyingly had permanent low-level lighting so I had to change tack. The suit disguise would be effective enough at a distance to hide my identity from him, but he would, rightly, be suspicious of anyone he saw out at that time of night. I had to content myself with following on a parallel street and just catching glimpses of him as he passed open grassy areas and intersections. He had sped up, which was probably an unconscious response to nearing his destination so I hurried to the next intersection to get ahead of him. I checked the tracker and saw that he had stopped about thirty metres back from my position. I walked to the path he was on and carefully peeked around the corner. He was standing in the middle of the path staring at one particular house then he backed away to stand in the shadows of the garden opposite. The house was a modern two-story building set back from the footpath to allow for a small front garden, just like all the others in this part of town. This one though had just a strip of neat grass with no borders or flowers or trees. The house was plain and unadorned. Absolutely nothing had been done to make it personal or individual and it appeared to be painted a light grey or possibly off-white. It was difficult to be sure with only the dim street lighting to see it by. The house was completely dark, but none of the other houses had any internal lights visible either. I guessed that could just be because their window blinds were very good.

Gernard was hesitating. He took a step towards the house then stopped and looked around, checking if he was being watched. I quickly looked up the address and wasn't surprised to see that it was Gernard's own home. He must have finally reached a conclusion as he suddenly darted across the path to the house. He ran his hands over the wall next to the door, feeling for the hidden access panel. Without his cuff the door wouldn't automatically unlock for him. He found the panel and opened it. I saw him pause to think and then enter some codes on a small keypad which opened the door. He glanced around once more and entered quickly after shutting the panel.

I pulled the earpiece from my cuff, undid the headpiece of the chameleon suit, popped it in and re-fastened the suit. If he contacted anyone, I wanted to be able to hear it. The cuff would automatically record anything he said. I heard him stamp up what sounded like wooden stairs, he wasn't light on his feet. I moved away from his house and back to the parallel street. It occurred to me that he might take a bubble somewhere and if he did, I'd struggle to follow him. I summoned one and while waiting listened to the sounds of a man used to living alone, muttering to himself. I heard the faint sound of something electronic being turned on with old fashioned switches. There were a few beeps then he spoke.

'Blessed be Gaea, source of all righteousness,' he said.

'Blessed are those who serve Gaea and accursed are the ungodly,' said an indistinct voice that sounded angry and concerned in equal measure. 'Where have you been? We've been trying to reach you,

'I don't want to talk like this. Let's meet. The usual place. Thirty minutes,' he said.

'Agreed. I'll see you in thirty minutes,' said the voice.

I heard a switch flick then silence.

Had he used a spare cuff? I didn't hear either dial or ring tones. This was the strangest Infosys call I'd eavesdropped on. Next I heard him take a shower and get dressed before he stamped back down the same stairs, which were now even louder as he must have had shoes on, then a door opened and shut.

My bubble hadn't arrived yet but I didn't want to lose sight of Gernard so I hurried back to the intersection and cautiously peeked over to his house. He was nowhere in sight. The tracker showed he was now one street away. He must have left his house by a back door, crossed his rear garden and was now moving at a brisk pace in the general direction of the central University buildings. I hesitated. I wasn't sure if I could catch him on foot or if I'd need a bubble. The decision was made for me by the ping from my cuff indicating the bubble had arrived. I sprinted back around the corner to it and jumped in. I programmed the destination to be a few hundred metres behind Gernard's current location and hoped he wouldn't radically change course. I made the bubble opaque and sat back as it accelerated away down the footpath. It wouldn't move quickly here in a residential area, even if I wanted it to, but it should be fast enough to catch a man on foot. I monitored Gernard's progress and noticed he'd sped up. He must have either been running or he'd also jumped into a bubble. I kept updating my bubble's destination to be slightly behind Gernard[1]. Soon we were right back in the centre of Transium. I saw the Fortitude Tower and the Astrophysics building dominating the skyline just ahead of me and I was relieved that there were one or two bubbles moving about and the occasional pedestrian. I kept an eye on the tracker as we headed through the quiet city centre and eventually it showed that Gernard had stopped so I had my bubble stop one street away from him, just out of sight, and got out ready to follow him on foot again.

I walked towards Gernard's position making sure I didn't make a sound. The street lighting was very subdued and there was enough shadow to hide an army in. The buildings were all extremely tall with variously sized open spaces consisting of combinations of grass, flowers, trees and water features in between them. The concentric circular footpaths radiating out from the very centre of the city were connected by a variety of smaller paths between the main five evenly

---

[1] As bubbles lack the ability to be manually driven the only option when following someone was to keep amending the destination co-ordinates.

spaced-out spoke-like paths. I cut through a garden that consisted of three almost dormant interconnected fountains and headed in the direction the tracker indicated. I couldn't see anyone but the tracker showed I was now on the same concentric circular path as he was, approximately one hundred metres behind him. I sped up a little and once I was only twenty metres behind I knew I should be able to see him, but I still couldn't. The tracker showed he'd stopped and I continued on as silently as I could until I ought to have been standing right next to him. I couldn't see Gernard anywhere. I glanced around me, wary of a trap, but there was nothing and no-one to be seen. Then I realised where he was, he was underground. He must have been in the maintenance tunnels below the paths. They would virtually guarantee privacy at any time of day. I pulled up the plans for that part of the city and searched for the nearest access point. The plans showed there was one back near where Gernard had slowed down, and presumably got out of a bubble, the next nearest one was about one hundred metres further along the path. For a moment I wondered which one to head for, as I was almost exactly half way between the two, then I heard Gernard speak.

'Blessed be Gaea, source of all righteousness',' he said.

'Shhh', said a voice.

'There's no one here', said Gernard, 'I wasn't followed. Pike's gone looking for you and thinks I'm tied up in Doctor Jones' cellar.'

'Shhh', said the voice again, this time slightly more insistently.

'What's that? What are you doing with it?' asked Gernard, sounding a little afraid.

There was a high-pitched whine, a loud crack, and then silence. The tracker icon on my cuff screen vanished.

I had to choose quickly, forwards or back? According to the plans there were no junctions, or turn-offs anywhere between the two points. I just had to pick one. I headed back to the entrance Gernard must have used. I hoped that whoever it was that he'd met wouldn't want to retrace their steps, so would continue onwards. I had a fifty-fifty chance I was right. I sprinted back the way I'd come as fast as I could, and found somewhere to hide near to the entrance. According to the plans it was hidden in a featureless section of wall right next to the entrance of a prestigious apartment building. I set the cuff to record what I saw and waited. Two minutes passed, then another two. I was itching to run to the other entrance and see if I'd guessed incorrectly but waited a little longer. After another minute a door outline lit up on the section of wall, flashed a few times to alert any passers-by what was about to happen, then opened smoothly outwards. The corridor behind the door had only low-level illumination but it was enough to see the person Gernard had been meeting was the old woman from the park and the restaurant.

She looked around cautiously and then stepped out into the street leaving the door to swing shut behind her. There was no sign of Gernard. Was he waiting until she'd gone before he left, or had he been instructed to continue on to the next exit? I had to ignore him, after all I did know where he lived and worked, so picking him up again shouldn't be too hard. I needed to follow the old woman and find out some more about her.

She set off at a brisk pace toward the city centre. I couldn't let her see me and I couldn't get a Spycomm tracker onto her from this distance so I pulled a microdrone from my pocket and launched it. Then I headed to a different path far to her left and stayed well back. The drone image on my cuff screen was excellent using the night-vision system and I locked onto the image of the old woman so the drone could automatically follow her without any further commands from me. It was easy to follow the microdrone, the cuff tracked it and gave me turn by turn instructions to stay reasonably close but completely out of sight.

From the direction she was taking I guessed she was heading for the Mag station. I sped up to get ahead of her and enter the station by a completely different entrance. The microdrone couldn't possibly keep up with a Mag, its maximum speed was approximately one hundred kilometres per hour, which was just enough to track a bubble but nowhere near Mag speeds. I entered the station and ran down the stairs to the split in the corridor that took you to one platform or the other. The chameleon suit would ensure she couldn't recognise me but neither would it stand scrutiny up close. Once again I had a fifty-fifty guess to make. Would she choose the northbound or southbound platforms? South took you to farmland, the spaceport, then to the ski resorts and finally to the southernmost city on this continent. Further south than that was just the polar wilderness. North seemed more likely as there were some local stops for commuter suburbs then nothing for a few hundred kilometres until Ghisto, the next major city.

My cuff showed her entering the station up at street level. I had to decide. I checked the arrival times for the Mags. There was a northbound one due in one minute and a southbound one due in three. I changed my mind and chose south then headed onto the platform. I had to hope she wasn't the sort of person that would risk missing the northbound Mag by arriving just too late to catch it. The platform was completely deserted so I headed down it as far as I could. The transparent tube that contained the Mag track was on my left, with airtight hatches spaced out evenly one carriage length apart. On my right was a pale tiled wall depicting stylized scenes of Transium, on the other side of which was the northbound platform. The platform was curved to the right, like everything else on Coronnol, but was it long enough to get me out of sight round the curve? I started to run, trying to stay as quiet as I could. I didn't want loud echoing footsteps to give me away. As I neared the end of the platform the view from the microdrone on my cuff showed that the old woman was almost at the bottom of the staircase and a quick glance backwards confirmed I was still easily in view once she moved out into the middle of the platform. Right at the very end I saw a plain metal door set into the wall. It had a sign proclaiming that it was for authorised staff members only. It must be an emergency access through to the northbound side. I pressed myself against the wall and pulled up the hacking menu on the cuff and started it scanning the door codes. This time I started the scan at the cheap end of the range, I couldn't imagine the transit authority springing for an Excelsior or a Stanton-Mayes door for something like this. I watched the screen as on one side codes flew up and the cuff flickered in time with them and on the other side I saw the old woman step out onto the platform. I risked a look to my left and saw her step forwards towards one of the tube hatches. All she had to do was look to her right and she'd see someone pressed up against the wall. I triggered the microdrone's recall and just when I was certain she was about to look my way I heard a quiet click as the door unlocked. I gave it a push and was relieved it opened quietly inwards, so I slid along the wall and stepped backwards through it and allowed it to almost completely shut.

Now I was out of sight I stared at the image on the cuff as she looked around her. She was good. She was definitely checking to see if she was being followed but doing it in a casual, almost carefree, manner. Like someone who was just interested in the station's art work and architecture. The drone was flying backward towards me but keeping focused on her. The Mag was due any second. I would have to wait until she was on board and then make a run for it. I readied another menu on the cuff, this time I would need to access the station's safety systems. If she was as good as she appeared to be, getting onto the same Mag as her was not going to be easy.

I heard the soft chimes from the platform indicating the Mag was approaching and a calm synthetic voice announced its destinations. Through the crack in the door I saw the sleek pods swoop into the station from my right, slowing rapidly to a stop with the pod doors perfectly lined up with the access hatches in the tube. There was a quiet hiss as the doors opened and on my cuff I saw the old woman walk towards the nearest hatch and stand half in, half out of the pod looking around, as if anxiously waiting for someone. No one else was waiting to board the Mag. Only two or three people had disembarked and they'd quickly made their way out to the stairs. There was another chime and a warning announcement to stay clear of the doors. The old woman stepped inside the pod, scanning up and down the platform as the doors all simultaneously started to close. I pulled the chameleon suit's hood off, as anyone in the pod nearest me would notice its artificial face didn't look quite right. I triggered a command on my cuff, which caused the doors of the end pod to reopen briefly, as I burst out of the doorway and ran to the hatch and threw myself through it to land sprawled on the floor, the door snapping shut again behind me. I felt the familiar rush of acceleration and looked up to see a sleepy night worker staring at me in alarm.

'Nearly missed it!' I said getting to my feet and taking a rear-facing seat.

He gave me a puzzled look and then closed his eyes and seemed to go back to sleep.

The microdrone had followed me into the pod so I sent it to the front window to see if I could see the old woman. We were still under the city, so it was difficult to see ahead but once we re-emerged above ground I caught glimpses of a grey head of hair three pods further forward. I hoped it was her.

The next stop was under five minutes away so the Mag wasn't going anywhere near its top speed but we were still moving pretty quickly. I could see the sky in the east out of the right-hand window was just starting to get a little lighter. It would be morning soon and I had no idea who I was following or what had happened to Gernard in the tunnels. The old woman had used some kind of device that had disabled my tracker but I doubted she had been able to detect it, it was probably just a precautionary and routine sweep. Our tech was fantastically hard to find once active unless you knew exactly what to look for. I wondered if Gernard was dead or dying down there. I found it hard to imagine her killing him in such an up close and personal way but as I had no idea of the kind of person I was dealing with I supposed anything was possible. I wouldn't mourn too much for him if that was the case but violence like that was virtually unknown in the vast majority of the galaxy. The myriad inhabited worlds might disagree on all manner of issues but a respect for, and holding sacred of, all life was as near a universal constant as you could find. Gernard's moral compass was clearly broken in this regard, so it was reasonable to assume this was also true of some of the people he was working with. There was a big psychological difference though between leaving someone to die in a disabled spaceship, or even rupturing an airlock seal, and killing someone standing right in front of you.

I felt the slight nudge of deceleration. We were nearing the first stop. I unfastened my seat belt, got up and moved to the door. I pulled the microdrone from my pocket and held it cupped in my hand. The Mag pulled into the station and as soon as the doors hissed open, I released it. It scooted towards the front pod then doubled back and hovered just outside the door. As soon as the doors started to close it flew back to my hand. As we accelerated away I reviewed the footage on my cuff. I got a good look at the old woman three pods ahead. The grey head of hair I'd glimpsed was her and she hadn't got out of the Mag at that station. The next stop wasn't for just over half an hour. I set my cuff to wake me as we approached the station and closed my eyes to nap. It had been a tiring night so far.

The cuff's insistent vibration woke me but stopped as soon as it detected I was awake. The station we were decelerating towards was in the countryside, it was a stop I'd not even noticed when I'd caught the spaceport express a couple of times. It was as near to the middle of nowhere as you were going to find between Transium and the spaceport. The faint dawn light showed nothing but fields and vineyards on one side and a forest on the other side of the Mag track. I readied the microdrone and took up my place by the door again. The drone zipped out as soon as the door opened, just in time for me to see the old woman step out of the Mag and head for the exit. The track was elevated here, so she was already heading down a flight of stairs to ground level when I stepped out of the pod just as the doors closed. I locked the microdrone onto her and waited on the platform as the Mag vanished south towards the spaceport. I pulled the chameleon suit hood up and reactivated its stealth technology. The sensors on the platform immediately lost track of me and to save energy dimmed all the lights to a negligible night-mode. The old woman had stopped at the bottom of the stairs and was looking up towards the platform. She seemed pleased when the lights all went out and turned and strode away from the station up a dirt track that led between two rows of vines. I waited until she was at least a hundred metres ahead before I cautiously followed her down the steps and away from the station. I avoided the track and walked into the vines and followed her from there, I couldn't risk her turning around and seeing me behind her. For all I knew she was the only person who lived out here. There certainly weren't any other people about that I could see. The microdrone was following her at a sensible distance and from quite high up. Its silent engine, size and adaptive paint scheme, the same as the scout ship's, made it as near to invisible as could be.

Up ahead in the distance the microdrone could see a small collection of buildings that looked older than any I'd seen so far on Coronnol. They were all low, in muted colours and appeared to be trying to blend into the countryside, rather than stand out from it. They were, of course, curved or circular like every other building here.

The track was as straight as a ruler and it took about forty minutes to walk from the Mag station to the buildings. The sun was now up properly straight ahead, casting long shadows behind me. This was good for the drone, as it did leave a small shadow and the laws of physics meant it wasn't possible to camouflage that, but it was a long way behind the old woman.

She turned off the track into the courtyard that led to the buildings and entered the longest one with the most windows. This I presumed was the main house for the winery, the other buildings looked more functional. I couldn't approach them without sticking out like a sore thumb, camouflage suit or not, but I couldn't stay in the vineyard either. An operational vineyard would soon have people turning up for the day's work and I didn't want them to find me. I needed to find a way to get close to the buildings without being seen.

I sent the microdrone off on a spiral course centred on the main building, moving further out as it circled. I soon found a way to get close. On the other side of the buildings there was a small wood and a good-sized stream that came down the gentle hill that rose up behind the winery. I could climb up the hill staying in the vines then cut across the track into the wood and come back down using the trees for cover until I was right behind the main house. I would be within ten metres of the windows by then and could hopefully stay there undetected as long as I needed.

I picked some grapes as I made my way up the hill as I hadn't had any breakfast yet. They were incredibly firm and juicy and had a sweet but tangy taste. I wondered which wine they would end up in. Grapes were good, but wine was definitely better. I could hear some activity starting up near the buildings. Someone was calling to an open vehicle that had come up from the Mag station with four or five people riding on it. I sent the microdrone to have a look. The vehicle looked homemade. It had a motor in a single spherical front wheel and four large circular wheels right at the back, two on each side. Above that were two benches running front to back facing each other across a narrow aisle. There was a single seat at the front just behind the wheel for a human driver. I guessed someone had put it together because they were sick of walking the few kilometres from the Mag station day after day. The driver hopped down, followed by the passengers and all but one vanished into the various buildings. The remaining person crossed the track and walked into the vines and appeared to be inspecting random plants closely as they moved systematically up and down the rows.

I hurried up the hill until I got to the top and was out of sight of the buildings then quickly darted across the track into the wood. It didn't take me long to work my way back down through the trees until I was right behind the main building. There was a low stone wall separating the edge of the wood from the collection of buildings but I stayed hidden in the trees with the chameleon suit doing its best to blend me into the natural colours and shapes there.

I flew the microdrone down to one of the windows so it came into contact with the glass. It was able to pick up the vibrations in the glass caused by conversations inside and translate that back into speech for me to hear. It would be tinny and low quality but it should be audible. I popped the earpiece out of my cuff and slipped it inside the chameleon suit hood and into my ear. I couldn't hear anything so I moved the microdrone to the next window, waited a minute or two and then moved to the next and then the next until finally I heard voices.

'…tonight, as soon as it's dark. There's no point staying here any longer.'

'I can't wait to get home. I feel dirty just being around these godless heathens.'

'Get some rest. I need to call Doctor Grippe and arrange to meet him before we go. He's coming with us.'

'What about Bertrand?'

'He's packing now. He'll meet us at Grippe's house later. He did well to escape but we don't know who Pike works for or how much they know, but once we leave Coronnol it won't really matter. They won't see us again.'

One person left the room and the other stayed quiet until I heard what sounded like snoring.

The tinny audio meant I couldn't tell which speaker had been the old woman I'd followed, if either. I moved the microdrone around the various windows but couldn't find the room the person who'd said they were calling Grippe was in. I wasn't surprised Grippe was involved as he was Gernard's immediate superior. I hadn't liked him much, and neither did Gernard it seemed as he'd labelled him as ungodly.

I had to find out how they planned to leave Coronnol. It seemed unlikely they would be going to the spaceport and catching a commercial star ship. The rescue ship I'd seen near Omega wouldn't be able to legally land anywhere as it had no transponder. I moved away from the buildings, deeper into the woods so I could make a call without being disturbed.

I stared at the blank screen on my cuff listening to the quiet sound of the ring tone. It rang three or four times before I saw Randolf's face appear, looking surprised.

'Per Pike, I didn't think we could communicate with you, or with anyone,' he said.

'You can't normally. While you're hiding in orbit the ship blocks your cuffs from making or receiving calls, but I've called the ship directly on a secure connection. I need your help.'

I explained that I needed him to scan for the rescue ship we'd seen at Omega, as it was possibly in orbit somewhere. I spent a few minutes teaching him how to operate the scanning equipment, unsurprisingly he picked it up quite quickly. I could do the scan remotely but it would be more efficient to have him do it, while I conducted a search down here.

He seemed excited at the prospect of being able to help.

'Is Doctor Jones alright?' I asked.

'Yes. She's busy working. She's adding in extra safeguards and security so what Gernard did couldn't happen again with the next prototype.'

'I'll call you back in about an hour or so,' I said. 'That should give you enough time.'

'That's fine Cemeron,' he said, 'speak to you soon.'

I dropped the call and made my way quietly back to the wall.

The microdrone was still tracking around the various windows cautiously listening for conversations. It hadn't detected anything significant.

I was really quite hungry by that point. I hadn't had a proper meal since the previous evening and I'd been awake all night following Gernard.

I had a couple of small bars of emergency rations in a pocket of the chameleon suit and decided now was as good a time as any to eat them. They weren't gourmet food by any means but they tasted sweet and sticky and I could feel a surge of energy infusing me as I ate.

I made my way to the stream for a drink of water and by the time I got back I felt ready to tackle a search.

Chapter 24
Hidden

The easiest way to search the buildings was using the microdrone but that meant there needed to be a door or window open and no-one about. Out in the open air the microdrone could follow someone easily without being detected as it could fly high enough above them to be out of their eye line, inside a building it was a different matter. It was only about one cubic centimetre in size but the human eye would spot it moving about. It was too big to pass for a fly and too small for a bird. If someone entered the room it would have to freeze and wait for them to leave the room or until they had their back to it.

The buildings made up three sides of the courtyard with the path to the dirt track being the fourth. The longest one with all the windows was facing the opening in the wall to the track. It was curved in two dimensions. It curved so the centre of the building was furthest away from the track, but the centre was also the highest point. At the edges it was barely a single-story building but the centre either had an upstairs or there was a very tall room in the middle. The building on the left side of the courtyard was an oval from above. It was just a single story with a doorway at the front that had large circular windows either side of it. Round the back were two sets of rectangular windows that came right down to the ground. All the windows were opaque from the outside, I presumed they were transparent from the inside. The final building was a very large circle from above. It looked more industrial than residential. It had a grooved conical metal roof. The building itself was slightly shorter than the others but the shallow conical roof made it the tallest one at the peak. It had a small door on the front facing the oval building and no windows. There must have been another door somewhere, it was illegal on most planets to build a structure with only the one entrance. I sent the drone to the oval building but the doors and windows were all sealed shut. The same was true of the main house. I then checked the circular building to see if I could find another door or entrance. On the rear of the building, the microdrone's camera showed what looked like a hidden door. It was just a faint outline in the paint but it looked promising. The problem was the woods petered out before reaching that far round the courtyard. There was a stone wall all the way round the perimeter of the buildings, that would have to do as far as cover went. I tracked along it and got level with the rear of the circular building. I hadn't seen anyone enter or leave it. The people riding the makeshift transport had gone into the oval building or the main house. I couldn't wait until night; I was going to have to chance it and hope no one noticed my approach. Once I was up against the wall I should be out of sight of any of the other buildings. That left just the vineyard on the opposite side of the track to worry about. I sent the microdrone to check on the worker that had been tending the vines and was pleased to discover they were about two kilometres away, tinkering with something that looked like irrigation equipment to my inexperienced eye. Once the microdrone was back I climbed the low wall and dropped onto the grass on the other side and lay down flat. The chameleon suit was trying its hardest to look exactly like the grass I was lying on so I stayed flat and crawled slowly forwards until I was at the back of the building. I pulled a scanner from my pocket, tapped it on my cuff and reached up as high as I could lying down. It immediately detected the hidden door. There weren't any controls or even a handle on the outside so it must be an emergency exit only, not meant to ever be opened from the outside. I couldn't find any alarms or sensors in the door, just a basic electrical lock. It was a simple matter to fool the door's circuits into unlocking the door, I used the scanner to emit a pulse that triggered the mechanism. There was a faint click as the door unlocked and it opened the tiniest fraction of a centimetre. It was enough to get my fingernails in, if I didn't have gloves on. I wriggled my hands out of the chameleon suit gloves and dug my fingernails into the edge of the door and pulled. The door resisted. Perhaps it hadn't been opened for years. I braced myself with one foot planted on the wall of the building, squeezed my fingers into the gap and heaved. The door gradually opened just enough for me to slip inside.

It was pitch black other than the thin column of light coming in through the door and I sensed a much larger than expected space. I put the chameleon suit gloves back on and pulled the door shut and was plunged into total darkness. I pulled up a small white screen on my cuff and turned the brightness all the way up as a makeshift torch. I was standing on a ledge about a metre wide with a thin metal railing ahead of me. The ledge disappeared off into the darkness on both sides. I looked over the railing and shone the light down. There seemed to be a very long drop. This building was simply a lid over an enormous underground bunker. I made the screen bigger and then bigger again to increase the light. Standing in the gigantic circular hole in the ground was a ship. It was pointing straight at the roof, standing on its tail. Anyone in the cockpit or flight deck would be lying flat on their back looking up. That wasn't the strangest thing about it though. The strangest thing was that it was identical to the one from the Omega star that had come to rescue Gernard, in fact I was almost certain it was the same ship.

I worked my way around the ledge to the opposite side of the ship and found, near the main door, a spiral staircase running down into the depths of the bunker. I made my way down it. The glow from my cuff's screen was enough to see this ship had done some distances, the surface was covered in micro scratches and the occasional dent. You didn't get that patina of wear on a brand-new ship. The staircase passed a standard looking access hatch, which was sideways due to the ship's peculiar orientation. It was quite a job of piloting to land the ship on its tail inside a building. I tried to open the hatch but it was sealed shut. I pulled up the hacking menu on the cuff and started a scan to find door codes that would open it. I turned the brightness on the cuff screen right down. If anyone came in through the door above, I wouldn't want them to spot the light glowing below their feet. The minutes ticked away and the cuff flickered as codes flashed up the screen. After almost half an hour the cuff had exhausted all the standard airlock manufacturer's codes and backdoor access features. This door was a custom made one. The hacking system now started working on directly cracking the algorithm locking the door, which might take some time if the people that designed it were particularly security conscious and competent. Another half hour passed without a result. I strained to hear anyone coming in, as I didn't want to get taken by surprise.

Forty more minutes passed and I was getting anxious and wondering if I should quit and leave, before I ended up being discovered, when suddenly there was a fairly loud clunk sound from the airlock and the hatch slid back into the body of the ship. I waited and no-one came running either through the entrance above or out of the ship. The gap between the staircase and the ship was about two meters, I looked around and found there was a lever on the staircase that when pulled opened a gap in the handrail and lowered a short flat walkway across to the airlock. I cautiously stepped onto it, as there were no handrails, and took the couple of steps to the now open airlock. I had to crouch down to get into the airlock as it was sideways but as soon as I got inside I felt dizzy and crashed heavily onto my left side, my orientation had switched ninety degrees. The artificial gravity of the ship was still on. It was keeping the interior of the ship oriented the way it would normally be when parked on its undercarriage rather than as it was now, on its tail. I got to my feet and looked back and saw the walkway was now sideways and the spiral staircase ran right to left instead of up and down. It looked completely crazy but it would make searching the ship a lot easier. I closed the outer airlock door and opened the inner one. The ship was in darkness and as far as I could tell there didn't appear to be anyone on board. I made my way left towards the front, or top, of the ship. The ship's control room definitely deserved the title flight deck. It was considerably larger than my scout ship's. There was a central captain's chair, in front of that on the left and on the right were two chairs and two sets of controls. There were two further stations slightly behind the captain's position, again, one on the left and one on the right. Those stations appeared to be communications and navigation. I looked at the two front stations and the left hand one seemed to be for the pilot but the other had controls that weren't familiar to me. I guessed it could be weapons and combat systems but as everything was powered down it was hard to be sure. I had no desire to power anything up as that would certainly draw attention. I was painfully conscious I had been inside the building for far too long for safety. I hurried aft and checked the other rooms. Most seemed to be living quarters and none were locked. The ship was functional and lean. It wasn't a pleasure craft, that was for sure. There was nothing personal displayed and nothing purely decorative. I needed to find something, anything, that gave me a clue as to its planet of origin. A ship like this shouldn't exist. Building a ship without a standard transponder meant it couldn't be licenced, insured or registered anywhere, but from what I'd seen it was no amateur effort. A good quality ship yard must have built it. I gave myself fifteen minutes to do a quick search. The lower deck had crew quarters to the front then a galley kitchen with the engine room at the rear, just like most ships but the rooms were smaller than I expected. Given the size of the ship there should have been more room on the main deck. Upstairs there were the captain's quarters, a small private dining room, what looked like a workshop cum laboratory and an armoury as well as several storage cupboards. The captain's quarters looked lived in. There was a small desk to work at with a fully adjustable comfy chair fastened to the deck. The bed hadn't been made and there were personal items in the small en-suite bathroom. I headed for the desk and sat in the chair. The desk had two small draws on either side. I opened them up one at a time. There was a handset in one that had a microphone and speaker on the front and some fiddly controls, it wasn't like any communication equipment I'd ever seen. There were some tiny tools for doing fine electronics work in another, nothing at all in the third but the fourth had a projector cube[1] in it. I picked it up, put it on the desk in front of me and activated it. The top square of the cube glowed white and then a perfect three-dimensional image faded into view above it. There was no flicker or transparency, there was just what looked like a window into a completely different part of the galaxy about two meters square in front of my eyes. There was a faint white edge around it, to help your eyes work out where the real world and the projection intersected. The image was of countryside on a summer day. There were hills in the distance covered in trees and nothing between the camera and them but rolling green pasture. On the left was a lake with some water birds paddling about on it. Right in the centre of the foreground were a family having a picnic on the ground. There were two adults and two children. The adults had their backs to me and the children were rummaging through a shiny metal picnic hamper. The sound was off and I couldn't find the controls on the cube to turn it on, or perhaps it was recorded without sound. The camera must have been mounted on a drone as the viewpoint started to move, rotating the image and bringing the adults into view. I could now see the adults were a man and a woman. The man was serious looking, with pale skin and blond hair. He had piercing blue eyes. He said something silently to the children and they laughed as they ate the food they'd retrieved from the hamper. He smiled briefly and turned to look at the woman next to him. She had a shock of medium length dark hair, which looked wild and unkempt with the beginnings of a

---

[1] A projector cube is the equivalent of a photograph album. It can be linked to Infosys but also has its own internal memory and power so it can be used anywhere. They're not as popular as they once were as cuff screens are now so good. They do still have the advantage over the cuff screen that they can project in three dimensions.

few streaks of grey at the temples. She had a similar pale complexion to the man but brown eyes. She looked familiar but I couldn't place her. She was wearing a one-piece jumpsuit in pale blue with darker blue piping that looked like a uniform of some sort. She was drinking from a flask and staring at the man. The scene continued to revolve until the children now had their backs to the camera. The woman put the flask down and turned to look at the camera and I suddenly recognized the old woman's face. It must have been her, but from decades ago.

I nudged the controls on the projector cube and a few other video clips appeared and all were of the two children either together or individually. The man didn't reappear in any of them and nor did the woman herself.

The old woman must be the captain of this ship. I replayed all the clips and recorded them on my cuff. I was no nearer finding out her identity but at least I had a good quality image of her even if it was from years ago.

I had overstayed my self-imposed fifteen minutes by some margin and decided I really needed to leave. I returned the cube to the desk drawer and ensured everything was in the exact position I'd found it.

I made my way back to the airlock using my cuff as a torch until I was inside then I turned the light off. I didn't know if anyone was in the underground hanger now so would have to be very quiet. I closed the inner airlock door and then opened the outer one.

The short walkway back to the spiral staircase was still there and I couldn't hear anyone moving about. Now the problem was how to get from the airlock back onto the walkway with a ninety-degree shift in gravitational direction. The walkway was sideways half way up the left-hand edge of the airlock from my current perspective. I couldn't just step onto it. I turned to the airlock controls to see if there was a local gravity generator that would allow me to change the orientation just inside the airlock. Frustratingly I couldn't operate anything other than the doors without powering up the ship properly and I didn't dare do that in case it alerted someone.

There was only one thing for it. I would have to jump. The top edge of the sideways platform was a little below my shoulder hight when standing up in the doorway, and I hoped I could jump outwards and upwards enough to land on it.

There was no room for a run up, I had one step and then a jump. I crouched and prepared for the most explosive jump I could manage. I sprang forwards and leapt, throwing my arms out to grab the top edge of the sideways ledge. As I left the airlock I felt the gravity shift in a most stomach churning way. The edge of the walkway now wasn't ahead of me, it was below me. I crashed into it face first, my hands scrabbling for grip on either side of it. My left hand overshot, I'd thrown myself with far too much force and my momentum was carrying me over the edge. I slid sideways off the thin metal and at the last second my right hand finally got a grip on the mesh of the walkway. I ended up dangling over a very high, very dark drop by one hand with my fingers hooked into the holes in the metal. My arm was aching from holding my whole body-weight, I needed to act fast before I lost my grip. I kicked my legs from side to side to swing my body so I could get my left hand up to the walkway too. Then at least I'd be hanging by both arms. I didn't try to pull myself up, I doubted I could manage that with such a narrow platform to get up onto. I moved my left hand a few centimetres along the walkway towards the spiral staircase, then my right. I repeated this a few times until I was able to hook my left leg over the handrail, then my right leg before I dropped onto the staircase. A spent a few minutes doing some vigorous rubbing and stretching to get the feeling back into my fingers and right arm. Once I felt some sensation had returned I climbed up one complete turn of the spiral, crossed the walkway to shut the airlock and then pulled the lever that retracted the walkway and closed the gap in the handrail. I went up the rest of the stairs as fast as I could while remaining reasonably quiet. At the top I made my way round to the door at the rear and cautiously pushed it open a little. I listened but couldn't hear anything. I sent the microdrone out first to ensure there was no one around. It looked like the coast was clear so I followed the drone, pushing the door shut tight behind me, lay down in the grass and crawled slowly to the wall. I waited a moment before I jumped over it and lay panting on the other side.

After a few minutes resting to get my heart rate back to something approaching normal I realised I was going to have to go back inside to the ship before it went dark. I was going to have to plant a hyperspace tracker somewhere on it.

Chapter 25
Rendezvous

I didn't have a tracker with me but there were plenty in the scout ship. It was just a shame the scout ship was in polar orbit. I headed back into the woods so I could call Doctor Jones and Per Randolf.

'Hello, Cemeron,' said Randolf, 'I haven't found the ship yet. I did a complete pass and didn't see anything so I've started again, just in case.'

'It's not in orbit. I've found the ship down here. It's hidden in an underground hanger at the winery,' I replied. 'Sorry I couldn't call earlier but I didn't dare risk it.'

He looked mildly disappointed.

'But thanks for looking and being so thorough,' I said.

I gave them the quick version of what I'd found out. Doctor Jones seemed extremely surprised when I told her that Doctor Grippe was leaving with Gernard and the other, as yet, unidentified conspirators.

'You're sure they said Grippe?' she asked.

'Absolutely. No doubt about it at all. They even called him Doctor Grippe, not just Grippe or Julius.'

'It's just that he and Gernard don't get along, in fact they seem to detest each other. Mind you Grippe doesn't get along with anyone on staff particularly well, he's much more interested in his students. I know I can't bear to be with him more than is absolutely necessary.'

When I'd talked with Randolf, in the core of the Transium laboratory he'd revealed that Grippe and Jones had been working on the secret project together, despite Jones stating they rarely spoke and their work had very little overlap. Jones herself had then confirmed their working relationship after I rescued them from Omega. There had to be a reason why she'd lied about her connection to Grippe, but was it the same reason she now claimed to dislike him so much?

'Unfortunately, I need some equipment from the ship,' I said.

'Why is that unfortunate?' asked Randolf.

'Let me ask you a question first. Have you eaten lunch yet?'

'No,' said Jones, 'why?'

'Because I can't land the ship at the spaceport as there's currently a drone impersonating the ship's transponder flying about down here, and I can't wait until night fall as these people may leave before then. This means you'll have to do what's called a fast-drop landing, which you really don't want to do too soon after a meal. It's unpleasant enough at the best of times.'

I described the landing procedure to them and told them I'd find a place nearby that would be suitable then hung up over Randolf's protests and Jones' questions.

I kept walking away from the buildings through the woods. I needed to get over the crest of the hill and a few kilometres away before I brought the scout ship down. I couldn't let anyone see it arrive.

After about forty-five minutes I was walking down the other side of the hill. The wood had thinned out and I'd seen no further signs of human habitation. I sent the microdrone off on a wide circuit around the area and confirmed that there were no buildings or people within sight.

I called the ship.

'I'm not happy about this,' said Randolf. 'It sounds dangerous. There has to be another way to get you this equipment.'

'There isn't,' I replied. 'It's not the sort of item you can easily make and they're not available to purchase anywhere. It's perfectly safe. It's just a high g-force landing. I've done it several times and while it's not my favourite way to land it'll be okay, honestly.'

He sighed and agreed. I could see Jones in the pilot's seat looking strangely excited.

'You can strap yourself into the bunk if you're worried. They're designed to cushion the body evenly and are the safest place to be, or you can strap into the seats there. But I need to manoeuvre the ship shortly to prepare for the drop so it's decision time.'

Randolf, looking very pale, headed out of shot and Jones confirmed he had gone to lie on the bunk. She pulled the seat belt across her lap and strapped into the pilot's seat. I accessed the ship's flight systems on my cuff and started it into a descent from orbit. It took about twenty minutes to get the ship to four thousand metres altitude then I paused. I programmed the fast-drop to put the ship down a hundred metres from where I was waiting. Theoretically I could drop it right next to me, but I've always been a bit too cautious to try that.

'Are you ready?' I asked.

I heard Jones call through to Randolf then she confirmed they were both ready.

'This should take approximately thirty seconds,' I said. 'Dropping in three, two, one…drop'.

I looked up to where I knew the ship must be. The stealth technology was so good I couldn't spot it at first. Then I caught sight of a slight ripple in the air plunging downwards, but unless you knew what it was you'd never work it out.

I heard a scream from my cuff and looked to see Doctor Jones beaming a huge smile and screaming with excitement.

There was an unnatural and powerful gust of wind and all the vegetation swayed back as loose leaves and other small items swirled up into the air. I was forced to close my eyes and turn away as dust and debris flew past me. When I looked back I saw the trees in the distance shimmer and look a little distorted for a moment then they settled down. I could just make out the outline of the ship as the imaging system in the hull recalibrated itself. The engines had been silent of course. No moving parts meant no noise, but the wind caused by the falling ship had been more intense than I imagined. I sprinted across the clearing, opened the hatch on the ship and rushed inside.

'Are you okay?' I asked Jones as I stripped off the chameleon suit.

She was panting and laughing, so I thought I could guess the answer.

'What a rush!' she said. 'That was incredible. I've always loved amusement park rides and I did some extreme sports in my youth, but that was a hundred percent pure adrenaline rush. Wow.'

I headed aft to check on Randolf. He was not laughing. He had unstrapped himself from the bed and was making use of a sick bag.

'I never, ever, ever, want to do anything like that again. Ever,' he said.

He looked awful. Shaken and sweaty. I got him a drink of water and told him to go outside, lie flat on the grass and breath slowly and deeply for a while.

I headed back to the workshop to get the equipment I needed. Jones joined me.

'What's the plan now?' she said.

'I go back to the winery and plant two trackers on that unregistered ship and then follow them wherever they go.'

'And us?' she asked.

'I will have to ask you to remain in your homes. I'll arrange with CI Andrews for local trustworthy police officers to be assigned to protect you.'

I saw the determined look reappear on her face.

'No. I'm coming with you. Randolf can go home, if he wants to. He'll be safe in a city centre apartment, especially with police protection. But if these people are all leaving taking Gernard and Grippe along with them then I think the danger to us here is vastly reduced if not eliminated altogether.'

'I can't take you. It's against the rules and I simply cannot guarantee your safety,' I said.

'You need my help. If these people are weaponizing my wormhole probes then other than Grippe and Gernard I am the only person with a full grasp of the technology. Which makes me indispensable to you. You don't understand it, your precious head-office don't and Randolf only understands the theoretical equations. I'll sign whatever waiver you want but I am coming with you.'

'I'll think about it,' I said but I didn't think I was going to be able to talk her out of it plus she did have a point about being useful.

I found the two smallest hyperspace trackers I had and fitted them into adhesive cases. I was going to fasten them to the outside of the ship. I didn't dare put them inside in case they found them.

'Before I head back and attach these to their ship I think we should have some lunch. I don't know about you but I'm starving.'

Jones agreed and we called Randolf and asked him to join us. He declined saying he felt far too sick to eat and wasn't sure he'd ever want to eat again. He stayed outside lying on the grass. I rummaged through the store of meals until I found something relatively interesting to eat and popped the two meals in the cooker.

I made tea for myself and coffee for Jones. I'd missed my breakfast tea and felt the need to catch up.

After we'd eaten, I got ready to head back towards the winery with the trackers.

'I think you'll be safe here in the ship until I get back,' I said to them both. 'But I'll pre-program the controls to return you to orbit with a single button push should it become necessary. The ship's stealth tech is good but not perfect. Someone passing nearby would be able to spot it if they were paying attention.'

'How long do you think you'll be?' asked Randolf.

'I'm hoping no more than a couple of hours. I'm planning on just planting the trackers and heading straight back. But what you plan to do and what actually happens can be two very different things.'

I put the chameleon suit back on and headed back through the woods to the winery. I made good time and got there in just over forty minutes. I hadn't seen a soul on the way back apart from a couple of people working in the vineyards a few kilometres from the buildings. Once I was back crouching behind the wall near the circular hanger I sent the microdrone to do a quick reconnaissance flight, but no-one appeared to be out and about. I slid over the wall and crawled to the door. I unlocked it again and this time it opened reasonably easily. I went inside and closed the door quietly behind me. The darkness didn't seem quite as complete as before so I froze and listened. There were voices coming from below.

'Sandora, I don't think that's possible,' said a male voice.

'Make it possible,' replied a woman. 'Get them to work around the clock if needed. We don't have as much time as I thought. The test was a success but with Jones and Randolf being rescued by Pike, and no doubt telling all, we need to act sooner rather than later.'

'It will still take a few hours to get everything packed on board but we should be able to leave soon after dark.'

'You stay on the ship Milton and supervise the loading. I'll tell the others to help. There's no need to keep up the pretence of running this place. We won't be coming back, thank Gaea.'

I heard an airlock open and close then footsteps on metal. I moved around the outer ledge so I could see the top of the spiral staircase and then lay down flat on the ground and hoped the relative darkness plus the chameleon suit would be enough to hide me from prying eyes.

The old woman stepped out of the spiral staircase and headed straight for the main exit without a single glance behind her. Now I knew her first name at least. I'd have to find out the rest of Sandora's name before I could research her, but it was progress even if quite slight.

I wondered what they were doing that required round-the-clock work. Clearly something other than loading the ship. I waited a full five minutes after I heard the front door close before I headed down the staircase. In the dim light I could see the shutters were over the flight deck windows so there was no need to worry about being spotted from within the ship. I took the stairs as fast as I dared and once near the bottom I pulled the two adhesive packages from the small knapsack built into the chameleon suit. I needed to attach them somewhere they wouldn't be noticed even if the pilot did a manual walk-around before take-off, which some still did, or when the ship was sitting in the more usual horizontal landing configuration. The ship was angular and didn't appear to have any wings, retractable or otherwise. It just had some small stabilising fins to help it manage atmospheric flight during take-off and landing. I pulled out the microdrone and attached the first tracker to it. The microdrone was a fraction of the size of the tracker, but it should be able to manage the weight for short distances. I flew the drone around to what would be the top side of the ship near the front. There was a sensor array sticking up from the hull in a dome shape that would hopefully provide cover for one of the trackers. I had the drone press it firmly down onto the bare metal beside it then flew it back to get the second tracker. This time I looked for the umbilical hatch that would be used to attach fresh and waste water pipes while the ship was docked. This usually had a somewhat irregular shape so should provide cover for the second tracker. I found it right near the back, or bottom, of the ship. The pipes were already disconnected so I planted the tracker near it. Hopefully it would look enough like a standard component to not arouse suspicion. The adhesive on the trackers would permanently bond to the metal surface within ten minutes. The only way to remove them then would be to destroy them.

I headed back up the staircase and as I stepped out at the top, I heard the front door open and people's voices. I sprinted quietly round the ledge until I was about half way to the rear door and lay back down. I heard what sounded like four or five people head down the stairs to the airlock. I peered over the edge to watch how they negotiated their way through the perpendicular gravity fields. The first person walked across the narrow bridge to the airlock and stepped in normally, ducking down to avoid the low roof. He then manipulated the airlock's wall controls and gradually slid down to the corner and stood up, sideways from my point of view, on what had been the wall. He opened the inner airlock door and went inside. After a minute the next person did the same and then the next. The ship must have a local gravity generator in the airlock itself, this allowed them to gradually replace the local gravity with the generated one inside the ship, and visa-versa. Once someone entered the inner airlock door the field inside the airlock was deactivated allowing the next person in. I hadn't seen Sandora. I crept round to the rear door and pushed it open as quietly as I could, slipped through and closed it behind me. I stood still and sent the microdrone for a quick look around. I had the horrible feeling I was being watched again. As the microdrone tracked around the circular building I saw the old woman, Sandora, coming out of the oval building opposite, she was heading my way.

I ran the short distance to the wall, threw myself headlong over it and pressed up against it. I watched on my cuff as she passed the entrance to the circular building and came round the back. I kept the microdrone quite high up out of her eyeline and pulled a stunner from my pocket. I didn't want to reveal myself to her but if she found me, I needed to be able to defend myself. She arrived at the back door and stared at it for a while then looked around carefully and slowly. I wondered if the grass was long enough or wet enough to have left noticeable footprints. I didn't think so but couldn't be sure. She moved towards the wall slowly, staring hard into the woods beyond as if possessed of x-ray vision. When she was a matter of half a meter from the wall I raised my arm very slightly and pointed the stunner at the exact spot her head would appear if she took one more step. She stood still for a couple of minutes then turned abruptly and retraced her steps into the circular building.

I heard the door slam and then a minute later came a loud grinding sound, like metal scraping on metal. I turned the microdrone and saw a gap appear in the grooved metal roof, right at the point on the top. The cone was splitting. The grooves were the edges of hundreds of long thin triangular metal sheets all leaning inwards from the rim of the circular building and interlocking to form a point in the centre. All the sheets were disconnecting from one another as they rose up to stand vertically, like points on a crown. Then they slid down into the circular wall until just the tip of each sheet was visible. That answered the question of how the ship left the building, that I'd been pondering. I stood up, recalled the microdrone and headed off through the woods back to my own ship as quickly as I could

.

Chapter 26
Protective Custody

As I walked, I recalled the drone that was zipping about pretending to be my ship, it would take a bit of time to arrive but I had until dark before I needed to be able to follow Sandora and her associates. Jones and Randolf were relieved to see me when I called. I let them know it was me approaching the ship so they wouldn't hit the button that would return it to orbit.

Once aboard I stripped off the chameleon suit again and returned it to its locker in the workshop. I called Kastagyr and updated them on what had happened and gave them the tracker details as well as the recordings from the projector cube.

'I'll start a search using that name and the images you captured of this woman,' said Kas. 'Perhaps we'll have success this time.'

'Thanks Kas,' I said. 'Keep in touch.'

I told Jones and Randolf I was going to get some sleep as I was exhausted having been up all night. I had at least three hours until the sun started to set and I planned to be asleep for a lot of it. I didn't bother changing or getting under the covers. I just lay down and closed my eyes. I had been on the bed no more than thirty seconds before I was fast asleep.

I woke up two hours later feeling a little better. I showered, changed and made three hot drinks, tea for me and coffee for Jones and Randolf before heading forward to the cockpit. Randolf was napping in the co-pilot's chair and Jones had her SSP sitting on the console and was working away on her cuff in the pilot's chair.

'Are you feeling better now?' asked Jones, turning to greet me with a smile.

'Yes, thanks,' I said. I handed her the mug of coffee then sat down in the spare seat.

Randolf woke up and seemed rather embarrassed that he'd been asleep but took his coffee gratefully.

'Thank you. I'm sorry I nodded off there. I must be more tired than I thought.'

I checked that the transponder drone had returned safe and sound and was back in the launch bay.

'We have a few hours before it's dark enough for a clandestine launch to orbit,' I said. 'I suggest we use the time to take you back to Transium, Per Randolf. I'll arrange with CI Andrews for some police protection at your apartment.'

He seemed relieved and didn't try to argue with me. We all swapped chairs so I could get into the pilot's position and we took off. I headed away from the winery and waited until I'd got an additional five kilometres away before switching the stealth systems off.

'You can land on the top of the Astrophysics tower in the centre of Transium,' said Jones. We have a landing pad on the roof. It's not used very often but being the head of department, I do have the right to use it.'

I programmed the destination into the nav system then sent a message to CI Andrews requesting he meet us at the landing pad with at least two officers he was certain he could trust.

Before long we could see Transium below us and the sea to the left. The sun was heading rapidly towards the horizon and it looked like there would be another beautiful sunset. The nav system pinged to indicate landing was imminent, and the ship banked left, slowed and then descended smoothly onto the roof. There wasn't even a bump as we touched down. I closed the window shutters and we headed for the airlock.

'I'll go first,' I said, 'just in case,'

I opened the airlock and checked around. There was no-one in sight and the only sound was the wind, which is pretty normal on the top of a hundred and twenty story building. I looked up and to my right and saw the transparent floor, walls and domed roof of the Forts restaurant at the top of the hotel next door. The lights inside looked warm and inviting but there was no time to eat somewhere like that tonight.

I made my way to the doorway into the tower and it opened as I approached. CI Andrews was there along with Examiner Pascal and another officer I didn't recognise who was introduced as Examiner Steel. Pascal nodded a greeting and I smiled back.

I waved to Jones and Randolf so they left the ship and hurried over to join us.

'I've got my vehicle waiting at the entrance and a bubble for Pascal and Steel,' said Andrews. 'We're not taking any chances. They're both armed with stunners, as am I.'

I patted my pocket to indicate that I also was armed.

'Let's go', said Andrews.

He hurried us to the lift which he said he'd kept waiting using a police override code.

'The lift won't stop now until we reach the street,' he said entering another code on the control pad.

The lift dropped quickly, so quickly it almost felt like free-fall. I saw Randolf's face drain of blood. He clearly did not cope well with rapid motion.

A sudden push of deceleration indicated we'd arrived on the ground floor and the door opened. Pascal went out first, stunner in hand, and once he was sure the coast was clear we followed Andrews to the ground car I'd been in before.

Andrews and I got into the front while Jones and Randolf took the back. The two officers jumped into the bubble that was sitting in front of Andrews' vehicle. It rolled off and Andrews' car eased out to follow it. As soon as we were moving, he seemed to relax a little.

'I've got another officer stationed in your apartment, in plain clothes. Her cover is that she's your girlfriend and she's visiting for a while,' said Andrews turning round in his seat to talk to Randolf. 'Pascal and Steel will take turns being in the apartment opposite yours, we've arranged for the resident to go on holiday for a couple of weeks.'

'Excellent,' I said.

'We've got microscopic cameras set up on all the entrances to your building and in all the rooms in your apartment apart from the bathroom. You'll be quite safe.'

Randolf looked relieved and anxious.

'What's the matter?' I asked him.

'I only have a one-bedroom apartment,' he said trailing off almost to silence at the end.

'That's fine,' said Andrews. 'Senior Examiner Scott is very happy for you to sleep on the couch, no-one is suggesting you have to actually sleep together.'

He winked at me and I suppressed a chuckle.

Randolf went crimson and Jones rolled her eyes at me.

'This is my building,' said Randolf, pointing to a low-rise block set in a stunning landscaped garden comprising terraces, lawns and flower beds in a complex interlocking pattern.

His block was curved, unsurprisingly, and approximately a quarter of the circumference of a circle, with the three other nearby blocks making up the other quarters. The garden the blocks were in was circular when seen from above, with a footpath on the outside edge and other paths at the four main compass points cutting through the centre. There was a small bubble park at the southern edge of the garden and our little convoy pulled up there. Pascal and Steel got out and looked around before Andrews indicated we should follow them.

We hustled quickly through the garden to the entrance in the nearest block and went up the stairs to the second floor. We walked down the curved corridor to apartment 202. Andrews knocked on the door and it was opened by a beautiful red-haired woman of about thirty years old.

Jones, Randolf, and I went inside with Andrews while Pascal and Steel opened the door to 201 which was opposite. Andrews made the introductions.

'Per Randolf, this is Senior Examiner Scott. She'll be with you for as long as is necessary. Do not leave the apartment for any reason unless you've cleared it with her or with me. If we do decide it is safe for you to leave, she will accompany you. Understand?'

Randolf nodded and looked like he wanted to ask a question but I jumped in first. I was impressed at Andrews' efficiency.

'You've done well to get all this set up so quickly,' I said.

'I've been working on this since yesterday,' said Andrews to my surprise. 'I got a call from Kastagyr Devon Marshall explaining that it was likely we'd need to set this up, so we started making the arrangements. I've got people ready at Doctor Jones' house too.'

'That won't be necessary, thank you CI Andrews,' said Jones firmly. 'I shall be accompanying Per Pike and not returning home just yet.'

Andrews looked to me and I nodded.

'So, I'm effectively under house arrest?' asked Randolf.

'I wouldn't call it that,' said Andrews. 'We prefer the term protective custody. Hopefully it won't be for too long, also we can arrange to have anything you need brought here.'

I indicated I wanted a private word with Andrews and he followed me out of the living room into the kitchen.

'How much did Per Marshall tell you?' I asked.

'Only that an attempt had been made on Doctor Jones and Per Randolf's life while they were off world, that you intervened and were likely to request protection services.'

'I'm hoping the danger is mostly passed now,' I said, 'but I'm not a hundred percent certain of that, so please ensure your people stay alert. I don't want their lives on my conscience as well as Randolf's.'

'The passport records show that a Doctor Bertrand Farley Gernard accompanied Doctor Jones and Per Randolf in their research vessel when they went off-world.'

I didn't respond and kept my expression neutral.

'Can I take it from your silence that the reason neither the research vessel nor Doctor Gernard have returned is because he was in some way connected to the attempted murder?'

I still didn't respond.

'I suppose the other reasonable explanation would be that Doctor Gernard was also a target and was, in fact, killed. But I can't think of a reason why you'd fail to mention that, especially as withholding information like that would be a serious crime. Is that the case Per Pike? Is Doctor Gernard involved in the attempted murders or is he himself dead?'

Damn Andrews for being so good at his job. I certainly couldn't tell him what Gernard had done or that he was currently on the planet awaiting pick up by his co-conspirators at Doctor Grippe's house. Andrews would be duty bound to arrest them all and I would then lose any chance to follow them and find out what was going on.

'I'm sorry CI Andrews,' I said, 'I'm not at liberty to discuss any operational matters, but I am extremely grateful for your assistance. May I remind you that you have been ordered not to investigate this matter?'

'If I get any evidence that you're covering up a crime Pike I will arrest you, or Jones or Randolf or all three of you, orders or not.'

He looked furious but unless he was more willing to disobey a direct order than I thought, I didn't expect him to actually do it. I went back into the living room to a curious glance from Jones, which I ignored.

'We'd better go,' I said. 'Thank you once again CI Andrews, Senior Examiner Scott. Danatis please stay safe and be careful.'

Randolf held an arm out to link with me, looking quite emotional. I stepped in to link arms and as I did so I leaned close to him and whispered in his ear.

'Don't tell the police anything at all about what happened with Gernard until you hear from me.'

He nodded.

Doctor Jones and I headed for the door expecting Andrews to come with us but when I looked back he was whispering to Scott. I presumed he was telling her to find out everything she could. I doubted Randolf would be able to keep much from either of them for long. He was far too easily swayed and far too eager to do the right thing. It didn't much matter once we were off the planet but I didn't want Andrews impounding my ship or arresting Grippe and the others before they could leave.

We walked down the stairs in silence and only once we were back in the car did Andrews ask us where we needed to go.

'Straight back to the Astrophysics tower please, we need to return to my ship.'

He didn't look happy but he took us back promptly and without complaint. We were riding up to the roof when he decided to break his silence.

'Per Pike, I know you think I'm just a provincial police officer who doesn't have a clue about what's really going on, but I have travelled, I haven't spent my whole life here on Coronnol. I was in the galactic navy for over five years, I've been part of peacekeeping missions, rescue missions and I've even been in a firefight or two. What I'm trying to say is that I can help. I'd like to help. You can rely on me but you have to give me more information for me to help effectively.'

He really seemed serious. I was touched by his sincerity and his eagerness to be useful. But I couldn't tell him more.

'Thank you, CI Andrews,' I said, 'I really appreciate your offer. Should I need your help I will call on you, you can count on it. At the moment though the best thing you can do is keep Per Randolf safe.'

It was a brush off and both of us knew it but it was the best I could do. I wouldn't even have taken Jones with me unless I absolutely needed her expertise.

We arrived at the roof and said our goodbyes. Andrews held his arm out to link and as we did so he squeezed my shoulder reassuringly with his other hand.

I opened the door onto the landing pad to discover the wind was now quite strong and very loud. It was just starting to rain so Jones and I ran to the ship and tumbled into the airlock. I sat in the pilot's seat and opened the shutters. I could see Andrews standing in the doorway watching as we lifted off, the stabilisers must have been having to work overtime to prevent us being thrown about by the wind. Once we were twenty meters or so above the roof, I angled the nose of the ship up by thirty degrees and did a fast climb until we were safely above the wind and the rain.

'Looks like a fairly powerful summer storm coming in off the ocean,' said Jones, pointing down to the coastline.

I could see some flashes of lightning and a lot of thick black cloud covering at least a fifty-kilometre square area stretching from the city centre out to sea.

'Do you get them often?' I asked.

'Two or three big storms each summer would be typical. They're usually at the end of the summer though, it's a lot rarer to get one midsummer but not unheard of.'

I was sorry to be missing it as I'd seen nothing but calm weather and sunshine since I'd arrived, apart from one day that had been cloudy in the morning. A good storm was exciting and invigorating so long as you were safe and appropriately dressed to be out in it.

A light started blinking on the console as I programmed in a return course back to the winery.

'What's that?' asked Jones.

'That is exactly what I expected' I said, removing my tunic. 'It's a rather good tracking device. When Andrews squeezed my shoulder I knew he was planting either a bug or a tracker on me. He's not the emotional sort. His whole speech about wanting to help could very well have been part of the build-up, to lull me into a sense of camaraderie. It may have been genuine but I wouldn't bet on it. The ship routinely scans for bugging devices and trackers before proceeding to a new destination.'

'It's microscopic,' said Jones peering at the tiny transparent disc stuck to the seam.

'It's nowhere near as good as ours, but it's pretty small.'

I peeled it off carefully and took it to the workshop where I stuck it to a drone. Jones followed me to watch. I put it in the launcher and ejected it.

'That will now fly randomly between various places Andrews might reasonably expect me to go, stopping long enough at some of them for him to be sure he'll be able to catch us there before moving on.'

'Places such as...?' asked Jones.

'Astrophysics Lab Two, Gernard's house, your house, the Astrophysics Tower, the spaceport plus a couple of random places I've not been. It won't go anywhere near the winery or Randolf. It'll keep him entertained.'

We headed back to the cockpit. Now the tracker had been ejected it was safe to get underway. The storm was firmly behind us but the weather wasn't great even further south. Heavy rain was making visibility atrocious out of the windows but the ship's sensors and cameras were unaffected no matter what the weather and it was perfectly safe to fly.

The sun had set so I expected the hidden ship to launch fairly soon. Sandora had seemed keen to leave as soon as possible. I activated the hyperspace trackers on one of the screens and a small ship icon showed up on the map, exactly where the winery was.

'Are we heading for the spaceport to take an orbital spiral?' asked Jones.

'No. We will follow them in stealth mode. The drone with Andrews' tracker on it is broadcasting my transponder signal so an official departure clearance would be difficult to obtain for this ship.

As we approached the winery I activated the stealth systems and slowed the ship to a crawl, then dropped down below the cloud cover.

'We'll slowly circle the winery at a distance of about five kilometres out. The cameras should be able to see them launch.'

I locked a night vision camera onto the circular building and zoomed in close. The detail was excellent even in the pouring rain.

'Are you sure they won't be able to see us?' asked Jones.

'Absolutely not. With stealth mode on we're impervious to any technological detection. The only way to find the ship is with your own eyes and the chameleon systems will make that virtually impossible from this distance.'

We impatiently watched the dot on the map and the camera feed, switching from one to the other waiting for something to happen.

'Could they have found the trackers and removed them?' asked Jones after about twenty minutes.

'They could have found them, but they couldn't have removed them. The cases I put them in bond to the metal of the ship so they become part of it. The only way to remove them is to cut a section of the hull away and patch the hole. That would destroy the tracker and I wouldn't be getting the two strong signals I'm seeing. If they found them they may have changed their plans, abandoned the ship and be trying to go off planet some other way. I think that's extremely unlikely though.'

The view of the circular building changed slightly. The nose of the ship appeared above the top of the wall and kept climbing. They were going very slowly and carefully as the ship was a very tight fit and manoeuvring out in the high wind must have been tricky. Once the whole ship was clear of the building the triangular metal sheets that made up the roof rose up to their full height then bent inwards to lock together and return the roof to its normal appearance. Sandora's ship turned slowly to point towards Transium then accelerated away so quickly it appeared to vanish from the screen.

'I presume you know Grippe's address?' I asked Jones.

'Not off the top of my head, but he's in my contacts,' she said.

She scrolled through a list on her cuff until she found him then flicked his contact info towards the nav system. The ship plotted a course and soon we were heading in the same direction. The icon on the map representing Sandora's ship was travelling very quickly, much faster than would be considered safe by the authorities.

'Why are they going so fast?' asked Jones.

'They don't have any stealth technology on that ship, so when local air-traffic control spot them, which they will shortly, they'll send someone to investigate an unregistered ship. They'll need to collect Grippe and Gernard as quickly as possible then escape to orbit and hyperspace before they're intercepted.'

We were following at several kilometres distance, and a higher altitude. I locked the camera onto the ship and we watched it fly over some impressive looking houses with huge gardens on the east side of Transium.

'That looks like the district Grippe lives in,' said Jones. 'I've not been to his house but I've heard stories about how wealthy he is and how he shows off to society types with his extravagant parties.'

Sandora's ship slowed and then lowered itself straight down into the garden of a huge house that had several ornamental ponds between the areas of lawn. Two figures came running out of the house, arm in arm, it was Grippe and Gernard. The moment the ship touched down Gernard bundled Grippe in through the open outer airlock door then scrambled up after him. The door shut and the ship tipped up to a forty-five-degree angle and shot upwards at high speed. The camera lost it momentarily then refocused in time to see a rear view of the ship as it shrank to a dot leaving the atmosphere.

'They are in a hurry,' said Jones.

'With good reason,' I said and pointed to a screen showing several police craft heading towards us. 'The response time is pretty impressive. We'd better get out of here too, just in case an eagle-eyed officer sees us.'

We tipped upwards and moved up through the clouds. Within ten minutes we were nearing orbit. The tracker showed Sandora's ship heading away from the planet at speed then suddenly the icon vanished.

'They've jumped through hyperspace,' I said

.

Chapter 27
Tracking

In under a minute the trackers had reported their new location. We waited in orbit to see if this was the final destination or simply a stopover. After ten minutes they jumped again, the trackers dutifully logged the new location. I used one of the screens to plot the jumps on a scalable galactic map, centred on Coronnol.

'I'm going to stay one jump behind them,' I said to Jones. 'I don't want them to get so far ahead we can't get to them in a single jump without it being dangerous.'

The stars outside the window flickered and changed completely.

'How did they manage a second jump so quickly? They barely waited ten minutes to recharge their ship.'

'I imagine they have a larger power cell on board, or possibly multiple cells. Perhaps it's part of their tactic to avoid being tracked. If they repeatedly jump very quickly most ships would be unable to follow due to the minimum half hour recharge.'

'Most ships? But not this one?'

'I can get a partial charge in ten minutes but we are going to deplete our reserves quickly if they keep jumping.'

'What happens if they transfer to another ship during one of the recharge cycles?' asked Jones. 'Couldn't we lose them like that?'

'Fortunately, that's not possible,' I said. 'The trackers we use have built in proximity sensors to detect another ship nearby. If another ship comes close enough to make such a transfer, I get an alert, the stealth systems activate and we automatically jump to their location. I only have about twenty seconds to override that automatic jump and if I don't do that then as soon as we arrive a special adhesive probe is fired at the new ship with a tracker built in to it. The fastest I've ever seen anyone do an airlock-to-airlock transfer is about five minutes, but that was very experienced pilots, with someone familiar with microgravity making the transfer. For an elderly woman and two senior scientists from a high 'g' world I'm certain it would take fifteen to twenty minutes.'

Sandora's ship jumped again. Then again, and again, each time with about ten minutes between jumps. The galactic map looked crazy, the stars they'd jumped to were highlighted in yellow with tiny labels next to them identifying the jump number and system name. Faint blue lines linked them all together, but there didn't seem to be a consistent direction. They were hopping about all over the place but always slightly further from Coronnol.

Jones was researching the names of the star systems, trying to spot a pattern. Neither of us had heard of any of the places they were jumping to.

'Do they know they're being followed and that's why all the seemingly random jumps?' asked Jones.

'Probably. They'll know it's impossible to follow someone through hyperspace without a tracking beacon. They will scan for one if they're smart but they won't detect ours. If they suspect there is one that they can't detect, then this would be a good way to shake your pursuer.'

I programmed the nav system to stay one jump behind their ship and closed the shutters on the windows. Seeing the stars flicker and change so frequently had made us feel slightly nauseous.

The map now also showed a green line, starting at Coronnol, following the blue one. Each time the blue one moved to a new star system; the green line jumped to the stop before.

'Is this kind of thing normal for you?' asked Jones.

'I'm not sure I know what normal is any more. I've been doing this job nearly fifteen years and the thing that's brought home to me most often is just how fragile civilization really is. I assumed this job would be long periods of inactivity with occasional bouts of frantic action, but it's not. It's constant painstaking research, detective work, dead ends, danger, frustration and disillusionment with humanity.'

'Disillusionment?'

'I guess. Perhaps that's a bit harsh when you consider how well we've been doing as a species for the last few thousand years compared to all the previous millennia. No more rival galactic empires, no hunger, no racial or gender prejudice, almost no sickness or disease, very little crime and virtually no war, it could be considered almost utopian. But there must be something not quite right. Why, with all that, are people like me needed, why a galactic navy? Why do we keep having to stop people like her,' I pointed to the icon of Sandora's ship, 'and who knows how many more?'

We sat in silence for a few minutes, watching the icon on the screen until it vanished once more and reappeared a minute or so later in another part of the galaxy.

'Why do you dislike Doctor Grippe so much and why did you lie to me about not working closely with him? I asked.

Doctor Jones paused. She looked as if she really didn't want to answer.

'Your secret is safe with me,' I said.

'You're quite right I don't like him. In fact, I can't stand the man. I lied about working closely with him because I don't want my career and my department dragged down when he inevitably crosses the line and ends up in disgrace.'

I waited until she chose to continue.

'I am fairly sure he has had inappropriate relationships with his students. I'm convinced he's using his position to elicit sexual favours from, primarily but not exclusively, the female ones. I haven't any conclusive proof but I've seen his body language around them and we've had higher than expected drop-outs amongst his students. None of them were willing to go on record and most have transferred to similar courses at other universities, each time with a glowing reference from Grippe. Which I presume is his way of paying them off to remain silent. Sooner or later he is going to slip up or someone who is willing to talk will come forward. I've reported my concerns and there has been a discreet investigation but he's extremely clever and no proof has yet been found. That combined with his powerful political connections both on Coronnol and Cestus mean without undeniable proof no direct accusation can be made. I suspect he's been doing it for years and no-one looked too closely for fear of the repercussions for the university.'

She looked relieved to have finally told someone but I could see the anger at this betrayal of a position of trust was fuelling her determination to expose Grippe.

'I presume you knew none of this when you appointed him deputy director?'

'Absolutely not! If I'd had the slightest inkling about any such activities he wouldn't never have got anywhere near that job. But until I have solid proof or someone willing to go on the record about his behaviour then there's nothing I can do.'

'Just another reason for my moments of disillusionment with humanity,' I said.

'Don't give up on humanity, the bad eggs are few and far between,' said Jones. 'You and your colleagues do an almost unimaginably important and stressful job completely without recognition, that makes up for the Grippes in the galaxy doesn't it? Perhaps you need a break. When was the last time you had a holiday, a proper one for weeks not days?'

'Years,' I said.

'You have to get away, to reset, to recharge, to re-establish a connection to your own life. I couldn't survive without my trips to the mountains, not just on Coronnol or Mirth but elsewhere too. I've even been to Earth and climbed some of the mountains there. To be a part of an unending chain that stretches back to humanity's earliest physical challenges grounds you. I've been three times. I climbed Mount Kilimanjaro, the first time unsuccessfully as I wasn't fit enough, the second was a year later and that was successful. Then on the last trip I did several smaller peaks on a trip to the European continent. Ben Nevis was a highlight.'

'I'm not much of a mountaineer, I'm afraid,' I said.

'It's extreme hill walking really. I'm not into scaling sheer rock faces or glaciers. It's the scenery I love and it is incredible. My heart belongs to the Eastern Rift Mountains in Africa, we should go together sometime, soon. It would do you good. I can show you where my ancestors came from.'

I looked at her beautiful earnest face. She was serious, she really seemed to care about people. It sounded interesting but I wasn't at all clear how she could know which part of Earth her ancestors came from as there were no surviving personal records from back when Earth was humanity's only home. I was gratified that my initial assessment of her as fundamentally an outdoor person who happened to work in a lab had been correct.

'You know I've never been to Earth? The job has never taken me there and I've never felt the urge to visit as a tourist. I'm just not that interested in gardening or ancient history. But a holiday does sound appealing. If you can guarantee that the food is good then I'll think about it.'

'Oh, and please will you call me Mal? I'm sick of being called Jones or Doctor Jones. We are going to be spending quite some time together and we may as well be friends,' she smiled at me and at that moment I knew I really wanted to visit Earth with her.

'I'd like that Mal,' I said.

I watched the screen and realised that Sandora's ship hadn't jumped again. It had been over fifteen minutes and they were still in the same star system.

I checked our power reserves and was concerned to see we only had enough power for one jump, with a little to spare.

'I'm going to catch them up,' I said. 'I'd prefer more time to recharge but if we wait too long we might lose them.'

'How?'

'The trackers can report location so quickly because they're only accurate to the solar system, it can take sixty minutes or more to be accurate to a few kilometres. If we let Sandora get too far away from the jump point we may not know for over an hour where she's made planet fall. There's usually only one planet in a goldilocks zone, but not always. Her ship may drop her off and then depart leaving us with one or more whole planetary surfaces to search.'

'Let's go then,' said Jones.

I activated the stealth technology then opened the shutters in time to see the stars flicker as we jumped.

'This system isn't recorded on Infosys,' Jones said in a very surprised voice.

'What?'

'It doesn't exist in the habitable planets database. The star is marked, obviously, but it has no name, just a number, it's recorded as having no planets other than a couple of gas giants. Why would they come here?'

'It's worse than that,' I said, pointing to a blue and white planet outside the window, 'the habitable planets database is incorrect. Which isn't supposed to be possible. That planet is smack in the goldilocks zone judging by the colour. Nothing looks quite like that except a planet with plenty of liquid water and an oxygen/nitrogen atmosphere.'

'Is the planet inhabited?'

'I can't tell from this distance. If someone's gone to the trouble to vandalise the Infosys database to remove this world they must have something or someone to hide. I'm not detecting any orbiting traffic control systems, there's hardly any artificial satellites at all. There's also no power grid on the planet, which implies it's not inhabited. Perhaps Sandora uses this planet for storage, but of what?'

I sped up as Sandora had quite a lead on us and was already entering orbit ready to land.

'Can you see her ship?' asked Jones.

'Not visually, but my sensors can detect both trackers.'

'Are we going to land?' asked Jones.

'Absolutely not,' I said. 'The energy cells are almost out following all those fast jumps. And this isn't a job for one person or even two. We'll get into a low orbit, then watch what happens after they land using the cameras, they're incredibly high resolution and we should be able to see everything in detail. Once we're sure they're staying put we'll contact Kas but if it looks like just a stopover we'll move closer to the sun to recharge so we can follow them.'

We were now almost at the right distance from the planet to enter orbit, so I slowed down and prepared to position the ship directly above the sensor image of Sandora's vessel. Gradually I eased the ship into a low altitude orbit. There was no automatic traffic control satellite so I had to do pilot the ship manually, which took all my concentration

'The tracking icons are fading,' said Jones.

I risked a glance at the tracker screen and she was absolutely right. The two icons were fading away to nothing. That shouldn't be possible. The trackers hadn't yet reported their precise location, I was relying on my sensors detecting them and they simply couldn't.

I checked the energy cell. It was very low.

'We know roughly where they went. That'll have to do for now. We need a recharge,' I said.

That's when it all went wrong.

'Damn it,' I muttered under my breath.

'What? What's wrong?'

'We've lost our Infosys connection. Something is blocking it. There's some kind of dampening field cutting us off. I'm breaking orbit.'

I re-engaged the nav system and tried to plot a course that would take us into orbit around the nearby sun, but without Infosys it couldn't calculate it. I would have to do that manually too. I boosted the power to the grav engines and started to climb.

'Shit!' I shouted. 'The dampening field is sapping our grav engines too. We'll run out of power before we manage to break orbit at this rate.'

'Can we land?'

'At the rate the power cells are draining that's not guaranteed, we're almost certainly going to crash.'

Chapter 28
Powerless

Jones looked at me and I could see the fear in her eyes for a moment, but only for a moment. She took a deep breath and focused.

I was scanning the surface looking for somewhere to land and was surprised to discover the planet was inhabited. There was a moderately sized city near where we'd lost contact with Sandora.

'What can I do to help?' Jones said.

'The beds have a crash protection feature, for use in emergencies. I don't know how it works as I've never had to even contemplate using it. Can you work it out and get them ready? I'm going to use what little power we have to try and do as controlled a landing as I can. I'm not going to be responsible for mass casualties on the ground, no matter who lives in that city.'

The lack of an Infosys link meant the automatic distress signal would not be working. We really were on our own.

'I'll work out how to configure the bed,' she said, 'how hard can it be?'

She disappeared into the living quarters leaving me wondering just what kind of inhabited planet had no power grid and no Infosys link?

I deployed the wings to their largest configuration and killed all non-essential systems, including all the stealth technology, to preserve what little power I had and got the ship into a spiral glide pattern that would hopefully allow us to descend in a reasonably controlled manner.

The landscape around the city was fairly arid, just lots of small pockets of green among a sea of pale brown earth. I couldn't see any surface water near it. No lakes, no rivers, no reservoirs. There was an ocean but that was several hundred kilometres away. Even at this altitude I could tell it was a fairly sparsely populated continent as I couldn't detect any large settlements other than the one city. This made choosing somewhere to land a lot easier. All I had to do was not crash on the city.

We were going far too fast and the diameter of the ship's descent spiral was enormous. I used a considerable amount of the energy reserves slowing us down, which allowed me to tighten the spiral. I had seen some farmland about twenty kilometres from the city that looked promising as a landing site. Where there was greenery there must be water, which we might need. There were also no buildings beyond a couple of small huts. As we looped back around over the city, which was now close enough to see properly, I wondered if there was anyone on the ground monitoring us. They had spaceships so they must have technology, even if their power source was completely different.

We orbited the city three or four more times before I eased out of the spiral at roughly two thousand metres altitude and headed towards the fields. The wings did not provide enough lift to fully maintain flight, they were really only to aid manoeuvring, the ship still relied on the antigrav engine to fly and that was draining the last of the power quickly. I slowed us some more and got us down to a few hundred metres altitude. By now red warning lights were flashing all over the cockpit warning me that power levels were critical. It occurred to me how completely absurd it was for the ship to use any of the remaining power to light up warnings that I was low on power.

'How's it coming with the crash protection?' I shouted through to Jones.

'I think I've worked it out but we'll need some power to engage the system, so don't use it all,' she replied.

I closed the shutters on the windows and locked the controls on the furthest edge of the fields which was near a small wooded area and as far from the huts as I could get, then ran through to the living quarters.

Jones was already lying on one of the fold-down beds, there were straps coming out of one side of the bed fastened across her chest and legs pinning her down. She held an oxygen mask ready to place over her face.

'Get on the other fold down bed,' she said. 'There's a red button by the hinge. Press it and hold it for five seconds then get your face mask on.'

I jumped on and looked for the button. It was small and not easy to spot, but I guess they didn't want you pressing it accidentally. I lay down then held the button for a five count. Thick soft straps snapped out of the side of the bed and snaked across my body, holding me gently but firmly down and a face mask with a small cylinder of oxygen attached dropped out of a hidden compartment. I grabbed it and pulled it over my face and saw Jones had already put hers on.

I heard the impact alarm sound in the cockpit then both beds snapped up back towards the wall. Hundreds of small nozzles appeared in the wall and began spraying a thick white foam all over us filling the gap between our bodies and the wall. The foam hardened almost instantly which made me very glad of the face mask.

I'd instinctively screwed my eyes shut, even though I already couldn't see anything because of the foam, then felt a colossal impact as we hit the ground at what must have been around three hundred kilometres per hour. I wondered if the ship would dig in then flip over and roll or if it would bounce and skip like a stone on a pond. Fortunately, it did neither. The ground was soft enough to absorb some of the impact, and we simply gouged a deep furrow into it like some sort of demented space plough. The noise inside the ship was deafening as we carved our way to a stop at the end of a kilometre long scar. As soon as the ship was stationary I heard something else spraying out of the nozzles then the foam melted completely away, the beds flopped back down to their horizontal position and the straps retracted back into the bed.

I scrambled off the bed, pulling my mask off. All the lights were off for a moment then the emergency low level lighting kicked in. Jones was still lying on her bed, not moving.

'Are you alright?' I asked.

'Yes. I think so,' she replied. 'I know I'm usually a thrill seeker but I never want to do that again. That was horrible.'

She pulled off her mask and smiled at me to reassure me she was okay.

'We have to grab some supplies and get out of here quickly,' I said. 'No doubt someone will be along soon to investigate and I don't want to be here when they arrive.'

I went through to the galley and opened a cupboard and retrieved lots of prepacked emergency ration packs. They were pretty boring to eat but they would keep you alive for quite a long time. I also retrieved a few items from the workshop that might come in handy on a strange and probably hostile planet. Jones was stuffing the ration packs into a couple of rucksacks when I came back from the workshop.

'I found these. Is that okay?'

'That's great,' I said shoving the equipment into a rucksack. I opened the fridge, grabbed as many bottles of water as I could and passed some of them to Jones. We crammed them into the rucksacks.

We headed for the airlock and I instinctively looked at my cuff to check the outside weather conditions but the faint red glow along its edge reminded me we were going to have to manage without Infosys.

I showed Jones the manual release and hoped there was enough power left to open the door, if not I'd have to use the explosive bolts to blast it off.

'I need to set the self-destruct,' I said. 'I can't have anyone getting hold of this ship or its contents.'

I went into the cockpit one last time and found the self-destruct sequence under the main control console. It had its own separate power source so that you could be certain of destroying the ship, even if it was completely crippled. I set the timer for ten minutes then headed back to the airlock. On the way the lights all went out.

Jones had the inner door half open.

'I guess the main power finally gave out,' she said.

Together we heaved on it and managed to push the door all the way open.

'Stand back,' I said as I triggered the explosive bolts.

Jones, ever the curious scientist, leaned forward to look at what I was doing. I had to grab her and push her back away from the airlock. There was a rapid sequence of twelve small explosions and the outer airlock fell onto the ground.

'Are you OK?' I asked.

She nodded.

The air outside was cold so I ran quickly back into the living quarters and felt around for some warm coats, gloves and hats in the store cupboard then I jumped down and looked along the dead straight groove pointing back towards the city. As our speed had slowed, the furrow had got shallower. The ship was now sitting on the crushed and burned grass. I had absolutely no idea what the local time was, but the city was only about twenty kilometres away so it wouldn't take long for a search party to arrive. It was fantastically unlikely that we'd managed to arrive without being noticed. If there were any occupants in the huts on the other side of the farm they would have heard the crash, if nothing else.

Jones dropped the rucksacks down to me then jumped down herself. I looked at the scout ship. One of the wings was badly damaged, a large section had been torn off. There was a crack in the hull on the underside, probably made by the initial impact, that ran three quarters of the length of the ship. Even if we could recharge the power cells there wasn't a hope it was still space-worthy.

'Let's go,' she said. 'I don't want to be anywhere near here if you've set the ship to self-destruct.'

'There's no danger now we're out of the ship. It's not an explosion. It's a molecular solvent. The whole ship is reduced to biodegradable mush. The self-destruct pumps the solvent solution through microscopic channels throughout the whole ship. It takes about half an hour before there's nothing left but a puddle of sludge that the rain will wash away.'

Together we dragged the broken section of wing until it was right next to the ship. I wanted to make sure it melted away too. Then we put our coats, hats and gloves on, strapped on our rucksacks and started walking away from the doomed ship.

'Where are we heading?' asked Jones, which was a pretty reasonable question.

'Cover. We could be out here for some time. We're going to need shelter, warmth and water. I saw a small wood a kilometre or so from here, on the far edge of this field. It wasn't much more than a few hundred trees but it'll have to do.'

When I guessed twenty minutes or so had passed I turned and looked back. The ship was losing its shape, melting like an ice-cream in the sun. It wouldn't be long before it was completely destroyed.

The trees were easy to see now and we sped up slightly as we neared them. Once we were in the wood we both started to relax. The cover wasn't brilliant and it wouldn't take anyone long to find us if they looked, but psychologically it felt safer.

We lay on the ground and I pulled out some optical binoculars from one of the bags and looked back at the ship. It was just a lump on the ground now. Black and shapeless. I followed the line of the crash back towards the city and saw far off in the distance something moving towards the ship. I couldn't make out what it was, but it was on the ground not in the air. It was going to take at least half an hour for whoever it was to get to the crash site.

We moved deeper into the woods to ensure we were out of sight of anyone approaching the crash. I rummaged through my rucksack and found a small flat package. I placed it on the ground below the largest tree I could find. It unfolded itself again and again and then expanded upwards until there was a pyramid shaped two-person tent standing in front of me. It was a neutral grey colour but quickly took on the colours of the woods around us as the basic camouflage system calibrated itself.[1]

I pulled the top off the pyramid and unspooled an almost impossibly thin thread with a hook on one end. I threw the hook up into the tree and it wrapped itself automatically around a thick branch high above me. I opened the front of the tent and unrolled a ladder. I touched a control on the base of the tent and the cable at the top of the pyramid was wound in until the floor of the tent was hanging more than a metre above our heads.

'It'll keep us warm and dry and, unless someone comes really close, it'll keep us invisible once the light starts to fade,' I said to Jones.

'That shouldn't be too long,' said Jones indicating the length of the shadows around us. 'It'll probably be dark in an hour or so.'

She looked up at the tent with some concern.

'Won't that sway about all over the place trying to get up there and once we're in it?'

'No. Once the tent is in position the cable it's hanging from and the ladder go completely rigid.'

I grabbed the ladder and pulled on it to demonstrate, it didn't budge.

She climbed the ladder and went inside. I started walking quietly back towards the edge of the trees to have a look and see what the search party was up to.

They ought to be at the remains of the ship by now and I imagined they'd be very disappointed not to find anything identifiable or useful. If they didn't believe that we'd died in the crash then they'd come looking for us next. The woods were an

---

[1] The survival tent had a rigid frame and floor so it could sit on the ground or be suspended overhead. The small built in power source could erect and collapse it automatically half a dozen times or so even without a power grid before the cell was exhausted. It didn't have the latest chameleon suit technology only a basic adaptive camouflage that blended into its surroundings. The great thing was once you were inside you were invisible even to infrared or electromagnetic detection. The material was a perfect shield.

obvious place to hide so we would be relying on the tent to hide us until we could find somewhere better to hole up.

I had no idea how we were going to get out of this mess but stealing a spaceship was going to have to be fairly high on the list of possibilities. The city was a long walk away and I hadn't been able to spot anything that looked like a spaceport as we'd circled it. The consistently low-rise buildings had all looked fairly rustic and had been scattered around in an organic and unplanned way, neither was there any consistent architectural style. Even finding a spaceship might prove difficult.

I looked through the binoculars and saw four people walking around the crash site examining the liquid remains of the ship. I didn't recognize any of them but they were far away so I couldn't see any details without the image enhancements Infosys would usually have provided. Their transport was fascinating. They had some kind of small four-wheeled wagon that was being pulled by a pair of large quadrupeds. One of the group was still sitting in the wagon, apparently controlling it. He was waving his arms and directing the others. He pointed our way and I guessed he was telling them where they were going to be searching next. He had something hanging round his neck, which he picked up and held to his face. It was a pair of binoculars. I kept very still. I didn't want a reflection off my lenses to give my position away. We were staring right at each other but as I was lying down in the undergrowth, I doubted he could actually see me.

The men on the ground clambered back into the wagon and the man with the binoculars lowered them and started the animals trotting our way.

I wriggled backwards on the ground, until I couldn't see them anymore, before I stood up and walked briskly back to the tent.

The light was definitely starting to fail and even though I knew exactly where the tent was I still had trouble finding it, which was reassuring. I called out to Jones as I didn't want to startle her before climbing up.

'They've found the remains of the ship,' I said, 'and they're coming this way.'

She was sorting through her pack, checking on the food supplies and looked up as I entered. She seemed concerned but not frightened. I made the ladder flexible again and pulled it up back into the tent.

'They won't find us except by chance. They're moving relatively slowly on some kind of animal powered wagon. By the time they get here it'll be almost dark.'

'Animal powered?'

'Yes. It's a four wheeled vehicle with two large quadrupeds harnessed to it at the front. I couldn't tell what kind of animal. They definitely weren't horses but I don't know what else you'd use for something like that. It'll be faster than walking I suppose.'

'What kind of planet has no power grid and no Infosys link? How do they power anything?'

'One that rejects all such technology,' I said. 'Is your cuff completely dead?'

She looked down and saw the red glow on the edge had faded away.

'The Primitives would feel right at home here, anyway. No technology allowed.'

Let's eat,' I said. 'We may not get a chance later.'

Jones looked at the uninviting emergency rations without enthusiasm.

'I know you're a food connoisseur and these are nothing like the fine dining you would normally enjoy…'

She interrupted me.

'It's fine, really. Needs must, and when I'm hiking, or camping, I eat simple food. It's just that I don't feel particularly hungry. I'm too anxious. I wouldn't say I was frightened, I'm sure you've been in worse scrapes than this and survived, so I trust you to get us out of it. But I haven't ever had someone try to kill me with a supernova, or found out my innocent research is being corrupted into a horrible weapon of mass destruction, or crashed on a probably hostile planet, all within the space of a few days. It's a lot to take in.'

She chose a self-heating can of risotto and opened it and reluctantly started eating it using the utensil concealed in the lid. I chose a mushroom stew.

We ate quickly. It was now getting quite dark and a lot colder. I sealed up the entrance to the tent and we kept the light off inside.

'Do you think it's winter here or is this planet's normal climate simply a lot colder than Coronnol?' asked Jones.

'I don't know. We're fairly far north of the equator, but not close enough to an arctic zone to make it uncomfortably cold even in summer. I didn't have time to read any of the stats the ship's systems had gathered before all hell broke loose. The lack of surface water is curious. I'm not sure why you'd settle on a continent with so little easily accessible water. There are large oceans so there must be rivers on other continents and the presence of farms, sporadic and spread out even as they are, means they must be getting water from somewhere. An underground source that they've drilled down to?'

'The sun is a standard M-type. You'd expect to find a terraformable planet in the goldilocks zone orbiting a lot of those. I didn't see any unusual radiation signatures listed when the tracker identified this system as our destination, so we should be safe from that particular hazard.'

We heard voices calling to each other in the distance and both stopped talking and instinctively held our breath. We could just make each other out in the gloom. I pulled a stunner from my coat pocket and offered it to Jones, but she shook her head. I held it ready.

Gradually we started breathing normally again but we both strained to hear if the voices were coming closer or getting further away.

I heard someone trip and fall over a tree root, swearing profusely, a few metres away from our position.

'This is ridiculous!' they shouted. 'I can't see a thing. If there's anyone here they could be right in front of us and we'd never see them'

Little did they know how right they were.

A chorus of agreement sounded from further away in two other directions.

'Santis! Santis, it's time to go home. We can come back in the morning,' said the voice of the person who'd tripped.

'Sandora won't like it,' said another voice, presumably Santis. 'But I agree. We'll head back. Everyone back on the wagon.'

There was some noise of people stumbling about in the undergrowth that got fainter and then silence.

'Well at least now we know Sandora is here,' I whispered.

Jones opened a bottle of water and sipped at it.

'I suppose we should conserve our supply until we know where to get more,' she said.

I nodded then put my finger to my lips and lowered the ladder.

'I'll go and check that they've really gone,' I whispered.

Once I was back on the ground, I made my way as quietly as I could back towards the edge of the wood. The binoculars didn't have night vision but I could just make out a faint light, swinging backwards and forwards on the cart as it trundled back where it had come from. The driver clearly didn't care about the crop in the field, as he wasn't bothering to go around it, but had cut through it diagonally.

I wondered how much trouble Santis was going to be in when they finally got back. I hoped it was a lot.

Chapter 29
Haven

Back in the tent we made ourselves as comfortable as we could, given the limited space, and settled down for an early night. We needed to be up and moving before dawn if possible but without a working Infosys connection between us we had no way to set an alarm, so I was relying on anxiety to wake me up on time. As it turned out I needn't have worried about oversleeping as I only slept fitfully all night. Jones' breathing was steady and deep and thankfully she didn't snore. If she wasn't really asleep she was very good at faking it.

I checked the light outside the tent from time to time and as soon as there was even a hint that the sun was coming up I nudged Jones awake and we prepared to leave. Back on the ground and shivering in the pre-dawn cold I unhooked the cable from the tree branch and stowed it back into the top of the pyramid. Pressing a button collapsed the tent back down into a small rectangular box, then we checked all about us to ensure we'd left no obvious sign of our presence. I looked at my useless cuff, the red warning glow had gone, it must finally be completely out of power.

Neither of us felt like talking so as we walked we munched on cereal bars and sipped water for our breakfast.

We didn't head back towards the crash site, that seemed far too risky, so we looped around the woods and the farm, as far away from the site as we could while still keeping it in view.

After about an hour Jones finally broke her silence.

'If you don't mind me asking, what exactly is the plan?'

'I don't mind at all. The plan is pretty simple; walk back to the city we saw, stay out of sight, find a spaceship we can steal or failing that find communication equipment so we can let Kas and the barbs know where we are. Hopefully they'll be looking for us, as our cuffs will have gone off-line as will the ship when we entered the dampening field. But they may not know exactly where we are in this system, so it could take some time.'

'What are we going to do about Gernard and Grippe? We need to find out what they're planning. They have to be stopped.'

'I agree,' I said, 'but we have no idea where they are, I'm fairly sure Sandora will have people on the lookout for us, and there's just the two of us. The first priority has to be to make contact with my people, that way if anything happens to us at least someone will be able to continue where we left off.'

The landscape was dry and fairly barren other than the farm we'd crashed near. Without the advantage of high altitude we couldn't see where the next farm was. The ground was quite flat, a few natural falls and rises but no hills or mountains as far as the eye could see. There were a few clumps of trees dotted about but nothing approaching the size of the wood we'd spent the night in. The sun was well up and the cold had eased off somewhat. We weren't in danger of overheating, even maintaining a brisk pace. I stopped us every twenty minutes or so to scan all around with the binoculars, I didn't want to get taken by surprise but in this landscape an ambush would be very difficult to mount. Unfortunately that also meant it would be very hard for us to hide from anyone searching for us.

After another three hours of walking we were finally close enough to see the city in some detail through the binoculars. It looked even more ramshackle from the ground than it had from the scout ship. It was large, spread out over a wide area and there didn't seem to be a single building taller than three stories. All the buildings were made from the same brick and their random arrangement really did indicate there was no centralised system for planning. The buildings had a few trees scattered about between them and a lot of the smaller ones, that would likely be private dwellings, had a thick low hedge around them with various different plants growing within. It was still quite early but there were people moving about. Some were tending the plants within the hedges, some pulling small hand carts, fewer still riding on a cart pulled by an animal.

I passed Jones the binoculars.

'Can you see anything that looks like a good place to hide a spaceship? Or even anywhere that looks like some kind of civic centre or communications hub?'

She studied the city carefully for quite a while.

'Nope,' she said finally, 'it's too hard to see anything near the centre of the city.'

'No, neither could I. We are going to stick out like a sore thumb down there. These clothes don't look like anything I saw anyone wearing. It's a pretty big city, but two strangers wandering about looking like us are going to draw attention. We need to get some suitable clothing and have a chat with one of the locals.'

She handed me the binoculars and I started scanning the buildings on the edge of the city.

'I can see a likely candidate,' I said after about fifteen minutes of watching the nearest buildings, 'let's go.'

We set off walking to a smallish building right on the edge of the city. There was a large building directly behind it but the immediate neighbours had their gardens between the house and the one I was interested in. I'd just seen someone go inside through the binoculars, but I hadn't seen them leave.

As we approached the building, I asked Jones to wait while I went inside alone. I wasn't sure what I would find but I didn't want to be worried about her safety while I searched. She sat on the ground with her back against the hedge and I gave her a spare stunner and showed her how to use it.

'It's fully charged so it should last quite a while,' I said. 'But please be careful, keep it on a low setting, and only shoot if you have to. I'm hoping to come and go undetected.'

I looked at the windows of the building. They had wooden shutters on that were fastened open with hooks embedded in the wall. Perhaps they never got shut. I couldn't see anyone moving about inside and I hadn't seen anyone watching our cautious approach but that didn't necessarily mean they hadn't been watching. I pulled my own stunner from my pocket, set it to the lowest setting and scrambled over the hedge then ran for the door in the centre of the wall facing me.

The door wasn't locked, in fact it didn't seem to have a lock. It opened smoothly and quietly so I went in and listened, trying to work out where the occupant or occupants of the house might be. There was a long corridor running to the other side of the house with doorless alcoves into the other rooms. There was a staircase to my immediate right. I decided to check the downstairs first and went from room to room. The furniture was basic and looked homemade. There were no images of loved ones on display and the only art I could see was that each room had a circular disc mounted on the wall that had a pair of straight rods connected to the centre point of the circle. It didn't take long to check the four downstairs rooms. There was a kitchen, a lounge, a basic workshop containing mostly gardening implements and what seemed to be a study. I made my way back to the staircase and moved cautiously up it. There were only three rooms upstairs. The first was a bathroom. It wasn't particularly fancy but it had everything you'd need, and it was the only room with a door on it. There was a small bedroom with a single, unmade, bed in it, a store cupboard and finally the master bedroom. This was messy and lying face down snoring gently was the man I'd seen enter the house. He was fully dressed, aside from his shoes which were on the floor, and he was lying on the unmade bed. He wasn't wearing a cuff, but without a power grid or Infosys link he had no use for one. I checked again to make sure there was no-one else about then I prodded his bare foot. It took a while to wake him up, he was a heavy sleeper. Finally, he stirred and started to cry out but I shot him before he could.

The stunner was on the lowest setting so it didn't even knock him out. It just paralysed him. I rolled him over and propped him up with his pillows so he could see me.

'I'm not going to hurt you,' I said in my most reassuring voice. 'Not unless you try to hurt me. I need to ask you some questions and I want you to answer honestly. I'm very good at spotting a lie and I will have no hesitation stunning you again, possibly on a higher setting, if I think you're lying to me. Is that clear? Blink rapidly if you understand.'

He blinked rapidly.

'Thanks. We're off to a good start. Now you'll be able to talk in a minute or two, but you won't be able to move for a bit longer. Bear in mind I can stun you again and again if necessary, so please don't try to attack me.'

He appeared to be in his mid-thirties. He was lean, had short badly cut brown hair and a scruffy beard. I saw him moving his mouth, experimenting, trying to talk.

'That's good. My name is Cem. What's yours?'

'Leeton Salvador Gains,' he slurred with some difficulty. His tongue probably still felt twice its usual size.

'Okay Leeton, first question. Do you live here alone or are you expecting any visitors?'

'Alone. Not expecting anyone.'

'Even better. Don't go away.' I said as I headed back down to the door.

I called to Jones that it was safe to come inside. I didn't want any passers-by to spot her hiding by the hedge.

I headed back upstairs as soon as I saw her clambering over the hedge.

'Now Leeton, this might sound like a stupid question but where are we? What's this planet called and what city is this?'

'Haven. The planet's called Haven and this city is Stronghold.'

Jones appeared in the doorway behind me.

'What have you done to him?' she asked.

'Just a light stunning. He's fine. We're having a nice chat. Why aren't you out working in your garden or somewhere else Leeton?'

'I work nights,' he said, 'I only got home half an hour or so ago. What do you want?'

'Just for you to answer my questions. That's all.'

Leeton closed his eyes and started a quiet chanting that sounded awfully like the prayers Gernard had been saying on the scout ship.

'Leeton, you can stop that please, or I will have to stun you again. Let's stick to Inglis, then we can all understand each other.

He opened his eyes and glared at me but stopped chanting.

'Thank you. The next question is really important, so take your time and think about your answer. Leeton , who is Sandora?'

'I don't know a Sandora,' he said instantly.

'Now Leeton, what did I say about lying? You answered me far too quickly there and I know it was a lie. Let's try again. Who is Sandora?' I said and pointed the stunner at his head.

'Sandora Willow Sylvester,' he said somewhat reluctantly. 'She's our leader.'

'Thank you Leeton, I believe you. So what is she the leader of?'

'This planet, our movement, the Radical Primitives. She's a visionary. You should talk to her, she'll explain it all to you. About how the galaxy has lost its way. It's trapped in ungodly complacency by technology,' he glanced at my lifeless cuff. 'She can explain how Gaea could sets you free from that shackle on your wrist. You can learn to think for yourself again, get back to being able to fend for yourself. Gaea is freedom. She could explain it better than me, obviously.'

I glanced at Jones, who mouthed 'This planet is Sandora's home.'

'Leeton I knew Primitives rejected technology, but I've not heard of Gaea before. Who is Gaea?'

'Who is Gaea? Are you serious?' Leeton seemed genuinely astonished. 'Gaea is the mother of life, the source of wisdom, the one that makes the harvest grow, the one who maps the stars, and knows our secret thoughts, who orders our steps and knows our future. Gaea is everywhere. Gaea is God. The path of Gaea leads to righteousness. To reject Gaea is to reject righteousness and become ungodly.'

'Normally I'd be quite happy for you all to reject the comforts of technology and live a simpler but much harder life. I can almost see the appeal. But Sandora is planning to commit an atrocity. Something more destructive than you could imagine. Something deadly to many millions if not billions. I need you to tell me what you know about that.'

Leeton looked extremely uncomfortable and more than a little confused.

'I don't believe you. She cares about Gaea and taking life is only permissible in extreme circumstances. Sandora cares about humanity's future. It's the reason she's taken on the burden of leadership. She can be tough, but the discipline is for our benefit, it's for our own good, it's not deadly or destructive.'

He wriggled on the bed, his hands and feet twitching with anxiety. The stun shot had almost worn off and he was getting some movement back. He looked thoroughly miserable.

'Leeton, my name is Mal. I'm a scientist,' said Jones. 'Cem is telling the truth. Sandora tried to have me killed along with an associate. If Cem hadn't been nearby she would have succeeded. She's dangerous. She's not telling you the whole story.'

'No,' he said, vigorously shaking his head, 'I don't believe you. Gaea is freedom. Gaea is peace. Gaea is life. I've known Sandora my whole life and she serves Gaea. She's not like you. She's passionate and dedicated and, and, determined but she's not a killer, she's not ungodly or evil, she couldn't be.'

He almost sobbed the last few words. I needed to get back on track and remember our first priority, find a ship or find a way to call for help.

'I'm sure you believe that Leeton. Our spaceship crashed here yesterday. We weren't hurt in the crash but our ship was destroyed and as you can tell we don't belong here on Haven,' I said, 'we need to leave. We saw Sandora arrive in a spaceship with some of Doctor Jones' colleagues. Where would her ship be now? Are there any other ships near Stronghold that we could hire or purchase?'

He looked confused.

'There are no spaceships here on Haven. We have no need for them. Sandora doesn't use a spaceship any more, she wouldn't. Why would any of us leave here before the Emancipation?'

'You didn't see the large grey spaceship that arrived here yesterday afternoon?' asked Jones.

'I was asleep most of the day but even if I hadn't been working nights, I haven't seen a spaceship for so many years I can't remember the last time.'

Jones left the room and motioned me to follow her.

'Do you believe him?' she whispered.

'I do,' I whispered back. 'With my cuff I could be sure, as I'd get all sorts of biometric feedback to confirm his stress levels, but even without it I'm pretty good at spotting a deliberate lie. He definitely believes there are no spaceships here. That doesn't mean that there aren't though. For some reason Sandora doesn't want anyone to know she regularly leaves the planet.'

'But how could she land a spaceship in broad daylight without anyone noticing?'

That was a question I couldn't answer as to the best of my knowledge only The Organisation had effective stealth technology and Sandora's ship that had been hidden on Coronnol certainly didn't have any. I returned to see that Leeton was now rubbing his wrists and ankles and fidgeting more. One of the side effects of the low-level stun was to make your skin itchy for a while once it started to wear off.

'Leeton, for the people who aren't on nights what would they typically be doing in an afternoon?'

'Working. Everybody works. I work at the water purification plant. I'm the senior supervisor on the night shift. Some people work on the outlying farms, some grow crops in their gardens, some are builders, some make furniture and household goods. There are teachers, healers, all the usual jobs.'

'But is there anything they have in common, anything they all do?'

'No. Everyone is different. We're not like you, we're not slaves to Infosys. We're individuals, unique. Gaea gifts each of us with our own strengths and abilities.'

'I don't mean like that. Is there a group activity?'

'Like prayers?'

'How do you mean "like prayers"?'

'Daily prayers in the Congressarium. You really are ungodly aren't you?'

He seemed genuinely surprised, as if he'd never met anyone from outside his religion. Perhaps he hadn't. I doubted he'd ever been off world.

'Explain the daily prayers to us Leeton. Where and what is a Congressarium?'

'Every day between three o'clock and four we gather in the Congressarium for prayers, if we're working near enough to the city. If you're out in the fields or mines or working away from the city for some reason there's always a small building dedicated as a Congressional. We spend the hour in quiet contemplation, thanksgiving and prayer.'

'And where is this Congressarium?' asked Jones.

'In the centre of town. It's the largest building.'

'Thank you Leeton, you've been really helpful so far. I'm sorry I shot you, but I didn't know if you were dangerous or not until I'd had a chance to talk to you. One last thing. If we needed to get in touch with our families on our home planets, to let them know we were all right and had survived the crash how could we do that? Where is your main communication centre?'

He thought about this for a little while but once again the puzzled look returned to his face.

'I don't know anyone off world. I wouldn't have a clue how to contact someone.'

'How about someone in another city?' asked Jones.

'There's a radio relay in the proctor's office in the Congressarium. I have a friend that works there and she's seen it being used to talk to other proctors elsewhere on Haven.'

I adjusted the stunner in my hand to a much higher setting.

'Once again, thank you Leeton you've been very helpful. Unfortunately for you, as I'd really rather Sandora didn't know we were here, I am going to have to shoot you again.'

He looked terrified and Jones looked worried too.

'It will just put you to sleep for about a day. You'll wake up hungry and thirsty, and I'm afraid the itching and tingling will be worse, but it doesn't last long. You'll suffer no permanent effects.'

He started to protest and plead so I shot him. He slumped back, out cold. I arranged him into a comfortable position and checked his breathing. He was fine so I covered him with the duvet.

'We need to raid his clothing and find something that will allow us to blend in with the locals,' I said to Jones. 'We are going to look around the Congressarium.'

Chapter 30
Congressarium

The cupboard in the upstairs hallway had almost everything we needed to blend in. The cold climate necessitated lots of layers of cloth. There were long undergarments, baggy multi-layered trousers and then three or four layers on the torso. All in subtly different shades of tan and light brown. Over that most of the people we'd seen had worn a cloak or shawl which covered the head and keep the ears warm. We examined Leeton's outfit carefully to ensure we didn't get anything wrong. From our earlier observations we'd noticed that there didn't seem to be a difference in attire based on gender, which made things easier. The only insurmountable problem we had was footwear. Leeton had large feet and both Jones and I had similar sized small feet, so neither of us could wear anything he owned. We ensured the baggy trousers covered our shoes as much as possible and were glad we'd both worn sensible plain items that didn't immediately give the game away. I was usually a big fan of brightly coloured footwear and was glad I hadn't worn any on this trip as they didn't really fit in with the Pike alias.

'What time do you think it is?' asked Jones.

'I don't know. I should have asked Leeton how he knew as I've not seen anything displaying the time. Without Infosys or complex electronic devices how would you know the time accurately anyway? We don't even know how long the day is here.'

'We'll just have to guess. It's early morning now so if they go to the Congressarium for three o'clock we must have at least five hours before the place will be swamped. Perhaps we should wait until then and go when it's busy. It might be easier to slip in unnoticed in a crowd.'

'I thought about that,' I said, 'but there's also a much higher chance of us being spotted as strangers, especially as we'd have no clue what to do when we got in there. I think we'll go now and try and get a look around. If we take some of the gardening tools from Leeton's workshop we can at least look like we're going to or coming back from our place of work.'

We removed our cuffs and put them in our pockets, if we managed to get an Infosys connection somewhere then we'd need them. I took a few small items from our rucksacks and stashed them in amongst my clothing, while Jones hid the rucksacks at the back of the cupboard and covered them with Leeton's clothes. We left the house and started walking towards the centre of the city.

'Act confident. Don't hesitate. Look like you're doing exactly what you're supposed to be doing at all times,' I whispered to Jones.

'Understood.'

There were fewer people out and about in the streets as presumably almost everyone was now at work. There were still some people in their gardens tending the crops. I had no idea what any of them might be, but getting anything to grow in this cold, arid land was an achievement. We were relieved when nobody paid us any attention as we carried our garden tools along the scrubby paths between the buildings.

After about fifteen minutes we saw glimpses of what must have been the Congressarium between the buildings ahead of us. It had the look of all ceremonial buildings. Larger than really necessary, more ornate than the surrounding buildings and with that indefinable architectural air that suggested importance.

'That's got to be it,' Jones whispered.

'I don't see any other candidates,' I agreed.

We headed towards it, intending to circle it once to look for a back way in. It had no ground floor windows; they were all high up just below the roof. They were large and made of coloured glass in angular geometric patterns. As we passed the last building with a garden I looked round quickly to ensure we weren't being observed before dropping my tools over the hedge. Jones did the same and shot me a quizzical glance.

'The Congressarium has no garden, so why would two gardeners be going in there?'

She nodded and we continued to the building and began our circuit, checking surreptitiously for entrances, especially discreet ones. The front right-hand corner was closest to us, so we started there and worked our way around towards the back. I wanted to leave the extremely exposed front steps, that led up to the ornate carved doors, until the end.

The walls were virtually featureless smooth bricks at ground level, above that and all the way to the roof was smoothly plastered.

The bricks seemed to be the same type as all the other buildings but much more carefully prepared. Once the walls were out of reach of even the tallest person there were patterns and images in the plaster. There were highly stylised representations of family groups, animals and plants, there were representations of rivers, mountains and lakes, there was the sun, the stars, planets; and everything looked perfect and idyllic. There were no other doors. It seemed there was only one way in and out of the Congressarium.

We arrived back at the front steps. They went up to a height equivalent to a first floor, and I immediately strode up them. Jones hesitated just for a moment and then fell into step next to me. Someone was coming down the steps. They were dressed almost identically to us. As they passed us they nodded, so we both nodded back and continued to the door. I hoped there was no lock or passcode to gain entry.

The doors were wooden and they were huge. They must have been three metres tall and two metres wide each. The old wood had been stained jet black and had strange symbols carved into it. As we approached I realised they were letters, but not quite the same familiar shapes that we were used to, these were more angular. The language wasn't Inglis either. I guessed this was what Latin looked like when written down. Without my cuff I had absolutely no way to translate it. I pushed on the left-hand door and it opened easily on a smooth sprung mechanism that hissed back shut as soon I let go of it. We were inside.

It was quite dark and it took our eyes a few moments to adjust. The floor was tiled in a checkboard pattern of black and white and the walls were wood panelled. The space felt vast and echoey and seemed to demand that the visitor be quiet and respectful. The entrance foyer was the height of the doors and ten metres ahead of us there was a wide gap in the wood panelled wall that opened into a huge empty central chamber that was the height of the building. Shafts of coloured light came in through the windows that both illuminated it and gave it an air of mystery and wonder. There were no chairs, benches, tables or other furniture. At the far side of the space I could see a small very slightly raised platform with a carved wooden stand in the centre of it, like a lectern. A heavy looking curtain, embroidered with Latin phrases and religious symbols, hung at the back of the stage, covering the whole of the back wall. At the far left and right of the foyer I could see there were corridors that ran down the sides of the central hall. We had been standing still for far too long, no one familiar with the place would have spent as long staring but fortunately there didn't appear to be anyone about. I headed right, towards the far corridor. If there was going to be communication equipment anywhere it wasn't likely to be in the central hall. Our footsteps echoed and sounded deafening, but there was no point tiptoeing about. Confidence was always best, so we strode on as if we owned the place. The wood panelling continued all the way down the corridor, which stretched right to the back of the building. The only light came through slats in the top of the wooden panels separating the corridor from the main hall. I could make out regular sized doors every ten metres or so down the right-hand side so headed for the first one and opened it. It was pitch black inside and smelled rather musty. Feeling about in the dark soon confirmed it was simply a store cupboard, I wasn't sure what the smell was but it wasn't technology, and that was all that I was interested in.

'I'll search the rooms down here,' I whispered to Jones, 'you keep an eye out. If anyone comes we can either hide or front it out, depending on the situation.'

We headed down the corridor and tried each door but the rooms were purely for storage. One was full of folding chairs, another folding tables, another had floor to ceiling shelves, stacked with books. We got to the end of the corridor and there was nowhere to go but back the way we had come. I hurried to the front of the building and we crossed the entrance to the empty main hall and headed down the left-hand corridor. The first room was empty apart from a small comfortable looking chair, a full-length mirror and a small wardrobe. The wardrobe had robes, sashes and ribbons in it. There was a connecting door through to the next room along the corridor. This was a change. I crossed to the door and listened. I could hear voices talking but I couldn't make out what they were saying. I put my ear against the door and strained to hear. There were two different voices but I still couldn't make out anything.

Jones looked at me quizzically and I touched a finger to my lips with one hand and held up two fingers with the other then pointed at the door. She understood and kept quiet. We headed back out into the corridor and continued down it. I missed the next door out as that room had people in it then stopped at the next one and listened intently. I heard nothing. I opened it a crack and peered in. It was slightly brighter inside than the rooms on the other side as there was a light fitting on the wall, which was emitting a feeble but warm yellowish light. There was a large desk and chair. This was clearly the office of someone important. The desk had a small speaker unit build into it and a microphone on a stand. There didn't appear to be any controls, so they must be elsewhere. A partially open connecting door led to the room on the left, back to where I'd heard the two voices. I stepped back into the corridor letting the door close quietly then headed to the next one which was at the very end of the corridor. I listened again but couldn't hear anything. I opened it and looked in. It was dark but it sounded bigger than it ought to, a hollow echoing quality to the sound. I took a cautious pace in then another and then felt a step going down. There was a metal hand-rail on my left and the stairs curved round to the right and down. This must go back down to ground level under the great hall, but I wasn't going to go exploring in the dark down there without a light. So far as I could tell from our walk-around outside there was no way out of the ground floor, other than back up these steps and I didn't want to get trapped.

'What is it?' asked Jones in a whisper.

'Stairs leading down,' I whispered back, 'but I didn't bring a torch with me from the rucksacks. We'll have to come back later.'

Jones started rummaging through her layers of clothing looking for something.

'I did,' she said.

She triumphantly produced two small self-powered torches, that I'd put in the rucksacks when we had been leaving the scout ship.

'I noticed you didn't get them so I did. I thought we might need a light.'

She turned her torch on and we headed down the stairs.

The light was fairly feeble because we kept it on the lowest setting, as we didn't want to lose our night vision completely. The stairs went round one hundred and eighty degrees before we got to the bottom. It was dusty and completely plain under the hall, no fancy carvings, no wood panelling, no tiles on the floor. Clearly this space wasn't used by the public. There were tracks in the dust that revealed people did come down here from time to time. We were in quite a narrow corridor with rough brick walls that led to a central aisle running from the back of the building to the front.

'I don't like it down here. There's no way out that I can see and it would be disastrous to get trapped down here. We'll make this go quicker by splitting up, I'll do the left-hand side and you do the right,' I said. 'If you see anything that looks like a comm system or even anything remotely technological let me know.'

Jones nodded, handed me the second torch and we split up, moving quickly checking all the rooms.

About half way to the front of the building I'd found nothing of interest but Jones called me over to the door she'd just opened. I looked inside and there was an electronic device of some kind. It was huge. It was a large metal cabinet with a built-in desk sticking out of it. The cabinet had indicator lights, dials and switches on it and some sort of analogue gauges as well as a speaker grille. The desk portion had more switches and a large microphone sticking up out of the centre. It looked prehistoric but it must have been some kind of transmitter. I couldn't imagine how it worked. I presumed it was switched off as there were no lights on and it was silent. There were two thick cables running up through the ceiling, presumably going to the desk I'd seen upstairs.

'Do you know how to operate it? asked Jones.

'Not a clue,' I said. 'But maybe we can find someone who does and coerce them into operating it for us.'

We split up and continued down the corridor. The next door was locked and had a small hole cut into it, at roughly head height, with a wire mesh covering the hole. Shining the torch in didn't reveal anything or anyone inside. The next room was the same, then the next. They looked like basic prison cells. I was nearing the last door; Jones had already checked all of hers and found nothing worth calling me over for. I approached the last door, tried the handle and found it locked, like the others, so lifted the torch up to the grille. There was someone in the room, curled up on a thin mattress on the floor. They stirred when the light filled the room and rolled over to see who was at the door. I found myself looking into the haggard face of Doctor Julius Markus Grippe.

Chapter 31
A Lie

Jones must have seen the surprise on my face as she hurried over and looked in through the grille.

'Doctor Grippe! Oh my god. What's happened to you?' she asked.

'Doctor Jones? What on Coronnol are you doing on this frozen gulag?' he croaked. 'Have you seen that snake Gernard? Watch out for him if you do. He's not to be trusted. He tricked his way into my house then he... he beat me... and forced me, using graphic threats of further violence that I found completely convincing, to go with him in a spaceship that brought us here. He's mad, I think, completely mad.'

I looked at the lock and decided it would be fairly easy to pick with some basic tools. I just needed to find some.

'You need to get me out of here.'

I wasn't convinced that was a good idea as it was going to be hard enough for two of us to avoid detection, a third person who was also an escaped prisoner would be much trickier. I was happy to rescue Grippe, but perhaps not just yet.

'Doctor Grippe,' I said, as he shakily got to his feet and came over to the door, 'why did they kidnap you? Have they told you what they want?'

He had bruises on his face and a sizeable cut that was just healing. He was limping and seemed to be in pain.

'I...I'm not sure. It has something to do with the hyperspace wormhole technology, Gernard told me they needed my expertise and if I cooperated they'd return me to Coronnol.'

'No disrespect Doctor,' I said, 'but why would Gernard kidnap you instead of Doctor Jones?'

'Several years ago Gernard recommended a woman who could discreetly test the wormhole technology for me. She started out sending probes and then she moved onto sending small ships through a test wormhole. The data she collected has been invaluable. But I think he's really working for her, rather than the other way around.'

'You've been pushing ahead with the wormhole transportation system without telling me?' asked an outraged Jones.

'Yes! Of course I have,' snapped Grippe, showing just a little of his normal arrogant self. 'Your obsession with stellar engineering is ludicrous. What the people of this galaxy need is a better way to travel around it and I'm going to be the one to give it to them.'

He stopped for a moment and glanced around his cell.

'Well I thought I was,' he sighed. 'Until Gernard brought me here.'

'Who was the woman Gernard recommended Doctor Grippe?' I asked.

'Some woman called Sylvester. Sandora Willow Sylvester. I don't know how Gernard knew her but she seemed smart, capable and guaranteed absolute discretion. I only met her the once, a few years ago just before I hired her. She's expensive but her results were impressive. Obviously I couldn't use the university's usual procedures without alerting Doctor Jones that I was going ahead with the project against her wishes.'

I stole a quick glance at Doctor Jones, she looked livid.

'We will get you out Doctor Grippe,' I said. 'But at the moment I don't have any way to pick the lock, nor have we found a way off this planet. As soon as we do we will come back for you, but in the meantime you mustn't let Gernard or anyone else know you've seen us. It's vital they don't know we're here.'

He looked deflated but he nodded and returned to his mattress on the floor. He seemed old and frail and very little like the confident man I'd had breakfast with five days before.

We headed back to the staircase.

'Sandora really is up to her neck in this isn't she? We've got to get in touch with Kas or someone at The Organisation.'

'Perhaps one of the people upstairs will know how that transmitter works,' Jones said.

We turned our torches off and I pulled out my stunner as we climbed the stairs. I stopped at the door at the top to listen. I couldn't hear anything. I opened it and peered out. There was no one around. We made our way forwards to the next door and listened again. I still couldn't hear anything, so we went in. There was no one in the room and the connecting door on the left was now shut. I moved close to the door, and listened. This time I could hear voices, so I readied the stunner and yanked it open fast.

There were four people in the room, two I didn't recognize and two that I did. I fired the stunner at the pair I didn't know, in two rapid bursts. They slumped down, paralysed. The other two were Gernard and Sandora. Gernard leaped to his feet looking furious and dangerous, I fired as he rushed towards me. He fell headlong, sprawled on the floor next to me. I turned the stunner onto Sandora.

'Please don't move Sandora,' I said. 'I will stun you. No permanent harm will come to you but I believe it's quite an unpleasant sensation.'

She sat completely still, staring at me.

'I presume you know how to operate the transmitter downstairs? If that's capable of getting a message off world then you'll show me how to use it. If it isn't then you'll take me to one that does. You must have comms equipment as you have spaceships that you come and go in, while the faithful are in here for their daily prayers.'

'I see you're competent enough to have discovered my name. Congratulations, but unfortunately for you the radio transmitter downstairs is planetary only. It has a range of a few hundred kilometres, and that's all I'm afraid. For Gaea's sake we have no galactic comms here as that would require a connection to Infosys, something our belief in Gaea makes us fundamentally opposed to. Even if we did have such a device, I wouldn't tell you where it was nor how to use it, nor could I be forced to do so. In fact, I don't see how you could force me to do anything I don't want to. You're too civilised to be capable of any meaningful violence.'

'I got Gernard here to talk,' I said, prodding him with my foot. 'And he seemed to think he was pretty tough, tougher than you certainly.'

'Only by drugging him,' she laughed as she said it. 'He told me all about it. You could have used simpler more effective methods but you're squeamish, weak, civilised. I doubt you brought any of your drugs with you when you abandoned your ship and without those I will not cooperate with you.'

The way she said the word 'civilised' it sounded like the most appalling insult she could think of. She folded her arms across her chest and stared defiantly at me, praying quietly under her breath.

I turned to look at Jones, who had followed me into the room.

'I'm not squeamish,' she said. 'You're perverting something I designed to ensure life has the chance to survive millions, possibly billions, of years longer than the universe would normally allow into a weapon of unimaginable destructive power. I think I could do you some harm in order to prevent that.'

I looked back at Sandora and saw a momentary flash of doubt. I pointed the stunner at her.

'Perhaps you're right Sandora. Perhaps I couldn't force you. But I'm absolutely certain my moral compass would be fine with me doing nothing to stop Doctor Jones here from forcing you. You say you have no comms connected to Infosys, and I might believe you, but that means you must have a ship. Maybe not the one you arrived here on, but a ship, otherwise you're just as trapped here as we are. So let's all go to the ship.'

I indicated she should stand and move. She stood up and reluctantly headed for the door. Jones followed her and I brought up the rear.

I heard a noise behind me then moments later something hit the back of my head and the lights all went out.

When I eventually woke up, an unknown amount of time later, with a thundering headache I decided to keep very still and not to try open my eyes for while.

'You probably have a concussion, keep still,' said a familiar voice.

'I intend to,' I croaked back. 'Who hit me?'

'Gernard,' said the voice that I now recognized as Jones'.

I felt like a house had fallen on me. Something touched my lips, it was a bottle, with fresh water in it. I drank gratefully and felt a little better and decided to risk opening my eyes. The pain pinged around inside my head as I did, even my eyeballs hurt. I closed my eyes again and focused on not throwing up.

'I'm guessing you still had the stunner on the lowest setting? Perhaps because he's from Cestus it didn't affect him as much as it would me or you?'

That made sense, someone from a high-g world might well be more resilient to the lowest settings. I should have turned it up, or shot him again to make sure. I struggled up into a sitting position and cautiously opened one eye then the other. The pain was bad but manageable. I looked around, moving my head slowly and as little as possible.

'Where are we?' I asked.

'I'm not entirely sure,' she said. 'After he hit you he also hit me, although nowhere near as hard. I was only stunned and groggy.

Several people appeared and dragged us down the steps at the front of the Congressarium and put us into a cart pulled by those animals you mentioned. Marcus was in the cart already. We bounced around in the back for quite a long time and I'm afraid I passed out. I woke up when we got here, and was forced to help carry you inside. We're underground at some sort of mine or quarry.'

She described the cart arriving at an enormous hole in the ground, more than a kilometre in diameter, with a track carved into the side that went down the hundred metres or so to the bottom. Once there she was forced from the cart and she and Grippe had to help lift me out and carry me through a short tunnel to a modern elevator that went down even further. From there we were shown to this room and locked in, Grippe was taken elsewhere.

The room was small, clean, modern and brightly lit, with the same ambient lighting used on most of the worlds I'd visited. A solid metal door with an electronic lock ensured we wouldn't get out without access to my cuff. I patted my pockets and wasn't surprised to discover it was gone.

'They thoroughly searched us I'm afraid,' said Jones. 'They took our cuffs and all the handy gadgets you'd hidden in your clothing. They did leave us some water, plus some pills for you.'

She handed over the pills. They looked exactly like the kind of thing you'd want to take if you had a headache and probably concussion. I wasn't prepared to risk it though; they could also contain the same drugs I'd used on Gernard to get him talking.

'Could you tell how far from Stronghold we were?'

'It wasn't in sight before we came down into the mine but I don't know how long I was unconscious for. The sun was pretty high in the sky still, so we can't be more than a few hours from the city by cart.'

'There's clearly power here. If we still had our cuffs perhaps they'd work. They may not connect to Infosys, so yours wouldn't be much use, but mine has some autonomy built in. The technology here is clearly compatible with the galactic standard. They've brought all this in from off world to save building everything from scratch. That gives us an advantage, it's familiar, unlike back in Stronghold. Perhaps they're building the probes here, and that's why they want you and Grippe. They'd have been better off leaving me in the Congressarium.'

At that the door slid open into the wall and Sandora stood there.

'I did consider leaving you in the Congressarium's cells Per Pike, but I wanted to talk to you. And as I need to be here for the time being, you're here at my convenience. Please come with me.'

She pointed my own stunner at me. I didn't move. I needed to try to assert some control over this situation and not let her have all her own way. She waited for a moment, then adjusted the controls on the stunner and pointed it at Jones.

'Per Pike I'm not overly familiar with these devices but I believe the highest setting can cause permanent nerve damage if used repeatedly. I'm sure Doctor Jones would prefer you to do as you're asked rather than end up crippled and unable to continue with her work.'

I looked at Jones, she was trying to be defiant and brave but I could tell she was scared of being shot.

'Fine. I'll come with you,' I said.

I got to my feet, slightly unsteadily, and walked towards the door.

'You should have taken the pills Per Pike, they're just analgesic with an anti-concussion component. But I suppose they'll still be there for you when you get back.'

I briefly considered jumping her even though the chances of success were tiny, especially as when I got outside the cell I saw she had two burly young men with her, also armed with some kind of weapon. They were dressed in a mid-blue one-piece item with the word 'Protectorate' embroidered underneath some kind of official looking logo. She put the stunner away then set off down the corridor, the two men took up very close positions either side of me and put their weapons right into my ribs. One of them looked familiar, he must have been in the search party at the crash site.

We walked like this down several corridors until we reached a large office. It was sparingly furnished, but comfortable. There were two small sofas, facing each other with a low table in between. On the right there was a desk with an office chair. The desk had some kind of virtual screen above it, but the interface didn't look like Infosys. There were no decorative images on the walls or any personal items. The only decoration was a large three-dimensional image of the planet Earth above a pedestal that must have contained a projector cube. It was about two metres in diameter and the image resolution was superb

There was a window on the wall opposite the door looking out into a vast workshop one floor below us. There were dozens of benches, on each sat a pair of probes virtually identical to the ones I'd seen in the Astrophysics lab back on Coronnol. I could see Gernard and Grippe working at separate benches. Gernard was on his own but Grippe had a minder hovering nearby.

Sandora pointed to the sofa facing the window.

'Take a seat. Would you like anything to drink?'

'Just water please,' I said.

One of the guards, for surely that's what these uniformed protectorate officers were, positioned himself right behind me while the other fetched a glass of water from the chiller in the corner of the room. Sandora remained standing watching Grippe and Gernard work for a little while, then she sat facing me on the other sofa. She removed the stunner from her pocket and placed it on her lap, pointing it at me, then dismissed the two guards with a wave.

The sofas were carefully placed, with a low table in between them, so there was absolutely no chance I could cover the distance between us before she shot me. I had enough problems with my headache and concussion so didn't fancy adding paralysed nerve endings to the list.

'Let us pray before we talk,' she said, bowing her head and placing her hands palms up on her knees.

'You can do what you like but don't involve me in your ludicrous superstitions.'

There was a brief flash of anger on her face, but she controlled it.

'Great Gaea, originator of life, director of the righteous and judge of the ungodly lead us away from darkness and towards your light. Thwart ungodly schemes, grant repentance and contrition to those who deserve it and punish those who resist you. Grant mercy to your humble servants. Blessed be Gaea.'

She glanced at me, I genuinely thought she expected me to intone the 'blessed be Gaea' part along with her. I didn't. She scowled then got down to business.

'I'm so pleased we finally get to talk. We're all intrigued to know who you work for Per Pike. You're not Coronnol police, I doubt you are galactic navy, there's absolutely no chance you're simply a journalist nosing around for a story, as you pretended to be. So, who are you?'

I didn't reply.

She reached into her pocket and put my cuff down on the table between us.

'No-one is coming to rescue you. One of the first things we did when I took over was put a dampening field in place in orbit. It targets any ships with an active Infosys connection or live transponder beacon. It emits a field that blocks the Infosys connection and has the side effect of causing the ship's power cell to drain extremely rapidly. I don't understand the details but Gernard designed it and it's worked well so far. Your presence proves that much. We didn't want any accidental visitors reporting the existence of our planet to the authorities. You were singularly uncooperative when Gernard questioned you back on Coronnol, and all we wanted that time was to look at your cuff. This must be a new one. The original had an unfortunate encounter with one of your shoes, didn't it? Gernard thought there was a good chance you were simply a journalist then, but perhaps one who was cooperating with some kind of authority. I didn't think so and now I know that's not the case. No journalist could have tracked our ship through hyperspace without access to some extremely sophisticated and probably illegal technology. I presume you purposefully let Gernard escape from Jones' house, in order to follow him when he met up with me? Then you somehow followed me on the Mag to plant a tracker on my ship. All without anyone seeing you. That's very clever. I don't suppose you'd care to tell me how you did it? What tipped you off that Doctor Jones' research and Per Randolf's breakthrough was being used for other purposes?'

I still didn't reply, but I was impressed she'd worked that much out. I was going to have to be on my guard with her. She was very smart and very in control.

'Gernard thinks you are dangerous and wants to get rid of you, but he's rather paranoid and prone to a simplistic approach to problem solving. I agree that you are dangerous but I think you might also be useful. I looked you up. Cemeron Argalion Pike looks awfully like an alias to me, the life story was just a little too neat and tidy. No previous bondmates that can be questioned, not many close friends from childhood, no siblings. What do they call it in the novels and dramas, a legend, is that it? I'm still curious to know who created that for you and why. I could threaten Doctor Jones' life if that would help you answer my questions.'

I still didn't reply.

'Fine. As you probably guessed I need Doctor Jones, so I'm unwilling to hurt her unless I really have to. She may be more useful than you Per Pike. Is that an alias or is it your real name? Tell me, just what do you think we're actually doing here?'

I waited a while before deciding to answer.

'Pike is the only name I'm using currently, so we'll stick with that please. What do I think you're doing? I think you're a lunatic who's planning on blowing up dozens, if not hundreds of stars and possibly killing billions of people. I think there's a good chance you doing that will shatter the peace and the galaxy could descend back into the anarchy and tribalism that almost destroyed our civilization five thousand years ago. I think you're planning to use the hyperspace wormhole technology to attack the galactic navy. Finally, I suppose you hope you can seize control of a sizeable percentage of the remaining inhabited planets and rule a new empire all because of the fear of annihilation via supernova.'

She stared at me incredulously for while then started laughing.

'What an imagination Per Pike. May I call you Cemeron, or Cem?'

'You may not.'

'Ruling the galaxy never even occurred to me, and I certainly don't want to return to the bad old days of military empires, war and fear.'

'What then? What possible use is the ability to destroy stars to you?'

'To save the human race of course!'

It was my turn to laugh.

'Save it by killing billions? That's new, are you worried about over population? There are plenty of planets left to terraform. We're unlikely to run out of resources or land for quite some time yet.'

'I'm serious,' she said and she looked it. 'You're barely human Per Pike, Doctor Jones is barely human, sadly I'm barely human. I imagine the only real human you've ever met was poor Leeton Salvador Gains who woke up an hour or so ago and went straight to the Congressarium to warm them about you.'

'An hour ago?'

'Yes. You were unconscious for rather longer than Doctor Jones thought. The sun was still quite high in the sky, when she woke up on the cart, but it was high in the sky of the day after the one you supposed. We used a soporific gas on you as you travelled, the same one we used to snatch you on Coronnol. We surmised you'd be easier to transport if you weren't conscious. Anyway, back to the matter in hand. Saving the human race.'

Sandora was calm, measured, serious. She sounded like she was conducting a lecture at a university.

'Humans have thrived for millennia, despite our primal instincts for violence, greed and destruction. Gradually we grew more civilised we left such things behind. Eventually we even left our original home and spread out throughout the galaxy. We learned to cooperate, to value others and to work towards a common goal. We settled new planets and we prospered.'

'Do you do anything besides state the obvious?' I interrupted.

She ignored me.

'That went well for thousands of years, but gradually the petty squabbles and tribalism that had so blighted our primitive past on Earth was repeated, but on a much grander scale across the inhabited galaxy. Empires were forged, kings anointed, presidents elected, territory was claimed and fought over until we'd exhausted our resources and were in danger of destroying ourselves.'

'You do know this is the elementary school version of our history? You're not saying anything profound, new or interesting,' I said.

She ignored me again, but there was a slight flash of irritation on her face.

'The cooperation and mutual respect that allowed us to expand from Earth was only possible because of Gaea. It was the faithful, righteous followers of Gaea that made the difference amongst the mass of humanity pouring out into the galaxy. But as the technology advanced and the terraforming became easier so came a decline in spirituality. We forgot our dependence on Gaea. We forgot even the name Gaea. Science and reason, technology and individualism became our gods. Then Infosys was created. A simple, easy, instant way to communicate over the vast distances between worlds. Suddenly you didn't need to send an ambassador to negotiate a treaty and maybe not hear back from them for days or even weeks. Messages didn't need to be couriered from world to world. As soon as every world had an Infosys link barriers started to come down. Cooperation became possible again. Inglis gradually became the language of the galaxy. Sharing resources was suddenly easy. Your planet has an excess of lithium, but you're running short of manganese? Simple! You connect with someone via Infosys who has the opposite problem and you share. Infosys got smarter, got more automated, the databases grew and grew and worked their way into everybody's lives. Soon human beings weren't even aware of the decisions being made about their planetary resources, it was all done by Infosys without any people being involved.'

'Sandora, that's a really simplistic view of history and I still don't see the problem you say we all need saving from.'

'I'm getting to it. I need you to think of the back-story, how we got to where we are. We didn't just become reliant on Infosys, we became addicted to it. It was perfect. It was inerrant. It's not just at the planetary scale we've abandoned our responsibilities and given control to Infosys, if personal too. If you need to know something then you check Infosys. If you aren't sure what to do next, you ask Infosys for suggestions. Infosys plans your journeys for you. Infosys automates your menial chores. Infosys restocks your fridge and your larder for you. Infosys arranges for your house to be cleaned, your lawn to be mowed, your laundry to be done. Infosys provides your news and your entertainment. Infosys monitors your health and diet. Infosys guides the doctors as they prescribe and investigate, the surgeons as they operate. Infosys finds you your bondmate. Infosys helps you chose a career. Infosys runs your life. All through the cuff on your wrist. They're well named those cuffs. Think of them as handcuffs, shackling us humans to our electronic overlord.'

She paused and looked at me for a sarcastic comment. I didn't have one.

'This is all as it should be, you may say, and has made everybody's lives easier. But it's also made us soft, dependent, lacking initiative and self-reliance. Other than a few psychological outliers such as yourself, the majority of the galactic population is sleepwalking through its existence. Even that, I might, just might, have been able to tolerate. We could, at least, choose to take the cuff off and go hiking, swimming, mountaineering, make love, stare at a sunset, write poetry, paint, whatever we felt like doing away from the monitored, measured and logged existence. Then I heard about the work being done on my own home planet, Scarlastion, to link the human brain to Infosys. That was the last straw. Our humanity was already under threat from the amount of technological dependence encroaching on our lives, but actually linking our minds to Infosys? Absolutely not. No.'

She stood up and started pacing up and down, holding the stunner in her hand, waving it about as she talked.

'The mind is what makes us individual. No one, no matter how close to us can ever really penetrate that fortress. They can only know us to the extent we're willing to share. Our thoughts are our own. Our desires are our own. Our creativity and intellect are our own. Once that final barrier is breached, we are no longer truly human. We're a partner in a symbiotic organism, and when the other party is a galaxy-spanning information system we are most certainly the junior partner. How could you ever trust your own thoughts? How could you tell where you ended and Infosys began?' she paused, reconsidered for a moment then continued. 'That would be a moot point. There wouldn't be a you and an Infosys as separate entities. You'd just be an organic terminal connected to a galactic computer system. It is the ultimate heresy, the ultimate blasphemy.'

She turned and looked right into my eyes. Hers were blazing with passion.

'And I won't allow it. I won't. Humans are worth more than that. The great messy, unpredictable, imperfect, wild, creative, feeling, loving, caring, angry, stupid lot of them are worth more than ending up as little more than bees in a hive.'

I sat still. Momentarily stunned by her rant and unable to marshal any coherent thoughts to refute her conclusions.

'I agree,' I finally said

.

Chapter 32
The Truth

'Liar,' she said.

'Not at all. I agree a direct brain to Infosys link is a very dangerous development. However, your objection to this particular advancement in technology doesn't explain why you want to blow up stars, does it?'

She rested a hand on the top of the Earth and only then did I realise it wasn't an image but a scale model. It was beautiful. A perfect glass sphere with superbly modelled continents, in three dimensions, and clever lighting effects on the inside that made the oceans appear to move and ripple. Sandora sat back down and repositioned the stunner on her lap, but still kept one hand on it.

'I'm getting to that. I grew up on Scarlastion in an academic family. My father was an anthropologist and my mother an ethnobotanist[1]. They both had a great deal of sympathy for the Primitive's movement. They tried to live simple lives themselves and we used to spend our holidays in Primitive communities. The religious aspect of it all looked unbelievable to us at first. There seemed little chance that there was a supernatural being in charge of the destiny of the whole galaxy, but you couldn't deny the fact that the Primitives believed it wholeheartedly and it gave them tremendous inner strength. Everyone else we knew at the University considered us eccentric but harmless. There's quite a variation amongst the Primitive communities, the fundamentalists won't use any technology that requires a power cell, the more liberal ones will use most current technology so long as it's not linked to Infosys. I met my future bondmate on my eighteenth birthday while we were holidaying on New France at a fundamentalist Primitive commune. Sacha was the son of one of the leading families. His mothers were both devout followers of Gaea and if we were to bond then I would have to convert. It seemed a small step really, at first. We had so

---

[1] An ethnobotanist studies how people of a particular culture and region make use of indigenous plants.

much in common already, what difference would it make to formally join them? But the more I studied their teaching and read their sacred texts the more I did come to believe.'

I took a sip of water as she continued.

'Life was hard in the fundamentalist communities. They had almost no technology, not even medical items. Death and disease were a part of everyone's experience. You lived life to the full because you knew it could be shortened if you got ill. No one welcomed an early death but they believed death isn't really the end. After our mortal body perishes there's rebirth in the hereafter. My bondmate and I returned to Scarlastion as I wanted to continue my medical training, he wasn't particularly happy about it but he was willing to indulge me. I was still trying to reconcile my love of medicine and healing people with my distrust of Infosys and related technology. Sacha remained unhappy until we had our children. He adored them and devoted himself to raising them and teaching them.'

'Are you still together?' I asked.

A black cloud appeared to cross her face. An old deep pain suddenly brought front and centre. Her hand twitched on the stunner controls and for a moment I thought she was going to shoot me.

'He died. He died along with my daughter Corinne,' she answered. 'There was an accident on the way to visit his mothers. He took Corinne, as she didn't get to see her grandmothers very often. Their shuttle had a defective grav unit and instead of entering the landing spiral, after detaching from the starship, it plunged straight down and crashed on the outskirts of their village.'

She stood up, got herself a drink of water and returned to the sofa.

'I'm so sorry to hear that,' I said and I meant it. 'I can't imagine the pain of losing them. It must have been unbearable.'

'Thank you. It was a long time ago now. I try not to think about it. Where was I? My other daughter and I moved here to Haven, a fairly moderate Primitive colony at the time. I never completed my medical training but I had learned enough to make myself useful. I kept in close touch with my father and mother and returned to Scarlastion as often as I could to see them. When my father died my mother stopped having anything to do with the Primitives and buried herself in her work. She never once visited me here.'

'Why are you telling me all of this?' I asked.

'I want you to understand. I'm not a monster. I'm not evil or deranged. I'm a human being. Like you. I just happen to have a clear understanding of the danger humanity is in, and I think I might be the only person willing to do what is necessary to save it.'

'So why the supernovas. What is that about?'

'You've heard of serendipity I presume?'

I nodded.

'On one of my last visits home, just before my mother died, an old colleague of hers had told her about a young post-graduate student working on research linking Infosys to the human brain. I was horrified. I spent months trying to work out how to stop this research from being pursued. Fortunately, it was in its early stages of development and his small team were having problems getting it to work reliably or even at all. I initially considered simply assassinating the researchers, but the problem with ideas is that they don't die with people. The research was on Infosys so even if I killed them, other teams maybe at other universities would access it and could continue it. I couldn't kill them all. Also killing people isn't as easy as all that, even when you're motivated by a noble ideal such as the survival of our species. I knew I couldn't personally do it, I'm not particularly strong nor adept at combat. I hoped the research would never amount to anything but made sure I kept an eye on it. That meant visiting Scarlastion regularly. Haven was gradually becoming less and less tolerant of off-worlders and we fundamentalists were gaining the upper hand in the Congressarium. That's why I have to time my visits off the planet and back with the daily prayer time. And then serendipity played its part. Just as I found out that their research was finally, after decades, starting to show some serious promise one of my counterparts in the Congressarium on Coronnol introduced me to a long-time secret member of the community there, a certain Doctor Gernard. His department head had asked him to join a project that would finally allow the colonization of another galaxy. Our path was suddenly so clear. I knew it had to be inspiration directly from Gaea. We would gather as many people as possible who shared our beliefs here on Haven and we would prepare ships to transport us away from the corruption and contamination in this galaxy. We would settle in a new one. One where we could live a simple life, use minimal technology and practice our beliefs as we see fit. Almost all the Proctors here and in the other fundamentalist Primitive communities agreed.'

She paused. I suspected the key point, the whole reason for my being here was about to be revealed. I wanted to scream 'GET ON WITH IT' at her but didn't dare. I took another sip of water. She did the same. Then she took a deep breath and continued.

'But I alone knew that wasn't enough. We had to leave, that much was certain. Our attempts to influence wider society by sending missionaries out had failed utterly. Our way of life was gradually being eroded away and it was becoming harder and harder to stay pure and uncontaminated by your civilisation. But I knew once the Infosys neural link was widespread and more and more people were swapping their cuffs for it then it wouldn't be long before this new lifeform, and don't have any doubt that it would be a completely new lifeform, would see our existence as a threat and we would be hunted down and wiped out. I estimated it would take a maximum of twenty years before the cuff users were a tiny minority and the default would be the neural link. This new decentralised galaxy spanning cybernetic organism would not tolerate the existence of us old fashioned humans, even if we were in a different galaxy. We wouldn't stand a chance against the sheer force of numbers it could deploy against us. Humanity, true individual humanity, would be extinct and all that would be left would be a soulless husk. That's when Doctor Jones' interesting use for the new hyperspace calculations developed by Per Randolf was brought to my attention, once again by Doctor Gernard. We will use the modified stellar probes to eradicate Scarlastion and every other major centre for research in this galaxy. We will destroy so many worlds that Infosys will crumble no matter how decentralised it is. The radiation from thousands of new supernovas will prevent the hyperspace communication, that Infosys relies on, from working. The humans that are left will have no choice but to adopt aspects of the Primitive life. We don't care if they don't follow our religious teachings. So long as they're no longer stultified by their addiction to Infosys that will be enough for us.'

'You are insane,' I said quietly. 'Absolutely insane.'

She shrugged.

'No,' she said slowly, 'no I'm not. But it's a new concept for you. It'll take you time to see that it's the only way. I didn't get to this position overnight, believe me, I looked for other ways for years. But Gaea assured me that it's the only solution. The existence of the human race itself is at stake.'

She sounded completely reasonable. As if discussing the pros and cons of moving house, not virtual genocide.

'Have you tried anything else? Did you talk to anyone at the university on Scarlastion? Did you notify the galactic council of your fears? Did you consider even for a moment that killing billions of people, innocent, carefree, normal people might not be the first, best course of action? How do you even know that you're right about the results of the neural link?'

She sighed then got up again. She moved to the small desk near the window and retrieved a projector cube, like the one I'd seen in her cabin on the space ship.

'As I said, I looked for other ways for years, I have done my due diligence,' she said and tossed me the cube.

I turned it on and placed it on the table between the two sofas. Sandora stayed where she was and looked out of the window at the workshop below.

The cube lit up and above it a largish projection appeared. There was the usual white fuzzy line marking the border of the image with the real world. It was hand held camera footage of what looked like a room in a hospital. There were medical monitors above a bed, which had rails to stop the patient rolling out, and padded restraints. The rails on one side were down and someone was sitting on the edge of the bed. It was a man of about forty years old. His close-cropped greying hair revealed a healed scar behind his left ear. The camera moved around until it was facing him directly. He had a vacant expression, was drooling slightly and didn't react to the presence of the camera operator. Someone spoke to him, probably the person holding the camera.

'Doctor Karshon? How are you feeling today?'

The man looked at the camera and the vacant expression cleared a little and he licked his lips, then smiled slightly.

'Hello Gerry,' he said, 'how long have you been here?

'I'm always here Doctor Karshon. How are you feeling?'

'I'm fine. A little busy, you know. Always things to do. There's no rest for the wicked, eh?'

'How's the pain today?'

The man called Karshon winced and a hand went up to the scar behind his ear. Then the vacant expression reasserted itself.

'Doctor Karshon?' said Gerry. 'Doctor Karshon, how are you feeling?'

His focus returned again.

'Gerry, my boy! How long have you been here? So sorry to have kept you waiting. It's been one of those…one of those…things…you know. Erm. Busy, busy, busy. You know how it is.'

The vacant expression returned and the camera moved away then the projection vanished.

'That was Doctor Runcible Artura Karshon,' said Sandora, 'the man who first proposed the direct neural link to Infosys. As you can see, he had the courage of his convictions and was the first to actually try it.'

'What happened to him?' I asked.

'As far as we can find out, and Scarlastion is very secretive about this project - that footage was smuggled out, he was fine for a few months. Perhaps as long as a year. He said he enjoyed a greater focus on his work, his productivity increased and he required less sleep. Then he stopped responding to his surroundings for short periods of time. He claimed to be lost in thought at first and everyone believed him, but over the next five years the absences got longer and the productivity tailed off until he was incapable of leading the team, then incapable of looking after himself. He's been hospitalised now for over ten years.'

'Why don't they remove the link?'

'They can't. It's an organic component. Anything plastic or metal would have been rejected by the body or prone to infection. They developed an organic interface and implanted it. That scar is the exploratory surgery when they looked into removing it and failed. It's now just part of his brain.'

'Well, what have you got to worry about? Surely you just make that public and no one in their right mind would get the interface implanted.'

'They've improved since then. Watch the next clip.'

I touched the cube again and another projection appeared above it. This time it was a large lab. There were three identical musical instruments in one corner, keyboards of some sort, plus three painting easels, and a large whiteboard. Three people walked over to the keyboards and one started playing a complex two-handed piece, then the second joined in playing harmonies on the second keyboard, finally the third joined in playing a different but complimentary tune on the remaining keyboard. It lasted a couple of minutes then all three finished with a flourish together. They then moved on to the easels and started sketching at the same time. One canvas each. One started at the top, one in the middle and one at the bottom. They sketched at speed using some kind of pastel pencils. They were clearly drawing the same picture but starting from different points. It was a countryside scene and all three were virtually identical when finished. Finally, they moved over to the whiteboard. The first person picked up a black marker and wrote a complex mathematical equation at the top. The second person then moved in, took the marker, and started to write a proof underneath it. Part of the way through the third person took over and then finally the first person finished it off, each handing over to the other seamlessly. The three people turned towards the camera, acknowledging it for the first time, then bowed as if it were the end of a play, then they burst out laughing and hugged each other.

'That was smuggled out just over a year ago,' said Sandora. 'Those three are volunteers. One is a musician, one is an artist and the third, as if you couldn't guess, is a mathematician. Neither the artist nor the mathematician could play an instrument before they got their implants, the musician and the mathematician couldn't paint or draw and the musician and the artist knew nothing of mathematics beyond simple mental arithmetic. They had only been linked for one week when this was recorded.'

'Impressive,' I said.

'Terrifying would be a better description. The musician said his playing had improved immeasurably since getting linked, the other two noted similar improvements in their own fields. This technology is creating a new species, one that will look at us in the same way we look at ants. Those three are abominations in Gaea's eyes. They've abandoned their sacred human souls to become little more than limbs for Infosys.'

'It's a lot to think about, Sandora.'

'It is. As you can see it's nothing like the information being made public by Scarlastion. That article you wrote was almost word-for-word the same as the information they're feeding the public. The press releases just say it's like having a cuff you control with your thoughts, saving you from manipulating it by hand. The reality is that it's full integration of your consciousness.'

She paused and closed her eyes for a moment. Rubbed them and then looked me in the eye, as if silently pleading with me to agree with her conclusions and not to oppose her.

'I need to rest. This has been tiring. I don't think I've talked for so long in years. I want you and Doctor Jones to understand. I want you to realise I have to do this. You could both be valuable assets in the struggle. The protectors will take you back to your room now.'

The door opened and the two men from before came in, drew their weapons and escorted me from the room. I looked back to see Sandora lie down on one of the sofas and close her eyes. We walked back down the corridors to the locked room and Doctor Jones.

She was sitting on the floor leaning against the wall, she looked up and appeared to have been asleep.

'You've been gone a long time,' she said.

'Yes, Sandora had a lot to tell me.'

I crossed the room, sat as close to her as I could and whispered in her ear.

'The room is bugged and they can hear everything we say.'

She nodded. I reached into my sleeve and pulled out the projector cube.

'I have some things to show you,' I said.

I activated the cube, expanded the image to be as large as it would go, turned the volume all the way up and set it to loop through the two clips.

Jones watched it through, at first horrified then fascinated. When it started to play again I moved closer to her.

'The sound from the cube should mask our conversation if we keep quiet.'

I gave her a brief run through of what Sandora had told me.

'She's telling the truth about the danger this research poses. It does have to be stopped. It's more important than ever that I communicate with my organization. But she lied too. We weren't unconscious for more than a day. She wants us to think that Stronghold is further away than it is. There's no way my headache would have been as bad if I'd been asleep for a whole day, plus we weren't hungry enough. I think you need to volunteer to help Gernard and Grippe complete the probes. I'm not sure why Grippe is helping them when he was so adamant that he wouldn't. He must be doing it under duress as they've got a minder with him. Perhaps you can sabotage them in some subtle way? I don't know how they work.'

'It would be very difficult to sabotage them in an undetectable way. I'll see what I can do, assuming they believe I want to help.'

'The best way to lie is to tell the truth about something similar. So convince her you find this Infosys neural link horrifying and you want to stop it. That is true so it'll ring true.'

I moved away from Jones slightly then stopped the playback.

'Somehow we have to get to Scarlastion and stop these people,' I said.

'Perhaps. I need time to think. Maybe Sandora has a point. Maybe we ought not dismiss her solution out of hand.'

'You're not serious?' I asked.

'I don't know. The consequences for humanity if they go ahead would be catastrophic. Perhaps extreme measures are called for? I need to think it though. Please, just leave me alone to process it all.'

She got up and moved over to the other side of the room and sat facing the door, ignoring me completely.

My head was throbbing again, but I still wasn't convinced the pills I'd been left could be trusted. I stood up and faced the door.

'I know you can hear me out there. You can't expect us to be sympathetic to your cause if you don't look after us. We need some bed rolls in here, access to a washroom, and a meal.'

There was a pause then a click from the wall behind me. A section of wall had opened slightly, it was a door into a washroom with a shower, toilet and a shelf full of towels and changes of clothing.

'You could have given us access to that earlier,' I said for the benefit of those listening. 'Do you want to go first Mal?'

She nodded and went in pulling the door shut behind her.

After a few minutes the door out into the corridor slid open. One of the guards from earlier stood there with a weapon in his hand. He waved me away from the door, then his companion came in with a bed roll under each arm and placed them on the floor. He left and reappeared with a large tray full of food, which he placed on the floor too. He held his hand out and I pretended to not know what he wanted. The guard with the weapon raised it a little and aimed it at my head. I handed over the projector cube I'd taken. They left and the door closed again. I unrolled the bed rolls and watched them self-inflate to comfortable looking single mattresses. There was a thick single sheet on each which looked warm enough. They weren't planning on subjecting us to any hardship, if we behaved ourselves, it seemed. The food smelled pretty good. There was a large bowl of some kind of stew with chopped vegetables floating in it, dark dense bread and two large glasses that had a decent red wine in. I knocked on the washroom wall and told Jones that food had arrived.

While she finished up, I served the stew into the two bowls provided and broke the bread into manageable chunks. For obvious reasons they hadn't provided a knife, just a couple of blunt wooden spoons to eat with. I doubted even I could get up to much mischief with one of them as my sole weapon.

The washroom door opened and Jones appeared looking more like her usual self, she had showered and changed into clean clothes.

We ate but didn't really talk much, we were both far too aware that we were being listened to, and possibly also watched.

Once we'd finished eating I went into the washroom and had a long hot shower. While the water was running I searched the washroom as carefully as I could for a camera and couldn't find one. I dried myself and put some clean clothes on. As I pulled my shoes on I slipped open the very well-hidden compartments in the heels and extracted a small device from each one. I was glad these people were amateurs. Anyone who knew what they were doing would have had us stripped naked and scanned to ensure we had nothing hidden internally, then given us new clothes and shoes, or possibly just left us naked. Some planets had nudity taboos but my home planet didn't. I was comfortable naked, but clothing did make hiding things easier and with Haven's climate it would keep you alive longer. I slipped the devices into my pocket and left the washroom.

'I wonder what time it is,' said Jones.

'I've no idea but I'm pretty tired. I'm going to sleep if that's okay with you? Assuming our hosts turn the lights off at some point.'

'That's fine. I'm ready to sleep,' she said.

I put the bowls and spoons back on the tray and put the tray by the door, then lay down on my mattress, pulled the sheet over me and fell asleep within minutes. I awoke briefly when the lights suddenly went out.

'Thank you,' I said.

I could hear Jones' breathing, but it wasn't particularly even or slow so I didn't think she was asleep.

Under the sheet I carefully extracted the two devices I'd got from my heels and clipped them together before returning the now single item to my pocket. The next time someone opened the door this simple scanner-repeater would record the command used to open the door and allow me to replay it any time. There were one or two other things it could do, but nothing terribly clever. Even in a tough pair of walking boots there wasn't a great deal of room in the heels to conceal things.

Chapter 33
Tank

I went back to sleep pretty quickly but slept fitfully. I had a few bad dreams about ending up like Doctor Karshon, lucid for a few minutes at a time before my mind wandered off to some synthetic attraction. I'm surprised I didn't wake Jones up. I was eventually forced awake by the light coming on and the door opening. The same guard was there with his weapon and the same companion took the dinner tray and dropped off a breakfast one.

'Be ready to leave in twenty minutes,' he said.

'Cheery fellow isn't he?' said Jones sleepily, as she rolled over to look my way.

'The life and soul,' I replied.

We ate quickly and used the washroom. While it was my turn in there I separated the small device, that hopefully had done its job, back into its two halves and returned them to their hiding places. Just in case.

The door opened and our humourless guards escorted Jones and me out of the room. We were separated at the end of the first corridor. Jones was taken down a flight of stairs, I presumed to the workshop, I was led back to Sandora's office.

She wasn't there when I arrived, so the guard and I just stood waiting. I saw Grippe and Gernard arguing down on the workshop floor. Grippe looked furious and was waving his arms about excitedly. Gernard just stood watching then he slapped Grippe, hard, across the face. Grippe reeled backwards from the blow, then he backed down and moved towards the first bench on his side of the room.

I saw Jones enter from directly below the office window. Gernard approached her and indicated the probes she was to work on. He handed her a ring bound pad opened to a particular page and pointed to a line. She shook her head but took it, approached the probes Gernard had pointed to, then leaned on the bench and folded her arms across her chest.

Gernard watched for a moment then walked over to her. He said something and she shook her head. I hoped she remembered she was meant to go along with him, and was only supposed to play hard to get. Gernard pulled his hand back and made to slap Jones but she easily dodged his swing and, while he was off balance, she pushed him over. He seemed about to attack her when Sandora entered through some double doors at the far end of the room. While they were open, I caught a glimpse of a long tunnel carved out of the bare rock on the other side. She shouted at Gernard who relaxed and reluctantly went back to his own workbench, shooting angry glances at Jones. Sandora spoke calmly to Jones then looked up and saw me watching. She nodded slightly then turned to leave. Jones turned back to the workbench, picked up a couple of small electronic tools and proceeded to work on the first pair of probes.

A few minutes later Sandora entered her office, invited me to sit on the same sofa as yesterday then she took out my stunner and dismissed the guard.

'Why are Doctor Grippe and now Doctor Jones helping you?' I asked.

'Enlightened self-interest I suppose you could call it,' she said. 'Doctor Grippe was adamant that he wouldn't help us. I pointed out that if he refused I would ensure Cestus was one of the first systems destroyed, but that his uncomplaining cooperation could earn it a reprieve.'

'Is that true?'

'The first part is certainly true. I only had one working pair of probes, but to get his cooperation I was happy to threaten his home system. Gernard understands most of the technology involved but Doctor Grippe designed these devices with Doctor Jones, together they will speed up the programming no end as they have a full understanding of the mathematics.'

'And Doctor Jones?'

'Similar reasons. I told her if she didn't help then firstly I would kill you, and then as well as destroying the Coronnol system I would also destroy Mirth. Coronnol is going to be destroyed, no matter what, as that university is far too likely to jump on board with the Scarlastion neural interface. Mirth is full of artists, poets and philosophers so they're going to be customers not developers of the interface, but Jones has sentimental attachments there.'

'I don't understand why you need them at all,' I pointed out the window, 'you have hundreds made already.'

'Thousands.'

'Thousands?'

'Thousands. To cripple Infosys I need to wipe out a significant percentage of the universities that provide the computational infrastructure and also contaminate the space-hyperspace boundary with radiation. Making the probes is fairly straightforward. We had the components manufactured by legitimate suppliers and then shipped to our facility on Coronnol for assembly. I needed Gernard to not only acquire the designs but also to test the ones we'd made, to ensure they've been assembled correctly, and to program them for each pair of stars we've selected as donor and recipient.'

'The winery!' I said. 'That's why you were at the winery.'

'Yes. The bottling plant machinery was replaced with a device Gernard built to assemble the probes from the constituent parts. We then brought them here in the ship that you somehow followed. What I didn't fully appreciate was that each pair of probes must be custom programmed for each pair of stars. The donor and the target.'

'How many have you programmed?'

'Not enough. Each pair of probes needs complex programming using Per Randolf's formulas or the portal isn't stable in the hostile environment at the core of a star. Gernard can get through ten to fifteen in a day if the probes are assembled correctly, but if they're not then things slow down somewhat. He either repairs the pair or rejects them as unusable. That's why we wanted Doctor Grippe on board. We were well into our plans to recruit him, or abduct him, when you showed up snooping around. I thought given time, and the promise of a prestigious position in the new colony, Grippe would have joined us voluntarily, but so far he's been rather resistant. It's all stick and no carrot with him. Doctor Jones on the other hand may surprise us both, it seems I was a little hasty in agreeing to Gernard's plan to leave her and Randolf in their spaceship to be vapourised when Omega went nova.'

'She'll never agree to your plans.'

'We shall see. Like most scientists she's incredibly pragmatic. Anyway, I've been civilized enough. I'm afraid it's time for you to tell me who you really work for and on what planet they are based. There will be no reprieve for them and I know you wouldn't believe me even if I told you there would be. Your choice is simple, tell me now voluntarily or tell me after you've been inside another of those rather unpleasant metal tanks that you encountered on Coronnol.'

I said nothing.

'As you wish. I don't like using the tank, but we've occasionally had to use it when disciplining some of the more recalcitrant citizens. They all saw sense sooner or later, as will you. Santis, who searched the crash site for you and utterly failed to find you, has been reminded of his responsibilities by spending some time inside, but I think it's time he vacated the tank for you.'

A guard appeared, I still hadn't worked out how she was summoning them, and escorted me from the room with his weapon jabbed into my ribcage. I wondered if I should try and escape from him but I decided the time wasn't yet right. It soon became a moot point as another guard joined him, together they took me along an unfamiliar corridor to a room containing an identical metal cube to the one I'd spent time in before.

The guards stopped me at the steps.

'Take off your shoes,' said one of them.

I sat on the edge of the steps and removed my shoes and put them neatly at the side of the steps, hoping that I'd get them back later.

'Take off your clothes,' said the same guard.

I stripped completely. I didn't bother trying to keep my underwear on, I knew I'd just be ordered to remove that too. I folded everything neatly and put it all next to the shoes. One of the guards opened the door and a painfully thin naked man gradually uncurled himself and walked unsteadily down the steps. He briefly glanced and me with haggard sunken eyes before falling to the floor.

'In!' said the guard.

I climbed the steps and went inside. The door swung shut and I heard it lock. I found a spot in the corner of the cube, sat down with my head low and my knees pulled up to my chest, clamped my hands over my ears and closed my eyes. I was as ready as I could be.

The noise and light started without warning. It was earth shatteringly loud and so bright I feared it would burn my eyelids off. It was impossible to think clearly, all I could do was hold on to my sanity. I was shivering with cold when after what felt like about an hour it went dark and quiet.

'Who do you work for?' asked Sandora's voice.

I didn't answer.

'What star system are they in?'

I didn't answer but I got up and moved about briskly, stamping my feet and rubbing myself to try and generate a bit of warmth.

The darkness exploded with light and sound so I returned to the corner and curled up as much as I could to block it out.

My head was throbbing. I wasn't fully recovered from Gernard's monumental blow and this was making things considerably worse. The minutes trickled by, slowly turning into hours. At random intervals the noise and light would stop and Sandora's calm voice would ask the same questions. I kept silent and after a pause the torture would resume. I'd always considered I was pretty resilient but wasn't sure how long I could last. I eventually lost all track of time and just hung on grimly. I must have passed out because the next thing I knew the door was open and one of the guards from before was shouting at me to get out. I wobbled and nearly fell as I came down the steps, he instinctively held a hand out to help but I didn't take it. There was no sign of Santis. At the bottom I struggled to pull my clothes back on as I was shivering so much so I just stuffed my feet back into my shoes without fastening them. I was led back to the room I'd been in with Doctor Jones and shoved inside. Jones was already there lying on her bedroll staring at the ceiling, lost in thought. As soon as she saw me she leapt to her feet and came to help me. She put an arm around me and helped me to my bedroll. I sank back onto it and thanked her.

'What have they done to you?' she asked, looking fairly horrified.

I suppose I must have looked pretty awful.

'Oh, just the usual. Stripped naked, locked in a tank and subjected to sensory torture,' I said and tried to laugh.

Jones left me for a moment then came back with a water bottle and helped me drink some.

'Enough of my day, how are you?' I asked.

She smiled, relieved I was able to make a joke, even one as feeble as that.

'A hard day's work. I don't really want to talk about it. It's easier if I don't think about why I'm doing this, just that it needs to be done.'

I pulled away and glared at her.

'You're not falling for Sandora's crazy bullshit, are you?'

'No. Not necessarily. Not completely. She does make a compelling argument and I agree with her aim of stopping the Scarlastion neural interface. As far as I can see she's the only one doing anything about it. I'll help her only so much, and will try to influence her plans to minimize the harm.'

'Oh right. If she kills a few hundred billion people that's okay but a few thousand billion and she's crossed a line?'

'I don't want anyone to die, but the important thing is the survival of the human race. Scientists are the best placed to look at this situation rationally. You're reacting emotionally. Which I understand, I do, but if we let Scarlastion proceed, in less than a generation humanity, as we understand it, won't exist.'

'I thought I could trust you!' I said.

I struggled to my feet and went into the washroom. I needed a shower and some time to think, away from irrational people.

When I came out again there was food waiting. Jones had divided it up. It was exactly the same as last night's meal. Lunch wasn't an important event on Haven or with the Primitives it seemed. Perhaps they thought two meals a day ought to be enough for anyone.

We ate in silence, not because we feared being overheard but because we didn't have a thing to talk about. As soon as we were finished I headed for the bedroll, stretched out and went straight to sleep.

They came for me a few hours later when I was fast asleep. The same two guards, perhaps there were no others, grabbed me by my ankles and dragged me out over Jones' shouted protests. Once in the corridor, and the door had shut on Jones, they got me to my feet and jostled me back to the tank. I was instructed to strip again. They lost patience with me folding my clothes neatly and knocked them out of my hands and onto the floor. I was shoved into the tank. The door had barely shut when the sound and light started.

I decided I had learned all I was going to learn from Sandora and it was definitely time to leave Haven. I had a couple of ideas how that might be achieved but first I had to survive the sensory torture. The first session felt like it lasted over an hour. I thought my head was going to explode and my ears were both deafened and hyper sensitive at the same time.

'Per Pike, I admire your resilience. But you know you will break sooner or later. Why damage your hearing, risk hyperthermia, experience excruciating pain for hours, or even days, when you must know you are going to tell us eventually?'

'Screw you,' I croaked from dry lips.

'Charming. Tell me who you work for and where we might find them.'

'No.'

The sound and light started again and went on and on and on, for hours and hours without interruption.

Chapter 34
Underground

Eventually I must have passed out again because the next thing I knew I was back in the cell. Jones was nowhere to be seen. My ears were whistling and buzzing horribly and I was naked, lying half on my bedroll and half off. I panicked for a moment until I saw my shoes and clothes by the door in a messy pile. I made use of the washroom before I got dressed then retrieved the water bottle from by Jones' bed. It was empty but I had no reason to suppose the water in the washroom wasn't drinkable so I refilled it from the sink and drank half the bottle in one go, then filled it back up. While I was in there I re-assembled the device hidden in my heels and tucked it out of sight in my clothing.

My head still hurt and I was feeling dizzy. I had no idea what the time was but as Jones wasn't here it was likely to still be the working day. I sipped at the water and wondered whether to wait for Jones to return or not. On balance waiting for her seemed best. I was reluctant to believe she'd been converted, even partially, to Sandora's cause so quickly. Perhaps she was playing along like I'd asked, but if she was then astrophysics' gain had been the theatre's loss.

I decided to sleep until she arrived back then put my plan into action. I lay down and was soon asleep.

The door opened and Jones was escorted back into the room by Gernard. He was his usual surly self and the look he gave me told me everything I needed to know about how he wanted to deal with me. Jones nodded at me and went straight into the washroom. She emerged changed and fragrant half an hour later.

'How are things progressing?' I asked eventually.

'I got fifteen probe pairs programmed today, Gernard managed twelve. Doctor Grippe however only completed eight and three of those were unusable due to his clumsy efforts at sabotaging them. Gernard punched him so hard he vomited. Where were you this morning? You weren't here when I woke up.'

'Sandora had other activities planned for me. I enjoyed more time at the sensory funfair, until I passed out, then they brought me back here. Torturing an unconscious person is rather pointless.'

The door opened and the two guards were there again, one keeping watch while the other placed a tray of food on the floor. Tonight we had something different to eat, I wasn't sure what it was as I was watching the guards carefully, and not paying attention to the food. They backed out and closed the door. I got up off the bedroll and stood right in front of the door, waited five seconds then triggered the device hidden in my clothing. To my delight the sneaky little gadget worked, the door opened. The two guards were standing talking, one had his back to me, the other was facing me. His eyes widened and he started to react. I squeezed the device hard and threw it to him, as I launched myself at the closer guard. He instinctively caught it and was immediately given a large shock that dropped him, unconscious, to the floor. I crashed into the guard with his back to me and we went down. I got my right arm hooked around his throat and applied pressure, trying to knock him out. He thrashed about on the floor, desperate to throw me off but I tightened my grip until eventually he went limp. Jones was standing in the doorway, watching with a look of complete shock on her face.

I put a finger to my lips then indicated that she should stay in the doorway. I pushed past her, grabbed one of the bedrolls and used it to stop the door shutting, then she helped me drag the guards inside the room.

I prized the shocked guard's hand open and retrieved my device. I doubted it had any useful charge left in it but I didn't want to leave it behind. Then I used the two bed sheets to tie them up and gag them. I looked at their weapons closely. They appeared to be some kind of projectile weapon. They used a compressed gas canister to fire metal pellets. No doubt they would do considerable damage to a fragile human body. I unscrewed the gas canisters and dropped them into the toilet bowl and flushed them away. I wasn't going to use them and I didn't want anyone else to either.

'Are you coming or are you a true believer now?' I asked Jones in an urgent whisper.

'I'm coming, obviously,' she replied equally quietly. 'I was only pretending to agree with Sandora, like you asked. I can't believe you even had to ask that.'

'You should be an actor. You pretty much had me fooled, hopefully Sandora too.'

I looked out of the door, cautiously, but there was no one around. Once out in the corridor I pushed the bedroll back into the room with my foot and the door slid shut.

We headed, as quickly as possible while keeping quiet, towards Sandora's office. I wanted my cuff back and my stunner. We didn't see anyone on the way. Perhaps everyone was eating. Her door wasn't locked but I didn't know if she was in there or not.

'Wait here,' I said to Jones.

I burst through the door and kept moving. If she was inside, I wanted surprise first, then a moving target for her to contend with, second. The room was empty and the light was off. Through the window I could see the workshop was in darkness too. I went straight to her desk and searched it. I found my cuff in the bottom draw along with another one I assumed was Jones', so I grabbed them both and put them in my pockets. My stunner wasn't there, which was a shame. That was a weapon I could use without any ethical concerns, but Sandora must have kept it on her person or locked it away somewhere secure.

I led Jones down the staircase to the workshop level and then to the double doors at the back that I'd seen Sandora come through. Once through them the floor, walls and ceiling were bare rock. I hoped this was the way into the mine, and that my hypothesis would prove correct.

'How did you get the door to our cell open?' asked Jones.

'I had a small lock scanner hidden in two pieces in the heels of my shoes. It's kept in half so it doesn't register as a device on any kind of scan. It only works when clipped together, even the power cell is completely inert when apart. I scanned the lock code when they opened the door yesterday and then re-transmitted it today. I knocked the guard out by overloading the power cell, a good hard squeeze triggered the release. You've got a couple of seconds to throw it before the whole device is live to the touch. The guard instinctively caught it when I threw it to him, and he got zapped. That was my only one, so if we get caught again, we're in really serious trouble.'

'I'm glad you didn't kill the guards. For a moment you had me worried when you were throttling the one you attacked.'

'I don't kill people, ever. The organization I work for has a very firm policy of non-lethal intervention. We cannot be the guardians of life in the galaxy if we don't value every single one, even a warped and damaged one like Sandora's.

We walked in silence for a while

'How many completed probe pairs do you think they have now?' I asked.

'I would imagine it must be less than a hundred,' she replied. 'Gernard's only been completing them for a few days, which is hopeful. Isn't it?'

'That's still more destructive power than has ever been deployed in every war in history combined. Sandora may be weeks away from having enough finished probes to fully complete her plan, but even with the ones she has she could wreak serious havoc. Not having you there will slow them down somewhat but it won't stop them. We need to get Gernard and Grippe away from her and let the barbs know where Haven is and what's happening.'

'There's something that's bothering me,' said Jones, 'If she's this close to being ready to unleash the destructive half of her plan, what about the colonizing another galaxy part?'

'She cannot possibly have found a habitable planet in another galaxy already. I expect she's found one here, nearby. Even if she's sent a ship through a wormhole, using Randolf's hyperspace calculations, to the next galaxy it could take them months or even years to find planets suitable for terraforming. Then that process would take decades or even longer. There has to be a part of this plan we don't know about yet. She's completely crazy but she's not stupid. So either there's a planet, in this galaxy, already terraformed ready for them or they're staying here on Haven until they've got a new home in the next galaxy.'

'In that case Sandora won't live to see humans settled in the next galaxy. She doesn't look well and she's clearly quite old,' said Jones.

'Which is more evidence that we're missing something. People like her, with a sense of destiny and purpose, are determined to see their plan succeed. She's focused on the end game but she wants to personally ensure victory is assured before she hands the reigns to her successor, no matter the personal cost.'

We'd reached the end of the rock tunnel by now. The lights had been getting further apart as we'd got further from the workshop, so now it was quite dim. I could make out a rough wooden door. I pulled it open and we looked through into the largest underground cavern either of us had ever seen.

The door was quite high up near the ceiling of the cavern and the floor must have been three hundred meters below. The cavern was roughly rectangular in shape and we were in the centre of one of the narrower sides. It was brightly lit but almost completely filling the space was an enormous spaceship. It was vast. I'd been on some large passenger liners in my travels but this one was twice the size. I couldn't see the other end of it. It vanished into the distance. It had an almost circular cross section, but with a flattened bottom to allow it to sit on the ground without rolling. The end closest us was the tail end, I could see the propulsion units below me.

'You must be able to get eight or nine thousand people in that ship,' gasped Jones.

'Or four or five thousand and a lot of equipment,' I said. 'I'm hoping there's another spaceship somewhere here, one similar in size to Sandora's as hers can't be here.'

'Why?'

'Because there's been no rescue attempt. Once we were cut off from Infosys Kas would have followed the hyperspace trackers to locate Sandora's ship. It's a standard rescue protocol. I triggered it when I was held prisoner on Coronnol by smashing my cuff. Rescue isn't here, therefore Sandora's ship isn't here. We're on our own for the time being. I wonder how we can get down to the ground level?'

We decided not to split up, with no way to communicate short of shouting or whistling, sticking together seemed the least risky way to search without being discovered. We also needed to be quick as sooner or later someone would notice those guards hadn't returned from giving us our food and I supposed all hell would then break loose.

'Two questions: Why ground level and why wouldn't Kas, even if they found us, just crash on the planet like we did?' asked Jones as we hurried along to the left looking for steps, or some other means of getting down to the floor of the giant hanger.

'I think there's a tunnel back to Stronghold down there somewhere and I suppose it's possible Kas could crash just like us, but I'm counting on the fact that Kas is very cautious and would scan the planet thoroughly before they attempted a landing.'

I spotted a set of plain metal doors in the wall that looked like a lift, there was a single button on the wall next to them. I pressed it and seconds later the doors opened. It was a lift, and there was only one button inside so I pressed it. The doors shut and we plunged down with very little attempt at inertial dampening. If there were only two destinations then one button was all you needed, just to tell the lift when to go. The lift stopped as suddenly as it had started and the doors snapped open. I peered out and saw a long retractable ramp sticking out of the side of the ship about half way along its length. The bottom of the ship was indeed resting on the ground, but the access hatch was set into the side of the ship about three meters up the curved side. I ran over to the base of the ship with Jones following closely. In the curve of the base of the ship we were hidden from anyone above looking down by the hull of the ship, and it was in deep shadow so hopefully anyone on the ground would also struggle to see us. I ran until we were behind the ramp. It was wide, at least fifteen metres, and long enough to make the gradient fairly gentle. I peered out from behind it and saw what I expected. A tunnel opposite. The tunnel was as wide as the ramp and had no doors. It wasn't lit. I looked around and couldn't see anyone around.

'Let's go,' I said as I pointed to the tunnel.

I stepped out from behind the ramp and walked purposefully but briskly in the direction of the tunnel. If you looked like you belong and should be doing exactly what you were doing then you were half way there.

'What if an alarm sounds? Do we run?' asked Jones.

'Why would they have an alarm? They never expected to have prisoners here. They barely had one room with a lock on it to put us in, and not a very sophisticated lock at that. Because Sandora and friends didn't expect to have hostiles on the loose here they haven't got any systems in place to deal with us. I'm sure they know we're out and about by now but they'll have to pass the news on in person and look in person. They don't have cuffs or Infosys to help them coordinate a search. We could be anywhere. The first place they'll look is the way they brought us in, the lift up to the mine floor, and then the track that leads back up out of the mine to Stronghold.'

We'd reached the tunnel entrance by now. There was very minimal lighting, barely enough to see where you were walking but we hurried down it as best we could. I could tell Jones had more questions as she kept drawing breath to ask and then changing her mind. I was glad not to have to explain anything else in case I was dead wrong. I didn't think I was but I needed to talk to someone and get some more answers before I could be sure.

Chapter 35
Emancipation

W e'd been heading down the tunnel for about an hour or so, jogging for parts of it, then walking to conserve energy but trying to make the best time possible. The tunnel was still very wide, but had narrowed slightly and was only half a meter or so taller than I was. It was mostly straight. The entrance had been a tiny bright dot far behind us before we'd eventually walked far enough to lose sight of it. If anyone was following us down the tunnel then it would have been impossible to see them. Looking at the walls and ceiling, when we passed a light, I could see that the tunnel hadn't been completely dug by hand or by machine. Parts of it looked natural, like an old watercourse for an underground river, but it had been widened and occasionally made taller using a focussed disintegration beam. That was pretty advanced technology for Sandora to have access to given her Primitive belief system. Perhaps she didn't do it. But if not then who did?

As we neared two hours in the tunnel, I felt the floor start to rise up, the ceiling rose too. We were heading upwards. The artificial parts of the tunnel were now more obvious and we appeared to have left the watercourse somewhere in the darkness.

Another half an hour went by and the tunnel came to an end.

'What now?' asked Jones. 'Where are we?'

'Find the door, there has to be one, a big one.' I said, ignoring her questions.

I slipped on my cuff, and tried to turn it on to use the screen as a torch, out of force of habit. Nothing happened, of course, the small power cell was completely empty. I started feeling along the end wall at the far right-hand side, leaving Jones to do the left.

'I've got something,' she called, 'it's some kind of handle or manual release.'

I hurried over and sure enough there was a large metal door with a manual lever next to it.

'Don't pull it. That's the main door. It'll be really noisy, but I'd bet there's a smaller one nearby.'

We split up again and traced the edges of door with our hands in the gloom, trying to find another door nearby. As I was about to give up in frustration I had an idea, and moved inwards towards the middle of the door. There it was, a door within a door. It had no lock just a simple handle. I called Jones over in a hissed whisper then opened it and stepped cautiously through. On the other side the floor was wooden and there was a heavy curtain in front of us about a metre from the door. I made my way to the edge of it and peered round into the room beyond. The Congressarium's main hall. I could just make out the lectern in the centre of the raised platform and the empty room beyond. The tunnel came out right at the back of the platform. It was dark outside. There was no sunlight streaming in through the coloured windows.

'Well, well,' said Jones as we stepped out into the room, 'that's interesting. Why did Sandora lie about the distance from Stronghold?'

'To make us believe it was too far to make it back here on foot. I had the idea when we were talking about the missing part of the plan. The colonization part. This continent is sparsely populated but perhaps other ones on Haven are not. If they're moving everyone they need a huge ship, if they have a huge ship it must be hidden, if it's hidden it's underground, if it's underground how do you get people to it? Through a tunnel. I image people will be making their way to Stronghold over the next few weeks from all over this planet. It'll be called a pilgrimage, or some such, and when they're here they'll be lead down the tunnel in groups of a few hundred at the end of a ceremony of some kind. They'll walk to the ship, move inside and when it's full they'll leave for wherever it is they're going.'

'You're sure of all that?'

'No. Not until we've had another talk with Leeton Salvador Gains. He knows more than he told us before. Hopefully he'll either confirm my theory or provide a better explanation.'

We made our way through the empty hall, out of the doors and down the steps at the front of the Congressarium. There was no one about. It was the middle of the night. I had a good sense of direction so we found our way back to Leeton's house without any difficulty.

There were no lights on so I tried the door. It was unlocked. We went in and looked for him, but he was nowhere to be found.

'He works nights,' I said to myself.

'Pardon?'

'He works nights. He's not here because he works nights at the water purification plant. The problem is we have absolutely no idea where that is.'

'So, what do we do?'

'We wait. But not inside, in case Leeton isn't the first person to come knocking. Let's see if any of our equipment is still here.'

I found the cupboard and amazingly the rucksacks were still there. No one had searched his house. Amateurs. There wasn't a lot in them but every little helps, as they say. We headed out of his house, across the garden and back over the hedge. One of the neighbours had some kind of tall crop growing in their garden, I wasn't sure if it was corn, wheat, barley or something else altogether. All I cared about was that it was almost head height. I set up the camouflage tent in the crop, but nearest the side facing Leeton's house. In the darkness it would be completely invisible, and hopefully as the sun came up it would remain almost as undetectable from a distance. Jones and I sat inside taking turns watching out of a gap in the door for when Leeton came home from work. I felt bad about crushing a few square meters of someone's crop but not very.

'How long do we wait?' asked Jones as she took her turn watching, about an hour later.

'I guess if he's not home within a few hours of the sun coming up, then he's not coming at all. Maybe Sandora stopped trusting his loyalty and has him locked up, or worse.'

The night dragged on and we tried to sleep when we weren't watching. After about four hours the first glimmer of light on the horizon indicated dawn was approaching. It was my turn to watch. It was cold but very peaceful. There was no sign of life anywhere, no lights on in the houses, no one moving about. I was so tired. My ears were definitely not back to normal yet and I could still feel the after effects of the concussion. The Organisation's medics would be keen to check me over assuming we made it off Haven and back to civilization.

At long last I saw a shadow moving, in the early morning light, towards Leeton's house. As it got closer, I could see it wasn't him. They went right past the house and disappeared into the buildings towards the centre of the city. A few more people started stirring and moving around. There were some seriously early risers in this town. I hoped that didn't include the occupants of the house whose garden we were in.

The sun was now just up and long shadows were being cast. There wasn't a cloud in the sky. I nudged Jones' foot. She was fast asleep, but I didn't think we'd be able to stay where we were much longer, someone was bound to see us if we didn't move. She stirred and sat up slowly.

'Is he here?'

'Not yet,' I said, 'but we're too exposed here now the sun is up. I think we're going to have to move. We may have to stun the occupants of this house and watch from inside.'

'You don't have your stunner.'

'I have the spare. The one I gave you the last time we were here. I put it back in the rucksack when you didn't want to keep it.'

Just then I saw a familiar looking figure trudging wearily towards the house.

'I think he's home,' I said.

Jones peered through the gap and nodded.

We saw Leeton enter his house and close the door. As we quietly left the tent, I pressed the button to collapse it but didn't wait while it folded itself up. We scrambled over the hedges and into Leeton's garden. I opened the door and went inside, Leeton was sitting in the lounge, with his head in his hands looking thoroughly miserable.

'Hello, Leeton,' I said brightly, 'you must be thrilled to see us again.'

'You can't be here again. You can't. You have to leave.'

He seemed very agitated, so I tried to reassure him.

'Leeton, it's okay. We're not here to cause any more trouble and if you help me with some answers then I won't stun you again. I promise.'

He looked doubtful and kept glancing at the door.

'I'm on my last warning. I've been given punishment duties because of you. The Proctors questioned me for hours and threatened to bring me in front of Sandora.'

He looked genuinely miserable.

'If you help us Leeton I can take you far away from Sandora and the Proctors. You'll never have to be afraid of them again.'

'I couldn't leave Haven. It's my home. I couldn't live out in Gehenna with the ungodly.'

'Gehenna?'

'The planets the ungodly live on. I know some of our people have to live there to do Gaea's work, but you need to be so strong to resist the temptations of the ungodly. Stronger than me.'

'How about if I promise that after Doctor Jones and I will leave we'll never trouble you again, and neither will Sandora, the proctors or the protectorate? But only if you answer some questions.'

'What kind of questions? I only know about water treatment. I'm not a Proctor. I'm not even one of the Lay Supplicants. I'm not sure I believe you can protect me from Sandora.'

He was squirming in his seat. He clearly wanted to help but he was frightened and worried about further reprisals. He kept glancing nervously at Jones.

'We've escaped from her fairly easily. I think we can look after you. The questions I have are quite easy ones. Simple theological ones and a few practical ones. Will you do your best to answer?'

Doctor Jones smiled and reassured him that we meant him no harm.

'A practical one first. When I stunned you, which I won't do again, you should have been unconscious for at least a day. What happened?'

'A neighbour came round when I didn't water the crop in my garden on schedule. It's very important to tend your crop daily and I didn't that day. They came in to chastise me and found me asleep, or so they thought. When they couldn't rouse me, they called the Proctors and one of them revived me with a stench stick. I was groggy for a while but they gave me a drink that helped and I told them about you questioning me. Then they got furious with me and called me a traitor and told me I was no longer in charge of the night shift, but demoted to second junior. I also have to do extra duties during the day to make amends. They said they would have to inform Sandora and she might want to speak to me herself, but she hasn't, yet.'

'Thank you, Leeton. I'm sorry you got in so much trouble,' said Jones.

'Okay,' I said, 'now a theological question. What is Emancipation?'

'It's The Emancipation,' corrected Leeton, automatically, 'It's when the faithful followers of Gaea are taken to paradise. The ungodly face judgement but the righteous experience The Emancipation. There's some debate over exactly what it means but every scholar agrees that the faithful are taken to a paradise. Sandora and other recent scholars say that the departure point for The Emancipation is here on Haven, although I personally doubt Gaea needs us to be here. Surely she can collect her followers from anywhere? It does mean that Haven has had a lot of immigration. Not many to Covenant, that's this continent, until quite recently. But people have been arriving at Destiny, that's the other continent, for years.'

'And you believe this is a real event? Not a metaphor about dying and some kind of afterlife?'

'Oh, there's an afterlife alright. But that's called heaven. The Emancipation is physical, it's freedom from the slavery of Infosys and the lies of your technological society. The faithful all live together on one beautiful planet where the crops are plentiful and life is easy. The ungodly are going to be judged. You seem nice enough, other than stunning me, so I'm sorry you will be found wanting and judged but there it is. If you repent and make penance, I think it's possible you could still be included...but you'd need to talk to the Proctors about that sort of thing. I've never been trained in missions work.'

He shrugged and looked genuinely concerned for us. What a strange thing belief is.

'And this judgement? How does that happen?' I asked.

'I don't really know. The scriptures are fairly vague on that one. It just says the unrighteous are found wanting and receive judgement for their unbelief. They definitely don't get taken to paradise in The Emancipation though. That much is clear.'

Leeton had a fairly uncomplicated and simple relationship with his faith and wasn't the sort to ask too many questions. Mind you, I doubted asking questions was tolerated. The power of religion was in the certainty of its answers, rather than in its embracing of questions and discussion.

'Thank you. Now a practical question. Where do you get your water from? There are no rivers nearby and I've seen no lakes or reservoirs.'

'Oh, there are rivers!' he said enthusiastically. 'They're just underground. This whole continent has a network of underground lakes and rivers. There used to be a gigantic underground lake near here that we used for all our water needs, but a few years ago the levels started dropping so Sandora said we had to find another source for our water. The new source is much smaller and the water has an unpleasant taste but we filter it through many layers of carbon rich mulch to make it safe to drink. I'm in charge of the filtration system. Well, I was.'

His enthusiasm died and I could see he was feeling anxious about helping us again.

'I have to go soon,' he said, glancing up to the circular ornament on the wall, 'my punishment shift at the waste plant starts soon.'

'How do you know?' I asked.

'The clock.'

'What clock?'

He pointed to the ornament on the wall.

'That clock. It's quarter to seven.'

He stood and pointed to the shorter rod which was almost pointing at the first dot up on the left from the bottom one and the longer rod pointed to the one at the extreme left.

I stared at it and suddenly understood. The rods indicated hours and minutes. What a way to tell the time. Elegant and ornamental but needlessly difficult to work out.

'I have to ask one favour of you Leeton, is that okay?' I asked.

'I guess so.'

He didn't look sure.

'I need you to keep our conversation secret. Don't tell anyone you saw us again. Will you do that for me? For us?'

Doctor Jones read the moment right, and smiled at him and reached out to squeeze his arm gently.

Leeton nodded and blushed.

'Thank you, Leeton,' said Jones.

We left, after cautiously checking around outside. I retrieved the collapsed tent, now back into its small rectangular package.

'Where to now?' asked Jones.

'Back to the woods near where we crashed to hide out, or back to Sandora's base to try to stop her seem to be the only two options.'

Jones looked surprised.

'Stop her? Just the two of us?'

'Yes. Once we're there I'm fairly sure we can count on Doctor Grippe's help. He seems determined to disrupt their plans, if he can. So that's three of us. Ideally, we would find a spaceship and leave to get help but if the only choice is that enormous one then we'll just have to find a way to stop Sandora. Did you really program the probes that you were working on correctly?'

'I did program the particle filters correctly to bring about a supernova, yes. But I also amended the shielding protocols in a virtually undetectable way. The probes will last no longer than half an hour inside the star before the shielding is overwhelmed and the probes will be destroyed. Only Doctor Grippe would notice the change, I don't think Gernard would. He had no involvement in the design of those systems, they're all mine. Half an hour wouldn't be anywhere near enough time to significantly change the star's composition.'

'Excellent. I trusted you had sabotaged them in some subtle way. We're going back to the Congressarium and then back down the tunnel. There're more people about but as Leeton told us there's been a lot of immigration into Haven and some to Stronghold we can just pretend to be new in town if we're challenged. Remember, be confident and act like you own the place.'

I strode off back through the streets towards the Congressarium and Jones fell in step beside me. There were people about but they too were moving purposefully, on their way to or from work. No one was paying us much attention. If anyone did glance our way I smiled and nodded to them, as if they were a familiar face but I wasn't sure of their name. A smile and a nod disarms ordinary people who might otherwise be suspicious. It didn't work with officials and police officers but ordinary folk assume they know you from somewhere and usually just nod back.

Soon we were at the steps of the Congressarium and as we started to climb them I whispered to Jones.

'They may well be on alert in here. Sandora must have some way to communicating with the Proctors, the radio or something or maybe she just sends a flunky with a message. In any case I'm going to stun first and not worry about the consequences. The time for subtlety is past. Try to stay close to me, they may have more of those gas-powered weapons our guards had.'

I closed my eyes tight as we climbed the steps and held on to Jones' arm. I couldn't afford to wait for my eyes to adjust to the dim light inside. I needed to be ready straight away, so I slipped the stunner from my pocket and adjusted it by touch to the maximum setting.

I heard Jones pull the door open, I stepped in and opened my eyes.

Chapter 36
Here today, gone tomorrow

There were four people in the foyer, all standing together talking in hushed reverential tones. Two were dressed in flowing robes and looked familiar, I think they were the people I'd stunned when I encountered Sandora and Gernard here previously. The other two were dressed in in the mid-blue uniform of the Protectorate and had weapons in holsters on their hips. That was really stupid. If you thought there was a threat you kept your weapon in your hand. They received the first shots from the stunner. They slumped unconscious to the floor and should remain that way for quite some time. I followed this with two fast shots to the robed figures who then joined them on the floor. The stunner was completely silent but four people falling to the floor wasn't. As I ran forwards into the main hall, with Jones on my right, I heard footsteps running towards us from the left-hand corridor. Two more guards appeared, these had their weapons drawn. I hit the first one easily and he fell face-forwards and slid along the polished tiles, his weapon clattering away from his limp hand. The other had enough sense to duck back round the corner and fire at me. There was a 'pfft' noise and then the hard smack of a metal slug hitting the far wall behind me. This fellow wasn't an idiot. He started shouting that I was in the main hall and he needed reinforcements. I ran to the inside corner of the hall closest to where he was sheltering. I looked at the wall, it was wood, but how thick was it? I pressed the stunner hard against the wood and fired. I heard a yelp and ran back out of the hall and round to my right. The guard was leaning against the wall twitching and trying to raise his weapon. I fired and he slumped down unconscious. Thank goodness the wall was organic matter and not too thick; it had conducted the stun field enough to partially disable him. Thick wood, a metal or other inorganic material would have blocked it completely.

I moved down the corridor as quietly as I could. There had to be other guards or else who had he been calling out to? A nervous head appeared from a doorway half way down the corridor. I fired and another guard slumped out onto the floor. I got to the doorway, pointed the stunner into the room and fired several times, then risked a look. A Proctor was slumped over the desk with the microphone and speaker on it. Another guard was on the floor. I shot them both again, just to be sure. I didn't want a repeat of Gernard's nasty little trick. I checked the nearby rooms and they were all empty.

Back in the main hall I saw Jones nervously standing by the curtain.

'Okay, I think I've stunned them all. Let's go.'

We pushed through the curtain and opened the door within a door and I peered through. There didn't seem to be anyone about so we headed back down the corridor as quickly as we could.

'What is your plan?' asked Jones as we ran.

'Find a ship. Steal it. Contact Kas. Stop Sandora.'

'So why the detour into Haven? We've lost almost a whole day.'

'I needed information. As I said before there's a part of Sandora's plan that she didn't tell me and I needed to confirm my suspicions. Leeton told me what I needed to know.'

I was gasping for breath a bit now and slowed down to a walk. I didn't want to run into any hostiles while out of breath.

We alternated walking and running as before. It had taken us about two and a half hours to travel the length of the tunnel in the opposite direction. I couldn't see any particular reason why it would take much longer to do it in reverse.

Jones looked at me quizzically but I wasn't about to share until I had proof. It would sound like I'd gone completely insane, especially if I turned out to be wrong.

We pressed on and eventually we could see a faint light in the far distance that must have been where the tunnel entered the cavern that housed the enormous space ship.

'How large is the wormhole your stellar probes create?' I asked.

'Fairly small. Too small to send a ship through, if that's what you're thinking. At maximum size it's about ten metres in diameter.'

'So how would you have made one large enough to use with a starship?'

'I can only assume they've done it with two pairs of synchronised generators. Years ago when I first started working on this with Randolf we called Grippe in as we needed his expertise to actually build the wormhole generator. Within days he'd realised the implications for interstellar travel but I was committed to getting the stellar probe finished and working first. I felt it was more important, long term, plus we needed to carefully consider the impact of a revolution in travel on the galaxy's ship builders and engineers. We have to consider the ethical, social and economic consequences of what we hope to do as well as the scientific impact. I thought we needed to perfect the technology before we even started a consultation period involving the starship engineers and associated specialists.'

'Grippe didn't agree?'

'Not in the slightest. He was determined that not only should interstellar travel be revolutionised but that it ought to be his revolution. He didn't care how disruptive it would be so long as the name Grippe was attached to it. He was even reluctant to acknowledge that it was Randolf's unique and innovative new equations, which truly are a work of genius, that made the whole thing possible.'

'Why isn't Per Randolf Doctor Randolf yet then?' I asked as an aside.

'Because until we've published the results of my stellar probe work his equations must remain secret. He's done more than enough excellent work to earn the title Doctor. As soon as the project is public knowledge the University will rubber-stamp his doctorate. It may be difficult to hold on to him after that. Every mathematics or physics department in the galaxy will want him.'

She paused and I could tell she cared about Randolf and was expecting to lose him.

'From what Grippe told us beneath the Congressarium he ignored your instructions to wait?'

'He must have, if Sandora's been conducting tests for him.'

'Do you have any ideas how they might be doing it?'

'We discussed the possible methods on occasions. To make a wormhole large enough for a ship to pass through, especially one as large as the one at the end of this tunnel we decided that you'd need four wormhole generators working in perfect sync placed at the four corners of the wormhole entrance. Then you'd simply fly between them to enter it. That was the idea, anyway. I can't think of any reason it wouldn't work.'

'How large would these generators be?'

'I don't know. I've never built one!'

'Mal, I need you to guess. Unless we're fortunate enough to find Grippe you're all I've got.'

'They could be really quite small. About the size of a large four-person bubble would be big enough. It would be powered directly by the nearest star. All you'd need is a large energy collector, a cell big enough to provide emergency backup power, the focussing array and the grav generator. The control circuits wouldn't take up much space and the Infosys link would be doing any live calculations needed.'

The entrance was quite clear now, but it looked different somehow. It was brighter than I expected. I couldn't work out yet what had changed. Had they turned the lighting up brighter to make intruders easier to spot?

'One more question, Mal,' I said. 'Could you disable such a wormhole if we encountered one?'

'No,' she answered simply. 'You'd need Grippe. He's the only one who'd know enough. He could probably modify a stellar probe to emit a disruptive grav beam that would collapse the wormhole safely.'

She paused.

'If the wormhole hasn't been created yet it's easy and you could do it.'

'Me?' I said incredulously.

'Yes. You could target one of the generators and destroy it. Assuming he's proceeded with the four-generator scheme then that would do the job. If only one generator went down that would put a stop to it. You mustn't try that if the generators are running and the wormhole has been created though, that would be extremely dangerous.'

'In what way?'

'The generators not only create the wormhole, they keep both ends at a fixed point in space, relative to a nearby gravity well, such as a star. An uncontrolled collapse causes those fixed points to move, in an entirely unpredictable way, before the wormhole itself collapses. We found that out the hard way testing early versions of my probe. We once had a power failure which caused the uncontrolled shutdown of a wormhole. The entry point suddenly jumped from near one of the outer planets deep into the inner part of the solar system. One of Coronnol's asteroids got ripped in half by the wayward wormhole collapse and was sent, somewhere. We never found it. Imagine if it had hit a ship, an inhabited space station or the planet itself? We conducted all further tests in uninhabited systems after that.'

The tunnel entrance was now close enough to see clearly through into the cavern and I realised what had changed.

The gigantic space ship was gone. The cavern was empty.

Chapter 37
Airless

'Where the hell is the ship?'

I didn't expect a reply. We stood for a moment staring at the gigantic empty cavern. There was an enormous hole out into the outside world at the far end where the front of the ship had been. From the look of the perfectly smooth edges of the hole they must have used an atomiser to crumble the rock away into dust which would have allowed the ship to fly straight out. It would still have been a tight fit out into the huge pit that Jones had seen when we were first brought here, but that was the only logical explanation for the missing ship. As if reading my mind Jones pointed to the hole.

'My guess is that it went that way,' she said, and then grinned.

We ran to the lift that would take us up to the top level and back into the base. Back upstairs we soon discovered that there was nobody around and all the stellar probes were gone.

'They must be on the ship,' said Jones.

I nodded.

'But they can't be ready to deploy them. They haven't had the time to programme them all.'

'I don't think that matters any more,' I said. 'If Sandora has a working wormhole hyperdrive she can finish them off at her leisure in the ship, I'm sure it's well equipped, then jump to her targets from anywhere in this galaxy or the next to deploy them. Our escape has forced her hand and she's reversed the two stages of her plan but it's still happening. They must be on their way to the other continent, what did Leeton call it?'

'Destiny, wasn't it?'

'The Emancipation is happening right now over in Destiny. But Leeton and the residents of Haven are missing out. I doubt Sandora will come back for them. She's cut her losses and run before my people found us or we worked out how to disable that huge ship.'

'If they have another terraformed planet to operate from, we'll never find them. A needle in a haystack would be child's play compared to searching the galaxy for them.'

'True. But we still have to get off this planet. There must be other ships hidden down here. That huge ship was built here, it must have taken years. They brought the machinery and parts in somehow. Also Sandora came and went, so it's possible others did too. All we need is one with enough power to break orbit and do one jump through hyperspace to make contact with Infosys. I think it's safe enough to split up and search. You take that side and check all the passages and side rooms and I'll take this side. We'll meet back here in about an hour. Okay?'

Jones nodded and turned to go.

'Take the stunner,' I said, offering it to her. 'Just in case.'

She took it and set off.

Sandora's base was large and split onto several levels. Without my cuff to map it I would just have to rely on my sense of direction and hope neither I nor Jones got lost. The living quarters were a mess, everyone had left in a hurry and no attempt had been made to evacuate in a tidy way. I presumed the majority of the proctors from the Congressarium in Haven and other key personnel had been quietly contacted while we were waiting to talk to Leeton and they'd left on the ship. The other residents of the town were going to feel betrayed when they found out but I doubted that would endear us to them. We would probably get the blame for forcing them to miss The Emancipation.

I felt like I was nearing the end of my hour when I finally found something that looked promising. It was a dark cavernous room at the bottom of a staircase not far from Sandora's office. I couldn't work out how to turn the lights on as they didn't detect my presence and come on automatically. In the dim light coming from the stairwell I could see what looked like a small tug. These tiny stubby craft were used all over the galaxy to tow things too large to fit into a spaceship hull. It was a metallic disc about four metres in diameter and a meter and a half thick, with a large transparent hemisphere for a cockpit mounted in the centre of the top surface of the disc. The single swivel seat inside had all the controls built into the arm-rests. There were sockets, hatches and brackets all around the rim of the disc that allowed all kinds of attachments to be fitted. They rarely had a hyperdrive as they were generally just used to ferry bulky items to or from orbit, but it was a start. The door was open and once inside I found the controls were completely standard. I turned on the exterior illumination and saw at the far side of the room, away from the stairwell, a huge wooden doorway. That must be the way out. It was the only doorway large enough to let the tug in or out. The tug's power cell was in pretty good shape and showed forty-five percent charge. More than enough to make it to orbit. I climbed out of the tug and checked the wooden door. It was locked shut and I couldn't make out any controls that would open it. That problem could wait. I returned to the tug and extinguished the lights, I didn't want to drain the power unnecessarily, and headed as quickly as I could back to the rendezvous point.

Jones wasn't there when I arrived. I called out and nobody answered. I sat down and waited. What felt like about half an hour passed and finally she appeared, looking rather glum.

'I found a ship, but it doesn't work. There's a hangar that way,' she pointed back the way she'd come, 'it's open to the outside world, but the ship has no power, the cell must be completely drained.'

I followed her back to it and sure enough there was a space ship. A really quite small ship. It wasn't as sleek as the scout ship, whoever designed Sandora's ships preferred slightly more bulbous shapes. Perhaps that was to accommodate cargo or larger power cells. It was grey, with stubby fins down the sides and the profile was like a squashed cylinder, the bottom was considerably fatter than the top. The front was rounded not tapered. It was really only large enough to accommodate two people. The docking port was low down on the left side at the front.

'You stay here,' I said. 'I've found a working tug, perhaps we can repair or recharge this ship using it. I'll go and get it.'

It took me about fifteen minutes to find my way back to the tug. I searched all around the wooden door for a lever or something that would open it but couldn't find anything. Giving up, I climbed back into the tug and started it up. The grav unit made an unpleasant rough humming sound. I wasn't sure if that was normal as I'd never flown one before. Given that it would have to have a powerful enough grav drive to lift many thousands of tonnes perhaps the noise was normal. It lifted off the ground smoothly enough and edged closer to the doorway. I pressed the tug against it and gradually increased the power. I could see the wood starting to buckle and bend where the curved front of the tug was pressing into it. I increased the power some more, but the wood didn't want to give. I kept increasing the power. The tug could lift objects many times its own mass, so breaking the door should be easy, but I didn't want to shoot through at speed and crash into whatever was on the other side. Eventually I saw cracks appearing in the wood and as I boosted the power one more notch the door shattered outwards and I was flying free.

The sun was still quite high in the sky and the day looked clear and bright. I'd come out of the hangar into the same deep pit the huge ship had flown out into. I could see the hole in the rock face below me to my left. I swivelled the chair to the right and the ship flew in the direction I was now facing along the rock wall. I was looking for the hangar Jones and the other ship were in.

I found them fairly easily. The rock face was covered in shallow caves and cracks but only one of them had an astrophysicist standing dangerously close to the edge waving her arms and jumping up and down. As I turned towards her she moved back inside and out of the way so I could land. The tug was nimble and easy to fly so I dropped it down right next to the broken ship.

Jones climbed up onto the disk and looked into the dome.

'Why don't we just use this?'

'There's only the one chair,' I answered. 'Plus, it has no hyperdrive I'm afraid.'

I started searching the tug's hatches for something that would help us get the other ship working. I eventually found a power transfer cable which I took back into the tug's dome, found the power cell's service hatch and connected one end of the cable. I dragged the other end out and into the broken ship.

The docking port came up right into the back of the tiny cockpit. To the right was a corridor through a small living area into the engine room. I headed for the service hatch above the power cell. When I opened it I discovered a much bigger problem, there was no cell.

Jones must have heard my shouted expletive as she soon appeared with a quizzical look on her face. I pointed to the empty socket in the floor.

'The reason you couldn't power the ship up, wasn't because the power cell is depleted. It's because they've taken the cell with them.'

She swore.

'What now?' she asked after a few minutes.

'Well, we have a working ship with power that can get to orbit, but that has no hyperdrive and a ship with a hyperdrive that cannot go anywhere as it has no power at all. The only option is to use both.'

'Both?'

I explained that we'd use the tug to pull the powerless ship up into orbit, then use the power cables to activate the hyperdrive and leap to a nearby system with an Infosys connection.

Jones looked extremely sceptical.

'Will the hyperdrive take the tug along when we jump? If not we'll arrive in a new star system but not have any power.'

'I think so. If we attach them properly, I think it should work. Besides, our only alternative is to stay here until the residents of the town find us, Sandora comes back or Kas and the barb's rescue us. The chances of those three are high, nil and low in order.'

She didn't look convinced.

'Why can't we take the power cell out of the tug and put it in this ship?'

'Do you know how to dismantle a tug without damaging the power cell?' I snapped angrily. 'Do you have the required tools and heavy lifting gear? I don't, nor do I see any of those things lying around.'

Jones looked a bit surprised and quite hurt at my tone.

'I'm sorry,' I said. 'I shouldn't have been so angry and rude. I'm just really tired and stressed.'

'Apology accepted,' she said. 'What can I do to help?'

'We are going to need spacesuits. Can you look for some please?'

She nodded.

I pulled the power cables back out and returned them to the tug then checked it over carefully, paying special attention to the power connectors. Smashing through the wooden door had done absolutely no damage to it. It was as robust as it was possible to make a ship. I climbed up onto the disc and stepped into the transparent cockpit. Somewhere in the floor would be a hatch to take the operator down into the disc. There had to be a standard docking port built into the tug. It was a legal requirement, and it couldn't be part of the cockpit as that was a transparent dome. I found a hatch in the floor, pulled it up and saw the emergency docking port directly below in the base of the ship. There was just a straight cylindrical tunnel through the base with handrails to aid manoeuvring in microgravity. I shut the hatch and called to Jones.

Jones came back and reported there was one suit. But it had no oxygen left in its tank.

'We'll have to manage then,' I said. 'Are you ready?'

'I suppose so if you really think there's no alternative.'

'I don't think so. Let's go. You'll have to ride with me in the tug. It won't be comfortable but it'll be safer. If that ship isn't airtight then you'd be dead by the time we got to orbit.'

I got into the spacesuit, didn't put the helmet on, but carried it with me into the tug's cockpit. I sat in the chair and Jones sat on the floor with her back against the curved transparent dome.

I lifted off just half a meter, then engaged two grappling arms out of their bays on opposite sides of the disc. They grabbed the small ship, like two small hands holding on to a large watermelon. Gripping it by squeezing tightly. I went up another half a meter and the grav unit's rough humming got considerably louder, then the other ship lifted up off the ground and I was able to back out of the hanger and out into the daylight. As we cleared the floor the arms swivelled ninety-degrees downwards and the hands holding the ship went slack on their pivots to allow the ship to hang below the tug. I boosted the power and we went straight up. I wasn't going to waste power with a spiral climb as there was no traffic to worry about. With the ship directly below us I couldn't see it at all. I studied the controls in the tug and found one for the screen. A small virtual screen appeared giving a crystal-clear view from below the tug's disc. The ship was still tightly gripped by the arms and coming up to orbit with us. I took my cuff off and placed it in the charging bay in the left arm rest[1]. After about twenty seconds I saw a flash of red as it gained enough power to start up. The red light pulsed faintly indicating low power but the pulses gradually faded and stopped as the cuff's cell charged.

'Why charge your cuff?' asked Jones. 'There's no Infosys connection here.'

'Just being prepared,' I said, 'hopefully there will be one when we arrive at our destination.'

After half an hour we were nearing orbit and the tricky work would soon start.

---

[1] Tugs always have a charging bay because they often operate outside of a planet's power-grid. They're used, amongst other things, to charge the operator's cuff if it runs low on power while in orbit.

The instrument console beeped indicating we were high enough and moving fast enough for a stable orbit. The power indicator was showing a drop of about five percent after dragging the ship up with us. A little worse than I hoped but not catastrophic.

'The moment of truth. Well, one of them. Let's see if I can dock with the ship.'

I rotated the hands to get the ship's hatch facing the underside of the tug then detached them and withdrew the arms back into the disc. It was going to be quite tricky as the docking had to be done manually because the other ship was completely inert. On the screen I could see the docking port on the other ship getting closer and closer. Once it was within range I pulled up the hatch in the floor and invited Jones to swap places with me and sit in the pilot seat.

'You're going to have to turn the internal gravity off so I can complete the docking procedure,' I explained.

Once we'd swapped places, she turned off the internal grav generator and I pulled myself down into the tunnel to the docking port. I put it in rescue mode and extended the docking ring to the ship's hatch. Without a working space suit this next part was pretty dangerous, but I didn't have any option.

I floated up and grabbed the helmet.

'I'm going to put this on. Then you shut this hatch and bang on it hard, twice. I'll know you're ready and I'll open the docking hatch. Once I'm in the other ship and have checked the atmosphere is holding I'll come back and bang on the hatch twice. You can then open it and follow me through. Is that all okay?'

'How much time will you have in that suit with no oxygen supply?'

'Only two or three minutes. I'll be quick.'

'Be careful,' she said.

I smiled, grabbed my cuff and slipped it on over the suit then pulled myself back down into the tunnel. It was extremely cramped in such a small space and it was worse when it went completely dark as she shut the hatch. I heard two muffled thumps as she banged on it.

I took several deep breaths, held the last one and then pulled the helmet on and fastened it shut.

I opened the outer hatch and pulled myself through the docking ring to the unpowered ship. The docking hatch was shut but I was prepared. This small ship didn't need powered hatches. It was stiff but it was possible to open the hatch by hand. Before I opened it I checked the air-pressure using the docking ring's built-in gauges. The air wasn't leaking. It seemed safe to proceed. I opened the outer airlock, then the inner one. There was a slight hiss as the pressures equalised.

I was starting to feel hot and light-headed. I must be running out of oxygen. I pulled myself back to the tug, unfastened the helmet and took it off. It was impossible not to gasp a lungful of the freezing cold air. When my breathing had calmed down I banged on the hatch twice and moved away as it opened.

'We're going to have to hurry,' I said. 'I don't want to trust this seal any longer than I have to.'

Jones pulled herself down and headed for the small ship. I grabbed the power cable, connected one end to the tug's cell and followed Jones through into the other ship bringing the helmet with me.

In the engine room Jones had the hatch open and was floating nearby holding on to a handle. I connected the cable then headed back to the ship's cockpit. There were only two seats, as I expected, in such a small ship.

I flipped the appropriate switches and watched as lights started coming on all over the instrument consoles. Jones strapped herself into the spare seat but was already shivering with the cold.

'You'll need to turn the heat right up, even if it's uncomfortable,' she said. 'Or when we lose power we'll freeze in no time.'

'There's enough power for full life support,' I answered, and turned the heat to maximum. 'But there's very little oxygen on board.'

Some heat started filling the cockpit.

'When I jump, the tug may not come with us,' I said. 'There's only one space suit and the airlock will be wide open on a ship with no power. You may have a better chance of survival in the tug. I mean, if the tug stays here when this ship jumps you could simply shut the hatch and fly back to Haven and wait for rescue. If the tug does come with this ship I'll join you in it, we cut this ship loose and head for the nearest planet.'

'Don't you know what will happen?'

'No. I don't think anyone has ever been stupid or desperate enough to try a hyperspace jump in a docked ship running solely off power transfer cables before.'

She thought for a minute, then appeared to reach a decision.

'We stay together. I'm not spending another moment on Haven that I don't have to. You'll just have to get the hatch shut quickly if the worst happens.'

The heat in the ship was now almost unbearable and the sweat was trickling down my face.

I pulled up the navigation system, it was extremely basic and wouldn't allow us enter a destination of our choice. The primitive's rejection of Infosys meant the ship had to have its own on-board computer which could only calculate certain jumps within a short distance from Haven. Perhaps that was why Sandora's journey from Coronnol to Haven appeared so erratic and random; she had to use whatever jumps were pre-calculated by the simple on-board computer. I scrolled through the list of destination systems. I didn't recognise any of the names. Not one. Jones looked at them as I scrolled up and down the list. The ship had only been to eight other systems, but I had no clue which of them might be inhabited worlds linked to Infosys, or which might be isolated like Haven. She wasn't sure either but thought Jaradon sounded familiar. It was the best of a small set of equally bad choices.

'Jaradon it is then,' I said.

I programmed the destination and set a thirty second countdown to the jump.

'Why thirty seconds?' asked Jones.

I undid my straps, got out of the pilot seat and braced myself next to the inner airlock as best I could.

'Someone has to shut the airlock if we arrive without the tug. Now the real moment of truth,' I said as I pulled the helmet back on.

Jones started to protest then the stars outside the window winked and all hell broke loose.

Chapter 38
Do it yourself

The atmosphere was rushing out of the open airlock through the shattered remains of the docking ring. I had seconds to pull the severed power cable inside the cockpit so I could shut the inner airlock before Jones died of asphyxiation. The inner door's manual override lever was spring loaded, so all it took was a shove on the release and it snapped shut with a bang.

To my great relief Jones was conscious and breathing heavily. I unfastened the helmet and then removed the space suit, which was easier said than done in microgravity in almost complete darkness.

'Are you sure you're alright?' I gasped.

'Yes. I think so.'

I pulled myself back into the pilot seat and fastened the straps. All the instruments were dead and all power was gone. Jones looked out of the window to her left and confirmed what I already knew.

'The docking ring is still attached to the ship but the tug is gone. Well technically I suppose, the tug is where we left it and we are gone. Can you see the planet?'

'No. This system's planet and sun must be behind us as I cannot see either.'

The air rushing out of the airlock had put us in a slow spin and the stars were moving from right to left across the cockpit window.

'We'll catch sight of one or the other soon thanks to this spin,' said Jones.

Sure enough within a minute the inhabited planet came into view. We were close to it, but not close enough for my cuff to pick up the planetary Infosys link. A few short bursts on the ship's manoeuvring thrusters would have us there in ten minutes, except they weren't working.

'We have a problem. We're not close enough to the planet to connect to their Infosys link. Normally my cuff would piggy-back to Infosys via the ship's link, but this ship doesn't have one even if it had any power. If we can get close enough for a low orbit my cuff will connect via the planetary link.'

'But we have no power. How are we going to get close enough? And what if this planet doesn't have an Infosys link either?'

I held my cuff up.

'This is fully charged now. I might be able to hook it up to the ship's systems and power the thrusters just long enough. If it turns out that this planet also doesn't have an Infosys link then we are screwed. The name sounded familiar to you though so we'll have to hope. It's all we can do.'

I had already unbuckled myself and had started stripping the covers off the underside of the control panels, looking for the power feeds.

'Why not hook the cuff up with the power transfer cable we already have?' asked Jones.

'The tiny cell in the cuff can't power the whole ship. We'll have to leave gravity, life support and everything else offline. I can only power thruster control and only directly, not through the instruments. Even that would drain the cuff in seconds.'

Jones joined me, pulling away panels and putting them in the living quarters to stop them floating around the cockpit. It took some time to find the thruster circuits and even then I was only about seventy-five percent sure we'd identified them correctly.

'There's only one way to find out,' I said.

I opened the cuff and isolated the tiny power cell. I used some of the torn power transfer cable to connect the cuff's cell and got ready to fire the starboard thruster, which I hoped would stop the spin when I touched the other end of the cable to what I hoped was the correct circuit.

As the planet came back around, slightly larger this time, I touched the cable and there was a brief sensation of acceleration and the planet froze. Almost froze. I'd overdone it a little and the planet was now moving slowly the other way, but very, very slowly. I tried the port side contact with the briefest of touches and our rotation stopped. I tried the main rear thruster for about five seconds and we felt the shove of acceleration until I removed the cable. The planet was now definitely getting larger.

'You do know the odds against manually achieving a stable low altitude orbit are gigantic, don't you? asked Jones.

I didn't answer. I waited until the planet more than filled the screen then touched the port side circuits for a few seconds then alternated the starboard and port in smaller and smaller bursts.

We waited anxiously in the now rapidly cooling cockpit. The planet was mostly on our left-hand side and we appeared to be maintaining a rough orbit around it, but was it low enough to connect to Infosys?

I removed the cable from the power cell and reassembled the cuff. We waited. A red flash showed the start-up but the gold flash of connection didn't come.

I ripped it apart again, reconnected the cable and blipped the starboard thruster to push us down, closer to the planet. Once, twice, three times. Tiny bursts, each time. That was all I dared risk.

'Try your cuff again,' said Jones.

I re-assembled it and we watched the red flash die away. Nothing else happened.

'By now if they have a planetary traffic control system they will be screaming at us,' I said. 'As we haven't answered they'll probably send a ship up to intercept us, but I doubt it will get here soon enough.'

The orbit appeared to be decaying and we were now brushing against the upper atmosphere. The noise level in the cockpit had increased and the ride wasn't smooth any more.

'How long before we crash?' asked Jones.

'We won't crash. We'll burn up in the atmosphere. Minutes I suppose. Sorry.'

'Don't you want to try and correct the orbit?

Jones looked like she really hoped I did want to do that.

'Let's give it a minute or two more. I can't have much power left in this thing. I daren't use it all or we can't communicate.'

The vibration in the ship was now fairly severe and the noise as we ripped through the upper atmosphere was loud enough to make talking difficult.

My cuff chimed. I looked down at it and was overwhelmingly relieved to see a faint gold glow indicating a connection to Infosys.

We both started laughing and crying so it was a couple of seconds before I placed a call directly through to Kas.

'Trace my cuff, quickly. Very quickly,' I said as soon as we were connected. 'We're in a decaying orbit somewhere called Jaradon but we have no power, very little oxygen and it's very cold. The cold won't be a problem for long though, as we'll be burning up on re-entry within minutes.'

I saw Kas call to someone off-screen and heard a familiar voice confirm that they had a positive fix on us.

'We'll be with you shortly. We're not far away,' said Kas.

'You're not? How?'

A cruiser class space ship suddenly appeared outside the window several kilometres away.

'Planetary Traffic Control sent up your exact trajectory. We can see you, don't try to manoeuvre. We'll bring you into the hangar. Sit tight,' said Kas.

The cruiser turned towards us and within seconds was filling the entire window. A large hatch opened in the underside and the ship started lowering itself towards us. The buffeting from the atmosphere was really frightening now. I was worried we might not remain airtight long enough to be rescued. The thinner metal around the cockpit window was glowing red as it heated up. There were several loud bangs from somewhere in the ship as heavy items broke loose from their mountings and crashed around in microgravity.

'Hurry!' I shouted into my cuff.

The cruiser's hatch appeared to be bouncing around to the left and right, but it was us that was moving. A ship that massive would barely be feeling the effects of re-entry yet.

The noise in the cockpit was now deafening, a roaring hissing that drowned out any other sound so I had no idea if Kas replied.

Suddenly everything went silent as the cruiser swallowed us up. We saw the hatch close and our ship dropped a few centimetres onto the now solid floor. We felt the artificial gravity build up to normal. Jones and I looked out of the cockpit window to see Kas and a few other people, familiar to me, enter the hangar and head towards us.

'Let's get out of this piece of junk,' I said to Jones.

'Agreed.'

We heaved on the manual airlock release and the inner door gradually slid back allowing us out into the hangar.

Kas ran over to me and ignoring all formality threw their arms around me in a hug.

'Don't touch the ship, it's rather hot,' I said.

'I'm so happy to see you're both in one piece,' said Kas, 'but there was no cause for alarm, we had everything in hand.'

'It didn't feel that way from in there,' Jones said pointing to the wrecked ship.

'Kas, I'd like you to meet Doctor Maldonaro Octavius Jones. Without whom I wouldn't still be in one piece. Mal may I introduce Kastagyr Devon Marshall, one of my oldest friends and regular rescuer.'

Kas held out an arm and linked formally with Jones.

'It's a pleasure to finally meet you Doctor Jones.'

'Likewise, Per Marshall,' said Jones.

'Enough formality, it's Kas and Mal from now on please,' I said.

I introduced Jones to the other people with Kas.

'Mal, this is Dharya Peeyush Patel and Praanvi Madri Jogalekar. They work with Kas. It was Dharya's voice you heard confirming they'd traced us.'

The other two people with Kas were from a planet called Bhaarat, they were both very young, tall and extremely elegant with dark brown eyes and jet-black hair. I'd known them both for a few years. They were two of the best scientists we had. Dharya was a physicist and Praanvi was a mathematician. Everyone presumed they were a couple, as they were inseparable, but they were extremely private and had neither confirmed nor denied it. Dharya had short straight hair and an immaculately neat beard while Praanvi's waist length hair was always interwoven with flowers or jewellery. Today was a flowers day. They briefly linked arms politely with Jones.

'Let's go back to the operations room. We can talk on the way,' said Kas.

I nodded and we set off.

'Firstly, answer me this Kas, how come you were so close?'

'Not that we're complaining,' said Jones.

'We were monitoring your pursuit of Sandora's ship through all the rapid hyperspace jumps. We could see the tracker location and then one jump behind, your cuff and the scout ship. When your cuff and the scout ship went off line virtually simultaneously, four days ago, we started to get concerned. I prepared to jump to your last known location, but then after about an hour the tracker jumped again, then again. I decided to continue following the tracker and sent Dharya and Praanvi, in a shuttle, to the system your cuff went off line.'

'We got into orbit around the only habitable planet and soon realised that there was no planetary power grid, said Praanvi. 'We had enough power for a safe landing and take-off, but not enough to enter the atmosphere to conduct a thorough search. We could only presume you were somewhere on the planet as we detected no sign of the scout ship in orbit around the sun or any of the nearby planets.''

'The two largest continents seemed the most likely place to look for you and we spend two days scanning the most populous one from orbit, but detected no trace of you, then a full day scanning the other continent,' said Dharya. 'But without hundreds of drones to deploy it wasn't the best search methodology.'

'We were in an underground facility near Stronghold, the large city on the sparsely populated continent,' I said. 'You couldn't have detected us even if you'd known exactly where to look.'

'As Haven isn't a member of the galactic council, we technically have no jurisdiction, so while we waited for permission for a full-scale on-the-ground search and rescue we decided that they should stay in orbit around the planet and observe. Dharya saw your cobbled together tug and ship combo break orbit so we jumped back here but before we arrived the ship vanished. We couldn't contact you over Infosys or follow you through hyperspace. But we knew you'd find a way to contact us so we waited until you did,' said Kas. 'We programmed the nav system with jump coordinates for all the nearby star systems so we'd be ready whichever way you went.'

'You mean if I'd been a bit slower hooking up the hyperdrive to the tug you'd have been rescuing us above Haven and we wouldn't have had to do that crazily dangerous jump?'

'I'm afraid so,' said Kas.

'Did you see Sandora's gigantic ship leave the mine near Stronghold?' I asked Dharya.

'What ship is that?'

'A huge ship, bigger than a liner. Big enough for thousands of people. If you'd seen it you'd know.'

'We didn't, we were searching for you. It was only because we were monitoring ships leaving the planet that we saw you break orbit and jump. We saw nothing else leave orbit while we were there.'

'If they didn't break orbit then they must have gone to the biggest city on Destiny to pick up the faithful, like you said they would,' said Jones.

'Perhaps you were on the orbiting on the other side of the planet, and they stayed in the atmosphere. That way you wouldn't have detected them,' I said. 'So it's likely that Sandora's managed to start the Emancipation. How long would it take to load everyone and everything onto that monster?'

'A long time, many hours,' said Jones.

'I think so too. Kas, we have to go back to Haven, right now. Sandora could still be there.'

Kas spoke into their cuff and ordered a rapid jump back and a low orbit over the most populated city.

We had, by now, arrived at the operations room. I was exhausted and flopped down into one of the comfy chairs. It felt like early evening to me but I had no idea what the ship's local time was. I hadn't eaten since the evening meal the day before yesterday by my own personal time.

Kas knew me well and recognized the symptoms so before long a large hot cup of tea and a plate of sandwiches was produced without me even asking. Kas had also done their homework and Jones had similar sandwiches but with coffee. As I ate, I filled Kas and the others in on everything that had happened since we had last spoken.

We watched on the screens as we approached Haven, passed over Covenant and headed towards Destiny.

'We're deploying drones now to search Stronghold and the surrounding areas,' said Kas. 'There's no point in secrecy and subterfuge, so we'll search properly.'

We were in a very low orbit and soon I caught my first sight of the other continent, Destiny. We were too high to see much detail, but it looked a lot greener than Covenant, from what we could see between the gaps in the clouds. It must have been early morning on large parts of Destiny.

'We're scanning for the energy signature of a large space ship. Anything big enough to carry thousands of people must have enormous grav generators just to fly so we should be able to detect it. I'm also deploying drones to each of the cities.'

'Thanks Kas,' I said.

I had a nagging suspicion that Sandora would be long gone.

One of the operators controlling the drones signalled Kas, who nodded for them to report.

'Per Marshall, the drones are showing just a few hundred people in Stronghold. Two hundred and eleven so far spotted.'

'Where are they all?' I asked.

'Almost all of them are in or around the large official looking building in town.'

'The Congressarium,' said Jones.

'They're probably looking for the proctors to find out what is going on.'

One of the screens lit up showing the familiar building in the evening light, and sure enough there were scenes of what looked very like an angry mob milling about. I hoped anger wouldn't escalate to violence.

'Put in a call for the navy to send a peacekeeping force there as soon as possible please,' said Kas to one of the operators. 'I've seen mobs like that go from shouting to killing all too easily. Make sure they're well equipped for relief aid.'

Another operator signalled for Kas' attention.

'I'm not detecting anything at all Per Marshall. No grav generators of any size, no significant power usage and no radiation other than the planetary background. If the ship is here, it's powered down and well hidden. Probably deep underground.'

'Keep scanning. If you spot anything like mine entrances or caves then send drones in to search.'

A third operator caught Kas' eye.

'The drones are reporting in now Per Marshall. The three cities are abandoned as far as I can tell. I've not encountered a single person.'

'Sandora's gone Kas,' I said. 'We've missed her.'

Everyone in the room turned to look at me.

'How can you be so sure?' asked Kas.

'The cities are empty. There doesn't seem to be any kind of underground cave system to hide the ship in, although I suppose we can't be absolutely sure of that for a little while longer. I think as soon as Mal and I escaped Sandora wasted absolutely no time at all looking for us, she just put her plan into action. She got everyone from the base on board, plus select key personnel from Stronghold then she headed straight for the cities in Destiny to start The Emancipation. You need to get the navy on high alert. She will target Scarlastion, Coronnol, Mirth and as many other advanced scientific university planets as she has stellar probes for. If she knows where the major navy bases are she'll probably target those too.'

'How do we find her?' asked Kas.

'It's going to be virtually impossible, isn't it?' asked Jones. 'Or do you know something we don't?'

'I know exactly where that ship is going,' I said. 'And we need to go there too before it's too late.'

'Where?' asked Kas.

'Earth. She's going to Earth.' I answered.

Chapter 39
Earth

'Why would she go there?' asked Praanvi. 'It's a museum, a tourist attraction.'

'To most people, yes, that's all it is. An interesting holiday destination, a curiosity. To terraformers and biologists though it's the template, the blueprint, the ideal to aspire to and crucially the nursery. All the plants and animals used to terraform a new world come from Earth, always. But to the Primitives it's so much more, it's a sacred place, a mythological homeland that actually exists. They resent the fact that humanity ever left, they consider it their birthright, their one true home.'

'Cem, I don't think you can be right about this,' said Kas. 'They wouldn't be able to take over Earth. We would have a dozen navy cruisers there in hours. Even if that ship has eight thousand people on it, that's nowhere near enough to occupy the planet and hold on to it. They'd struggle to take over the capitol city let alone the whole planet against what would certainly be spirited resistance.'

I looked round the room, everyone seemed to be agreeing with Kas and they were looking at me like I was mad. I took a deep breath and pressed on.

'They're not planning to occupy Earth. At least not initially. Sandora is stealing it.'

There was a stunned silence.

'What?' exclaimed Dharya, incredulous. 'How?'

'She considers this galaxy to be a lost cause. As far as the Primitives are concerned there are too many people, too dependent on technology. The Scarlastion neural interface was the last straw for Sandora and her inner circle. They want to leave us behind and start again, live a simpler life without technology, but they want to do that far away in the next galaxy so they're safe. Sandora said as much. It would take far too long to terraform a suitable planet there, she doesn't have the time. It could take years to find one, then decades to make it habitable. But it wouldn't take years to find a suitable star that doesn't have a planet in the goldilocks zone. That's all she needs. She's going to create a gigantic wormhole and take the Earth and put it in orbit around the star she's found. This solves all her problems. Her devoted followers get to live on Earth, something they've no doubt dreamed of[1]. Humanity here is crippled, we're deprived of the source material for any future terraforming, plus we'd be so busy dealing with the aftermath of her supernova attacks we wouldn't even notice the Earth was gone for some time even if Infosys survives her attack on it.'

'I think you're right,' said Jones. 'It's possible. The maths would be absolutely horrendous but there's no reason, theoretically, why it wouldn't work.'

'She may even go one step further,' I said. 'It's just occurred to me that perhaps she plans to destroy Sol, the Earth's sun. If she did that just after she'd taken the Earth through a wormhole, we wouldn't even know she'd stolen it. We'd assume she was so crazy she'd destroyed it in a supernova.'

Kas didn't look completely convinced but called up the captain to order the ship to Earth in the fewest possible jumps.

'We need to get in touch with Randolf,' I said. 'If the maths is horrendous, for moving a whole planet, then we need him here. He, Praanvi, Dharya and Mal between them should be able to come up with something as we don't stand much chance of rescuing Grippe just at the moment.'

Jones looked down at her cuff, which was finally active again since we'd boarded Kas' ship. The internal power grid had started charging it the moment we arrived. She stroked it almost affectionately.

'I'll call him,' she said.

'We're a long way from Earth,' said Kas, turning back to me. 'It's going to be at least a dozen jumps, and that's six or seven fewer than the captain is really happy with. It'll give you some time to rest. We should still arrive before Sandora. A ship that size won't be able to skip so many jumps and will take longer to re-charge. Unless she's set up a wormhole straight to it. Then we'll be too late, much too late.'

I nodded but I doubted she'd had time to do that.

'Keep someone on a continuous live call to our office on Earth so you know if anything happens. We don't want to pop out of

---

[1] The galactic council hasn't allowed immigration to Earth for millennia. The population is very carefully controlled.

hyperspace into the middle of a supernova. I presume you've already dispatched the nearest naval ships?'

'I have. There's only two able to get there faster than us. I didn't tell them much, only that an unregistered liner-class space ship may try to enter the Earth system and they were to stop it at any cost. Other ships will arrive as and when they can. Are you absolutely sure about this Cem?'

'I am, but I wish I wasn't. It occurs to me that Sandora must have tested moving a planet through a wormhole. Her whole plan depends on knowing it will work, unless she truly is deranged and doesn't care one way or the other and I really didn't get that sense from her. She's calm, reasonable and competent, within certain crazy parameters. Can you put some people on checking for any unexplained planetary disappearances or appearances? It won't be an inhabited world, that would have been noticed immediately, but it would have to have an atmosphere and be roughly Earth sized. That should narrow it down somewhat.'

'Do you have any idea how many planets fall into that category? Hundreds of thousands.'

'You'd better get on with it then,' I said, with my best cheeky grin.

I looked over at Jones, she'd finished her call. She looked tired, and very worried.

'What's the matter?' I asked.

'I couldn't get hold of Danatis, so I contacted CI Andrews. He's going to call me back in a few minutes when he's checked in with the team guarding him.'

'That's a bit worrying, but I'm sure Danatis is fine. That beautiful redhead, Scott, is probably distracting him. You must have noticed the way he looked at her? We've been assigned quarters on this deck, so we're near the operations room. We'll be at least six hours getting to Earth. I need a shower and some sleep. It would be a good idea to get some rest if you can.'

We headed for our assigned quarters, our cuffs guiding us. We were standing outside Jones' room when her cuff chimed.

'It's CI Andrews. Hello? What news?'

The call was audio only, which seemed odd. Then I found out why.

'Doctor Jones I'm afraid I have some bad news for you. Per Randolf is missing. I'm at the apartment building now, Examiner

Pascal is dead and Senior Examiner Scott is seriously injured. There's no sign of Randolf. I'm having the security camera footage examined and when I know more you'll be informed. It's a real mess here. The door to Randolf's apartment has been forced open. We found Pascal in the corridor. He must have tried to intervene. Someone crushed him, just squeezed him until his ribs snapped and his lungs collapsed. Scott is in a coma with a shattered jaw, spinal fractures and internal injuries. She may not survive. I'm instructing you to return to Coronnol immediately to help us with our enquiries.'

Andrews' normally steady calm demeanour had crumbled and his voice was shaking with raw emotion.

Jones looked at me with tears in her eyes. I felt sick. I shook my head to let her know not to reveal she was with me.

'I'm so very sorry CI Andrews but that won't be possible for the foreseeable future. I can't explain but I will return, and tell you what I can, as soon as I'm able. Please do pass my condolences on to Examiner Pascal's family and I wish a full and speedy recovery to Senior Examiner Scott.'

She cut the connection over Andrews' urgent insistence that she return.

'It has to be Gernard,' I said. 'He's from Cestus. He could easily kill someone like that. Sandora has clearly not headed directly to Earth. She's stopped off at Coronnol to grab Randolf on the way.'

'We have to get him back,' said Jones, her voice breaking with barely repressed emotion.

'We will, and Gernard will answer for what he's done,' I said grimly.

That news put paid to any idea of getting some sleep. We headed for my quarters to find out more in private.

The guest quarters on the cruiser class ships were superb. There was plenty of room on board, so the cabins were always on the generous side. A snack and drinks bar, a double bed, a pair of comfortable arm chairs and a wet-room all to yourself. Under the bed was copious storage space, half was full of clean clothing in assorted sizes, half was empty for those travelling with rather more luggage than we had, which was none. The carpet was deep, soft and warm, the room had subtle under-floor heating.

'I've been on worse liners than this,' said Jones, clearly surprised.

'Did you expect hard metal bunks and cold ceramic tiled floors in the navy?'

'Frankly, yes. Yes, I did.'

I got two shots of a good whisky from the snack bar then we sat in the arm chairs, sipping them.

I pulled up a large virtual screen and connected to Coronnol's police department. As I was calling from a naval vessel and using my own special cuff, I was able to bypass most of their security and was soon allowed into even the most sensitive parts of the police's Infosys domain.

'Let's see what Andrews' cameras saw,' I said.

I located the feed from Danatis' apartment. The apartment complex appeared on four screens from four different cameras. One was looking at the main entrance from inside, two showed the view down his corridor from opposite ends, and the last was in his apartment, focused on the front door.

'Is this live?' asked Jones.

I confirmed that it was. The door looked like it had been hit by a rhinoceros, the hinges were shattered and the wood splintered. The inside of the apartment was trashed, completely. There had been quite a struggle in there. I guessed that would have been Scott rather than Randolf. He wasn't a fighter. There were four uniformed police on guard. Not that the attacker was ever coming back, I'd see to that. I found the time index controls and started winding backwards fairly quickly. We watched the guards twitch jerkily as the clock sped backwards, then they vanished and the figure of CI Andrews appeared. We saw some paramedics rush about urgently, they delivered an injured looking Scott to the apartment and the inert shape of Pascal to the corridor. Andrews moved around the apartment cautiously, kneeling for a moment next to Scott and Pascal then ran down the corridor in reverse. A few moments passed with nothing much happening. Then we saw a short powerful figure bring someone in through the front door over their shoulder, carried them, backwards, down the corridor and into the apartment through the smashed door before going off camera into another part of the apartment. They returned alone then proceeded to tidy the apartment, hindered by Scott who seemed to be trying valiantly to stop them. The short figure then went out pulling the door back into place and shutting it. It took some doing to get the door back into the frame. There was a lot of frenzied shoulder charging and kicking, interrupted briefly by Examiner Pascal, who got up off the ground and wrestled with the figure before going back into the apartment opposite. The short stocky figure walked backwards down the corridor and out of the building. I froze the image on the figure as they passed through the doorway, where it was brightest. I zoomed in on the face. As we'd known all along it was Doctor Bertrand Farley Gernard.

I clicked on play and we watched the whole scene forwards at normal speed. Pascal stood no chance. He should have stunned Gernard first and asked questions later, but he was too civilized. He'd approached him and spoken to him. The ferocity of Gernard's attack had taken him completely by surprise. Gernard had slammed him into the wall then wrapped his arms around him, pinning Pascal's arms to his sides, and squeezed, just as Andrews had said. They'd staggered around in the corridor for a short while as Pascal thrashed about trying to break free but it was over for him before he knew what had happened. We could clearly see the moment when he took his final painful breath as his ribs snapped under the relentless pressure from Gernard. He was held, for a further thirty seconds then dropped like a broken toy. Gernard's rage was then turned on the door, when Randolf and Scott refused to open it. We saw Scott send Randolf into the bedroom and try to call for backup on her cuff, but they were too far away to be of any use. Gernard had reasoned that the locks might be reinforced but it was unlikely the hinges had been, so he attacked there. The structure of the door had simply given way. Scott had rushed at him and had got some good blows in; she'd taken Gernard by surprise; her martial arts skills were impressive but he was just too strong. Once he'd got hold of her he'd thrown her around the apartment like a doll, smashing her into the furniture until eventually she stopped getting up.

I stopped the playback and sent a copy of the footage to Kas. When we caught up with Gernard I wanted this on record so I had greater freedom of action with him.

The feed started again and we saw Gernard come out with Randolf over his shoulder. He was clearly unconscious, but I couldn't see any significant injuries. I shut down the connection.

I was trembling and could feel hot angry tears burning on my cheeks. Jones had put her hands over her face and was sobbing. I had liked Pascal. I was furious that his plans to becoming an Investigator working for Andrews would now never be realised.

'How could anyone behave like that?' she finally managed to ask. 'Leaving us to die in our crippled space ship was bad enough but I've never, ever, seen anyone capable of violence like this.'

'He's sick,' I said and took her hand. Something in his heart or his head is broken. We'll probably never know what. We will get Danatis back, I will do everything I can to do that. As you've seen, I am pretty resourceful.'

Jones politely smiled at my poor attempt to lighten the mood. She got up and went to sit on the bed.

'I need some sleep,' she said. 'But I don't want to be alone. I think my head might pop if I'm alone with my thoughts.'

She kicked her shoes off and lay down. I joined her and dimmed the lights to minimum. We lay side by side, then she took my hand and we went to sleep.

I woke up a few hours later, alone. I felt grubby, tired and hungry. There wasn't much I could do about being tired just yet but the other two needs were easily taken care of. A long hot shower then a short cold one cleaned and refreshed me. I threw the clothes Sandora had provided into the recycler, then found some suitable items from under the bed. The snack bar provided me with tea and a selection of fruit.

I wondered how long it was since Jones had left. I hadn't heard her leave. The door chimed and my cuff lit up showing it was Kas outside.

'Come in,' I said.

The door opened and Kas stood on the threshold, looking a little uncomfortable.

'Are you alone?' they asked.

I confirmed that I was and Kas came in and sat themself down in one of the chairs.

'We've finally found Sandora's Infosys records. She did a very passable job of removing herself and her whole family from the databases. She must have hired someone very resourceful and skilled to unlink all the information and scatter it. We have her full information and most of her bondmate Sacha's. Other family members, if any, will appear in time as we rebuild the files.'

'Thanks for that. I'll review it later when I have time. How far from Earth are we now?'

'We're almost half way to Earth. I need you to ask Doctor Jones to work with Dharya and Praanvi. As we don't have Doctor Grippe, to disable any wormholes that Sandora creates, those three are our best hope. If she will explain her stellar probe technology and Randolf's mathematics to them I'm hoping those giant brains will be able to design something that will help. We have almost complete simulations ready to go thanks to your scans back at the lab on Coronnol. So if she fills in the blanks we can fabricate the real thing. What do you think? Will she cooperate?'

'Why would you think she wouldn't? The stakes are so high. As long as we ensure the technology is used only for this one purpose. You can't take this away from her, it's her life's work.'

'No one is suggesting we appropriate it. I wouldn't allow that. Talk to her. We don't have a lot of time.'

'I will. Assuming we can resolve the Sandora issue, we then need to talk about what we do about Scarlastion's neural interface. Sandora's plan may be an extreme and horrifying overreaction but she's not wrong about the danger it poses to the human race.'

'That problem is, I think, above our pay grade. The galactic council will have to discuss that and reach a decision.'

We both left my quarters. Kas went back to the operations room and I went next door to Jones' room. I pressed the chime and waited. The door opened quite quickly and I saw Jones sitting on the bed with several virtual screens projected from her cuff. She too had changed her clothes and showered.

'Come in,' she said.

'Are you alright? What are you up to?' I asked.

'No, I'm not alright. I'm worried sick about Danatis and, I'm ashamed to say, considerably less worried about Grippe. I'm working on Randolf's equations and Grippe's wormhole generator. I've got the full specs up and I'm trying to work out how we could adapt one of my probes to interfere with the wormhole creation. It's tough going.'

It seemed we weren't going to talk about falling asleep holding hands and her quietly leaving.

'I'm sorry about running off, but I hadn't intended to change the nature of our relationship unilaterally,' she said, proving me wrong. 'I do like you but I should have kept things professional. I only slept for a short while and when I woke up I realised how inappropriate I'd been and just knew I had to leave and get to work. You needed to rest so I thought it best to come here. Are you alright?'

'Tired, but I didn't sleep for long either. You're right about needing to stay professional, at least until we've stopped Sandora, but I was very happy to hold hands. I think we both just needed some human contact after what we watched and the experiences of the last few days. On the subject of work, Kas came to see me and they offered Dharya and Praanvi's services to help you.'

'Really? That's what Kas said?'

'Well not exactly. Kas wanted you to help them design a countermeasure, but it's your project, your technology and you are the only person who understands Randolf's mathematics and the new hyperspace equations. If Praanvi can't understand them after you've explained, I would be amazed. She is one of the smartest people in the galaxy. The two of them can help you. We have incomplete simulations of your probes and I'm certain the three of you together can do what Grippe could. The Organisation have no intention of stealing your research. It's yours. But we do need to use it to stop Sandora. They'll have some unused SSPs here, you could encode one of those to your cuff and your project. That way you protect your research if you don't trust Kas.'

'Okay. Let's go and see them.'

Our cuffs guided us to one of the labs on the ship. They were fantastically well equipped as you'd expect. Dharya and Praanvi were both waiting when we got there. Dharya opened a cupboard and handed a familiar looking device to Jones. She tapped her cuff on the SSP to sync it, pulled up a screen and started entering her security information.

'We completely respect your intellectual property Doctor Jones,' said Praanvi. 'We wouldn't do anything to compromise the publication of your work, your reputation or that of Coronnol University.'

'Understood,' said Jones. 'This will take a couple of minutes to finish synchronising. In the meantime, let me explain the principles of the wormhole hyperspace generator.'

I didn't understand more than one word in ten of the complex mathematics and physics being discussed but I could tell from Praanvi and Dharya's faces that they both completely understood her and were suitably impressed.

I left them to it and headed back to the operations room. Kas was there finishing off a call with someone dressed in a captain's uniform in the galactic navy.

'Captain Raven has arrived at Earth. He's taken up a high orbit around the planet and has his sensors set to maximum range. Another ship will arrive within the hour then they'll start elliptical orbits to cover a greater area. If Sandora somehow gets there before we do, they will disable her ship and take it under tow.'

'Great. Let's hope it's that easy,' I said, knowing it absolutely wouldn't be. 'How's the search for a planet that's moved coming along?'

'It's not. We've found nothing. We're trawling through every known system and we started the search centred on solar systems near Haven, as it's likely they wouldn't have gone too far to test it.'

'Start another search centred on Coronnol's star with the same parameters. Sandora manufactured the probes there at the winery, so she may have done her testing near there as well.'

Kas nodded and passed the instructions along to one of the people running the screens, who quickly started composing the search.

We watched and saw no results even as the search radius wound further and further out from Coronnol, just as the one centred on Haven was now many light-years away from its centre but was also producing no hits.

I had a feeling I was missing something, something obvious. I stared at the search results willing them to change.

'Doctor Jones is working with Dharya and Praanvi down in one of the labs. I assured her you're not going to appropriate her work and she's set up an SSP to protect it. Her last one was destroyed when we crashed on Haven.'

Kas frowned but didn't object.

'How many completely uncharted solar systems are there within the search parameters?' I asked.

'None at all' answered the operator. 'Unless Infosys is wrong.'

'That's it!' I exclaimed. 'Sandora has hidden the test planet by altering the data in Infosys somehow, like they managed to hide Haven by making it appear to be a system with no habitable planets. She's chosen a planet, amended our records to remove it then removed the planet. That way as far as Infosys is concerned all is well. Set two more searches running looking for systems that have inconsistent data between now and, let's say, the Infosys archive from six months ago. Centre one on Coronnol and one on Haven.'

The operator's hands flew and two additional screens appeared showing the parameters I'd just suggested. This search went much faster and pretty soon was scanning systems tens of light-years from the centre with no hits.

'Start it again,' I said. 'but use the archive from a year ago and from two years ago.'

The Haven search continued to be blank but after a minute or two the Coronnol centred one spat out a single result.

'That's it!' said Kas.

'I'm afraid not,' said the operator, 'that planet is still where it's supposed to be. It's just a minor data correction.'

'What kind of correction?' I asked.

'There was an update on the orbital statistics, correcting what appears to be bad data from the previous survey.'

'Show me,' I said.

The data on the planet's orbit appeared. The planet was in the exact same orbit around the star but it was six hours behind where it was expected to be in its journey around the star.

'That is it, Kas. That is most definitely it. They knew snatching a planet would be discovered, even one that's uninhabited, so they put it back! But they didn't have Randolf with them to help with the mathematics. They took it somewhere else, presumably in our galaxy, but once it arrived they moved the wormhole generators, using a space ship, to the destination system. They re-programmed them and sent the planet back where it came from. But what they couldn't do was correct for the six hours it took to move and reset the wormhole generators, so it went back to exactly where it came from. Six hours behind where it should be in orbit.'

'Is there anybody on that planet?' asked Kas.

'Yes, a research team. It's earmarked for possible terraforming within the next few years. They're geologists. They've been there since before the data change,' said the operator.

'Call them,' said Kas.

After a moment a screen popped up in front of us, full height for a regular sized person. We heard a ring tone then someone shuffled into view, obviously struggling to wake up. They were completely naked apart from the cuff on their left wrist.

'What do you want?' said the naked man.

'I'm calling from the Galactic Navy, I'm Commodore Jareth Mythias Denham,' said Kas, using one of their more impressive aliases. 'What is your name please?'

'I'm Doctor Albrecht Linus Vorsheer, it's the middle of the night here. What. Do. You. Want?'

He seemed quite angry. We heard a voice from off camera complaining about being woken up then a pair of trousers were thrown at Doctor Vorsheer. He caught them and pulled them on, without any sign of embarrassment.

Kas checked the date of the wormhole jump and asked the Doctor if he'd been on the planet at that time.

'Of course I was!' he snapped. 'We've been here for just under two years. Got about six months to go before we submit our report to the terraforming council.'

'You didn't notice anything unusual?' I asked, stepping into the frame at our end.

'No, nothing. Everything is fine here. Why? Should we be worried?'

'Not at all. Thank you Doctor. If we need you again we'll be in touch,' said Kas then they signalled to cut the connection.

The angry Vorsheer was cut off mid-swearword and the virtual screen vanished.

'That's definitely the place. They must have done it at night while Vorsheer and his people were asleep. He never even noticed. Sandora would have needed to know that organic life could survive the trip through the wormhole. The doctor and his team will be in bio-domes as the planet's not been terraformed yet, but it tells us that it is possible to move a planet completely, without killing everyone on it or causing it to break up. Get him back on the screen please.'

Kas nodded to the operator who made the connection again.

The screen re-appeared and Vorsheer stamped back into the frame. He was naked again.

'What now!' he bellowed.

I pulled images of Sandora and Gernard up on my cuff, enlarged the screen and showed them to him.

'Do you recognize either of these people Doctor Vorsheer?' I asked.

He looked at them for a moment.

'Yes. I've seen them both. They were here around the time you asked about. They landed on the planet, they said they had engine trouble. They were here for a couple of hours. We gave them a meal, any company is welcome company after eighteen months alone, they repaired their ship and they left. Can't remember their names, the woman was nice enough but the man was very unpleasant. My bondmate didn't like him one bit.'

A voice off camera said something we couldn't catch.

'Sandra and Bertrand or something, he says. Now leave me alone to sleep will you.'

Vorsheer cut the connection this time and our screen vanished.

'That's close enough for me,' I said.

'And me,' said Kas.

The next few hours dragged by anxiously as each jump brought us closer to Earth. Captain Raven informed us the other navy ship had arrived and they'd, as yet, detected no unauthorised ships, in fact no ships at all. All legitimate traffic to Earth was suspended both inbound and outbound. I resisted the urge to go and check on Jones and the others. If they managed to find a way to prevent the wormhole formation, they'd let me know. There was nothing I could do to help. I'd just be a distraction. I was not comfortable waiting, but sometimes there was literally nothing else to do.

After what seemed an eternity we were informed by the captain that we were about to make the last jump, the next stop was the home of humanity. In fact, the home of virtually all life in the galaxy. The planet Earth.

Chapter 40
Moon

I headed for the bridge. It felt like the place to be at such a moment. It was near the operations room, right at the front of the cruiser, and when I entered I could feel the tension. The cruiser class ship typically has seven stations on the semi-circular bridge. The captain is right in the centre, in front of her were the pilot and the navigator, facing the windows. Then from the captain's right-hand side, working around the outer wall behind her to the left-hand side were communications, science, engineering and weapons. One of the other bridge officers would be doubling up as the second in command.

I stood in the doorway, as protocol demanded.

'Permission to enter the bridge, captain?' I asked.

Captain Yoshi Asano Tamaki didn't even glance my way, but I could tell from a slight stiffening in her posture that she wasn't particularly pleased to have a spectator on the bridge.

'Granted,' she said cordially enough.

I moved around to my left and sat at a spare seat near the weapons console.

The navigator and the pilot worked seamlessly together plotting the jump to Earth.

'Be ready to get moving the instant we exit hyperspace,' said the captain. 'If something's gone wrong I don't want to present a stationary target.'

I noticed a discreet countdown timer overlayed on the bottom left corner of the window, which doubled as a gigantic screen.

'Weapons ready,' said the person next to me, which was followed immediately afterwards by the rest of the bridge crew.

'Engineering ready.'

'Comms ready.'

'Science ready.'

'Navigation ready'

'Pilot ready'

The countdown hit zero and the stars winked into a different formation and then lurched sharply left and down as the pilot immediately banked hard right and upwards.

The Earth came into view with the sun in the far distance behind it. A tactical overlay started appearing on the window, showing the positions of the two navy ships already on patrol and other pertinent data. I was intrigued to get my first ever view of Earth in such a stressful situation. It looked peaceful and serene. The side facing us was in darkness, but between the gaps in the cloud cover I could see a few bright patches of light that could only be major cities.

'No vessels beyond the two navy ships detected so far,' said the science officer, who had four medium-sized virtual screens in an arc around his station. Data streamed across two of them and complex visuals filled the other two.

'Co-ordinate with the other two ships to ensure the widest possible scanning range as we orbit the Earth,' said the captain.

The navigator went to work, linking their console to the other two ships to generate a complex three-ship interlocking search pattern centred on the planet. As I watched I saw the tactical view shifting to reflect the new orbits calculated by the addition of a third ship.

'How certain are you that there's a threat to the Earth?' asked Captain Tamaki, who finally turned to look at me.

'Absolutely certain,' I replied.

The Earth now filled the viewscreen. I could see the terminator as our orbit brought us round towards the daylight. It was a stunningly beautiful planet.

Then I noticed something. Something someone more familiar with Earth would have known immediately. The Earth had a huge natural moon, about a sixth of the size of Earth itself.

'Captain, what's that moon called?' I asked.

'The Moon.'

I wondered if the captain was being deliberately stupid. I thought I'd asked a fairly simple question.

'Yes, the moon. That moon there. What's it called?' I tried again.

'It's called The Moon. That's it. Nothing else. Humanity evolved here. There was just the one moon so it was called The Moon.'

I thanked the captain, pulled up a virtual screen from my cuff and spent ten minutes querying Infosys about moons and the Moon in particular. Then I left at a run and didn't stop until I found Jones, Dharya and Praanvi's lab.

They looked around in some surprise as I burst in.

'There will need to be two wormholes. With two absolutely horrific sets of calculations. The Earth has an enormous natural satellite called, prosaically enough, The Moon. They'll have to take that too. The Earth and the Moon orbit each other, though the barycentre[1] is within the Earth's surface. If Sandora takes the Earth and not the Moon, then the Earth will not survive long. Every living organism on it has evolved with its influence factored in. Without it there'll be no tides, for a start, and the whole ecosystem will be unbalanced. I grew up on a planet with a very large satellite. It influenced the tides, the currents in the sea, the weather, everything. Apparently, it made terraforming the planet a nightmare back when it was founded. But Sandora's from Scarlastion and has lived for decades on Haven, Gernard is from Cestus, Doctor Vorsheer was on, an as yet, unnamed planet designated for terraforming and the one thing they all have in common is that none of those planets have any satellites larger than a small meteorite. They're merely a hazard to navigation, whereas the Moon has a medium-sized city on it. If Sandora hasn't factored in taking the Moon she's not just depriving life in this galaxy of its origin and its nursery she's destroying the Earth and likely killing every living thing on it. I have no precise idea what will happen to the Moon and the people on it if it gets cut adrift from the Earth but I can't see a scenario where it ends well.'

'What made you think of this?' asked Jones.

'I saw the tactical display on the bridge and the orbits the navy ships are doing looked especially complex and then I realised that was because of the Moon. I did a bit of research and then came straight here. Is it possible to set up a wormhole to take the Moon too, or one massive wormhole to snatch both?'

Jones and the others turned to their respective screens and their fingers flew over the controls for a few minutes. There was a lot of mathematical chatter between them and equations flew up the screens, all of which was completely indecipherable to me.

'Yes and no,' said Praanvi.

'What?'

'Yes, it is theoretically possible to take the Moon too, but no, not with one giant wormhole.'

'Why?'

---

[1] The barycentre is the centre of mass of two or more bodies that orbit one another and is the point about which the bodies orbit.

'For two wormholes the timing is absolutely crucial. The difference in the relative diameter and mass between the Earth and the Moon makes positioning the two wormholes, so that the two bodies enter and exit them simultaneously, extraordinarily difficult. It would take Infosys hours, if not days to run those numbers and if they were out even by the smallest margin you would end up with earthquakes, tidal waves and atmospheric disruption on Earth so bad it would devastate the planet. We think a stable wormhole large enough to swallow the Earth and the Moon just wouldn't be possible, the power requirement alone would be prohibitive. Even if you could solve the power problem,'

'Which you can't,' interrupted Dharya.

'You'd have the same problem with timing too, only worse. You couldn't position one wormhole so that the two bodies entered and exited with their relative positions intact.'

'I think the three of us agree that it's unlikely that Sandora has considered this,' said Jones looking at Dharya and Praanvi, who both nodded.

'When she arrives let's hope she's amenable to reason then,' I said.

I think we all knew how likely that was.

'How are we going to communicate with her?' asked Jones. 'She won't have an Infosys link on her ship.'

'Radio. There must be a radio. She had to have called Destiny on one before they took off from the mine to get everyone ready to board. I'll go and find the chief engineer and get them to find or build a radio. Keep working on a wormhole countermeasure. We may need it more than ever if we're now preventing the destruction of the Earth not just its theft. How's it going, by the way?'

Dharya started to explain, as I headed for the door, about wave-points, harmonics, quantum fluctuations and other phenomena so I interrupted.

'Short version, Dharya. Very short version.'

'We have a promising model in the simulator. We're running some tests. It definitely collapses the wormhole but it does it in a very unpredictable way and we think there's a good chance anything nearby will end up pulled inside and be ejected at an indeterminate location.'

'We will have it working for you in time,' said Jones. But I could tell from her body language she wasn't completely convinced of that herself.

I waved a goodbye and headed off back to the bridge to find the chief engineer.

The captain granted me permission to enter and I stood politely next to the chief engineer until she asked me what I wanted. When I did, she looked extremely puzzled.

'A radio?' she said, as if I'd just asked for two pieces of flint to start a fire with.

She was a serious looking woman in her mid-to-late fifties. She was tall, thin, with short grey hair cut in a very fashionable style. She also had more piercings in her ears than anyone I'd ever seen and the edges of complex tattoos were just visible at the collar and cuffs on her uniform.

'An actual carrier-wave based electromagnetic spectrum communication device?'

'Yes,' I said.

'I'm aware of them, but I've never seen one in use. I doubt anyone has since shortly after the invention of Infosys.'

'Sandora and her primitives have. They use them instead of Infosys. I guess that means you don't have one?'

'No.'

'Could you build one?'

'Yes. We could do it in a few minutes. I'm sure there are plenty of designs in InfoSys,' she pulled up a screen from her cuff and started flicking through a menu of design schematics. 'The fabrication facilities onboard are cable of making almost anything. There are half a dozen ways to encode speech into radio frequencies though. Which one will they be using on board the ship we're looking for?'

'How should I know? Can't you make one that works on all the known systems?'

The engineer rolled her eyes. I knew the look. It was the look an expert gets when a layman asks them for something stupid.

'Yes. I can. But we won't be able to tell the difference between them not receiving our transmission, because we're transmitting using the wrong system, and them simply refusing to answer us. Which makes working out which system they have problematic.'

'They don't use Infosys. That's their fundamental principle. So I'm guessing they'd use whatever system was easiest to build without access to that. Something basic. Something with a range of only a few hundred kilometres on a planet. Start there and add on whatever else you think is likely. Let me know when it's ready, please.'

The engineer reluctantly went to work and I went to find Kas.

The operations room was as busy as ever. Kas was working on something on their cuff but flicked it closed when I sat down next to them.

'Progress?' asked Kas.

'Some. Jones, Dharya and Praanvi have a simulation of a device that can close a wormhole, but not safely. They're going to keep working on it but I think we need to fabricate one of them, just in case. We may decide it's better to risk some collateral damage than risk the Earth.'

Kas agreed, passed the order on and then I brought them up to speed on the issue regarding the Moon and that the chief engineer was building me a radio.

'Do you honestly think Sandora will be amenable to reason?' Kas asked.

'No. I don't. Gernard most definitely won't. But there have to be others on board who will be. In any group like the Primitives there's always a fanatical few in control driving the agenda but there will be those who aren't fully committed. We need to talk to them.'

'Those people won't have use of the radio though. We need a way to communicate with the mass of people on board. I have an idea about that. I also have a way to get someone on board. It's experimental and potentially very dangerous so I'm probably going to go myself. I can't order anyone else to try it.'

I insisted Kas show it to me. When they did I agreed that it looked absolutely crazy but I knew if anyone stood a chance of making it work it was me rather than Kas. In this instance being a field agent trumped whatever seniority Kas may have had.

'How are we going to stop the ship when it arrives?' I asked.

'That, we're not certain of. We can't just open fire on it. The galactic council will likely consider the majority of the thousands of people on board to be victims rather than perpetrators, and I'm very much inclined to that view myself. They've probably no idea what's really going on. As the ship isn't a standard model and has no

Infosys connectivity, we can't commandeer it remotely and without a reasonably detailed schematic we wouldn't even know how to disable the engines. It will take time to scan the ship and work out how to fire on it in such a way as to disable the engines or any weapons systems.'

'So what's it to be?'

'We're going to start by tagging it with trackers in case it jumps again trying to get away, then we'll physically block it with our ships to prevent it entering any wormhole while we scan it for vulnerabilities.'

'It's at least three times the size of this ship.'

'It's handy we have three ships then, and more on the way. The last thing I want is mass casualties but if it's a choice between that and the destruction of the Earth...' Kas' voice tailed off and they looked pale and ill. 'Well let's say I'm hoping that's a decision I don't have to make.'

Kas' cuff chimed and Captain Tamaki's face appeared.

'A very large ship has just dropped out of hyperspace and is heading towards the Earth at high speed. Our ships have tagged it with several hyperspace trackers already and we're moving to intercept, they won't get away,' she said.

Chapter 41
Interception

K as activated a large screen, so we could see the same view that the captain was seeing on the bridge, complete with tactical overlays. We were the furthest ship from Sandora's monster vessel, but we were fast, manoeuvrable and closing quickly. The other two ships were almost on her.

I checked with the chief engineer and was told the basic radio was complete and that new circuits, to work on alternative radio systems, were being added constantly. A new menu option appeared on my cuff granting me access to the transmitter. I activated it.

'This is the navy cruiser, Rubicon, calling Sandora Willow Sylvester, Doctor Bertrand Farley Gernard or anyone on the ship from Haven. Your plan to transport the Earth will result in death and destruction, you must not proceed. Please respond by radio,' I said, and set it to auto-repeat on every frequency until I got a reply.

I then called Jones to check on her progress.

'We're really close. Just give us a little longer,' she said.

'I'd love to,' I replied, 'but it's not up to me. Sandora's ship is here and as soon as it starts creating a wormhole we have to shut it down.'

'Cem!' shouted Kas. 'Look.'

I look at the screen just in time to see that Sandora did not share our scruples about collateral damage and the use of deadly force.

There was a pulsing ragged beam of energy coming from near the front of her ship which was hitting the closest naval vessel. The ship veered away, trying to break free but the energy beam stayed with it until the ship lost power and began to drift. The beam vanished. The second ship had retreated and was keeping a reasonable distance.

'Was that their one shot, do you think?' asked Kas.

'I have no idea. I wouldn't want to bet on it. Are you able to contact the ship they hit?'

'No.'

Sandora's ship wasn't getting larger on the screen so our captain was also playing it safe and not getting any closer than necessary.

'So much for physically blocking Sandora from the wormhole,' I said.

One of the operators signalled to Kas, who nodded their permission to speak.

'We're reading a massive build-up of gravitic waves right in the orbital path of the Earth.'

'On screen,' said Kas.

The viewscreen shifted. At first we could see nothing apart from the stars then the camera systems focused in and we saw four small ships. They must have been inside the gigantic ship but were now moving away from it and getting further apart, each at the corners of a square that was getting larger and larger. The ships were linked by six green beams of light that comprised the four edges of the square, plus two going across the diagonals.

'Mal, are you seeing this?' I asked Jones over my cuff.

'Yes.'

'What's the green light?'

'It must be a targeting beam to ensure the four ships stay in a precise square as they move apart. That's my best guess. It's nothing directly to do with creating the wormhole. Our instruments can detect it, but it's currently tiny. It's about the size of one of those ships. The wormhole itself will eventually become visible as it grows, simply because it will be opaque. You won't be able to see the stars that are behind it. At the speed they're moving we estimate it will take roughly thirty minutes for them to be in position at the corners of a square large enough for the Earth. It will take another ten to fifteen minutes before the Earth's orbit carries it into the entrance, based on the current relative positions. Sandora's ship is station keeping just a few minutes ahead of the Earth.'

'Can't we just target one of those ships and destroy it?' asked Kas.

'Absolutely not,' said Jones, 'the wormhole exists and the gravitic beams from those ships are keeping the entrance at a fixed point. If you sever any of the beams the entrance will move unpredictably, and it could take one or more ships in or maybe a big chunk of the Earth or the Moon.'

My cuff chimed.

'This is Doctor Gernard. Do not approach our ships or we will fire again. I have no problem disabling your other ships. Our weapon destroys every electrical system on board the target, the crew will be alive but only until they run out of oxygen or warmth. If you want a chance to rescue them you will leave us alone.'

'How did he send that?' asked Kas.

I asked the chief engineer who confirmed it had come in via radio and that it wasn't coming from the huge ship but from one of the smaller ones creating the wormhole.

'How can you tell?' I asked.

'Unlike Infosys radio is directional, we can triangulate the source of the signal. The other two ships also built radio transceivers as I thought locating the source of any returning signal might be useful. It's the top left-hand ship as you look at them on the main viewscreen.'

I was impressed, and told her so. She shrugged and hung up.

'You're not the only one good at their job, you know,' said Kas.

'It's time I tried out your new toy. I need to get to that ship and convince Sandora to stop Gernard. If that doesn't work you must use whatever means necessary to stop the Earth entering that wormhole, even if we have to take a chance on a ship being pulled in.'

Kas told me to follow them and we headed back down to the hangar deck at a brisk jog. As we entered the hangar Kas pointed to a small pod-like device, just taller than a regular sized person.

'That's it, are you sure you want to risk it?' they said. 'We've tested it in the lab but never in the real world.'

'I don't think we've got any choice. I have to get on board,' I said as I struggled into a space suit, then slipped my cuff back onto my wrist.

The pod was the shape of a tear drop that had been sliced in half vertically. It was open on the flat front and there was room inside for one person to stand in the hollow. The rim around the opening was flat, plain metal and about forty centimetres thick. There were two rows of small circular ports every few centimetres all around the rim, dozens of them. I climbed in and turned to face outwards, gripped the hand rails at chest height and pushed my boots into the hoops in the floor.

'Are you ready?' asked Kas.

'No, not really' I replied but then I nodded and gave a thumbs up.

A hatch opened in the floor, the pod and I dropped through it and then through another one and out into space. The pod rotated until I could see Sandora's ship ahead of me then a powerful thruster kicked in and I was propelled at speed straight for it. My vision to the left and the right was restricted by the pod, all I could see was what was right in front of me. The pod was on automatic pilot, all I could do was press an abort button to return to the ship or hang on until the end of the ride. Sandora's ship now filled my vision and the acceleration suddenly stopped and braking thrusters fired just enough to stop me being pulverized against the side of the ship. We still hit the ship pretty hard. The flat front of the pod was flush to the skin of Sandora's ship. The outer row of ports on the pod contained small drills that bored into the skin of the ship, pulling the pod tighter and tighter against it until a perfect seal was established.

I wriggled my feet out of the hoops and waited. The inner row of ports fired atomiser beams at the hull, dissolving the metal into the finest dust. I kicked at the hull again and again until a large oval piece detached and dropped down into the gap between the outer and inner hull. The atomizers detected the outer hull was gone and now started working on the inner one. Soon I could see dozens of holes that almost connected up with each other, so I started kicking again. This was a bit easier as the inner hull wasn't as strong. With what I hoped wasn't too loud a crash the oval section fell into the ship. The pod itself created a seal preventing decompression. It was a nifty gadget, so long as the hull you were trying to attach to was almost completely flat and smooth.

I stepped into the ship, stripped off my space suit, retrieved my cuff and set off to find Sandora. I was armed with a stunner in each hand. I wasn't stopping to chat with anyone. I'd put the setting high enough to ensure anyone I stunned would be out for several hours. I hoped I'd be able to find the bridge, as that was where Sandora was most likely to be and even if she wasn't whoever was there ought to know where to find her. I set off towards the front of the ship down empty corridors.

That was when Kas' other bright idea, the one about communicating with the people on board, came into effect.

'People of Haven, you have been lied to by Sandora Sylvester Willow and her associates,' came Kas' voice, from all around me. 'The journey you are on is not to your long foretold idyllic planet but back to the original home of humanity, the Earth. This is not the Emancipation, this is a concocted phoney hiding a terribly destructive true objective. The plan Sandora has involved you all in will result in Earth's destruction and the death of every living thing on it. Please, you must help us stop her and take control of your ship.

We will return you to Haven, or any other welcoming planet, and assist in your re-settlement. You will be taken care of to the very best of our ability.'

There was a pause then the message started again. Kas had fired hundreds and hundreds of microscopic communication drones at the ship. They had landed all over the surface, attached themselves to it and were now broadcasting, on repeat, using the hull of the ship as a resonator.

I hurried up. I suspected it was about to be bedlam on board. The pod had been targeted at the front of the ship where the bridge was likely to be and I was absolutely certain no-one knew I was on board yet. The pod would have been virtually undetectable in flight, but now there was a large hole in the side of the ship and a discarded space suit. As soon as that was discovered they'd start looking for me. Our scans of the ship had been concentrated on the front to start with, and the operations room was sending updates to my cuff in real time. The cuff guided me towards what was presumed to be the bridge.

Two people appeared out of a doorway ahead of me, they were in protectorate uniforms and armed. I fired before they even had time to realise that I didn't belong. I was equally good with either hand and they slumped unconscious to the floor. A door to my left opened and a nervous man looked out, I whirled toward him ready to fire, but stopped.

'Don't shoot!'

'I wasn't going to unless you presented a danger.' I shouted over the sound of Kas' repeating message.

'What is going on? Who are you?'

Other doors started opening revealing frightened looking people. I pushed past the nervous man to see what was inside the room. There were a hundred, or more, people sitting on rows of simple moulded chairs. There were all sorts, from children and babies to elderly people. It looked like they were in family groups and they all looked frightened. I didn't suppose many of them had ever been on a spaceship before.

'I'm here to help. Sandora is not what she appears to be. She's not guided by Gaea or acting out of care or compassion. She's deluded. She's lied to you all. I have to find her. If she carries on with her plan she will kill billions of people all over the galaxy, including everything and everyone on Earth and then all of you.

You're not going to have a paradise planet to live on, it will be nothing but a devastated wasteland.'

The man hesitated for a moment, but he stuck to his guns.

'I don't believe you. You're ungodly. You're a liar.'

Everyone started shouting, some were agreeing with him but some were questioning him. I glanced around and people were coming out of the other rooms, hesitantly.

'Please stay in your rooms,' I said, raising my stunners and pointing them their way. 'These are stunners, but they will knock you out for several hours. I don't want to hurt anyone.'

I turned back to the man who'd confronted me.

'Why would I lie? Why would I want to stop you going to paradise? Although I implore you to consider the question, why does Gaea need a spaceship for the Emancipation?' It seemed a reasonable thing to ask. 'Just think about that. If I'm wrong then there's nothing I can do, a mere human and an ungodly one at that, to interfere with Gaea's plans, but if I'm right the consequences for billions of people are horrific and I'm sure Gaea wouldn't want billions of innocent lives to be lost.'

'The ungodly will be judged,' he said, but he didn't sound completely convinced.

'So I've been told,' I said, 'but until that happens I'm going to do everything I can to find Sandora and stop her.'

He lunged at me suddenly, so I stunned him. He lay sprawled at my feet. I rolled him over and sat him up against the wall.

'He's only unconscious. Look after him please, and think about what I said,' I called into the room.

More armed men appeared at the end of the corridor, they must have been sent to find out what happened to the first two. These ones were more cautious and fired down at me from cover. They had the same kind of weapon I'd seen in the Congressarium and Sandora's base. The gas-powered weapon only made a quiet sound but the projectile hitting the metal wall behind me was loud enough to hear over the broadcast. I lunged through the door as two more shots were fired.

'Is there another way out of this room?' I asked.

Everyone just shook their heads. Which was what I expected.

I heard another projectile hit the wall but there was only one this time. I pulled the door open slightly and saw blood pooling next to the leg of the man I'd stunned. The idiots had hit him. I risked a peek out but couldn't see my attackers. I grabbed the man's arm and heaved. He flopped sideways towards the open door and I heaved with all my strength and managed to drag him partially into the room.

'Help me!' I shouted.

A young man came running over and grabbed the man's clothes and together we got him into the room.

'He's my brother,' said the young man.

I ripped his trousers open and saw the wound. The projectile was still in his leg. It could have been a ricochet off the wall, a direct hit would probably have gone straight through.

I tore the rest of his trouser leg off and tied a tourniquet just above the wound. I had no medical kit with me, all I could do was slow the bleeding.

'Press here,' I said to his brother. Then I looked round the room. 'Is anyone a doctor, a medic, a nurse, anything like that?'

Everyone just stared or shook their heads.

I called Kas and explained we needed a medic as soon as possible and to get someone on standby. I went back to the door and adjusted the controls on one of the stunners. I turned the power all the way up and pointed it back to where the idiots had been firing from. I pressed the trigger and held it down. It would emit a continuous stun beam for only about ten seconds so I had to be quick. I ran diagonally across the corridor towards them keeping the beam pointed their way. They heard my footsteps and one person risked a look only to take the stun beam straight in the face. The other just fired blind and wild from inside the elevator. I heard the projectile hit the wall near me, but by then I could see into the elevator and I shot him with the stunner in my other hand. There were now four unconscious figures, two outside the elevator and two half in, half out. I dragged them out and dropped them by their comrades.

The faces at the other nearby doors had vanished, everyone had retreated back inside their rooms. All except one. A grey-haired very elderly woman.

'I believe you,' she said.

'You do?'

'Yes. I was a proctor for years until Sandora and her cronies came to power. I always understood the Emancipation as a metaphor. The sect I was a part of wasn't large, but we were influential. We emphasised kindness and compassion. But gradually we saw our influence diminish and I found myself having to remain quiet on so many issues that I resigned. You're quite right, Gaea wouldn't need a spaceship, we are Gaea, you are Gaea. We all are. Sandora's sect preached fear and division. Being in the right, and everyone else being in the wrong is seductive when you're poor and hungry.'

I didn't really have time for a theology lesson, but I did have need of an ally.

'Can you help me take control of this ship?'

'I'm not sure what help I could be, I'm old and was never much good at fighting.'

'I don't want you to fight. I want you to talk. I want you to convince as many people as you can that Sandora has to be stopped.'

I took my cuff off and put it on the woman's wrist. She flinched but allowed me to do it.

I contacted Kas and explained what I was doing. The recording of Kas' voice stopped and the ship went quiet.

'I'm Cemeron. What's your name?' I asked.

'Marriam. Marriam Flower Walker.'

'Marriam you just speak into this and your voice will be heard all over this ship. Tell your story. Speak to your people. Remind them about kindness, compassion and care. Let them know we don't mean you any harm but we have to stop Sandora.'

I briefly explained to Marriam about Sandora's plan to steal the Earth and why that would result in its destruction. She was appalled and promised to help.

Marriam started speaking, she was startled by the sound of her own voice being broadcast over the ship but she rallied.

'This is Marriam Flower Walker,' she said. 'Many of you will know me and many more will have known my late bondmate Maxim. This isn't the Emancipation, you know that. We're not thieves or murderers and I've just seen someone we would call ungodly risk their own life to save one of our own. But Sandora is doing something that will result in the Earth, humanity's original home, being destroyed. If Gaea's principles are about anything they're about life; natural, uncomplicated life. Most of the galaxy don't share our beliefs but that doesn't give us the right to kill them or take the Earth away from them.'

She carried on talking and I took the elevator up to the bridge.

Chapter 42
Gernard

The elevator door opened onto a bridge in chaos. I saw Grippe tied to a chair. He looked barely conscious and had a cut on his head which was bleeding. I saw some of the proctors from the Congressarium at the controls but they weren't doing anything. They were frozen in fear staring at the proctor who was sitting in the captain's chair, and all of his attention was on one of the protectorate officers who had a weapon pointed right at his head, it was Santis. The two others protectorate officers had their weapons pointed at Santis. The proctor in the captain's chair and all three officers were shouting at each other and no-one was listening. I could hear Santis loudly insisting the ship return to Haven where Sandora would face an ecclesiastical tribunal, the others were calling him a traitor and ordering him to repent and hand over his weapon. No-one had yet noticed me, other than Grippe. I checked the settings on the stunners then stepped out of the elevator and stunned the two protectorate officers with my right hand and the Santis with my left. Then I stunned everyone else, just to be on the safe side, except Grippe and the proctor in the captain's chair.

'Where are Sandora, Gernard and Per Randolf?' I shouted, keeping both stunners pointed at the proctor's head.

He refused to answer. I dialled one stunner up to maximum and put it right against his temple.

'Where are they? This stunner is on maximum. Repeated shots from this, as Sandora herself knows, would do serious damage to your nervous system. Now talk!'

'I will not tell you anything,' he spat back at me.

'Gernard is in the wormhole control ship with Randolf. He took him as a hostage and to help refine the wormhole calculations,' croaked Grippe's voice from behind me. 'He told Per Randolf they would kill me if he refused, then he beat me unconscious to show how serious he was.'

'And Sandora?'

'I don't know,' said Grippe. 'I don't think he knows either. She slipped out as soon as your cruisers attempted to intercept us.'

I stunned the proctor, but not with the one set to maximum power. He slid out of the chair onto the floor. I frisked the protectorate officers and deprived them of their projectile weapons, just in case. The elevator door opened behind me and I turned, ready to stun whoever came out. Marriam stood there with her arms out at her sides, palms facing me.

'Don't shoot,' she said, and her voice rang throughout the ship.

I smiled and put the stunners away then retrieved my cuff from her.

'I won't, thank you Marriam,' I said, then turned the broadcast off.

I studied the bridge controls and was glad to see they were pretty standard.

I turned the ship towards the Rubicon, Kas' navy cruiser, moving it out of the path of the wormhole entrance, which was now large enough to see clearly.

'What is that?' asked Marriam, who was staring at it out of the window.

I looked out properly for the first time. The four ships were too small to be visible to the naked eye, but the green beams to keep them perfectly positioned in a square could easily be seen. It was what was in the middle that fascinated me. Outside the square was the usual backdrop, the scattering of living diamonds that was the Milky Way galaxy. Myriads of pinpoints of light, so many of which were considered home by millions, or even billions, of people. Inside the square was something else entirely. Jones had been right when she said the wormhole entrance would be opaque but she had never actually seen one this large, nor one formed by the four-generator system. It was jet black but flecked with countless curved red streaks that pulsed and throbbed angrily as they formed out near the corners of the square and then were pulled in a spiral as they descended in towards the centre, getting brighter as they neared it before vanishing in a small flash of white light. It looked absolutely terrifying. I would no more fly into it than I would into the heart of a star.

'That's the wormhole. That's what Sandora, Gernard and these people,' I kicked the senior proctor in the ribs for emphasis, 'want to send the Earth through.'

As mesmerizing as the sight out of the window was, I kept glancing back towards the door. Marriam noticed.

'You can relax. The remaining protectorate and proctors will have been overpowered by now. No-one is going to storm the bridge. There's a lot of theological bickering and arguing going on about the nature of the Emancipation but one thing the overwhelming majority are agreed on is the respect for life. Sandora kept her true plans secret from everyone but her select few precisely because she knew the majority of us would never have agreed to it.'

My cuff chimed. It was Kas.

'Cem, we're docking with your ship now. Help is on the way.'

'I'm fine Kas. You shouldn't meet any resistance. How long do we have until the Earth hits the wormhole?'

'Fifteen minutes or so.'

'Doctor Grippe is here on the bridge with me, but he's been badly beaten and is barely conscious. He's not going to be in any fit state to help Mal and the others defuse that…thing…out there. Sandora isn't here as far as I can tell and it's Gernard in the control ship. He has Danatis with him.'

'Shit!'

I'd rarely heard Kas swear.

'I have an idea. But I'll need another one of those pods of yours. I need it modifying and very quickly. Can you do it?'

The elevator opened again and Kas stepped through, with a couple of navy hard-cases for protection, along with a medic.

'Yes,' they said. 'We can and we can be fast. What do you need?'

The medic untied Grippe then started treating him.

'We need these proctors here taking back to the ship, and locking up in isolation from the others. You may want to wake them up from the heavy stun I just gave him, the rest I'll explain as we go. Time is short.'

I hugged Marriam and thanked her profusely then Kas and I headed back to the Rubicon leaving the navy personnel to manhandle the proctors.

Kas and I ran most of the way while I explained what I needed. I can't say they were delighted with my plan but as no-one, as yet, had a better one and our three geniuses still could not be completely certain they could shut down the wormhole safely it seemed the least worst option.

'I want a medal and a large pay rise if this works,' I said, back in the hangar as I got into another space suit.

'You can have the medal but after we've deducted the costs of the scout ship and all the spacesuits you've gone through, you'll still end up owing us,' said Kas, grinning.

'Have we moved closer to the entrance?'

'Yes, as close as we dare.'

'I want you to back off, as far as you can, when I launch,' I said. 'This may not work and if we do lose the Earth I don't want to lose all of you too.'

Kas reassured me they would do so.

I checked the equipment I'd asked for was inside before I climbed into the modified pod. It was larger than the previous one, but I still wouldn't have called it roomy. As soon as I was clamped in, and ready, I gave Kas the thumbs up.

'You have just under ten minutes,' they said.

The floor opened and I dropped through, as before.

The pod swivelled about on its vertical axis until it faced where Gernard's ship would be, then the powerful thruster kicked in. I couldn't see the ship, it was still too far away and had no navigation lights, but I could see where three of the green beams all met up, so knew that must be it. I was at full acceleration for just over one minute, then the braking thrusters kicked in. I could clearly see Gernard's ship now. It was small and spherical, about five meters in diameter, there was a large complex emitter array sticking out of the side facing the wormhole. Whatever energies were pumping out of it to create the hyperspace effect were not visible to the naked eye. We'd scanned his ship but the only thing we were looking for was a space on the hull big enough for me to cut through that wasn't full of dangerous machinery. This meant I couldn't make a direct approach. As I slowed down, the pod passed the sphere then looped back to attach itself right next to the emitter. The front face of the pod was flexible rather than rigid as I'd initially thought. It moulded to the curvature of the sphere and the drills bored into the shell, pulling the pod snuggly against it until the airtight seal was achieved. I checked the cargo was securely fastened to the inside of the pod, unclamped myself, then triggered the atomisers.

I knew I'd have to act fast. I couldn't beat Gernard in a fair fight. I'd been fortunate once. I couldn't bank on it again, so I'd have to cheat. I couldn't even rely on a stunner, although I had one in my gloved hand. If Gernard was expecting a rescue he'd probably be wearing a spacesuit, and a stunner would not work through most spacesuits.

The outer hull collapsed into the gap and the atomisers started work on the inner hull.

The inner hull fell into the sphere and I threw myself through the hole head first. I crashed onto the floor suddenly feeling like I weighed a ton. Gernard had set the internal gravity on the small ship to be around the norm for Cestus, almost twice that of Earth. In a one 'g' environment he already had a considerable strength advantage, but in a two 'g' one I was put at a large disadvantage. I struggled to my feet and looked around. The lighting was down low which revealed the inside of the ship made no concession to creature comforts. Most of the interior was taken up with the wormhole generator. There was a huge power cell, embedded in the centre of the floor, from which sprouted a dozen thick cables, and hundreds of thinner ones. They trailed across the floor and up the walls to connect to all manner of incomprehensible equipment. At least half of the walls were covered in circuits and intricate readouts. Immediately ahead against the opposite wall there was the usual pilot's controls, but next to it a fearsomely complex control unit like nothing I'd ever seen before. Gernard wasn't in the pilot's chair. Randolf was. He was tied to it, unconscious and bleeding. Gernard, wherever he was, certainly loved hurting people. I swept the inside with the stunner, looking for the slightest movement in the dim light. He stepped out of the shadows to my right, I fired without any noticeable effect. He was wearing a full space suit.

'Not this time Pike you ungodly bastard,' he screamed as he ran at me. 'I knew you'd have one of those ludicrous civilised weapons. It doesn't work through a spacesuit.'

I couldn't dodge him in this high gravity, so I dropped to the ground, which happened so quickly it winded me. Gernard had spent far too much time on one 'g' worlds and his coordination was slightly off. He couldn't stop so he tripped over me and fell with a crash, but was scrambling back to his feet before I'd even got up off my backside. The double gravity was crippling. He opened his arms wide and moved in slowly this time, savouring the moment and fighting to get his rage under control. He was going to crush me. The suit I was wearing wasn't armoured, it was simply airtight. I dropped the useless stunner, and unclipped the weapon I'd taken from one of the guards on Sandora's ship. I pointed it at Gernard.

'You recognise this don't you?' I asked as I struggled back up to my feet.

He paused. He clearly did recognise it. I needed to get to Randolf, so I backed away from him slowly, treading extremely carefully over the cables on the floor. If I tripped now, that would be the end.

'You won't shoot. You're afflicted with this so-called civilisation's ethical weakness that prevents you from doing what is necessary. Sandora has the foresight, purpose, and clarity; I have the strength metaphorically and, as you well know, physically.'

I was right next to the pilot's chair now. I could see the pod directly opposite and Gernard had moved round to my left gradually getting closer. He looked confident, knowing I wouldn't, couldn't, kill him.

I fired. I wasn't aiming to kill. I wasn't even really aiming to wound. I just needed a distraction so I could cut the cords holding Randolf. I fired directly at Gernard's helmet. It's the toughest part of a spacesuit and since I'd lowered the gas pressure on the weapon to the lowest setting the projectile would have just made a loud bang and done minimal damage. He flinched and put his hands up to his helmet, instinctively. After a moment he realised both he and the suit were undamaged. He laughed.

'I'm going to kill you now, Pike. Got any clever last words?'

'I have as a matter of fact. Pod, open,' I said.

The curved back of the pod snapped back ninety degrees on its recently installed powered hinges. This opened the whole of Gernard's ship to the vacuum of space. He was pulled off his feet, but he was strong so grabbed hold of a thick cable and hung on. I had grabbed Randolf, in a bear hug, as I spoke. We flew straight past Gernard, carried along in the escaping atmosphere, straight towards the gaping hole in the ship.

As soon as the pod detected us close to it, the back of the pod snapped shut and we slammed into it. I was still hanging on to the unconscious Randolf.

'Pod, release,' I said. A force field snapped into place, covering the hole at the front of the pod as it detached from Gernard's ship.

I was dazed but had to move quickly. I fumbled for the cargo I'd brought into the pod, and smashed my hand down on the quick release lever on the top of it. Fresh, warm air started immediately filling the pod. It only took seconds to return the interior to normal atmospheric pressure.

'Jones, fire your probe at the wormhole now. Gernard is busy and I've got Randolf,' I shouted into my cuff.

'Done,' she replied. 'We made some changes since you saw our last simulation. We're reasonably confident this one will shut the wormhole down with minimal disruption.'

'How confident is reasonably confident?'

'About fifty percent.'

The probe Jones fired would only take about thirty seconds to get close enough to start emitting the wormhole cancelling field. All I could do was hope she was right.

It was unbelievably cramped in the pod. Randolf was unconscious and so tall he would have barely fitted in the pod even without me. I wriggled in the microgravity and managed to turn us both so he was against the back of the pod, and I could see out through the transparent forcefield. I could see into Gernard's ship through the hole in the side. The pod engines were only designed for one journey so it was simply the momentum of the expelled air after our release that was pushing us slowly away from Gernard ship and towards the wormhole entrance.

'Kas, how long until the drone grabs us?'

'Seconds. We've almost got you.'

'Hurry. We're really close to taking a very long one-way trip.'

I felt a thud against the side of the pod, then a gentle tug of acceleration. Gernard appeared at the hole in his ship, he pointed something at us. It was the weapon I'd fired at him. I'd dropped it in order to grab Randolf. He must have fired as I heard a couple of loud pings as the pellets hit the pod. The forcefield held and soon we were out of range and moving away from the wormhole as the drone towed us back towards the safety of the Rubicon.

We were still too close to the wormhole to properly see it so I pulled up a screen on my cuff and accessed the feed from the Rubicon. I could see the green lines and the black red-streaked wormhole with a tiny graphic overlayed marking the approach of the probe. I wondered if it ought to have been having a noticeable effect yet, but I couldn't see a change. The Earth must be coming up behind us very fast, we really were between a rock and a hard place.

Then I noticed something, the red streaks had sped up and started zigzagging wildly, the black space within the square started to ripple and pulse. The ship diagonally opposite Gernard's looked like it was shrinking in size as it moved from its corner towards the centre of the square. It dawned on me that it wasn't shrinking, it was going into the wormhole, it was getting further and further away. The green beams connecting the four ships bent and twisted, trying to maintain their connections then they all flickered several times before going out. The cuff showed enhanced images of the three remaining ships as they too were pulled towards the centre of the collapsing wormhole. They vanished one at a time, followed by the wormhole itself. The stars that had been behind it reappeared as if nothing had ever happened. I zoomed the image out and saw the Earth, glorious in its blue and white beauty start to pass the point where the wormhole entrance had just been.

I checked on Randolf. His breathing was shallow and he was deathly pale. Gernard had really gone to town on him.

'Mal, well done. Were there any casualties other than the wormhole ships?'

'No,' she replied. 'Gernard never left his ship, he must have managed to hang on until all the air had escaped.'

'I know, he shot at us with the weapon I took from one of the protectorate.'

'We watched his ship spiral round and round into the centre then it vanished. We've no idea where he is now, or if he's alive.'

'Our best guess is that he's in the next galaxy,' said Dharya. 'He's probably in orbit around the star the Earth was supposed to end up orbiting. But as the wormhole was collapsing, he and the ship could be almost anywhere.'

'Wherever he is, he can stay there for all I care,' I said. 'I'm not going looking for him. Randolf is alive, but he's in a bad way. Have medics standing by, we'll need to get him to the sickbay immediately you get us on board.'

Chapter 43
Sandora

T he drone dragged the pod into the main hangar. As soon as we were inside I deactivated the force field so the medics who were waiting could grab Randolf and take him away.

'We've put an alert out to every inhabited system to be on the lookout for Gernard, just in case the wormhole dropped him out somewhere other than the intended destination,' said Kas as they helped me out of my spacesuit. 'Plus we fired trackers at all four of the wormhole ships. If any of them pop back into real space anywhere in range we should soon know.'

'The ship didn't appear to have a regular hyperdrive so if he ends up anywhere, other than near a populated planet, he's had it.'

We headed towards the operations room, at a gentle walk this time. I'd done enough running for one day, plus I was pretty bruised from my activities rescuing Randolf.

'Did the proctors tell you where Sandora went?' I asked.

'No, they refuse to say anything other than accusing us of religious persecution, blasphemy, and sinful interference with Gaea's will.'

'Blasphemy? What's that? Never mind, it doesn't matter, I don't care. I know where she's gone. Well, I'm pretty sure I know.'

'Scarlastion?'

'Yes. How did you know that?'

'Once again I'd like to remind you that you're not the only one who's good at their job. We're already on the way by the fastest route possible, we jumped the moment you were on board.'

'She's got to assume the navy will do everything possible to intercept her ships carrying the stellar probes. You are intercepting them, aren't you?'

'We destroyed a probe fired at Cestus' star and impounded the ship that launched it. The two people on board are refusing to cooperate. We may have to use veraserum on them to find out anything. They had several other sets of probes on board, which means they had other targets. We've not heard anything from the other systems, but we now have ships at all university planets with a major science centre, plus two extra ships have arrived at Earth.'

'Sandora doesn't make idle threats, it seems.'

I told Kas about her threat to destroy Cestus if Grippe didn't help her. She must have decided he'd hindered more than he'd helped.

'How long until we arrive at Scarlastion, and is there any way we can know if we'll arrive before or after Sandora does?' I asked.

'We'll be about two hours. Sandora has only a small lead over us, but the number of jumps will be about the same so we can't make up much time. There's a navy cruiser in orbit ready and waiting for her. As soon as she arrives her ship will be boarded and she'll be taken into custody.'

I hoped it would be that simple.

'As we've got some time, I'm going to shower, eat, find Mal then go and check on Danatis. Probably in that order. I'll see you later.'

I left Kas in the operations room and headed for my quarters. I assumed Mal would already be with Randolf so I had the quickest shower I could, changed and grabbed some food to eat on the go. The ship's infirmary, or sickbay, was in the centre of the ship, as this was the most heavily protected and the safest place to be.

Jones was, as I suspected, already there when I arrived. She looked up, smiled, then got out of her chair to hug me. It was a proper embrace, rather than a quick greeting and I returned it eagerly.

'Thank you for rescuing him,' she said.

'It was my duty but I also wanted to do it. He's a remarkable young man. Imagine what other breakthroughs that huge brain might be capable of. How is he?'

I looked around the infirmary. There were four smallish private rooms and a much larger general treatment area. As you'd expect for a sterile environment it was all pale pastels and brilliant white to make it easy to keep clean. Randolf was in the first small room. I couldn't see Grippe, but the glass on one of the end rooms was currently frosted so perhaps he was receiving treatment.

The doctor that had been in with Randolf had just come out of the room and had heard my question to Jones.

'He's conscious, but sleepy,' she said. 'He's out of danger but I can only let you have five minutes with him, he really does need to rest. The gravity in there is turned down to Fortuna's norm, so be careful as you go in. It'll take a little getting used to. We need to give him every advantage to aid in his recovery.'

'How badly did Gernard hurt him?' asked Jones.

'Most of his ribs were cracked or broken, he had a skull fracture, a broken jaw, he'd lost several teeth and there's some internal injuries we're keeping a very close eye on. The good news is there's no sign of a brain injury. I've seen worse but only rarely. The tissue and bone regenerators have repaired the major damage but the organs will need time to heal. He'd be in a lot of pain without the medication, which he will need for several days. We won't replace the teeth until he's well on the way to recovery. This Gernard person, whoever he is, needs to go to prison for a long time.'

'He's almost certainly dead and if he isn't he's so far away from civilisation he won't be hurting anyone else ever again,' I said.

The doctor looked satisfied with that answer.

We opened the door and stepped into Randolf's room. It did feel strange suddenly being in roughly three-quarters of a 'g'. It brought a spring to my step. Randolf's eyes opened as we entered and he tried to smile, but winced instead. His face was black and blue and I could see gaps in his teeth. I was glad I hadn't had to arrest Gernard, his fate seemed appropriate as far as I was concerned.

'Don't try to move or talk,' said Jones. 'We're just glad you're going to be okay.'

'You'll be pleased to know Doctor Grippe is alive and well too, but Gernard almost certainly isn't alive and if he is, he certainly isn't well.'

Randolf nodded, slightly, and mouthed 'thank you' to me.

'You're welcome. You grabbed my leg and saved my life at Omega; I was simply returning the favour.'

Jones pulled up a chair and sat, holding Randolf's hand. He closed his eyes and seemed to be back asleep.

'I'm going to check on Grippe for a minute,' I said. 'I'll leave you two alone. He'll be up on his feet in no time.'

Back in the main infirmary I looked around for Doctor Grippe and found him inside the room with the frosted glass. He was alone.

'How are you feeling Doctor Grippe,' I asked.

He looked a lot better than Randolf. He was bruised and battered but intact and alert.

'Even when I set the glass to privacy mode it seems I get no peace. I'm doing much better now. No thanks to you. You never did rescue me, did you? You were happy enough to risk life and limb for Randolf though, I see.'

'Doctor Grippe, I'm only here because we could do with your help. If I send two of our experts down here to talk to you, could you design some kind of detector that would allow our ships to locate and destroy Sandora's probes?'

'It may be possible. But I'm not feeling particularly well disposed to you at the moment. You made me promises and then left me in the hands of those…people.'

He almost spat the last word.

'I'm a galactically renowned physicist. I've won countless awards and I'm on the verge of revolutionising space travel. Do you have any idea the loss to the galaxy if I hadn't managed to survive? Yet you did nothing to ensure my safety, but when that young fellow's life hung in the balance you suddenly turn heroic and there's no obstacle that can't be overcome. I don't really see why I need to, suddenly, be so very grateful.'

He was working up quite a head of steam. Grippe was a man used being the centre of his own personal universe, he couldn't conceive of a situation where his needs weren't paramount.

'Doctor Grippe,' I said, 'there are two ways we can do this. One way involves you cooperating with my people fully, willingly, perhaps even enthusiastically, and will result in you receiving grateful thanks and due consideration for your achievements. The other way still involves you cooperating fully but you receive absolutely no credit and we ensure your inappropriate relationships with your students aren't just extensively and comprehensively investigated, that will happen no matter what – let me assure you, but they will also be very publicly reported. We have arrived at what might be called 'a reckoning'. It is time to decide. Do you want to be forever known as the flawed genius who mended his ways after a traumatic experience or the predatory scumbag who abused his status and authority and lost everything?'

He barely paused.

'The hyperspace mechanism in them emits certain frequencies that are unique to my design. It should be fairly straightforward to design such a detector. But why is that necessary? Haven't you got Sandora in custody?'

I explained the situation, then I called Praanvi and Dharya and asked them to come and work with Grippe.

'The navy managed to intercept the attack on Cestus,' I said, when they arrived. 'But we can't rely on them hanging around these systems for days, weeks or even years waiting for Sandora's disciples to strike. We need an automated system that can orbit the star, detect a probe fired at it and neutralize it immediately. I want the three of you to work on it and I want it done fast. I want prototypes in place ready to deploy as soon as possible. I don't fancy heading down to Scarlastion for any length of time knowing there's the possibility I could be reduced to my constituent atoms by the star going nova while I'm there.'

Praanvi and Dharya escorted Grippe out of the infirmary to one of their labs and I headed back to the operations room. I needed time to think about what to do next and also to discuss it with Kas.

We were one jump away from Scarlastion when we got the news we'd been waiting for, Sandora's ship had been intercepted by the navy cruiser protecting the planet. There had been no weapons fire exchanged. It seemed the ship she'd used was very similar to the one I'd found hidden at the winery which was unarmed. Kas and I waited in the operations room for a live feed from the leader of the boarding party.

We watched on multiple screens as several space suited figures made their way through the rigid docking ring that was clamped firmly on the side of the ship, preventing it from escaping. The leader of the assault team had a helmet camera and we saw them enter the ship.

'They're extremely experienced,' said Kas, 'if it's possible to take everyone alive and unharmed they'll manage it.'

We needn't have worried, as we saw them go from room to room, lightly stunning anyone they found then putting restraints on them, they encountered no resistance. The stun was set low enough that it merely impeded motor functions. We knew we might need to interview them so we didn't want them knocking unconscious. It took fifteen minutes for the small team to thoroughly search the ship. Sandora wasn't on board.

'Ask the proctor, who was piloting the ship, where Sandora is,' said Kas.

The sullen angry face of the large sweaty man sitting uncomfortably in the pilot's seat with his hands cuffed behind him remained impassive as the question was put to him. He shook his head and turned away.

'Perhaps she was never on board,' said Kas to me.

'She was, I'm sure of it. They hadn't yet fired a probe at the Scarlastion sun. The only reason not to do that was because someone important to them was down on the planet.'

Kas instructed the assault team leader to search again. A few minutes later they came back with the news that while Sandora was definitely not on board an escape pod was missing.

'I'm going down to the university,' I said. 'Please get a landing shuttle ready for me.'

'You're not going alone,' said Kas, with a look on their face that told me I wasn't going to win this argument.

'Fine. But you can't come. You're needed here to keep Grippe, Dharya and Praanvi focussed on their probe defence project. Send that assault team down. We'll rendezvous on the surface.'

I headed to the hangar deck and chose a small surface shuttle. Within minutes I was on my way down to the surface of Scarlastion. I needed to be quick, I didn't really want a load of enthusiastic military types following me everywhere.

Infosys provided me with all the information I needed to plot my destination precisely. Planetary traffic control were not happy about me refusing to land at the spaceport on the outskirts of the city, but there wasn't time for that. I sent them my authorisation codes and they ensured I had a clear path straight to the university's main campus. Sandora wouldn't have had the advantage of Infosys to pinpoint her landing, but she wouldn't have needed it. This was her original home planet; she would know the university well.

I set the nav system to use the smallest tightest spiral it could for landing. These little shuttles didn't have the fast drop system, and I doubted Kas would be happy about me using it, without appropriate camouflage, even if it had.

The half hour landing procedure seemed to take forever, but it gave me time to review the information Kas had uncovered about Sandora, her history and her family. One item of information in particular caught my attention and clarified certain things enormously.

Once I could see through the clouds I saw the university campus was a much larger facility than Jones' one on Coronnol. I'd not been to Scarlastion before so wasn't prepared for the bold architecture they favoured. The buildings were brutal angular shapes, in bright metallic colours. They looked like assorted knives planted handle first in the ground, the lower floors were dark matte colours, but once

the building reached somewhere around the tenth floor the materials
changed to highly polished metal and glass. The nav system showed
a clearing, possibly a public park, in the middle of some of the tallest
buildings, as my destination. It was evening on this part of the planet,
it looked like sunset was only a matter of an hour or so away. I
checked the local gravity and was relieved to see it was fractionally
below one 'g'. That would make moving around bearable. I scanned
the park as the ship lowered itself smoothly to the grass, there was a
metallic object hidden in some bushes on the edge of the lawn that
could very well be an escape pod.

I grabbed some equipment from the storage units in the cockpit
and pulled on a chameleon suit. I didn't want Sandora recognizing
me from a distance if I could help it. I set it to mimic the uniform of
a local maintenance worker, but kept it switched off for now.
Someone who would realistically be wandering around any part of
the complex shouldn't raise her suspicions.

As I stepped out of the shuttle a small crowd of students had
gathered at a safe distance to watch. I headed towards where I
thought the escape pod had landed and asked the curious bystanders
if they'd seen anything else land in the park. They pointed in the
direction I was going, and one of them confirmed an escape pod had
landed, but the occupant had waved away all offers of help before
heading off into the university.

'How long ago was that?' I asked.

'Maybe, about an hour,' said one of the crowd, looking around at
the others for confirmation.

'Did you see the occupant?'

'Not properly. An older person, maybe a woman. Lots of long
grey hair, anyway,' said the unofficial group spokesperson.

The local police had been warned by Kas not to interfere,
otherwise there would already have been emergency responders in
the park to deal with the escape pod and my shuttle landing in a
public place.

I headed towards the university buildings, but stopped by the
escape pod to have a look. It was a standard model, with room inside
for just one person. There was nothing of interest to see.

I activated the chameleon suit as soon as I was out of sight of the
small crowd of bystanders and followed my cuff's directions into the
building.

My cuff chimed. It was Kas wanting me to wait for the assault team to join me. They were ten minutes from landing, but I really didn't want them following me. I disabled the location tracking on my cuff, something we are never, ever, supposed to do before sending a short message to Kas asking them to deploy the team around the building to ensure no-one got out if I failed.

I was nearing my first destination when the alarms went off. There was a low-pitched siren and flashing red lights in the corridor. My cuff informed me that I was to evacuate the building by the nearest exit. I ignored it and continued following the map. A few people passed me at a brisk walk, nobody was panicking, perhaps they thought it was a drill. They gave me funny looks but I wasn't sure if that was because I wasn't going the right way or if it was the slightly artificial look of the chameleon suit's disguise.

I reached my destination, a door with the name Doctor Runcible Artura Karshon embossed on it in the stylised script favoured on Scarlastion. The door was ajar. I pulled out my stunner and set it to a medium heavy stun; enough to knock anyone out for several hours, even if they were from Cestus or another high 'g' world. From what I'd read on the way here I knew that although Doctor Karshon was no longer able to work, his office and laboratory had been converted into a small apartment where he was looked after by his carers. Every time they'd tried to move him to either his home, or a medical facility, he'd become unstable and aggressive. I pushed the door with my foot and it moved smoothly inwards. I risked a quick glance in and saw nobody. I shoved the door all the way open and went in, firing a broad stun pattern, but there was no one in the room. It was furnished with three comfortable arm chairs and a sofa. A few pot plants and some soothing animated scenes of tranquil countryside completed the rather bland décor. I crossed to the door to the next room, the one that used to be the laboratory but was now the main care facility, where I presumed the video clip of the doctor had been taken. This door was wide open and the room inside was a mess. There was a body on the floor, lying face down in a pool of blood. It was such a large pool I didn't think there could be any way they were still alive. I had to check though. They were lying right next to the medical bed I'd seen in the video. The rest of the room was clearly unoccupied, there was nowhere to hide which meant Doctor Karshon was definitely not here.

I checked for a pulse on the prone figure. There was a very weak thready one, but I didn't think they'd last long. I triggered a medical emergency alert on my cuff, then rolled the person over. The name badge said 'Gerald' but I didn't recognise the face. This must be the Gerry that Karshon had been talking to, the one who had recorded the video Sandora had shown me. He had a nasty wound to the neck. I zoomed in with the cuff on the wound and could see a metal pellet lodged deep inside it. His breathing was shallow and slow. Someone had shot him with one of the gas-powered weapons. I wondered if it was by accident or by design. It had to be Sandora, there was only room for one person in the escape pod. I grabbed the pillow from the bed, pulled the case off it, tore it open and tied it around the wound. It might slow the bleeding enough until help arrived. Gerry's eyes opened as I worked and he stared straight at me. His mouth moved but no sound came out. I couldn't work out what he was trying to say. I held his hand and stroked his hair, hoping to provide a little comfort. His eyes went wide with fear for a moment, then he died. I felt his hand go limp and saw the eyes lose focus. I knew absolutely nothing about Gerry, other than he'd cared for another human being who needed him. He didn't deserve this end. I heard running feet in the corridor and called out that we were in the next room. Two medics ran in, one gently pulled Gerry's hand out of mine and helped me up, the other started working on him but quickly realised it was too late. He'd lost too much blood. I looked at Gerry's cuff and saw it was he who had triggered the evacuation alert. It must have been the last thing he'd done.

I was a little dazed as I walked back out into the corridor. I had Gerry's blood on my hands, shoes and knees. I forced myself to focus and think about where Sandora would have taken Doctor Karshon. There was really only one possibility. I looked it up on my cuff and set off along the corridor towards the neural link laboratory. If she had Doctor Karshon with her she couldn't be more than a minute or two ahead of me.

The cuff showed the entrance was one floor up, on the west side of the building and the lab took up most of the floor. By the time I got there the shock had turned into anger and I knew I had to stay in control and not let my feelings override my good judgement. My cuff had chimed several times on the way. It was Kas calling for an update, but I didn't want to talk so had just sent a terse 'stand by' response.

The reception was deserted, as I expected and none of the doors were locked. That was probably part of the evacuation protocol. I listened but I couldn't hear anything. The alarm had stopped on the way here and now there was just the flashing red light to warn people to leave. I started working my way along the corridor, checking rooms as I went and leaving the doors open so I'd know which ones were safe. Doctor Karshon would be no help to Sandora in stopping the neural link. He was too far gone to give her access to their Infosys domain, even if by some unthinkable lapse in security they'd left his access codes functional. For research this sensitive it would be bound to be controlled via one or more SSPs so I didn't know what she hoped to accomplish by taking him.

I could see through a small glass panel in the doors that the end room was a large open-plan lounge. In it, standing together were the three volunteers from the video Sandora had shown me. The three of them were facing Sandora who had hold of Doctor Karshon by the collar and was pointing a gas-powered weapon at his head. I wondered if the stunner would disable her quickly enough to be absolutely certain she couldn't fire. I didn't know for sure, so I opened the door and stepped through with my stunner held out in front of me.

'Sandora, please lower the weapon,' I said.

She glanced my way and looked confused.

'Who the hell are you? If you don't get out, I'll kill Karshon.'

The chameleon suit was preventing her from recognising me. I deactivated it and removed the hood.

'Sandora, it's me Cemeron,' I said. 'Please can you put the weapon down, then we'll talk.'

'If you throw your stunner over here and empty your pockets then maybe, just maybe, I won't kill Karshon,' she said.

I knew that was a lie but I threw the stunner over to her and saw it land right at her feet, almost buried in the thick carpet. I removed the chameleon suit, left it crumpled at my feet and showed her that my pockets were empty.

'Now your cuff too,' she said.

I reluctantly took it off and threw it next to the stunner. The three volunteers looked calm and unconcerned by the danger they were in, poor Doctor Karshon had the glazed far-away look on his face I'd seen on the video clip. He didn't seem to be aware of anything that was happening.

'I think you should know that the Earth is safe and sound just where it's always been, Gernard is either dead or all alone in another galaxy,' I said. 'The passengers seized control on your giant colony ship once they were told the truth about you and your plans. Those that want to go are on their way back to Haven. The rest will be resettled wherever they like and looked after as they reintegrate into normal life. The proctors are all under arrest.'

She looked momentarily angry but took a deep breath and maintained her composure.

'You could have just doomed the human race Pike. I pray I managed to program sufficient probes to inflict serious damage on Infosys, enough to wake the galaxy up to their enslavement, even if I cannot now destroy it completely.'

'That won't be happening either, Sandora. Grippe, Jones and some of our brightest people are already building a defence against the stellar probes, so you won't be destroying any more stars. It's over. Your deranged plan has failed. You may as well surrender to me. You will have to stand trial for killing Gerry, but nobody else needs to die.'

To my surprise Doctor Karshon turned to look at me. The eyes focused on me and he seemed to become aware of his surroundings.

'Did you say that Gerry's dead?' he asked.

'Yes, I'm afraid he is. I'm so sorry Doctor Karshon.'

Karshon seemed to sag, like a puppet whose string have been cut, then he started crying. Silent tears trickled down his face; the face of a man who had now lost everything.

'Gerry, my Gerry,' he said sadly, then gradually the previous vacant expression returned and the tears stopped.

'What happened to Gerry, Sandora? Why did you kill him?' I asked.

Just for a moment I could see she was struggling with her feelings.

'It was an accident. He wouldn't do as I said so I fired a warning shot, he thought I was shooting at Karshon so he threw himself in front of me. I didn't intentionally kill him, but he'd have died anyway when the system's sun goes nova. The ungodly will have judgement visited upon them, his just came sooner. It's his own fault, he shouldn't have interfered.'

She didn't sound completely convinced by her own justification.

'I know you agree with me about the neural link Pike. You do, don't you?' she pleaded. 'I may not have the Earth, I may not have my ship or my proctors but I do still have a righteous purpose. This…this…has to stop. It has to.'

She waved her free hand towards the three volunteers and Karshon.

'If we don't put a stop to this technology now it will be too late for us all. You need to get them to call the research team back in and we need to deal with them. You agree with me, don't deny it!'

'I do agree, that something must be done,' I said. 'But violence isn't the answer. You can't kill your way out of a problem like this Sandora, you can't kill an idea and I'm certain you can't kill Dominique, not your own daughter.'

Chapter 44
Mutual

The three volunteers turned to look at me as one. The tallest, a red headed woman I recognized from the video as the artist of the group, was Sandora's surviving daughter according to the information Kas had retrieved. She spoke first.

'That used to be my name. But it doesn't really seem relevant anymore.'

She turned to address Sandora.

'We sent everyone out when the alarm went off,' she said. 'The scientists who have been helping us with the neural interface will not come back in. We won't allow you to hurt them.'

The door behind me closed automatically and I heard a lock click into place.

The man next to her then spoke. He was stocky and strong looking. He could have been from Cestus or another high 'g' world, or maybe he just liked working out. He had the darkest skin I'd ever seen and a smooth closely shaved head. He was the musician.

'We are pleased to see Doctor Karshon, thank you for bringing him. We don't want any harm to come to him either, so please lower your weapon. We intend you no harm, mother.'

Sandora forced Doctor Karshon down to his knees in front of her. Despite her age her hand holding the weapon was as steady as a rock. She pointed it at the musician.

'Shut up. Don't call me that. You're not my daughter,' she turned to the red-head, 'and neither are you, you're a sin against Gaea. You are abominations, perversions of Gaea's design for humanity. It wouldn't even be a sin to kill the four of you, you're no longer human, not in any way that matters. Now unlock that door, call the research team back in or I will kill Karshon, then I will kill one of you every time you disobey me. Do it. Now.'

She put the barrel of the weapon tight against the back of Karshon's head. I moved slightly towards her, just half a step. She had good peripheral vision because she spotted it immediately.

'Pike, get on the floor. Sit cross legged and keep your hands where I can see them. Do it!'

I sat on the chameleon suit and crossed my legs, resting my hands on my knees with my palms up.

The mathematician then spoke. She was just a shade taller than the musician. She was extremely pale with a shock of white-blond hair.

'Sandora our abilities have grown exponentially. We, ourselves, are now the lead researchers on the neural interface, we know more about it than anyone else.'

'You're just saying that to protect them. Tell them to come in here, I'm not bluffing. I will shoot.'

'Truly Doctor Karshon isn't a threat to anyone, as you can see. The only people standing in your way are the three of us and Cemeron Argalion Pike who has done an excellent job so far in foiling your plans.'

'I had plenty of help,' I said.

'You have no idea what I'm capable of,' said Sandora. 'My disciples and I have sacrificed everything to protect humanity. Infosys is weakening the human race, corrupting us, making us dependent and decadent. It is an idol, an ungodly device trying to usurp Gaea's place but even that wasn't enough for you three. No! You had to go further, you had to submit your very soul to it, surrender your identity completely. That's the ultimate betrayal.'

'Sandora, you may not believe this but we have always been concerned about you. Even though you cut Dominique out of your life we kept watch, in case you ever left Haven. We tracked your visits here to Scarlastion and your enquiries into Doctor Karshon's work. We spotted your repeated visits to Coronnol, your meetings with Doctor Gernard and the others at the Congressarium in Transium. We tracked your purchases of equipment and ships. We eventually deduced that your interest in Per Randolf and Doctor Jones' work was not benign and alerted The Organisation to intervene.'

That sat me up straight.

'Excuse me Dominique,' I said to the red-headed artist, 'Are you saying you arranged the whole investigation?'

'Per Pike,' she said, 'our name is Mutual. We had our own names when we volunteered for this experiment but they seem irrelevant now. Please just address us as Mutual. It expresses our relationship well. Everything we do is for each other.'

'To answer your question,' said the musician, 'we merely prompted your own systems to look into Doctor Jones. We didn't help you in any way. We felt that would not be appropriate. We were confident that you and your colleagues would work out the rest once you realised something wasn't right.'

'Shut up! All of you shut up,' screamed Sandora.

The encounter was not going the way she intended and she had seen her command of the situation slip away.

'May I remind you all that I am in charge here.'

She fired the weapon at the musician in the middle and the pellet tore a hole in his thigh. All three of them screamed in pain but he fell to his knees, clutching his leg as blood began to ooze from between his fingers.

'Sandora, please,' I said, 'don't shoot again. You've lost. Your plan wouldn't have worked even if the wormhole had transported Earth away. You hadn't accounted for the Earth's moon. Without it the Earth would have been devastated and uninhabitable. All your people would have died alone, cut off from help from anyone in this galaxy. Your anger and your grief over Corinne and Sacha deaths has corrupted everything good about the Primitive's beliefs. You're the one that's betrayed humanity, not Mutual. You're also betraying your living daughter, Dominique. How would Corinne and Sacha have felt about that?'

Sandora composure snapped, the anger and disappointment overwhelmed her. The weapon came away from Doctor Karshon's head and she pointed it directly at me.

'Don't you dare speak their names,' she ranted with tears pouring down her face. 'Corine was my beautiful, sweet, innocent baby and Sacha was a good man, a good father, a righteous and devoted follower of Gaea. She was only ten years old. Flawed ungodly technology got them both killed. Can you imagine their terror as they fell? Can you? I lost one child to it and now it's…it's…stolen my only remaining daughter. It's corrupted her into an abomination, a blasphemy against Gaea.'

The artist reached out to Sandora.

'Mother, we can help.'

'You're not my daughter. Dominique is gone. She abandoned us years ago, she ran away from the community. She ran from our pure and simple life in Gaea, from our divine purpose. Maybe she wasn't strong enough, wasn't righteous enough and perhaps some of that is my fault. My fault that she was too weak to cope with the hardship. But that was then and this is now. She has been judged ungodly and I absolutely am strong enough to do what needs doing.'

'She was young and grieving, she needed her mother,' I said.

'Enough. That's enough talk. I have a purpose, a holy purpose, and I will not be diverted. Gaea's justice demands that I use your own precious technology to do everything I can to set people free from the tyranny of Infosys and to stop this…this…evil from spreading.'

She was so lost down the rabbit hole of her own pain and anger I didn't expect logic and reason would be able to reach her. But I could reach something. She'd made me drop my cuff and turn out my pockets, but in forcing me to sit I was now within easy reach of the spare stunner in the chameleon suit. I wanted to try to save Doctor Karshon if I could, but I was determined to save Mutual.

She was focussed entirely on me, the weapon still steadily aimed at my head. I could see the knuckle on her trigger finger whitening as she tightened her grip. I had slipped my hand into the chameleon suit's pocket and had the stunner held ready. I had no idea what setting it was on and could only hope it wasn't the lowest one.

I took a deep breath and prepared to pull it out and fire as I dived to one side, as best I could from my seated position, when Doctor Karshon's head suddenly snapped up, he rose to his feet and in a smooth flowing motion span around and grabbed the hand that was holding the weapon. Sandora fired. Karshon's intervention saved my life. He'd moved the weapon enough so that the pellet hit me in the left shoulder instead of in the head. He pulled her weapon hard upwards and towards himself as Sandora screamed and pulled the trigger again. There was a second pfft of gas discharge, instantaneously followed by a hard metallic ping as the pellet hit the roof. Doctor Karshon fell backwards onto the floor, still holding onto Sandora's weapon. The pellet had left a gaping exit wound in his head and blood was soaking into the carpet. There was no doubt at all in my mind that he was beyond medical help.

Mutual ran to Sandora and pulled her to the ground. I was too shocked to really notice exactly what the three of them were doing until it was too late. I saw Dominique holding her mother's head while another the mathematician grabbed a device from a nearby workbench. Sandora was shouting and thrashing on the floor but they were too strong for her. They placed something in her ear and her shouts became screams. By the time I'd got, unsteadily, to my feet she had stopped screaming. Her head was thrashing from side to side and her hands were clenching and unclenching, over and over. Her eyes were screwed shut but her mouth was muttering silently. The musician sat down on one of the chairs as the mathematician fetched a first aid kit then began to cut his clothing away to tend to the wound in his leg. It didn't look too bad. The projectile had gone straight through, rather than sticking in, so it had missed the bone.

Dominique came and checked my shoulder. I noticed the blood soaking my clothes and wondered why it didn't hurt. She tore the material away and placed a self-adhesive gauze over the wound.

'The pellet is still in there, but that will stop the bleeding. You're in shock, but the pain will kick in soon, you need to see a medic as soon as you can.'

'I'm so sorry about Doctor Karshon,' I said, as I picked up Sandora's weapon and pocketed it. I felt light-headed and slightly numb.

'Doctor Karshon wanted to end his life. We knew once he was out of his shielded quarters we stood a chance of reaching him. It was extraordinarily difficult to break down the walls his damaged mind had built up but we eventually managed it. The last years have been appalling for him, his once brilliant mind was trapped in a mixture of hallucinations, pain and confusion, but the love he and Gerry shared kept him going. When he understood that Gerry was gone he had no adequate reason to endure the suffering.'

'I didn't know Gerry was his bondmate, I thought he was just his carer,' I said rather lamely.

The mathematician continued.

'They were very private. Relationships with colleagues were discouraged back then. But when Doctor Karshon became almost completely withdrawn Gerry gave up his promising career to look after him. You distracted Sandora and we helped Doctor Karshon back to lucidity for just long enough for him to intervene to both save your life, ours and to put an end to his torture.'

The musician spoke up.

'We did not make him kill himself, we merely helped him regain control of his own body and senses to allow him to act as he saw fit. We hoped in time we might be able to help him recover, but he chose a different path.'

My shoulder was throbbing, the initial shock must have begun to wear off. I pulled a chair near to them and sat down.

'What have you done to Sandora?' I asked.

'We have given her the chance to atone and find peace. She too will become Mutual in time,' said the artist.

'What!' I exclaimed. 'You're not serious, are you?'

'We have implanted a neural link and she will join us. We can help her. Already we are able to access her memories and understand her motivation. It will take her some time before she is fully able to do the same, many weeks or perhaps months. She is older and her mind may find it harder than our younger ones did.'

'Then what? The Organisation are going to want to arrest her and put her on trial. For the killing of Gerry at least, never mind plotting genocide, theft and countless other crimes.'

'We think Kas and your superiors will agree to let us look after her. A public trial will only cause upset, panic and fear. We don't think the galaxy needs to know that a weapon exists that could annihilate entire solar systems nor how close Sandora came to using it.'

It was like talking to one person. I forget now which of the three of them was doing the talking. It seemed like it could be any one, or maybe each in turn.

'What about me, and my objection to the neural link becoming widespread? It may be dangerous for me to say this while I'm locked in here with you, but I think you are the real threat to humanity. I will do whatever I'm allowed to, to stop this neural link technology being adopted.'

'We agree,' said Mutual. 'The merging of consciousness was an unintended consequence of the procedure. We noticed it happening a month or so after we received the implants and the integration was fully complete within six months. The implant was only meant to allow the sharing of ideas and experience and to give the human mind instant access to the whole of Infosys. However, the brain is a complex and poorly understood organ. While we appreciate being who we are and have no wish to return to our isolated individual minds, if that were even possible – which I assure you it isn't, we recognize that inflicting this on the population of the galaxy without consent would be unethical and we will not allow it.'

'I'm very happy to hear this but I'm not entirely sure I believe you.'

'The SSPs will be destroyed and all the records of this technology on Infosys will be erased, you are welcome to witness this. We are sure we can persuade the other non-linked researchers to move on to other exciting and beneficial projects and we will provide The Organisation with their names so you can also keep them under surveillance to ensure compliance. We will monitor Infosys to make sure no-one continues the work in secret. It's not ideal but it should work. We will take Sandora with us to a remote sanctuary, here on Scarlastion, where we can continue to help her with the healing process.'

'But why?' I asked. 'She was prepared to kill you.'

'She was our mother, the part of us that used to be Dominique. We love her. We understand her pain and her confusion. Now we can do something about it. It didn't take us long to have doubts about the vast mass of humanity sharing in what we experience. There are advantages to being Mutual but we recognized the dangers too. As your own colleague Kas is fond of saying "You're not the only one who's good at their job". Humanity, overall, is doing well and there simply isn't enough data for us to know for certain if widespread adoption of the neural link would be good or bad in the long term. The link is not reversible, we would not survive having the implant removed. So, on that basis we will not allow this experiment to go any further. There may come a time, far in the future when humanity's best interests lie in a shared consciousness but that time is definitely not now, and certainly not without a lot more research and, crucially, informed consent.'

Sandora staggered to her feet, brushing aside Mutual's help and looked around for her weapon.

'No...no...be quiet, I won't calm down. I can feel you in here,' she said pounding her head with her fists.

'Stop it. Stop it,' she turned to me. 'Pike, help me! I can hear them in my head!'

I could see the panic in her eyes as she realised what they'd done to her.

'You ungodly heathens what have you done to me? I can't...I can't...I won't live like this...don't make me ungodly...Gaea....Gaea...help me...you abominations...'

The expression of Mutual formerly known as Dominique picked up a medical injector from one of the workbenches and pressed it against the side of Sandora's neck. She slumped to the ground muttering prayers in Latin until she passed out.

'When she wakes we will help her understand and accept all that she has done,' said Mutual. 'It will be hard for her, and by extension for us, but we will ensure she poses no further danger to the galaxy or anyone in it.'

'I think what you've done to her is probably worse than any possible sentence a court could have passed, from her point of view,' I said.

'We are hopeful she can be helped, and come to accept her place as part of Mutual in the time she has left in this life.'

The door unlocked behind me with a click and then opened. The same two medics were waiting outside to treat the injuries.

'Goodbye,' said Mutual, as they closed ranks around the musician as he was tended to.

'Goodbye,' I said, but I already think they weren't really listening.

I picked up the stunners and my cuff, triggered the chameleon suit's self-destruct then let one of the medics check my shoulder before I headed back to the shuttle. I preferred to let The Organisation's doctors treat my shoulder, plus I had a lot to discuss with Kas.

Chapter 45
Epilogue

By the time I arrived back on the cruiser the pain was really quite extreme so I was taken to the sickbay promptly. The medics numbed the pain then removed the pellet and started work on repairing the damage to my shoulder. There was nothing wrong that would be permanent, but I did need a few days to recover full use of my arm. Kas was the first to come to see me, but it was a business visit so it was private and all alone. I wasn't particularly surprised to discover they had seen the whole confrontation on their cuff. Mutual had activated some cameras in the room and invited Kas to watch as an impartial witness on condition that what they saw was for their eyes only.

'You were really stupid trying to get to the stunner in the chameleon suit's pocket,' they said. 'If the late Doctor Karshon hadn't intervened you'd be dead. Sandora was a good shot and our medics, good as they are, couldn't fix a hole in your head.'

I shrugged.

'It seemed the only thing to do. I was determined to give Mutual a chance to overpower Sandora. It seemed a reasonable trade. I wasn't expecting Karshon to save me, nor was I expecting Mutual to do what they did. I thought they'd just hit her with a chair or something.'

'Do you think we can trust Mutual?' said Kas.

I glanced at my cuff then felt worried.

'It's alright, the room is completely screened. Mutual cannot overhear us. Your cuff won't work and all the other devices linked to Infosys are physically disabled.'

I checked my cuff and discovered Kas was correct, it was offline and inert.

'I don't know. I want to trust them, I really do. While we couldn't properly understand the technology rejecting Primitives' belief in a supernatural deity like Gaea it seems Scarlastion, a beacon of rational scientific reasoning, may have just created its equivalent. Those three, well now four, people are able to access know and understand anything on Infosys, if they so choose. If that's not god-like then I don't know what is.'

'We can't use any of our normal methods to monitor them,' said Kas. 'We will have to invent new methods, ones not linked to Infosys. Which will be a challenge. I will have to prepare two briefings for our superiors, one leaving out Mutual's involvement which I can send via the usual channels and another more detailed and truthful one that I'll have to deliver in person in a secure room.'

Worrying about this was above my pay grade and I was pretty good at focussing on the task in hand. I would leave Kas and our superiors to decide how best to deal with Mutual, but my instinct was that they could, in fact, be trusted. I hoped I wasn't wrong.

Kas told me that Grippe, Jones, Dharya and Praanvi had successfully designed and built a defence against the destructive stellar probes. The schematics and build instructions had gone out to every inhabited world. Six probes had already been intercepted, the ships launching them had been impounded and the proctors piloting them arrested.

Randolf's family were on their way from Fortuna to take him home to recuperate before he returned to Coronnol where he would be awarded his doctorate.

Grippe was under investigation by CI Andrews and Coronnol university for his inappropriate relations with students and was unlikely to come out of that well. I knew Andrews would ensure justice was done.

That just left Doctor Jones. She was still on board and I was pleased to hear she wanted to see me. I wasn't sure exactly what I wanted to say, but I knew I wanted some time alone with her.

She knocked on the door of my room.

'Come in,' I said.

'I'll leave you two alone,' Kas said as the door slid open.

Kas left and Jones came in. She took one look at my heavily bandaged shoulder and shook her head.

'What happened to you at the university?' she asked.

'I'm not really allowed to tell you,' I said. Then I shielded the room from prying eyes and ears and told her everything.

'I was wondering about taking some holiday time now this is all over,' I said. 'Earth seems an appropriate destination. Do you have any plans?'

'Yes. I have lots of plans. I have to get back to Coronnol as I have a mountain of work to do to prevent anyone else from corrupting my work into a weapon. I have Randolf's doctorate to submit. I need to recruit a replacement for Gernard and, in all likelihood, one for Grippe too. I am going to be very busy.'

'Oh. That's understandable. Perhaps I'll go on my own then anyway. It looked beautiful.'

She glared at me.

'What?' I said.

'After everything we've been through together. Don't you know?'

I was very good at my job, but perhaps not so good at relationships as all that. It took me a couple of minutes to think it through.

'I would like to visit Earth but only with you,' I said. 'I would like you to come with me and show me all the places we talked about. I want to spend time with you and get to know you properly.'

'That's better,' she said. 'I'd like that, but on one condition.'

She moved closer until she was standing right in front of me, almost touching.

'What's that?'

'You tell me your real name. I'm not going anywhere with you until you tell me that.'

I told her, then she kissed me.

THE END

Glossary

Bubble
: A standard driverless mode of ground transport used galaxy wide. A sphere that can roll in any direction. Seats between one and four people depending on size. Usually transparent but may be made opaque for privacy.

Cestus
: A planet with an unusually high surface gravity. Almost twice that of Earth at 1.84 'g'.

Chameleon suit
: A flexible controllable suit that gives the wearer multiple appearances, when worn with the hood also disguises the features. Only realistic from about ten metres distance.

Coronnol
: A university planet. Specialisms include physics, astrophysics, psychology and Information Technology.

Cuff
: A personal interface for Infosys, worn on the wrist. Available in myriad styles and colours. Projects crystal clear virtual screens that are re-sizeable and maintain their relative position to the user regardless of arm/cuff movement. Cuffs provided by The Organisation have many additional features not found in

standard ones.

Excelsior	Manufacturer of high security doors and hatches.
Fortuna	A planet with a considerably lower than average surface gravity. Approximately three-quarters that of Earth.
Goldilocks Zone	Properly known as the circumstellar habitable zone, is the perfect orbit for a planet to be in where temperatures and solar radiation will be such that water can exist in liquid form and carbon-based organic life is possible. Most yellow suns have such a zone, but not all will have a planet in it.
Grav unit / Grav engine	Grav is short for gravity. A grav unit or generator creates artificial gravity inside a starship. Grav engines provide lift to allow ships to fly and enter/leave orbit.
Ground-car	A four wheeled driven vehicle generally only used by police or military when complete manual control is required. May also be used in driverless mode like a Bubble.
Infosys	Galaxy spanning information processing, storage, retrieval and communication system. Every known inhabited world is connected to it.
Mag	Surface transport similar to a railway. A chain of driverless pods travels at

extremely high speed through low atmospheric pressure tubes on a magnetic track.

Microdrone

A tiny flying surveillance device. Almost undetectable outdoors, but not really suitable for indoor use as the camouflage is good but not perfect.

Microgravity

Known to lay-people as zero 'g' or weightlessness. If far enough from a planet, or in a stable orbit around it, the effects of the planet's gravity are negligible.

Mirth

A university planet. Specialisms include philosophy, music and art.

Orbital spiral

To maximise the number of take offs and landings all ships are assigned to a spiral course that guides them to and from orbit. So long as all ships stick to the correct rate of ascent or decent in their spiral multiple ships can use the same one. A spiral is one way traffic, it's either going to or from orbit, never both.

Per

The title Per is universally used to formally refer to someone who doesn't have an occupational or academic title such as Doctor. It's short for Person. It's gender neutral.

Power grid

Every inhabited world has a wireless power grid that provides power to all mobile or portable equipment, such as cuffs, bubbles, ground-cars and starships.

Scarlastion	A university planet. Specialisms include medicine and biomedicine.
SSP	Secure storage and processing unit. Used to encrypt sensitive work done on Infosys. The user's cuff communicates with Infosys via the SSP ensuring security and privacy. SSPs are tied to specific cuffs and location aware so cannot be stolen and used elsewhere to decrypt information.
Stanton-Mayes	Manufacturer of high security doors and hatches.
Stunner	A small hand-held weapon that can fit in the palm of the hand. Fires an invisible beam that affects the nervous system. Low power may briefly paralyse or at full power knock someone unconscious for a day or more. Preferred weapon of The Organisation's agents and many police forces.
Terminator	A terminator is a line, visible from orbit, that divides the daylight side and the night side of a planetary body.
Terraforming	The process of modifying the ecosystem of a planet to make it habitable for humans. This includes one or more of the following: increasing the amount of oxygen in

the atmosphere, introducing non-human life, such as plants, microbes, insects, fish and animals, removing poisonous gases. May take anywhere between several decades and hundreds of years to complete.

The Organisation   A secret organization whose sole job is ensuring the continuity of human life in the galaxy. Comprised of field agents and back-room boffins. Has links to the galactic navy and can call on it for support and resources but operates independently of it. Reports directly to the galactic council.

Transium   The capital of the planet Coronnol and home to the physics and astrophysics department.

Veraserum   The name of a drug occasionally used when questioning suspects. Relaxes them and makes them eager to please. Not exactly a truth drug, but the next best thing. Highly addictive may only be used sparingly.

About the author

P hilip Alan Tyler has been writing since high school but Coronnol is his first completed full length novel. He reads, plays the drums, rides a motorbike and walks the dog for recreation. He has been happily married to Mags for over thirty years and is a proud father to three talented grown-up children and a grandfather to one incredible miniature human.

His next novel is a caper set, more or less, in present day Britain and should be out before the end of 2022.

He is on Twitter as @PhilipAlanTyler, Facebook and Instagram as @PhilipAlanTyler.Writer

Polite and respectful engagement is always welcome, trolls will be immediately blocked.

While plenty of proof-reading has occurred mistakes may have slipped through so please report any typos to…

typos@philipatyler.co.uk

Printed in Great Britain
by Amazon

80316454R10212